T0398931

THERESA HOWES lives in London, and has a background as an actor. Her work has been longlisted for the Mslexia Novel Award, Bath Novel Award, Caledonia Novel Award, Lucy Cavendish College Prize and the BBC National Short Story Award.

Also by Theresa Howes

The French Affair
The Secrets We Keep

A Matter of Persuasion

THERESA HOWES

ONE PLACE. MANY STORIES

HQ
An imprint of HarperCollins*Publishers* Ltd
1 London Bridge Street
London SE1 9GF

www.harpercollins.co.uk

HarperCollins*Publishers*
Macken House, 39/40 Mayor Street Upper,
Dublin 1 D01 C9W8

This paperback edition 2025

2

First published in Great Britain by
HQ, an imprint of HarperCollins*Publishers* Ltd 2025

Copyright © Theresa Howes

Theresa Howes asserts the moral right to be
identified as the author of this work.
A catalogue record for this book is
available from the British Library.

ISBN: 9780008666842

Printed and bound in the United States

For Bill,
my very own Wareham.

Chapter 1

1882

The artist's studio was in Hell's Kitchen, New York, an area of grubby streets and overburdened houses, where well-to-do men like Wilbur Eaton and Eleanor, the eldest of his three daughters, never usually visited.

It was left to Amy, the middle Eaton sister, to instruct the coachman of the coupe they'd hired on the most efficient route from their brownstone townhouse in the exclusive Silk Stocking District, to the fraying edges of the city, where Mr Justin Jones could just about afford the rent on the tiny attic space in the five-storey walk-up he grandly referred to as his studio. Ordinarily they'd have travelled in their own brougham with a pair of steppers, but Mr Eaton had been reluctant to risk his own carriage and horses in this part of town.

Mr Jones must have heard the progress of their feet on the bare wooden stairs as they made their way up to his attic, because the studio door swung open even before they'd reached the landing, before Amy had caught her breath enough to prepare Eleanor and her father for the artist's enthusiasm.

'Good afternoon. I'm delighted to see you all. Come in. Come in.'

He was wearing a yellow waistcoat and plaid trousers, and for once, had gone to the trouble of brushing his hair. He beamed at his guests, his eyes unnaturally bright for the time of day.

'The portrait is ready for you to inspect.'

The studio smelled of turpentine and damp cloth, of the accumulation of dust and yesterday's beer. Eleanor lifted the hem of her pink satin skirt to avoid it picking up the grime, curling her lip as she approached the painting, which had been set upon an easel by the window to catch the best of the daylight. 'So this is what all the fuss is about.'

Reluctant to cross the dirt-scrabbled floor, Mr Eaton raised his chin and squinted at the portrait from his place by the door. 'He's caught your likeness, Amy. I'll say that much.'

Never one to disagree with her father, Eleanor gave a grudging nod. 'It's like I'm looking right at you.'

Amy examined the picture of a woman in an oyster grey dress, a lilac wrap draped around her shoulders. Whichever way she looked at it, her own familiar face stared back at her, wearing the half smile she'd presented to Mr Jones during the long hours she'd sat for him. To his credit, he'd replicated the arch of her eyebrows, the curve of her lips, just as they greeted her in the mirror each morning as she pinned her hair and checked her starched collar and cuffs for dirt, but that was all he'd done. For all the hours she'd sat for him in this gloomy little attic, he'd failed to capture a single one of her thoughts. He'd caught every feature, but beyond the surface, the image could have been of anyone.

'Does it please you, Miss Eaton? I've caught your quickness, don't you think so?'

No, she didn't think so. Somehow, she had to find it in her heart to break it to him. Despite his best efforts, the portrait was a failure. Her enduring silence, during which she swallowed back a variety of tactless replies, was all the answer he needed.

'There's no obligation to purchase the painting, Miss Eaton. We agreed that when I asked you to sit for me.'

It seemed unfair not to buy the picture after he'd gone to so much trouble over it, and yet as far as Amy was concerned, the portrait might as well have been of a stranger. Even if it had pleased her, hanging it on a wall in the family home would have shown a lack of self-awareness on her part, bordering as it did on flattery. At twenty-seven, she'd passed the bloom of youth. Her complexion was no longer as luminous as Mr Jones had painted it. The unease she'd feel every time she looked at it would cause her to avoid the room where it hung. She should never have let him persuade her to sit for him in the first place.

'What will you do with the painting if I don't buy it?'

He bowed his head, indicating he was in her favour, that there were no hard feelings. 'I'm planning a touring exhibition of my work. Your portrait will be the main attraction. When the public sees I've painted a famous authoress, they'll line up for me to paint them too. America is advancing. Men are growing richer by the day. Many of them will want their portraits painted.' He smiled, bowing his head once again. 'The fact that you sat for me will draw their attention and help to advance my career.'

'You make it sound as if she's doing you a favour by refusing to buy the painting,' said Mr Eaton, retrieving a silk handkerchief from his pocket and pressing it against his nose to avoid breathing in the dust.

Mr Jones was too polite to give a direct answer. It stood to reason he would rather sell the portrait, but Amy had never agreed to buy it, and had only sat for him after he'd begged her to do so. If it secured his reputation as an up-and-coming society portrait artist, then it would have been a worthwhile use of both of their time.

Bored by the talk of her sister's portrait, Eleanor scanned the studio, her eyes picking over the unfinished paintings, the pencil sketches scattered across the desk. 'You'd have been better off painting me rather than Amy. I'm the eldest Miss Eaton.' She examined herself in the full-length mirror, propped at an awkward angle in the corner of the room because it was the only place it would fit. 'I'm also the prettier one.'

Having conquered his aversion to the dust, Mr Eaton joined her at the mirror and compared his reflection to his eldest daughter's. Both were tall and fair-haired, with long-limbs and slender frames, which after years of studied self-improvement, they'd trained to appear elegant rather than clumsy.

'You were blessed with my good looks, Eleanor. I'll give you that. No one would guess you were twenty-nine.' He pulled in his stomach, lifting his chin to improve the profile of his jaw in the mirror. 'Given the right light, I could pass as your brother.'

Amy was the odd one out, having inherited her mother's brown eyes and dark hair, her small stature and steady nature. She'd been gone so many years now, Amy would have had difficulty remembering her face if it wasn't for the miniature she kept on the table beside her bed.

Sensing the opportunity for another commission, Mr Jones adjusted the angle of the easel, allowing Eleanor a clearer view of Amy's portrait. 'I asked your sister to sit for me because of her fame as an authoress. I'd be delighted to paint you as well, but I'd require you to pay for the work.'

Eleanor turned from the mirror, fixing him with a frown. 'Are you saying my portrait wouldn't be as valuable as my sister's?'

'It's simply that . . . you're not famous. No one beyond your family would want to buy it.'

'But I'm prettier than my sister, admit it.'

'Beauty is in the eye of the beholder.' Mr Jones gave a nervous laugh, trying to distract from the unintended insult. 'Isn't that what they say?'

'You value my sister's image because of her novels and nothing else. I could have written books, if I'd had a mind to do it. It can't be that difficult. I chose to put my duty to my family first, running the house for my father and taking my mother's place at the table and in society. You say this isn't of value?'

Amy placed her hand on her sister's arm and led her to the door before the discussion could get any more heated. 'We mustn't keep the coachman waiting, Eleanor. Thank you for your time, Mr Jones.'

But Eleanor refused to be silenced. 'When I sit for my portrait, I shall select one of the more celebrated artists. Mr Sargent did a marvellous painting of Rosa Ledyard when she visited Paris last summer. He knows how to flatter a woman. When he comes to America, I shall insist he paints me.'

Red-faced from Eleanor's barrage, Mr Jones opened the door to see them out. Amy wished him luck with the touring exhibition before summoning her father, who was still admiring himself in the mirror, smoothing his moustache with his fingers and examining the lines around his eyes. Already, his thoughts had moved on from Amy's portrait to matters of his own reflection.

'Thank you for sitting for me, Miss Eaton. It's been a pleasure getting to know you. Your portrait will give my reputation the advancement it needs.'

As far as Amy was concerned, that was still to be seen. Anyone who really knew and understood her would see he'd failed to capture her character. Once again, she called her father to join them, encouraging him to step away from the mirror. Appearances were only skin deep. Surely any fool could see that.

Chapter 2

Mr Eaton was unusually silent during the carriage ride home. Eleanor was complaining so much about Mr Jones's failure of taste that Amy didn't think anything of it. It was only after she'd paid the coachman, adding a generous tip to thank him for waiting for them in such a low part of town, that she realised he wasn't himself, standing on the Dutch stoop in front of the house and staring into the distance.

The street was quiet for the time of day, with barely a curtain-twitch from the row of elegant five-storey brownstones that lined each side of the road just off Fifth Avenue. *Sedate* was the word used for the area, where old colonial families, Amy's own included, with plenty of money and time on their hands, had settled decades earlier, a place where advancement and newcomers remained unwelcome.

Still, there were new developments all around that refused to be ignored. Human nature and its desire for progress had seen to that. Since the Civil War, vast fortunes had been made from the building of the railroads and the steamships, from steel production and oil refining and all manner of other things. Whether the self-proclaimed New York aristocracy liked it or not, entrepreneurs were forcing the country through an industrial revolution, modernising and disrupting the old world, the old ways of life with their new ideas and their new money. It was this modern thinking that gave Amy the hope that women would one day be granted the right to vote, even though as things stood, it still seemed a long way off.

It was north along Fifth Avenue, a world removed from the overcrowded tenements of Hell's Kitchen and Five Points, where the new money now gathered, where vast houses of cream stone, built in the image of grand European palaces, with ballrooms and picture galleries, were steadily growing in number. Yet for all the gilding the newly rich added to their lives, nothing removed the taint of war-profiteering and political bribery that dogged many of them in the eyes of the old New Yorkers.

Along with the industrial progress had come mass immigration and the appalling living conditions brought on by a city unable to cope with its sudden rapid growth. It was a crime that buildings were built without running water or the basic means of sanitation. Nothing had been learned from the repeated epidemics of cholera and yellow fever that had struck the city in recent years, and all the while the rich grew richer, the poor became ever more destitute.

Amy encouraged her father inside the house and removed her bonnet, using it to fan her face. The streets boiled with the late summer heat and she was glad to be out of it. Already Eleanor had stormed off to the drawing room, her parasol abandoned on a nearby chair.

Amy's eyes followed the lazy movement of her father's fingers as he pulled off his gloves and removed his hat. 'Are you all right? Would you like some tea?'

He nodded, his attention drifting to the mirror on the wall, his expression clouding at the thin glaze of perspiration that had added a shine to his face. 'Bring it to my study. I have to talk to you. Tell Eleanor to join us.'

It was an unusually sombre exchange. Mr Eaton rarely

requested Amy's company and never at this time of day. His afternoons were usually reserved for playing whist and solitaire, for walking in Central Park with Eleanor, or simply doing nothing. He made no secret of the fact that he found Amy's conversation unbearable. He'd never forgiven her for being like her late mother, for reminding him of the love that had been taken from him so early in life.

It wasn't only Amy's resemblance to her mother that continued to be a source of pain to him. Instead of being proud of what she'd achieved as an author in a world dominated by the male pen, he saw only degradation in it. It was a sorry state of affairs when a daughter of his stooped to earning money through her labour and he would never forgive her for it, while the public attention it drew only served to mortify him. It saddened Amy that however hard she tried, she always disappointed him. Eleanor, who was like him in so many ways, was the only daughter he had time for.

Since the death of his wife, Mr Eaton had drifted into the life of an aimless widower. Despite attempts by several women to lure him into a second marriage, he had stubbornly refused to yield. Having already fathered three daughters, the thought of having more was too much of a burden when there was nothing to be done with them beyond marriage, and that in itself was not always a certainty, as both Eleanor and Amy had proven.

Hot tea with lemon was the habit, whatever the weather. In the Eaton household, traditions were upheld, no matter what. Once the tea had been served, Amy sat in an armchair near her father's desk, her small frame consumed by the red velvet upholstery that had been chosen almost a lifetime ago to match the fringed curtains and the cabbage-rose-patterned carpet.

Nothing in the house had changed since her mother's death. Her touch, frozen in time, remained on every item in the cluttered space, from the brass gas mantles to the glass-fronted bookcases of calf-bound volumes that no one but Amy ever opened.

Every room was scented with patchouli, the walls decorated in crimson or sea-green, the contrasting chintz pouffes and brocaded armchairs filling every corner.

Each table top and cabinet displayed silver gewgaws and jardinières of artificial flowers. Every room boasted a gilded mirror that reflected the chaos back on itself, multiplying the number of paintings by minor French masters that hung on every wall, the varnish on the canvases darkened over the years until the images were nothing but shadows.

There were times, usually after long hours spent working on her latest novel, when Amy felt stifled by so much decoration, as if one more breath of it might suffocate her. Despite her mild suggestions of removing some of the clutter, nothing would ever change. Her father and Eleanor clung to their possessions just as fiercely as they clung to the ways of old New York society.

'Was there something you wanted to talk to us about?' Amy smiled at her father, drawing him out of his unusual quietness.

'It's the household accounts,' said Mr Eaton, retrieving a pile of papers from the drawer and placing them on the desk. 'You've been keeping an eye on them, Eleanor?'

Eleanor picked up her embroidery and put it aside again. She'd been working on the same handkerchief for months and never seemed to get any nearer to finishing it. 'Of course I've been keeping an eye on them, just as Mother used to.'

'Only these demands for unpaid bills are piling up. The fools at the bank have said we've run up too many of them and something has to be done.' He leaned his elbows on the desk, dragging his fingers through his thinning hair, not fair any longer as he liked to pretend, but grey. 'I'm confounded if I know what to do about it.'

It was the first Amy had heard of these unpaid bills. As the eldest daughter, Eleanor had taken on the management of the household immediately following their mother's death, with no instruction other than what she'd observed of the general running of the house while growing up. The loss of their mother had been unexpected, and they'd been unprepared for the challenges that lay ahead.

As the years passed, and Eleanor's hopes of marrying and having her own home faded, it became the one area of her life where she was able to exert independence. Whenever Amy had offered to help, she'd been refused, until she'd finally given up trying, burying the disappointment she felt at the rejection deep and going to great lengths not to show it.

Eleanor had never forgiven Amy for being her mother's favourite, for sharing the same bookish interests and having the same curious mind. It was their mother who had introduced Amy to the pleasures of reading when her other daughters showed no interest in it, and encouraged her first attempts at writing stories, much to the ridicule of her father and sisters.

Since their mother's death, Eleanor had gone out of her way to punish Amy for the connection they'd shared, even at the cost of missing out on what could have been a close sisterly relationship. Not only had Amy lost her mother at an early age, but in doing so, she'd also lost her big sister.

It was during her mother's last days, as Amy sat beside her bed, willing her to fight off the influenza that had claimed the lives of so many New Yorkers, that she promised to take care of her father and her sisters, no matter what, to make sure they were comfortable and always loved. It was the reason Amy put up with their thoughtlessness and their open dislike. Her loyal nature meant that even after all these years, honouring her mother's deathbed wish was all that mattered, however roughly they treated her.

Eleanor shot Amy an accusing look. 'It's a good job you decided not to buy your portrait. Such extravagance will have to stop if we're not to run up more bills.'

Amy bit back her reply. A trunk had arrived only yesterday from Paris, packed with new dresses, each designed by Worth, the most exclusive couturier in the world, the silks, satins and brocades wrapped in delicate layers of tissue paper. All of them were for Eleanor.

Unlike her sister, Amy covered all her own expenses with the money she earned, and always with an eye to moderation. Rather than looking to Europe for fashion, she bought her dresses in Bloomingdale Brothers, choosing classic styles that lasted for multiple seasons. She wasn't responsible for their current financial difficulty, and until that moment, she'd known nothing of it.

She cast her eyes over the stack of bills and sighed. 'Why haven't you mentioned this before?'

Eleanor shrugged off Amy's question. 'They're not your bills. It's not your concern.'

'They can't be ignored. People have to be paid.'

As their exchange grew more heated, their father vacated his desk, wiping his hands down the front of his trousers as if to rid himself of the problem. 'It's none of my doing. Your mother always took care of these things. After her death, I left it to Eleanor. I'll leave you and your sister to work it out.'

Once her father had left the room, Amy went over to the desk and examined the unpaid bills, her eyes widening at the extravagant spending, not only on dresses for Eleanor, but on shoes and face creams for her father, jewellery and perfumes, the carriage and horses they rarely used. Their mother had always kept a tight control on the household economy, keeping it within their considerable means, but Eleanor had too much of her father's temperament to be any kind of steadying influence, and both enjoyed spending freely.

'Did you never think to look at the outgoings and compare them to the incomings?'

'If we owe people money, they'll just have to wait until we can pay them.'

'You can't expect the people who supply you with luxuries to wait indefinitely for the money you owe them. They rely on it to feed their families and to keep a roof over their heads.'

Eleanor averted her eyes from the stack of unpaid bills. 'I don't know what you expect me to do about it.'

'To begin with, you can return that trunk of dresses to Paris. Then we'll look at other ways to reduce the household spending until we've paid what's owed.'

'You won't make me shop at Bloomingdale Brothers just because you don't like good clothes. Imagine what people will say if I'm forced to appear in last season's fashions. I owe it to our family name to maintain a decent position in society.'

'You owe it to our family name not to leave unpaid bills all over town.'

'Then you'd better add these to the pile.' Eleanor retrieved a dozen notes from her sewing basket and threw them onto the desk. 'I've had a run of bad luck playing bridge lately. This is what I owe.'

Amy sifted through the notes and did a quick calculation. It came to a considerable sum, much more than the amount either Eleanor or Amy received as an annual allowance from the family investments. When Amy looked up, Eleanor had already left the room. The message was clear. If the family was to be saved from financial disaster, it was up to her to work out how to do it.

Chapter 3

Amy spent the next few days going through her father's financial affairs. It wasn't only the extravagant spending that was to blame for their current difficulty, but his failure to manage the capital he'd inherited. The family fortune was based on real estate, much of which had dropped in value since the Civil War and the economic depression that had dogged the following decade. Having never had an occupation, Mr Eaton had no alternative method of improving their income and it was unthinkable that he should ever consider working for a living.

She paid the most pressing bills using the money she'd saved from the sales of her novels over the past seven years. Her bank account was now almost empty, but the debts to those who could least afford to wait for their money had been settled.

After some hard decision-making, Amy devised a plan that would put their finances back on course within a few years and without any real hardship. Now, she faced the challenge of persuading her family to accept the proposal. She called everyone to a meeting the following afternoon. The sooner they made the changes, the sooner the situation would improve.

Marion was the first to arrive. As the only one of the sisters to have married, she assumed a superior status over both Eleanor and Amy, despite being the youngest of the three. Her husband, Charles Morton, was from an old New York family, whose descendants could be traced back to the earliest European settlers. The fact that they'd come over on the *Mayflower* was the thing that gave them precedence in their self-aggrandised social circle.

As a wedding present, Charles's parents had given them a brownstone across the street. Living in such close proximity meant Marion was never far from her father and her sisters. Some days, she called in so often, it was as if she'd never left home at all, leading Amy to conclude that her marriage had been nothing to do with love, and everything to do with achieving a higher status among the New York social elite.

She bundled into the parlour, a tornado of ostrich feathers and lace, her four-year-old son already ahead of her, running around the furniture and making whooping sounds at the top of his voice.

'I've brought Charles Junior with me. When he knew I was visiting his aunt Amy, he insisted on coming along.'

No sooner had Marion spoken, Charles Junior ran up to Amy and threw his arms around her legs, hugging her with all his might. Amy placed her hand gently on the top of his head to steady herself as he knocked her off-balance. For all she adored him, his boundless energy would test the patience of a saint.

'It's going to be a grown-up talk. It'll be rather dull for him, I'm afraid.'

Already Marion had begun picking at the plate of bread and cold chicken Amy had laid out. 'You're the only one who can do anything with him. It makes me nauseous just seeing him run around. He'll sit down and be a good boy for you.'

If only it were true, Amy would have a much better time of it in Charles Junior's company. She smiled as he made a grab for the slice of blueberry tart she'd put aside for him on his special plate, having guessed Marion would bring him along.

'Would you like to look at a picture book while I talk to your mama?'

Eleanor entered just in time to hear Amy's offer. She rolled her eyes in disgust. 'Don't give the boy a book, Amy. It's too weird. You don't want him to turn out like you.'

She was wearing a china blue silk dress, edged with cream chiffon. Amy recognised it as one of the new dresses that had recently arrived in the trunk from Paris. Tea with the family was hardly the occasion for such an exquisite outfit. It was Eleanor's way of showing that Amy's request for her to return the dresses had been ignored.

Since her marriage, Marion had followed the old New York society tradition of dressing in muted tones. She ran her eyes over Eleanor's hourglass figure and her coveted sixteen-inch waist, which had been created at yet another great expense by the purchase of a new whalebone corset.

'Goodness, don't you look fine. Anyone would think you were still trying to catch a husband.'

It was ten years since Eleanor had been disappointed in love. She'd been all set to marry a wealthy distant cousin. There was never an official engagement, but she'd been led to believe there was an understanding between them. She'd already made plans for her wedding dress, and decided on the flowers she'd carry down the aisle, when one day, he stopped calling.

The next time she saw him he was at the opera, sitting in the orchestra stalls with the daughter of a newly rich industrialist who'd made his fortune manufacturing refrigerated carriages to transport fresh foods on the railroads. They were married before the season was out.

It was some years before Eleanor could bring herself to eat lobster or clams again, knowing how the seafood made its way to New York. She managed the public humiliation by cultivating an image of heartless elegance, turning her undeniable beauty as ice cold as the refrigerated carriages that had thwarted her dreams of marriage.

Growing a protective shell over her disappointed heart, much like the seafood she could no longer face, also had the effect of giving her a reputation for being untouchable, and it was this that had prevented her from finding another suitor. Now at the age of twenty-nine, she had long passed the age when any man would consider her as a wife, just as at twenty-seven, Amy had suffered the same fate. It was a cruel fact of their society that women had no value or status beyond their youth and eligibility for marriage, both of which were fleeting and harshly judged.

Knowing what it was like to suffer a broken heart, Amy had tried to infiltrate Eleanor's protective shell in the years since her disappointment, attempting to become a friend as well as a sister, but despite her well-meaning efforts, the shell remained impenetrable. Her humiliation was too great, her pride too wounded to admit how deeply hurt she felt at being rejected by the man she'd set out to marry.

Eleanor's reply to Marion's comment was stalled by the arrival of their father and Mrs Rawle, who rushed over to Amy and put her arms around her, just as her mother would, if only she'd been there.

'My dear, is everything all right? You're looking terribly pale.' She pulled back from the embrace, frowning at Amy's simple muslin house dress. 'I'd worry less about you if you gained a little weight.'

As a widow, Mrs Rawle was answerable to no one, and wealthy enough to please herself. Intelligent and astute, she prided herself on being well-read and boasted opinions on many subjects. Although Amy relied on her good sense, many people considered her formidable. Despite the expansion of her figure in recent years, she still dressed in the latest fashions, and took pride in being seen in all the right places. She also missed nothing that went on in their closed New York society.

After the death of Amy's mother, she took Amy under her wing, offering advice and affection the way no one else in her family ever did. Over the years, Amy had grown into the habit of never making a decision without first asking her opinion. For all she was surrounded by her family, Mrs Rawle was the only one who was ever on her side. Now, Amy had invited her to the gathering, hoping she'd support her suggestions and defend her against the wrath of her father and Eleanor. What she had to say wasn't going to please them at all.

'Thank you for coming. We're very informal this afternoon. Help yourself to the food.'

Before Amy could say anything else, the door flew open and Mrs Canby entered, the housemaid trailing behind her in a fluster, miming her apology for the intrusion she'd had no power to prevent.

'I'm not late, am I? I came as soon as I received Eleanor's note. Well, not immediately, because I had to change out of my sage silk into this marvellous satin. It's quite autumnal, don't you think? And so very *now*.'

She ran her hands over her skirt, drawing attention to the oak leaf pattern woven into the delicate fabric in tones of yellow, russet and brown. She'd been widowed for less than a year, and had been quick to cast off her mourning clothes, claiming they were too dowdy for a woman of thirty-five to be expected to wear. Given the forthrightness of her character, nobody had been surprised by her assertion, or dared to question it to her face, although it didn't stop the subject being raised in whispers whenever her back was turned.

Amy had never understood why Eleanor valued Mrs Canby so much as a friend when their temperaments and interests beyond fashion were so wildly different. She could only suppose it was the energy Mrs Canby created that appealed to Eleanor who was generally so languid.

Once Eleanor had finished fawning over the oak leaf pattern, Amy took her aside. 'Why did you invite Mrs Canby? This was meant to be a family gathering.'

'Mrs Rawle isn't family, and yet you invited her. It's only fair I have someone on my side too. You can't expect to have all your own way in whatever it is you're about to inflict on us.'

It was impossible to argue with Eleanor's point on principle, even though it wasn't strictly correct. As godmother to all three sisters, Mrs Rawle had always been considered part of the family, whereas Mrs Canby was a relatively new friend of Eleanor's, and as far as Amy was concerned, an unsteadying influence.

Eleanor's defence of her friendship with Mrs Canby, which amounted to no more than the fact that she came from old New York aristocracy, was indisputable, her descendants, like so many others, having come over on the *Mayflower*. The Frost family had gone on to make its fortune in banking, and her father was now a senator in the United States Congress.

Since becoming a widow, Mrs Canby's disreputable behaviour had led to her being ostracised by her family and that of her late husband, both of which had cut her off from any inheritance or allowance. She was now reduced to living with her maternal aunt, who had also been good enough to provide Mrs Canby's two young daughters with a home, as well as giving Mrs Canby a small allowance on which to live, the amount designed to keep her in basic necessities, without leaving her the means to get into trouble.

Despite the reality of her financial situation, Mrs Canby succeeded in presenting herself as a wealthy woman, and no one who didn't know her would think anything different. At the root of her pretence lay her unshakeable belief that her aunt would one day make her the sole beneficiary of her vast fortune.

Amy kept her voice low, not wishing to cause a scene. 'Can we trust Mrs Canby to be discreet about our situation?'

Eleanor shrugged. 'I don't see why not. It's not as if our predicament is any worse than hers.'

Resigned to the fact that Mrs Canby wouldn't be budged, Amy presented her proposal to the gathering.

'To put it simply, we have to reduce our spending, so we can start to pay off your debts. If we're sensible, and are prepared to make sacrifices, we can clear what's owed within a few years.'

Everyone in the room, apart from Charles Junior, who had recently learned to whistle and was determined to demonstrate his newly acquired skill, remained silent as they took in Amy's words.

Eleanor curled her lip. '*Sacrifices*. What does that mean, exactly?'

'*Sacrifices* is perhaps the wrong way of putting it,' said Amy, already regretting the word. 'Think of my proposals more as *changes*, temporary ones.'

'*Years*, you said.' Mr Eaton wagged his finger at Charles Junior to silence his whistling. 'That doesn't sound temporary.'

'It will be temporary in the sense that it won't be permanent,' said Amy.

'At least you'll be able to see an end to your penury,' threw in Mrs Canby, 'which is more than can be said for me.'

Eleanor and Marion began complaining in the background, drowning out Amy's attempt to explain things in more detail, until Mrs Rawle clapped her hands to silence them.

'You should listen to what Amy has to say before you criticise. She always speaks sense.'

Once the room had quietened, Amy handed her father two sheets of closely written notepaper. 'I've drawn up a list of unnecessary expenses we can rid ourselves of straight away.'

Mr Eaton bawled as he read the items. '*Sell the carriage and horses.* That's impossible. *Give up gambling and cigars*, but I hardly ever . . .' He faltered, his eyes focusing on the carpet. There were things on the list he'd taken for granted all his life, things he couldn't possibly do without.

Eleanor was next to read the list. '*Stop playing bridge.*' She shot a pleading look at her father, who instantly interjected on her behalf.

'Steady on, Amy. Society expects a young woman to play bridge.'

'Only if she can afford to lose the vast sums of money she's

19

been gambling.'

'*Avoid buying fashion items for the next half dozen seasons.*' Eleanor tore the list in two and tossed the pages to the floor, glancing at Mrs Canby for support. 'I refuse to look dowdy in society. I've already made that clear. I have nothing more to say on the subject.'

'Don't look to me for help,' said Marion, picking up the torn pages before Charles Junior could put them in his mouth and start chewing on them. 'I can't ask Charles for anything. His father controls the family capital. We live off his allowance, and will continue to do so until he inherits the estate. Considering the robust health of his father, that could be years away.

'And then there's Lucy and Hester,' she continued. 'They're staying with us while Charles's mother and father are travelling in Europe. They're likely to be away for the best part of a year, which means we've got their expenses on top of everything else. It's not cheap, having two girls out in society at the same time. I only hope they find suitable husbands soon.'

At twenty-one, Hester was already attached to Conrad Harris, a promising young architect. The fact that he was of the professional class and without a good name or fortune, meant her parents didn't approve of him and neither did Marion or Charles. For this reason, they liked to pretend he didn't exist. Amy wished she could do something to help their plight, but the Morton family refused to allow Hester to enter into an engagement with anyone who didn't match their wealth and social standing. It was a situation Amy understood only too well, having faced the same disappointment herself some years ago, and it broke her heart to see it happening again.

She wrung her hands, waiting until the general grumbling had died down before she raised her final point. It was something she'd considered long and hard.

'If you don't want to give up your carriage and horses, Father, and you don't want to give up your new dresses, Eleanor, there is another way of reducing expenses.'

Eleanor looked at her with suspicion, but Mr Eaton's face instantly brightened. 'What is it, Amy? What miracle have you come up with to save us?'

'Rich husbands for you both,' barked Mrs Canby. 'Perhaps you can find one for me as well, while you're about it.'

'Not a miracle, a compromise,' replied Amy, ignoring Mrs Canby's unhelpful comment. 'We could let this house for a few years. It'll save us the cost of running it and bring in extra income. I'll pay for us to rent somewhere smaller, somewhere away from New York, where you can still keep up a decent standard of living but without so much expense.'

Mr Eaton's face fell. 'You want us to give up this house?'

'Only for a few years. Once your debts are cleared, you can return. Many old New York families are resorting to similar measures. No one need know it's due to our financial difficulties. We can say we're doing it by choice, that we'd like a change.'

All this time, Eleanor had remained quiet. Amy placed a gentle hand on her arm. 'What do you think of the idea?'

Eleanor shrank from her touch. 'You've obviously got it all worked out. Where are you planning on sending us?'

'Not far away. Newport, Rhode Island. Many of the good families we know spend their summers there. You won't be completely giving up society.'

'But you hate it there,' said Eleanor. 'You complain whenever we propose a trip.'

Following their mother's death, Amy had spent the summer at Mrs Rawle's villa in Newport. Mrs Rawle thought the change would do her good, when all it did was heighten her sense of loss and disorientation, confirming that without her mother, she didn't belong anywhere or to anyone. For all the sunshine and the sea air, the beautiful landscape and the sunsets, she would forever associate it with the early days of her grief, with foggy mornings and the mournful cry of seabirds.

'I know how much you and Father like the town. It's the next best thing I can offer you to New York. That's why I'm suggesting it.' Now wasn't the time for Amy to consider her own feelings. She had to do what was right to rescue the family finances.

'It's a splendid idea,' added Mrs Rawle. 'As you know, I spend part of every year there myself. We shall see each other often.'

Mr Eaton reached for the torn pages of the list and considered it again. 'We can still keep up our standard of living if we leave New York, you say? Nobody will know of our difficulty?'

'No one will see any difference. As long as you moderate your spending and stop gambling. I'll cover your basic living expenses. We won't be able to entertain the way we're used to doing, and we'll have to make do with one maid. I'll make it a condition that whoever rents this house also takes on the responsibility of our staff.' Amy turned to Eleanor, who was forcing another slice of blueberry tart on Charles Junior to distract him from running around the room. 'What do you say, Eleanor? Do you agree to the terms?'

'It depends on whether you're able to let this place first, doesn't it?'

'Can I take that answer as a yes?'

Eleanor gave a grudging nod. 'I suppose Newport isn't so very bad, and at least I won't have to cancel my next order with Worth.'

There were no thanks, and Amy had never expected any. No one in the family ever considered her with fondness, in spite of everything she did for them. She was just Amy, the slightly strange middle sister, whom none of them understood nor loved, the outsider, even as she lived in the heart of the family and tried every day to please them.

With everything settled, Marion took Charles Junior home to wash the squashed blueberries off his knickerbockers before he spread them on the sofa. Eleanor and Mrs Canby went to take the air in Central Park and discuss between themselves everything that had passed, while Mr Eaton drifted off to his study, his head full of his own concerns. This left Amy to sit with Mrs Rawle, who was quick to congratulate her as soon as they were alone.

'Well done, my dear. Your family doesn't deserve you.'

'Thank you for supporting my plan. I don't think they'd have agreed to it if you hadn't spoken up for me.'

Despite Amy's words, there was no victory in what she'd achieved, only a determination to bring financial stability back into their lives. Eleanor had no prospect of marriage, and with no way of making her own living, she would depend on the family income for the rest of her life. If nothing else, Amy had to ensure their long-term financial security for this purpose alone.

'The next challenge is to find a suitable tenant for the house. Someone prepared to put up with its old-fashioned character. Father won't want any changes. This house is his history, his life. I'll send a note to his lawyer. He might be able to help us find the right person.'

Mrs Rawle gave her a fond look. 'Aren't you glad I persuaded you all those years ago to concentrate on your ambition to become an authoress instead of marrying that young man, who didn't have a cent to his name? If you hadn't let me guide you, you'd have been too busy fulfilling your duties as a wife and mother to write those lovely novels that many of us are so proud of.'

Amy's delight in her achievement had always been tinged with the heartbreak of what it had cost her. Whenever she doubted her choices in life, it was Mrs Rawle she turned to for reassurance.

'Think how your success and fame as an authoress has enabled you to help your family. The financial rewards you've gained are a credit to your talent and your years of hard work.'

Perhaps Amy wouldn't have written any of those novels if she hadn't been persuaded to break off her engagement all those years ago. She was admired by readers all across America, but the general adoration had come at the cost of a particular love. She stared at the cold cuts of chicken forgotten on the plate, the tender flesh drying out in the overheated room. There was no comfort in dwelling on what was lost when it could never be regained.

If Amy was to help her family, she had to focus on writing a new novel, one that would sell even more copies than her previous books. With her savings all gone, she needed to start making money if she was to pay off their outstanding debts and cover their living expenses in Newport. She was fortunate to have achieved recognition in a world dominated by the male intellect. She had a voice and would continue to use it for good. Her father and Eleanor were relying on her. This was not the time to consider what alternative life she might have had if she'd ignored Mrs Rawle's advice and followed her heart. It was time to set to work.

Chapter 4

Rather than seeing the relocation to Newport as giving something up, Eleanor and Mr Eaton decided to view it as gaining a second home. It was nobody's business why they'd chosen to let their New York house, and with the Eatons being such an old and respected family, nobody would presume to ask the question, and if they speculated on it in private, it was never raised in public.

Marion was horrified that her father and Eleanor would be moving to Newport just as the summer season was ending, and claimed never to be seen dead there when all the fashionable people were returning to New York.

When it came to it, she also refused to be parted from Amy, who was such a great help to her in looking after Charles Junior. Even though she never alluded to it, Amy sensed Marion's frustration at trying to manage the house with little support from her husband and with Charles Junior in constant need of attention.

Marion professed to be desperate to engage a new nursery maid, but it was proving impossible to find just the right girl. Hiring new staff was such an expensive business these days and if Amy was there to keep an eye on the boy, there'd be no hurry to find a replacement.

And so it was decided that, for the time being, Amy would

move across the street and stay with Marion, Charles and Charles Junior, rather than relocating to Newport with Eleanor and her father, where she'd be no use to anyone. As Charles's sisters, Lucy and Hester, were also visiting, it proved to be a full house.

While Mr Eaton's lawyer set about the task of finding suitable tenants, Amy went to see Mr Farrand, the editor of *Scribe*, one of America's leading literary magazines, who had published one of her previous novels in serialised parts to great success. He didn't think twice about publishing her next work, agreeing to accept it in monthly instalments, beginning immediately, with payment upfront.

He was so in awe of Amy's reputation that he accepted her proposal without obliging her to admit that although she was determined to write a novel, and quickly, to help the family's financial situation, she hadn't the slightest idea what it would be about.

After she left the magazine office, Amy paused in the street to savour her victory, gripping the cheque for the first instalment, which she would use to pay the first month's rent on the house in Newport. Having the money in her hand was all that mattered. It was too soon to worry that she'd promised to deliver the first chapters of the unwritten novel within the next few days.

The rattle of the carriage wheels on the busy street was almost deafening after the relative quiet of Mr Farrand's office, the dust from the road, thrown up by the horses' hooves, gritty in the air. The sun had finally come out, adding a bright sheen to the sultry heat of the afternoon, and the women of the leisured classes were out to be seen, parading in their open-topped carriages with their lap dogs and their lovers, displaying their finest silk and muslin dresses, their fringed parasols propped against their shoulders at unruly angles.

Despite the heat and the noise, Amy decided to walk home. It was only a few blocks and the exercise would help her mind to focus on an idea for the new novel. Activity inspired her imagination much more than sitting alone in her room staring at a blank page.

It would be a love story; she'd decided that much, but that was all she knew. The prospect of having to come up with a compelling plot so quickly was terrifying. She looked left and right, checking it was clear before preparing to step out into the road, her mind already mulling over the possibilities of a setting, and the kind of challenges her hero and heroine should be made to endure. There could be no satisfying ending to a love story without first testing the lovers with cross-purposes and misunderstandings.

And that was when she saw him. At first, she thought her eyes had deceived her. It wouldn't be the first time it had happened. For months, years after he'd gone, she'd imagined seeing him repeatedly, not only in her dreams, which were vivid and startling, and real enough to touch, but on the street too as she went about her daily business, or as she sat staring out of the window, when even the power of a good novel couldn't hold her interest or alleviate her mind from the constant remembering, the regretting.

All those times she'd been mistaken. It had only been her wishful thinking that had conjured him. Now, those wishes were long passed, and yet there he was, on the other side of the street. Frank Wareham.

She barely caught a glimpse of his face, which was shadowed by the brim of his hat, but his gait was unmistakable, his bearing the same as before, the way he angled his shoulders as he crossed the road, politely stepping aside to allow an elderly woman to pass. Her breath caught in her throat as she realised his intention. He must have spotted her before she'd spotted him and he was heading straight towards her.

Before she could fully realise his presence, a presence she'd longed for every day for almost the past eight years, he was standing in front of her. She blinked once, twice to dispel the image of him, of his grey suit, tailored to every familiar contour of his body. Still, she refused to believe it. It had to be her imagination, summoning a vision of the romantic hero she needed for her new novel.

'Miss Eaton.'

The sound of his voice broke the spell. He was no illusion. This man who'd remained at the forefront of her mind for so many years, was here, now, when she'd least expected him, when she'd given up hope of ever seeing him again.

His eyes, cold and hard as stone, examined every line and blemish on her face. For all the effort he'd made to cross the road to speak to her, his expression betrayed no delight in seeing her again, only recrimination.

She gripped her parasol to stop her hands trembling and fought to keep her voice steady. She wouldn't let him see how much he affected her. 'Mr Wareham, I . . .'

Before she could continue, he raised his hat and continued on his way. It seemed he had no more words for her, and wasn't interested in staying long enough to hear anything she might have to say. It made her wonder why he'd bothered crossing the road to speak to her at all, if the pronouncement of her name had been his only intention.

She watched him make his way along the busy street until he finally disappeared into the crowd. He didn't look back, however much she wished it. He'd examined her face and after so many years apart, had found it disappointing.

Had she changed so much? Of course, she had. Now nearer thirty than twenty, she was thinner than when he'd known her, paler, her complexion suffering from long hours spent at her writing desk, compounded by the sorrow of lost opportunity and the anxiety that came with striving not to let anyone down.

Where her looks had faded, Wareham had grown into himself. Well-dressed and more handsome than ever, he had the same air of self-assurance he'd displayed as a younger man, when the certainty of success had hung about him like an expensive cologne. Even the sight of Amy, so unexpected as it must have been, had failed to stir him as he stood beside her on the pavement.

He'd gone as quickly as he'd appeared, and yet their brief meeting was enough to bring everything back, the agony of feeling, the acute sensation of loss, tender as a bruise on her heart every time she pressed it.

Suddenly she was that young girl of nineteen again, crying among the parlour palms in Mrs Rawle's conservatory, as the older woman persuaded her to break off their engagement. Amy would never forget the arguments she'd used. She'd run them through her mind repeatedly over the years as she'd tried to convince herself she'd made the right decision.

'He might be charming, but he's nothing more than a student at Columbia. He has no money and no prospects, no family name, and no fortune to fall back on if his professional ambitions fail.'

But he was clever and determined, and Amy had faith in him.

'He's studying to be an engineer. At least if he was a lawyer, that would be somewhere near respectable.'

Amy had sobbed, her heart too full to counter Mrs Rawle's arguments.

'You think marrying for love will bring you happiness, but it won't last, not without the security that money and social standing bring. You'll be nothing in society if you marry him.'

Amy didn't care about money or social standing. She loved him. That was all that mattered.

'Remember your aspiration to be an authoress. How do you expect to write novels if you're encumbered by an impoverished husband and countless children?'

She would have managed it somehow. She would have made it work.

'If you won't think of yourself, think of him.'

It was then Mrs Rawle had delivered the death blow to her hopes, forging the argument that would change everything.

'If you love him, let him go. Leave him free to make his way in the world. If he's so confident of making his fortune, don't stand

in his way. The responsibility of a wife and a family will only hold him back.'

In the end, Amy had allowed Mrs Rawle to persuade her she was letting Wareham go for his own good. There was no one on the side of Amy's heart to tell her she was making the wrong choice. Mrs Rawle and Mr Eaton had been in agreement in trying to stop the marriage, and they made sure no one else in their circle found out about the attachment. Marion had been away at school and Eleanor had been abroad for the summer, sailing the Mediterranean with family friends. If Amy had been considered interesting enough to have been invited along, she would never have met him. Without that summer of love and the following years of longing and regret, how different her life might have been.

There was no time to dwell on these things now when there were more important matters in hand. It was pure coincidence that she'd met Wareham in the street. The last she'd heard, he'd settled in California. He must be visiting New York on business and so it was unlikely their paths would cross again.

She mustn't hope for it, or confuse reality with the new fictional world she was trying to create. Nor could she allow her imagination to run away with her, leaving the door open for Wareham to slip inside. Their meeting had happened by chance and been fleeting, with barely a handful of words passing between them. There'd been nothing more to it than that, and there never would be.

Chapter 5

With Marion and Charles's house already fully occupied by Charles Junior, Lucy, Hester and an array of household staff, Amy found herself sleeping in a tiny attic room adjacent to the maids' rooms, a place reminiscent of Mr Jones's studio, only without so much dust or the lingering smell of beer.

The rising heat made the small space too oppressive when Amy sat down to write and so she wandered downstairs to find a cooler place to work. As she entered the drawing room, Charles Junior, who was lying on the rug pretending to be a fish, swam towards her and grabbed her ankles, until she reminded him that fish don't have arms, and he unwrapped himself, wriggling back to the centre of the rug, where he continued to amuse himself in his make-believe underwater world.

She left him to his fishiness and settled at the small three-legged table near the window to begin the first chapter of what she'd decided to call *Missing in Love*. Having failed to come up with an overall plan for the story, she had no choice but to plunge straight in, trusting inspiration to strike as she went along. After all, if she didn't know where the story was going, her readers wouldn't be able to guess either. Keeping them in suspense would be the thing that would encourage them to buy the next edition of *Scribe* magazine, which would in turn keep Mr Farrand happy, and as long as he was happy, he would keep writing the monthly cheques.

If her readers were intrigued by the new story, they might search out any previous novels of hers they hadn't yet read, and improve her sales there too. Her intention was to create a sensation, so the popularity of the latest book would feed into the others. The more money she could earn, the more she could contribute to paying off the family debts and the quicker they could all go home. It was so easy in theory. All she had to do was set her mind to it.

What she hadn't anticipated was bumping into Wareham outside the magazine office. Now, if she was to get any work done, she had to push all thoughts of a second encounter to the back of her mind, or better still, dispel them altogether. If he'd wanted to see her again, he would have said so, rather than simply stuttering over her name before carrying on along the street. He was probably already on his way back to California by now in any case.

An hour later, she'd completed the first page. Encouraged by her productivity, she convinced herself that the story wasn't going to be so difficult to write after all. She was halfway through the second page when Lucy and Hester burst into the room, quickly followed by Marion, fresh-faced from their walk in Central Park and waving a letter.

'It's done, it's all arranged.'

Amy looked up at her sister. 'What is it? What's all arranged?'

The answer was stalled by Charles wandering into the room. 'What's all the fuss about?'

'Father's lawyer has written to inform us that a suitable tenant has been found,' announced Marion. 'The house is let.'

Amy peered over Marion's shoulder, checking the name at the top of the letter. 'This is addressed to me. You shouldn't have opened it.'

'It was sent to my address,' snapped Marion, pinning the letter to her chest. 'Anyway, the house has been taken by a Mr Craig and his wife.'

Craig. The name had been familiar to Amy for a number of years. Not that she'd ever had the opportunity to meet Mr and Mrs Craig. And it couldn't possibly be the same people. It would be too much of a coincidence. After all, Craig wasn't such an uncommon name.

'They're new money, of course,' said Marion. Now she'd delivered the news, she tossed the letter to Amy, as if it were no longer of interest. 'Apparently, they made their fortune from the manufacturing of steel. He's decided to relocate his business to New York and wishes to rent the house until his own mansion has been built on Fifth Avenue. No doubt it will be a vulgar creation in the French style, just like Vanderbilt is building.'

From what Marion had said, it had to be the same Mr and Mrs Craig. There could be no doubt about it. Amy sank into a chair, gripping the letter in her hand, her eyes suddenly too blurred to read it.

'It's bad news that it's been let to an outsider,' said Charles, 'and an industrialist at that. We have to hope he treats the house with respect. People like him lack any kind of morals and have no idea how to behave in a civilised society.' He scratched his beard and yawned. 'I'm going back to my study. Don't let your womanish chatter disturb me again.'

'It's not only the Craigs who'll be living there,' said Marion. 'They'll also be joined by a Mr Wareham, who is something to do with the railroads. Apparently, he's Mr Craig's business partner. Presumably Wareham has no wife of his own and will be relying on Mrs Craig for his domestic comforts.'

The jibe was lost on Amy. Her mind had already drifted back to her chance meeting with Wareham in the street. She'd convinced herself he'd only been on a brief visit to New York, that already he'd returned to California, but her attempt to settle her heart had only served to mislead it.

She'd always known Wareham would make something of himself and her enduring belief in him had been justified. Now he was close by, she would have to face the reality of his success rather than imagining it from a distance. She was bound to see him again. There would be no avoiding him. He was here. He was back. And he would be living in her home across the street.

Lucy, who'd been silently taking everything in, snatched a piece of shortbread from the plate as the maid entered with a tray of tea. 'If Mr Wareham is rich and unmarried, then he must be looking for a wife.' She nibbled the corner of the shortbread and grinned. 'I hope he's good-looking.'

'Don't be absurd,' said Marion, handing Lucy a plate to catch the crumbs by way of a reprimand. 'The man is of the professional class. We won't see him socially, or Mr and Mrs Craig for that matter.'

At the mention of marrying into the professional class, Hester's lips twitched. Lucy glanced at her sister, shrinking quietly in the corner, and gave her a sympathetic look.

The two sisters couldn't have been more different. Lucy was small and full of energy, as fine-boned as an exotic bird, with a wide-eyed expression, a sharp tongue and a mind that missed nothing. She'd made her debut in society the previous year and had gained the reputation of being a beauty and a great catch for any man, as if she were some kind of wild creature in need of taming.

Hester was two years older and quieter in every way. Large-boned with ungainly limbs, she was conscious of not carrying off the latest fashions to best effect, and lacked the spark of her younger sister. Her sense of not quite being up to society's mark made her reserved, and more considered in her thoughts and actions. In spite of their differences, or perhaps because of them, the sisters were inseparable.

'It's too cruel of you to expect us to follow your old-fashioned rules, Marion,' said Lucy. 'Times are changing. New York is filling up with eligible men with new money, who you say are out of bounds. You forget how many young men were lost during the Civil War. Are we all meant to remain spinsters to suit your prejudice?'

Marion gave her a disparaging look. 'There's no need to be so dramatic.'

But Lucy wouldn't be silenced. 'We're in a changing world. Our values have to reflect that if we're not to be left behind. You can't expect us to live in the past.'

'You don't know what you're saying,' replied Marion with a visible shudder.

'I know exactly what I'm saying. Hester is in love with Conrad, but because he's of the professional class, working to establish his reputation as an architect, you all look down on him and refuse to approve their marriage.' She turned to Hester, who was doing her best to disappear into the corner. 'Look at her. She's heart-broken. It's unjust to keep the two of them apart, just because he wasn't born into our limited social circle, and has no name and no fortune.'

Amy remained silent, staring at the pattern on the carpet. Hester's plight was no different to the one she and Wareham had suffered all those years ago.

'How can any of you judge someone for being a member of the professional class,' continued Lucy, 'when one of our own flesh and blood is an authoress. The fact that she earns money by her pen has degraded the standing of the whole family. We either accept that times are changing and get on with it, or continue to live as hypocrites.'

It was too much to listen to. Amy's heart was still raw from meeting Wareham in the street, from seeing the disappointment on his face when he realised how much she'd aged. She didn't need this further humiliation. Nor did she need to hear Lucy discuss the only man she'd ever love as if he were nothing more than a financial commodity, someone to be valued for his wealth above all else. She got up from the chair. 'Please excuse me.'

For all they thought of her, Amy might as well have gone against the family and married Wareham when he asked her, rather than deferring to their prejudice. Instead, she'd devoted herself to a life of loneliness and duty. In spite of everything she'd done, Mrs Rawle was the only one who was proud of her achievements, and that was only because she'd encouraged her ambitions to write in the first place, and she wasn't strictly family.

It frustrated her to think the sacrifice had all been for nothing, that the family couldn't have thought any worse of her if she'd stood up to them and become Wareham's wife after all.

Chapter 6

Amy was sitting at the small table in the drawing room, keeping one eye on Charles Junior who was lying on the rug pretending to be a fish again while she continued to work on the first instalment of *Missing in Love*. Despite her promising start, she'd already stalled. It wasn't the work that was the problem. She never usually had this much difficulty. It was having Wareham so close by that was causing the distraction. Just knowing he was across the street had thrown her ordered mind into disarray, prompting her to constantly relive their parting moments all those years ago.

'I'll accept a long engagement, Miss Eaton, if that's what your father demands. I'll take you on any terms, if it means that one day, you'll be my wife. I'll wait a lifetime for you, if I have to.'

Wareham's words still haunted her, even after all this time. The tears had run down his face as he'd said them. He hadn't been ashamed to reveal his heart to her, even as she fought to hide her own pain.

Despite his pleas, she'd broken it off with him, believing he needed his freedom if he was to fulfil his dreams. Her father wouldn't have allowed a long engagement anyway and she hadn't had the courage to go against him.

During the weeks and months that followed, she'd expected

daily to receive a letter from him. Their hearts were too entwined to untangle so entirely, but nothing ever arrived. He'd taken her at her word. Their separation had been complete, absolute. It was years before she stopped rushing to the door every time a letter arrived, before she was able to accept that she would never hear from him again.

Her writing became a refuge, a way of occupying her mind and shutting the world out. Creating stories with happy endings stopped her dwelling on her own lack of a happy ever after. Her success as an authoress had been unexpected and the satisfaction she took from it went some way to making up for what was lost, until eventually, she convinced herself that her work and fulfilling her duty to her family were enough.

Marion wandered into the drawing room and rang the bell for tea, ruminating on the best way to enjoy it. Amy dipped her pen in her inkwell and forced her mind back to the present. She had to remain focused if she was ever to get any work done.

The discussion over whether Marion wanted lemon or cream with her tea dragged on. 'The cream tastes so good, but it does terrible things to my digestion. Lemon, on the other hand . . .'

Amy closed her eyes and wished herself somewhere else. Had Jane Austen suffered the same frustrations as she wrote her novels, sitting at a tiny table in the parlour at Chawton? She suspected the answer was probably yes.

The tea things had been cleared away and Charles Junior carried off for his nap when Lucy burst into the room, throwing her parasol aside and pressing a card to her chest.

'I've done it and you mustn't scold me for it.'

Marion lifted her head from the sofa cushion and opened her eyes. 'Where's Hester? I thought she was with you. I've told you not to go out alone. If you can't chaperone each other, you must take Amy with you.'

'Hester has been with me all afternoon,' declared Lucy, her face reddening as she said it. 'She's just this minute gone up to her room to lie down. She has a headache.'

The explanation was too emphatic. Amy suspected Lucy was covering for her sister, that she wasn't upstairs sleeping off a headache, but had gone to meet Conrad.

'Then what is it, Lucy?' asked Marion. 'What have you done that either has or hasn't earned you a scolding?'

'I've secured us an invitation for dinner at the Craigs for tomorrow night.'

There was a beat of silence before Marion responded, her eyes wide with horror. 'Then you must refuse it. We don't mix with people of that kind.'

It was then that Charles drifted into the room and asked if there was any tea. With everyone's attention focused on Lucy's announcement, nobody had a mind to inform him he'd missed it.

Lucy stamped her foot, counting on a display of petulance to get her way. 'Mr and Mrs Craig are living in Amy's home. We have a duty to know them, even if it's just to check they're looking after the house properly.'

Her desire to know Mr and Mrs Craig was nothing to do with checking the house, and all to do with meeting Wareham, the most eligible bachelor to have appeared in their limited social circle for years. It was ridiculous to feel possessive, but still Amy's heart stirred at the thought of Lucy's interest in him.

'Will it be just Mr and Mrs Craig at dinner, or will there be other guests too?' Amy despised herself for asking the question, but was unable to stop herself.

'I've been assured that Mr Wareham will be there,' replied Lucy, displaying a sense of victory. 'The evening would be too dull otherwise.'

'It's not a bad idea to meet the Craigs,' said Charles, after giving it some thought. 'Your father would appreciate us checking on the people living in his house. It would offer him peace of mind to know the old place is being looked after.'

Amy had to admit he had a point. She had no objection to

socialising with Mr and Mrs Craig. Wareham, however, was a different matter. She couldn't face the humiliation of seeing him again after the disparaging way he'd looked at her in the street.

Lucy stifled a squeal. 'Then it's agreed. I'll send a note telling them we accept.'

'Whatever possessed them to invite us in the first place?' asked Marion, snatching the invitation and interrogating it for correctness. 'It was rather forward of them.'

'I left a calling card the day before yesterday. It seemed only right, given the circumstances.'

'Tread carefully, Lucy,' said Marion. 'Your mother will never forgive me if I return you to her with your reputation in ruins.'

Marion's warning was interrupted by the sound of a carriage pulling up outside. Lucy dashed to the window and lifted the lace curtain to get a clearer view of the street. 'That must be Mr Wareham now, come and see.'

How was Amy supposed to concentrate, knowing she only had to look out into the street to see Wareham? And if he happened to catch sight of her, she knew the look of disdain he'd give her. She pushed the thought to the back of her mind and ordered Lucy to move away from the window.

'But it's him. It's Mr Wareham. He's standing on the Dutch stoop of your house, searching his pockets for the door key. He's staying with the Craigs, so it must be him.' She hid behind the curtain while she studied him, ignoring Amy's repeated pleas to step away from the window.

'He's very good-looking and well-dressed. Come and see. Look how fine he is.'

Amy didn't need to look out of the window to see how fine he was. His image was planted in her mind and had been so for a very long time. She couldn't trust her reaction if she crossed the room and watched him enter her home, couldn't trust herself not to betray her overwrought feelings to everyone who saw her. No one here knew of her past association with him, but it wouldn't take much for them to notice something was wrong.

This time, it was Marion's turn to scold. 'Come away from the window, Lucy. You'll see him all in good time.'

'Is it wrong for Wareham to know I'm curious about him?' asked Lucy, her eyes fixed on the street like a hunter studying its prey. 'I'm sure he'd be flattered.'

In spite of everything, Amy's heart went out to her. At Lucy's age, love was an adventure, a game of cat and mouse, determined by chance and luck. It only needed one cruel twist of fate to turn it from comedy to tragedy.

'Don't build up your hopes, Lucy,' warned Amy. 'Mr Wareham might not be everything you'd want him to be.'

'He's rich and good-looking. What more could I want him to be?'

Gentle and kind, thought Amy, *and generous of heart*. No woman who knew him could be blamed for falling in love with him.

'Do you think he's the sort of man who would buy his wife diamonds from Tiffany's and indulge her with the latest clothes from Paris?' asked Lucy. 'Will he keep a box at the opera, do you think?'

Marion gave her a disdainful look. 'Don't forget he's an engineer. He made his fortune on the back of the railroads. His fingers are probably covered in oil and grease. He won't care for satins and silks, never mind jewels or boxes at the opera.'

The judgement was too cruel. Amy turned her attention to the half-written page on the table in front of her, resisting the urge to respond to her sister's comments. If only she'd had an ounce of Lucy's boldness, how different her life might have been today.

The more she thought about seeing Wareham again, the more her courage failed her. She couldn't do it. She couldn't face him again, not after meeting him in the street the other day, not after everything that had passed between them all those years ago.

'It might be best if you all go to dinner at the Craigs without me tomorrow night. I have to finish writing the first instalment of *Missing in Love* for Mr Farrand. The publishing schedule is very tight.'

Charles peered over her shoulder, his eyes narrowing on the closely written page, the rough crossings out, and giving every indication that he was looking at it rather than reading it.

'Of course you must come. Your father will be relying on you to report back to him. It's your home, after all. You must be curious to see how those rough industrialists are treating it.'

There was to be no way out of it. After suffering his disdain in the street, she would be forced to see Wareham again soon, not at some vague time in the future, but tomorrow night. Her heart could hardly stand it. She took a deep breath to steady her pen as she angled the nib on the page. Another day, and then the evening, and it would be over and done with. He'd already seen the changes in her, seen how thin she'd become and pale, seen how the years of missing him had taken their toll on her looks and her character. And she'd seen in his face how glad he was that he hadn't married her after all. All she could do was reassure herself that the worst had already passed. Surely, there could be nothing more terrible to endure?

Chapter 7

Amy had been restless all day at the prospect of seeing Wareham that evening. She'd failed to meet the deadline for delivering the first instalment of *Missing in Love* and been obliged to send a note to Mr Farrand, begging for more time. Presenting polished work on such a regular basis didn't allow for the luxury of a bad day, a sleepless night or for taking time away from her desk to look after Charles Junior when Marion declared herself too busy or too ill to attend to him.

Since meeting Wareham in the street, she'd kept to the house, trying to concentrate on the story, grabbing any solitary hour she could between looking after Charles Junior and Marion's demands for her company. After all, as her sister reminded her whenever Amy expressed her need to work, why else was she staying in her home as their guest, if not to serve her family?

Her domestic responsibilities weren't the only reason for Amy's slow progress. She hadn't anticipated Wareham reappearing in her life or the emotional turmoil it would generate. She'd only seen him for a minute in the street, but it had been enough to feed her imagination. Now, the memory of him was in every word she wrote.

He'd grown better looking in the years they'd been apart, as many men did between the ages of twenty-three and thirty-one. His body had filled out to become the mature man he was always destined to be, while everything she knew of his success persuaded her that his character hadn't changed.

Amy was still thinking of this when Lucy burst into the drawing room with an evening dress draped over her arm, the acres of fabric billowing across the floor behind her.

'Will this lemon silk enhance my complexion over dinner tonight, bearing in mind the number of candles the Craigs are likely to use to light the table, or will it make me look too pale?'

Complexion was everything. To be fashionable, the skin needed to radiate a shell-like transparency, enhanced by a natural blush. This bloom, as it was known, had to be achieved without the help of powder or paint.

Amy glanced at the dress. 'It depends on how much wine you drink. You know how it brings the colour to your cheeks.'

'I don't want to end up looking like a rooster, or one of those peach-fed hens everyone serves at dinner these days.'

'Make sure you show our hosts respect this evening. It's very generous of them to ask us to dine with them.'

'They're not like us. You don't have to credit them with such fine sensibilities,' said Lucy, abandoning the dress in a crumpled heap on the sofa. 'I don't know what's got into you lately. You're no fun at all.'

'I'm busy with my work, that's all.'

It would have been too mortifying to admit the truth. For the sake of her dignity, it was best to pretend what had passed between them all those years ago had never happened. Judging by the way Wareham had reacted to her in the street, she was sure he felt the same way.

The hand-holding, the stolen kisses were long passed. It was almost possible to believe those moments never happened, but for the lingering memory of them, the physical sensation of his touch that had stayed with her, and would do so forever. Instead of mourning what was lost, she told herself to feel lucky that she'd experienced Wareham's love at all, that once she'd been fortunate enough to have been the most important person in the world to him.

Amy was still brooding over her work an hour later when Marion interrupted. 'You'd better get ready for dinner. We have to leave in a few minutes. I've sent Lucy upstairs to change. The pink dress she'd put on was a mistake. She's too high-coloured for it. She'll end up looking like a fighting cock after a second glass of wine. She said you told her not to wear the lemon silk, but I disagree.'

'I won't go tonight. Will you give Mr and Mrs Craig my apologies?' Now it came to meeting Wareham again, she couldn't face it. 'I have to deliver the first instalment of my novel tomorrow. Mr Farrand has already given me extra time to work on it and it still isn't finished.' It wouldn't do to let him down a second time and if she didn't deliver the work, she wouldn't be paid.

'It never usually takes you this long. What's wrong?'

Amy stared at the blank page, cursing herself for the precious hours she'd wasted, mooning over her romantic hero.

'The characters are proving difficult to work out, that's all.'

Charles wandered into the room, fiddling with his emerald cuff-links. 'Can someone see to Charles Junior? He's hiding under the desk in my study and refusing to go to bed.'

Marion tipped her head towards Amy, imploringly. 'Will you go to him? You're the only one who can do anything with him.'

It was quicker for Amy to check on Charles Junior than to argue that one of the maids was capable of taking care of him. She slipped across the hallway to the study, calling Charles Junior's name in a sing-song manner to jolly him along. He was more likely to be pliable if she made a game out of persuading him to go to bed.

When he didn't respond, she put her head around the door and smiled. 'Charles Junior . . .'

The smell of vomit hit her before she could finish the sentence. She held her breath, trying not to retch and stepped into the room. 'Are you all right? Where are you?'

He wasn't under the desk as his father had claimed. She checked his usual hiding places beneath the sofa and behind the curtains, but he was nowhere to be found. The only clue to his presence was the dark pool of vomit congealing on the edge of the rug.

'You can come out now, Charles Junior. There's nothing to be scared of. No one's going to scold you.'

Charles Junior stepped out from his hiding place behind the door, his face lined with tears, the front of his pyjamas sodden with sticky lumps of vomit. Whatever he'd eaten was brown and had probably contained a large amount of butter. He ran forward and threw his arms around her. Amy tensed, trying not to heave at the smell.

'What have you been eating?'

'Mama's molasses candy. Don't tell her.'

He sobbed through the words. No punishment could be worse than the one his stomach had already served on him. Amy peeled him off her dress, trying not to show her revulsion.

'Let's take you upstairs. We'll get these clothes off and give you a bath. How does that sound?'

He nodded, wiping the back of his hand across his face, spreading tears, mucus and vomit into his hair. There was no point scolding him for stealing his mother's sweets. He'd learned his lesson and she could have cried for him.

There was nothing for it but to pick him up and carry him. Her dress was spoiled in any case and it was the quickest way to get them both upstairs. She gathered him up in her arms, turning her head from the worst of the smell and hurried him out of the study.

Marion was in the hallway, fixing her hat in the mirror. She gave Amy a cursory glance as she passed by. 'Is he all right?'

'He's been a little sick, that's all. Too many sweets. I'll wash him and put him to bed.'

Charles was standing by the front door, checking his pocket watch. 'Leave it to one of the maids. Go and change, quickly. We're already late.'

Marion gave him a horrified look. 'Don't be ridiculous. We can't leave Charles Junior in the care of one of the maids when he's so sick. Amy must stay and look after him.'

'Can't someone else keep an eye on him once I've cleaned him up? I have to finish the instalment of *Missing in Love* this evening.'

'Don't be selfish, Amy. You must think of Charles Junior before you think of yourself.'

Charles slipped his watch into his waistcoat pocket. 'You're his mother, Marion. Don't you think you should stay with him?'

Marion lifted her face to the mirror, titivating the feathers in her hat, as if he hadn't asked the question. 'Lucy and Hester are already waiting for us on the stoop. We can't leave them standing on the street like common harlots. It's time to go.'

'Yes, my dear.' Charles gave Amy an apologetic shrug before following his wife out of the door, pulling it closed behind him as he went.

The house fell into quietness. With the family gone, the staff would be putting their feet up below stairs. Amy didn't begrudge them a night off, and there was no time to think about her own supper.

Once she'd bathed Charles Junior and got him off to sleep, she changed into a nightdress and settled down to work in the nursery where she could keep an eye on him, placing her paper and pot of ink on a tray, which she balanced on her knees. The four-hour candle at her feet gave off just the right amount of light without disturbing the sleeping child.

Soothed by the comforting atmosphere of the nursery and the sound of Charles Junior's steady breathing, Amy lost all sense of time. In this gentle space, she was able to throw off all doubts and distractions, and the opening pages of the novel finally began to flow from her pen.

She was replacing the candle, which had already burned down to a nub, when she heard a disturbance on the other side of the door. She looked up at the sound and whispered.

'Marion, is that you? There's no need to worry about Charles Junior, he's—'

'It's me.'

Lucy flung open the nursery door, her eyes glittering in the candle flame as Amy held it between them. 'I went to your room but you weren't there. Why are you sitting up so late? Don't you know what time it is?'

'Where's Marion? I thought she'd come to check on Charles Junior.'

'Marion's gone to bed. Mr Craig's guffawing gave her a headache.'

'You need to do the same. It's late.'

'Yes, but first I need to tell you about Wareham.' She grabbed Amy's free hand and gave it a squeeze. 'What a fine man he is. What a glorious evening I've had.'

Amy's heart turned to lead in her chest. 'You were pre-disposed to like him. You said as much yourself.'

'Forget what I said. That was just foolishness. Even if he was poor I'd adore him. He's so charming and well-mannered and very handsome.' She suppressed a giggle, squeezing Amy's hand harder than ever. 'Did I mention he was handsome?'

'You've only met him once. First impressions can be deceiving.'

Lucy dropped her hand as if it were a hot coal. 'Don't spoil this for me, Amy.'

'Tread carefully, that's all I'm saying. You hardly know him. You don't want your heart broken.'

'He's not the kind of man to go around breaking hearts. Mrs Craig wouldn't think so highly of him if he was.'

'What does Marion think of him?'

'She kept her head turned away from him all evening, which

was quite a feat considering she was sitting opposite him all through dinner. She'll have a sore neck tomorrow from all that looking the other way.'

'That might explain the headache.'

Lucy giggled, revealing the playfulness of the child that was still within her. She was so pretty, so unencumbered by cares. How could Wareham resist her?

'What does Charles think of him?'

'You know Charles. He thinks whatever Marion tells him to think.'

Why should it matter to Amy what Marion and Charles thought of Wareham? There was nothing to be gained from it. It was Lucy now who would fight for him to be accepted by the family. Lucy, who was used to always getting her way.

'I haven't told you the most exciting thing of all.'

Amy didn't want to hear anything else. She'd already learned more than she wanted to know. She'd hoped Lucy would be unimpressed with Wareham, that his steady character wouldn't be lively enough for her, but he'd clearly charmed her, or at least, his wealth and success had done so.

'He has stated his intention to marry.'

The words were a hammer blow to Amy's heart. 'Who is he intending to marry?'

'He hasn't decided yet, but I plan to make up his mind for him. I don't think it'll be so very difficult.'

'There'll be many women clamouring to be his wife, I'm sure.'

'I intend to capture him before anyone else in New York claims him. No one will care about his lowly origins now he's made his fortune.'

The sickness Amy had felt earlier while cleaning the vomit from Charles Junior rose up again in her throat. She took a deep breath, pushing the feeling down. If Wareham married a fortune hunter, he'd be marrying for the wrong reasons and his good heart would be squandered on a woman who didn't appreciate it.

'He deserves to be loved for himself.' The words escaped from Amy's mouth before she could stop them.

'You're so old-fashioned, Amy. And why would you care who he marries? He's nothing to you.'

Amy's eyes focused on the candle flame as it danced on the breath of Lucy's laughter. 'It's late. You should go to bed.'

Once Lucy had gone, Amy blew out the candle and made her way to her room, feeling her way in the dark. There was something consoling about the blank night, where there was nothing to see and no way of being seen. If only she could remain in the darkness forever, smothering herself in anonymity, creating within it a place where she didn't have to hide her regret or the pain of her loss.

Perhaps when she saw Wareham again, she wouldn't feel the same about him. After so many years of going their own way, they were different people. It was ridiculous to worry that he might still have any power over her heart. She'd met him briefly in the street, and it had caused a pang, but that was just sentimentality, an understandable regret for what was lost, for what might have been. None of what was passed had survived. She was free of him, and he was free of her. It was just her own fanciful notions telling her differently. None of it was real. Wareham wouldn't have expressed his intention to marry, giving hope to a beautiful young girl like Lucy, if his heart wasn't free.

Tomorrow, after the steadying influence of a good night's sleep, she'd no longer care about Lucy's plans, or Wareham's intentions. She would put it out of her mind and concentrate on her writing. She'd had her chance with Wareham, and squandered it. The situation was of her own making and she had to resign herself to it. Saving Eleanor and her father from their financial disgrace was all that mattered. This was where she could make a difference, even if she received no thanks for it.

Chapter 8

It was already the afternoon when Amy dashed out of the house, closing the front door quietly behind her, conscious that Charles Junior was still sleeping off the sickness that had plagued him the previous evening. Marion was also resting, having claimed that eating at Mr and Mrs Craig's table had been too much of a strain on her constitution, and that the disruption to her digestion had brought on one of her heads.

After Lucy's visit to the nursery, Amy had stayed awake for most of the night, polishing the first instalment of *Missing in Love*. Never had a piece of work been such a struggle, but at last it was finished and there was no going back on it. If Wareham was there on the pages, then so be it. He was never going to read it, and wasn't vain enough to recognise himself even if he did. She could only hope the work would please her loyal readers and keep them anticipating the next instalment, for without her readers, Amy was nothing.

There was an art to picking up a hansom cab on the New York streets, which usually involved going into battle with a smart-faced city banker or a society grand-dame, her maid laden with packages from Bloomingdale Brothers bringing up the rear guard. But today, Amy was in luck. The late summer heat had grown sultry and the clouds had turned the colour of lead. With the threat of thunder keeping everyone indoors, there was no one to challenge her for the cab that had just turned into the street, its wheels throwing up the grime on the dirt-strewn road.

The cab rattled to a halt in front of her, the horse snorting dust from its nostrils as it pulled against the reins. The driver stared straight ahead as Amy gave him the address of *Scribe* magazine, his eyes heavy with the heat beneath the brim of his cap. She put his lack of response down to the humidity, and was about to reach for the door handle when a man in a well-cut grey suit emerged from the cab. The driver hadn't stopped for her to get in, but to let the passenger out.

'Please forgive me, I—'

The stranger looked up. But it wasn't a stranger at all. It was Wareham. Amy felt the colour drain from her face. It was inevitable their paths would cross now he was living on the same street, and yet somehow, she hadn't prepared herself for the awkwardness of it.

He lowered his eyes, staring at the dust from the road that clung to the hem of her skirt. 'Ma'am.'

Amy too looked away, staring at the space between them as if it were an abyss. The muscles tightened in her throat as the seconds seemed to spread out into minutes, his movements, as he stepped aside to allow her more room on the pavement, appearing to happen in slow time rather than at a normal human pace. After all these years of being apart, it was impossible to believe he was here now, close enough to touch.

'Mr Wareham, there you are.' A light-tailed voice drifted through the quiet stillness of the afternoon. 'Don't you dare run away from me.'

Amy looked up from under the brim of her bonnet. Lucy was charging down the front steps of the house, restraining the energy in her youthful limbs that urged her to break into a run.

'Stay right where you are, sir.'

She must have been watching from the window and spotted Wareham getting out of the cab. Her pink silk day dress shimmered along the lines of her slim figure as she moved through the air, unhindered by the humidity that slowed down the afternoon. In her hurry to catch Wareham, she'd failed to put on her outdoor shoes. Amy frowned at the unseemliness of her behaviour, a nymph in high-heeled slippers and openwork lace stockings, tripping along the street without a hint of self-consciousness.

The neighbourhood would run wild with gossip if Lucy was seen unaccompanied in the street talking to a man who was neither her brother nor her father, which meant Amy was obliged to act as her chaperone, however uncomfortable it might be. Like it or not, she was trapped.

Wareham lifted his hat like the respectable gentleman he was always destined to become.

'Miss Morton. It's nice to see you again.'

Lucy paused to catch her breath, the image of the child she'd been not so long ago evident in her excitement. In that moment, she displayed every advantage Amy had lost in the years since Wareham had known her. Advantages she'd lost more rapidly for the wanting of him.

'I've been looking out of the window all day in the hope of catching you. I mean to invite you to dinner. You must bring Mr and Mrs Craig. They've been so generous, having us to dine last night.' She glanced at Amy. 'Everyone here is so dull. We long for fresh company.'

Amy cringed at Lucy's innocence, her lack of worldliness. 'It's not a good idea to linger in the street, Lucy. There's a storm due any minute and you've neglected to put on your shoes.'

The words seemed to knock a little of the puff out of Lucy's manner. 'You're quite right, Amy. Thank you for pointing out my failings in front of our Mr Wareham.'

Our Mr Wareham. Not *Amy's*, not *hers* any longer. Already Lucy had claimed him, the man that those closest to Amy hadn't wanted her to have. What a difference a few years could make to how a man is perceived, not for his character which is generally constant, but for the wealth he has accumulated, the success he has achieved.

The conversation moved on. The time and the day for the dinner were agreed between Lucy and Wareham, while Amy stood mutely to one side, assuming a neutral countenance, so as not to betray her regret for what might have been, or her eagerness to get away. Once the arrangements were settled, he gave Lucy a polite bow, gesturing his own desire to leave. Amy couldn't help feeling he was as keen to have the meeting over as she was.

Lucy's eyes ranged from Wareham's face to Amy's and back again as she searched for a reason to detain him.

'Oh, but I haven't introduced you to Amy.' Lucy grabbed Amy's arm, pulling her off-balance and displaying her to Wareham as if she were a prime chop in a butcher's window.

'This is Miss Amy Eaton. Her younger sister, Marion, is married to my brother, Charles. She's a famous authoress. If you don't believe me, just look how she grips those pages to her chest as if they were the dearest thing in the world to her.'

Wareham stared at the ground, still refusing to meet her eye. 'Miss Eaton.'

He was still angry with her, unable to forgive her. Even after all these years, Amy could read his every gesture, his every thought.

If Lucy noticed his coolness, she didn't respond to it. 'You might be familiar with her novels. She's written at least six. Isn't that so, Amy?'

'I'm sure Mr Wareham has no interest in my novels.'

'Novels are for the leisured classes. I'm far too busy for such trivial pastimes.'

His eyes remained fixed on the ground as if he were searching for something lost. Whatever it was, Amy knew there was no way of finding it.

A strand of hair had come loose from one of Lucy's silver

combs. She twirled it around her finger, coiling it like a snake. 'Mama says I'm not allowed to read novels until I'm married. She says they might corrupt me in some way.' She shrugged, displaying a calculated smile. 'I can't imagine what she means.'

It was bad enough to be ignored by Wareham, but to have her work, her success disregarded and diminished was mortifying. She didn't claim to be a great literary talent, or to be producing fine literature. Her novels were meant to offer an escape from the disappointments of everyday life, to give solace to the lonely and the broken-hearted. All the small comforts she gained from writing them she hoped to pass on to her readers. They were designed for distraction. She claimed nothing else for them.

The cab was still waiting, the horse irritably scraping the ground with its hooves. The driver frowned at Amy. 'Are you getting in, or is the gentleman planning on paying for me to wait here all day?'

Wareham stepped forward to pay his fare, adding extra to cover the time the driver had been kept waiting, while Lucy stood by, insensible to the awkward situation she'd created.

Desperate to be gone, Amy climbed into the cab. 'Forgive me, but I must leave now. I promised my publisher these pages by three o'clock and it's already half-past. Lucy, I beg you to go home before the storm comes. You'll ruin your slippers.' She couldn't stand to chaperone her any longer. She simply couldn't do it.

The atmosphere was heavy inside the cab, the threat of thunder looming as if it too were trapped in the enclosed space. The scent of Wareham's cologne filled the air, its citrus notes catching on her tongue, pricking the insides of her nostrils. She held her breath, but still she couldn't shake off the sensation of his lingering presence, the intimate part of him that he'd unwittingly left behind.

She'd allowed herself to believe she was over him, that in the years since they'd parted, her heart had healed over. It had only taken the brief meeting with him the other day, the minutes spent with him now, to realise she'd been deceiving herself. Her heart would never be free of him, and in spite of everything, she never wanted it to be.

The cab pulled away from the pavement. Amy watched Lucy and Wareham through the window, as arm in arm, he walked her to her door. What an elegant couple they made; Wareham, full of the dignity of his success, and Lucy, with her youthfulness and her whole life ahead of her.

Still, it wasn't Lucy but Wareham who held Amy's attention, her eyes refusing to shift from his commanding presence as the cab continued on its way and eventually passed him by. Even then, she looked over her shoulder, watching his figure diminish in the distance, until the cab turned the corner and he was no longer in her sight.

She leaned her head against the seat and released the sigh she'd been holding in. Wareham's reaction when Lucy introduced her weighed heavily on her heart. This was how it was going to be from now on. Now he was part of her social circle, she'd have to get used to being in his company, to suffering the brunt of his long-held disdain.

She ran her fingertips over the loose pages on her lap. The joy she took in her work, the satisfaction she gained from her success was all there was now. There was no hope, and no way back to the intimacy she and Wareham had once shared. They weren't simply strangers, but estranged, and she had to accept that that was how it would always be.

Chapter 9

Amy finally received a letter from Eleanor, informing her that she and her father had settled into a cottage, which they'd found for themselves in Newport, with *cottage* being a rather misleading term for what she went on to describe as a spacious six-bedroom house overlooking the Atlantic Ocean.

They also seemed to have befriended the people at the centre of the so-called *good* society who remained out of season, many of whom had relocated from New York for similar reasons to themselves. Despite the cost of renting the house being more than Amy had anticipated, she was relieved to know Eleanor and her father were adjusting to a new way of living, even if they only intended it to be temporary. There was no shame in trying to salvage what had been lost. Only pride made it seem so.

Amy was still thinking about the letter when Hester knocked on her bedroom door.

'Am I disturbing you? May I come in?'

Dressed in a pale green silk dress, with fresh flowers woven through the loops of her hair, Hester could have passed for the goddess of spring. She gripped a lace handkerchief in her right hand, crushing it repeatedly against her leg as she paced the small confines of Amy's room.

Amy pointed to the chair in the corner. 'Please sit down. You'll make your face all red and blotchy if you carry on and Marion will refuse to let you out of the house.' Although spoken in jest, the threat of being kept at home by a heightened complexion was real.

'Don't be mad at me, Amy, for what I'm about to say. Everyone is quick to tell me what's best for me, but nobody will listen to what I really want. No one knows my heart better than I do.'

These words could have come from Amy's mouth almost eight years ago, but it wasn't the time to think about that now. 'Is this about Conrad?'

'Is it wrong to want to marry the man I love? I know he's not rich, but he has good prospects. He's hard-working and smart. He's not from our small society, but few people are. Why should that matter if we're in love?'

It was too cruel to have to consider these questions when Wareham's reappearance in Amy's life had brought so many raw feelings back to the surface. 'It's not my place to give you permission to marry, or to tell you that you shouldn't. Marion has been charged with taking care of you while your parents are in Europe. She's the person you need to convince.'

'There's no hope of her support. She objects to anything or anyone new.'

'What makes you think I'd feel differently?'

'You're not like her. Everything you say and do is more considered. You always have everyone else's best interests at heart. I thought you'd understand how we feel, that you might take mine and Conrad's side.'

'You're asking me to go against her?'

'You're the only one in the family with a sympathetic heart.'

Was a sympathetic heart the same as a wounded heart? Hester was confusing the real Amy with her reputation for writing love stories. Amy had learned the hard way that what happens in romantic novels rarely happens in real life. It was the escapism

58

the stories offered that drew readers to them. To achieve this, she'd learned to separate her head from her heart, dividing herself into two beings as she wrote. The author inside her always strived for a happy ending, while in reality, Amy was resigned to a life of loneliness.

'Are you sure you love him, Hester? Are you prepared to spend your life with him, even if he's poor, even if the family disowns you?'

'Can't you persuade them to accept him?'

'You overestimate the power of my influence.'

'Are you saying you won't help us?'

'I won't speak against Conrad, but perhaps we should give him a little time to prove himself. You're both still very young.'

Were these the words she'd liked to have heard when she pledged to marry Wareham? The acceptance of a long engagement could have made all the difference. After all, time had proven his worth. If only she'd had the strength of mind not to let others persuade her out of it, or had the resolve to marry him anyway and let everyone else be damned. Then, just as now, his wealth was the last thing that mattered to her.

Hester sighed. 'You're right. If Conrad has to prove himself to the family, then that's what he'll do. No matter how long it takes. Do you believe true love endures, that it can last forever, no matter how much it is tested?'

The question was too close to Amy's heart. How could she answer without betraying herself? She pushed her feet into her slippers, displaying her intention to go downstairs. 'There's no more time for talk. Marion will scold us if we're late for breakfast.'

Chapter 10

Amy sat alone in her room, watching the minutes on the clock tick by. She dreaded going downstairs, knowing that tonight, Marion and Charles would be entertaining Mr and Mrs Craig, and that Wareham would be there. Marion had been furious when Lucy told her she'd invited them without consulting her first, but once the invitation had been made and accepted, it would have been impolite to cancel it, and Marion didn't want to risk the speculation spreading through old New York society as to what the reason for it might be. Cancelling a dinner party at the last minute with people such as the Craigs would be worse than actually entertaining them. Continuing with the spirit of rebellion, Lucy had also taken it upon herself to invite Conrad, even though Hester had been forbidden to see him.

Amy had put on the same grey silk dress she wore for every formal dinner. It didn't bother her that she'd been seen in it many times before. It was elegant and understated, and it suited her complexion, such as it was these days. Some women needed acres of lace and silk ruffles, ostrich feathers and jewellery to make them feel secure in society in the same way that soldiers needed battledress to face the enemy, but Amy was long past any desire for pretence.

To survive the evening, she needed to feel like herself and not stand out. This in itself would take courage enough. She would slip into the background and say as little as possible, observing the domestic social comedy that would play out in front of her as the evening progressed and the wine flowed, a comedy that would serve as meat for her new novel.

In spite of everything, she was eager to meet Mr and Mrs Craig, and keen to know what they thought of her beloved home now they'd settled in. Everything else, she would put to the back of her mind. She and Wareham were strangers now, and she would treat him as such. After almost eight years of silence between them, and his obvious coolness during their last two meetings, there could be no reason to do otherwise.

She was pinning up her hair when Lucy charged into the room, her peach satin dress, trimmed with cream lace, a compromise between the pink and the lemon dresses that Amy and Marion had failed to agree on before the previous dinner.

'Don't let me interrupt you, Amy. I've just remembered something Mr Wareham said and I'm desperate to share it with you. I don't know why I didn't think of it before.'

'It can't have been very important. Otherwise, you wouldn't have forgotten it.'

Amy checked her reflection in the mirror, trying not to feel disappointed by the face that stared back, at the cruel tricks age had played. Her youth had deserted her, slipping away unnoticed while she'd been concentrating on other things.

If Lucy noticed the collapse of Amy's spirit as she looked at herself in the mirror, she didn't comment on it. 'It's very important, because now I know you've been keeping secrets from me all this time.'

Amy wrung her hands. 'Secrets? What secrets?'

'After you rode off in the carriage the other day, Mr Wareham told me he knew you from before.'

'It's true.'

'Why didn't you mention it when I spoke to you about him?'

'I had nothing to say about it, and it was a long time ago.'

'He had much to say about you.'

'What did he tell you?'

The words were out of Amy's mouth before she could stop them. If he'd told her about their broken engagement, she had to be prepared for the difficulties it would inevitably create between her and Lucy. Would Lucy be so keen to catch Wareham if she considered him to be Amy's cast-off? And would it be such a terrible thing if she was no longer interested in him? She scolded herself for the thought, for the glimmer of hope it generated in her heart.

'He said how much you'd changed. He was quite shocked by it. He wouldn't have recognised you if he'd seen you across the street.'

But he had recognised her across the street. The sight of her had even prompted him to risk his life, dodging the oncoming carriages as he rushed over to speak to her. It was just a turn of phrase of course, and she shrugged off the comment, pretending it hadn't cut deep.

'I was your age when I last saw him. I've changed a lot since then and so has he. He's different to how I remember him too.'

Lucy grinned. 'He's so handsome, but I don't have to tell you that. You saw him for yourself, and will again as soon as you come down for dinner.' She checked her face in the mirror, the reflection prompting a smile of satisfaction. 'He was wearing a very fine coat last time. I wonder what he'll be wearing tonight.'

Wareham always used to think girls who behaved like Lucy were foolish. She wondered if he'd still think so now, or whether his age and his success had changed him and made him more susceptible to flattery, to the power of a pretty young face to seduce.

'Beware of showing too much interest in him, Lucy. You have your reputation to think of. Your mother would never forgive me or Marion if we allowed you to damage your chances of finding a suitable husband.'

'Are you saying that Mr Wareham, with all his wealth and good looks, wouldn't be a suitable husband?'

There was an archness to Lucy's question that stung Amy to the core, despite the innocence that lay at the root of it. If Lucy knew what had passed between her and Wareham, she wouldn't be so cruel.

'You know how people talk. It would only take one word to be said against you and nobody would want to know you.'

She didn't examine her motives too closely, whether she was warning Lucy off Wareham for her own good, or for herself. It was foolish to think there could be any hope for her where Wareham was concerned; still the thought of him loving someone else was too painful to bear.

'Don't worry, Amy. I won't spoil myself or bring the family into disrepute by doing anything as shocking as writing a novel.'

'You have no idea how cruel society can be.'

'You must accept that there'll be men who'll want to marry me, even though it's too late for you.'

'Nothing would please me more than to see you settled with a suitable husband.'

'You never know, Amy. You might find a widower willing to take you on, someone who needs a wife to look after his children and run his household. It must be hard for you, knowing you'll never be a man's first choice.'

The words cut like a knife. 'Lucy, that's enough.'

'Mrs Rawle admires you for making something of your life as a spinster, but I don't want to end up admired by women instead of being loved by a man. And I won't be someone's second choice, living in the shadow of a dead first wife. I'll persuade Wareham to love me, if that's what I choose to do. He'll fall for me so hard he won't be able to help himself.'

'You're being ridiculous. You don't even know him.'

'I don't need to. I'll make him into whomever I want him to be. And if I can't love him, his wealth will make up for his shortcomings. I'll have a fine life and far more independence as his wife than I have now, when I'm answerable to everyone but myself.'

'You wouldn't be so cruel as to trap him.'

'Just watch me.'

There were tears in Lucy's voice as she stormed out of the room. Surely, she couldn't have meant everything she'd said. She envied the love Hester had found with Conrad, even if it was forbidden, and craved a similar intoxication. That's all it was. She was also tired of being treated like a child, and was ready for the independence that marriage would bring. Amy couldn't blame her. Lucy was the same age as she was when she fell in love with Wareham.

Had Lucy been correct? Was she really jealous of the attraction Wareham was bound to feel towards a younger, prettier woman? Was she ready to stand by and watch him fall in love with someone else? If he married Lucy, he'd be a part of the family forever. There'd be no escaping him. It would be agony. And all the while, she'd be invisible to him.

This was no thought to carry as she braced herself for the evening ahead. She tried to settle the cauldron of emotions that were threatening to overwhelm her, as once more she frowned at her image in the mirror.

There was no reason to be anxious. She'd been in Wareham's company a hundred times before. Nothing he could say or do would surprise her. No one was interested in what had happened in the past, least of all Wareham. The world had moved on and she must do the same.

Chapter 11

The guests had finished their drinks in the drawing room and had already sat down for dinner when Amy finally gathered the courage to go downstairs.

'There you are,' said Marion, frowning at her late arrival. 'I thought you'd decided not to join us.'

The only available seat at the table was directly opposite Wareham. Amy had misjudged the timing of her entrance. Now, there would be no way to avoid meeting his eye repeatedly over dinner.

Mrs Craig stood up to shake Amy's hand, the warmth of her greeting registering not only in her words, but in her smile. 'Miss Eaton. I'm so pleased to meet you at last, my dear.'

Dressed in an understated mauve tulle dress, her generous proportions were corseted for comfort rather than style, her hair held in place by a series of tiny mother-of-pearl clips. Her only other adornment, beyond the simple gold band of her wedding ring, was a cameo, displaying the silhouette of a young man, which she wore on a black velvet ribbon at her throat. Amy returned her smile, matching its sincerity. Here was warm-heartedness and wisdom, here was someone who instantly put her at ease.

'I hope we haven't dragged you away from your work.'

'Not at all,' said Amy. 'I've been looking forward to meeting you.'

Amy took her seat at the table, placing herself directly in front of Wareham. If he thought she'd arranged the seating deliberately, then he'd misjudged her character.

'I believe you already know our Mr Wareham?'

How much did Mrs Craig know about her and Wareham? Her easy manner suggested he hadn't told her of their broken engagement. His pride would never have allowed it.

'Yes, we . . .' Amy faltered.

'We knew each other briefly during my time at Columbia,' said Wareham, rescuing the silence as she hesitated, his eyes fixed on the arrangement of tumbling geraniums in the centre of the table.

They might have only known each other for a matter of months, but the intensity of their acquaintance had made it seem much longer. Their attraction had hit them like a fever the first moment their eyes met, and had quickly turned from youthful infatuation to mutual understanding, and in no time at all, deep love. That summer, they'd spent every possible moment together. They'd had so much to say to each other that no one else had existed for them. Set adrift by her mother's death, Amy had gone about with him unchaperoned. She'd needed someone to love and her heart had settled on Wareham.

Lost in her reminiscences, Amy was unaware of the conversation going on around her until Mrs Craig placed a hand lightly on her arm.

'I can't spend another minute in your company, Miss Eaton, without mentioning your novels. I'm one of your most loyal readers. Please tell me there's to be another one soon. I've read everything you've written at least twice and I'm impatient for something new.'

'You're very kind.' Amy would never get used to the responses she received from her readers, whether they were flattering or otherwise. 'The first instalment of my new novel will be appearing in the next edition of *Scribe* magazine.'

'We'd better mind our manners if we don't want to find ourselves in one of your stories,' said Mr Craig, toying with his empty wine glass.

Beyond the playful twitch of his whiskers, he betrayed a directness of manner that trod a fine line between straightforwardness and appearing brusque. It was this approach, Amy imagined, that made him such a successful businessman.

Marion cringed at his bonhomie. Amy gave her a warning look. If the evening was to be a success, she had to stop bristling every time Mr Craig spoke.

Mrs Craig smiled at Marion, her fingers absently smoothing a tiny crease in the tablecloth. 'Do you scour your sister's novels to see if she's slipped you onto the page?'

'I have no taste for reading,' said Marion, rolling her eyes as if the idea was ridiculous. 'If Amy has stolen my character for one of her stories, I'd rather not know about it.'

An awkward silence settled around the table. Mrs Craig looked from Marion to Amy and back again. 'You haven't read your sister's books?'

'Having a novelist in the family isn't one of our proudest achievements. That sort of thing isn't done in our social circle.'

Astonished, Mrs Craig asked the same question of Lucy and Hester. 'Have you read Miss Eaton's work?'

They both shook their heads.

Mr Craig leaned over to his wife and whispered loudly, 'Reading's not for everyone, my dear.'

'I suppose not.'

There was no hiding that Mrs Craig was appalled by the family's lack of interest in Amy's work. 'I have to say, I'd be flattered to be immortalised in one of your stories, Miss Eaton. Use me as you will. I don't care how ridiculous you make me appear.' She paused, glancing with mischief at Wareham. 'I feel I must apologise for Mr Wareham's lack of enthusiasm for your novels. I've tried to encourage him to read them, but he doesn't have the time. He has no idea what he's missing.'

Amy shot a look at Wareham, whose eyes were still fixed on the tumbling geraniums. 'Mr Wareham has far more important things to do than read my novels.'

Was it her imagination, or did he shudder as she spoke, as if a serpent had crossed his path?

Mrs Craig raised her glass to Amy. 'Don't underestimate the importance of your work, Miss Eaton, or take any notice of Wareham. You bring happiness to countless readers, including myself.'

Wareham cleared his throat, appearing to choke back a comment as Mrs Craig stressed the word *happiness*.

Amy lowered her eyes, focusing on the plate of food that had just been put in front of her. Marion had refused to go to any trouble or expense to feed the Craigs, and had insisted on serving boiled turkey with stewed celery and tomatoes rather than the canvas-backed ducks or soft-shelled crabs she'd offer to guests she wanted to impress.

What was it Wareham had been about to say? It was probably nothing. And even if it was something, what did it matter? She forced a piece of turkey into her mouth. She had to stop reading significance into everything Wareham said or did. It would only drive her mad.

Silence never reigned for long with Lucy at the table. She batted her eyes at Wareham. 'So tell me, Mr Wareham, what is it you do all day?'

Marion gave a dismissive gesture with her hand. 'We don't want to hear all about that. Let the gentleman eat his dinner.'

'But Mr Wareham's work is important and I want to know all about it.'

'That's very kind of you, Miss Morton.' He fixed Lucy with his charming gaze. 'Most women have no interest in engineering.'

Amy swallowed another mouthful of turkey. The only interest

Lucy had in engineering was in the wealth it had created for the man sitting next to her. Lucy had recently seen a magazine article that said the best way to get a man's attention was to show an interest in his passions, and from what Amy could gather, she was putting it to the test.

'I'd like to know how it made you such a very rich man.'

Amy tried not to choke on the stewed celery. People of their social standing didn't talk about money. They weren't even supposed to think about it. It was too vulgar. To his credit, Wareham appeared unruffled by the question.

'The real value of engineering lies in the way it can make people's lives safer. The fortune I've made simply happens to be a consequence of the success of my invention, although not an unwelcome one, of course. Having financial means opens up many more opportunities to a man such as me, who started with nothing but ambition and a determination to work hard.'

The colour burned on Amy's cheeks. Did she imagine it, or did he throw her a glance as he made his last comment?

'Much of what I've earned will be used to fund the development of future projects.'

Lucy leaned forward, placing her chin in her cupped hand in a way that would later gain her a scolding from Marion for being *fast*. 'How fascinating. You must tell me more.' She was drawing him out like a soft-pawed cat toying with its unsuspecting prey.

'My objective is to improve safety for the working man. Many of the new industries, such as steel production and oil refining have created deadly environments in the factories. A man shouldn't have to put his life at risk just to earn a living.'

It was all Amy could do to remain still in her seat. Here was the same Wareham she'd fallen in love with all those years ago, a man of principle and integrity, and he was fulfilling his ambitions, just as he said he would. Money and success had done nothing to change him. If anything, it had improved him.

Marion dropped her fork a little too loudly on her plate. 'This conversation is far too serious for the dinner table, Mr Wareham. You're as bad as Amy, who talks of the importance of debating political reform, and of giving people ideas above their station.'

'There's nothing wrong in encouraging women to campaign for the right to vote,' replied Amy, jumping to her own defence, 'or in giving them the right to fight for decent, safe employment.'

Wareham cut her a glance, but she was too caught up in her indignation to pay any attention. If women like Marion wouldn't support the fight for women's rights, it would be a much harder struggle.

'If you ask me,' said Marion, 'we should leave all the decision-making to the men. It's the natural order of things.' She nudged her husband. 'Don't you agree, Charles?'

Charles, who appeared to have been paying no attention to the conversation, put down his wine glass and nodded. 'Yes, anything you say, my dear.'

Amy caught Mrs Craig's eye and suppressed a smile, suddenly glad to have a new friend and ally at the table.

Once the plates had been cleared and the fruit salad served, Lucy returned to her own personal campaign. 'Last time we had dinner, Mr Wareham, you told me of your desire to marry. Have you thought any more about the kind of wife you're looking for?'

'We've been trying to persuade him to marry for years,' roared Mr Craig. 'We've put every eligible young lady we could find in his path, but not one of them, no matter how pretty or accomplished, has been able to tempt him.'

Lucy gave Wareham an arch smile. 'There'll be someone to tempt him in New York, I don't doubt it.'

'I hope you're right,' said Wareham, dabbing his lips with his napkin. 'I shan't put it off any longer.'

'Tell me, what qualities are you looking for in a wife?'

Amy cringed at Lucy's forthrightness, but the blush on Wareham's cheeks suggested he didn't mind. She'd even go as far as to say he was enjoying himself.

'I don't care if she's tall or short, fair or dark as long as she knows her own mind, and doesn't allow herself to have her judgement swayed. Weak-willed women are too easily persuaded to abide by the will of others, whether right or wrong. You only have to look at Mr and Mrs Craig to see the kind of marriage I wish for. They're a true meeting of minds and an example of faith and constancy.'

Amy couldn't bear to look at him as he spoke. Everything he wished for were the things she'd failed him in. Every word had been aimed at her, and he couldn't even bring himself to look at her as he said it.

Lucy leaned back in her chair. 'Is that all? That can't be too difficult. Is there nothing else you wish for?'

'Beyond that, any woman who sets her mind to it is likely to capture me.'

'How about love, my dear Wareham?' asked Mrs Craig. 'Doesn't that have a part to play in it?'

The conversation stalled at the question. It was a moment before Wareham had an answer. 'I don't see what love should have to do with any of it. It failed me in the past. I see no reason to trust it again.'

Each word, each sentiment, stung Amy more than the one that went before it. She wanted to run from the room, but wouldn't give Wareham the satisfaction of seeing it.

Lucy played with the lace collar at her throat, drawing Wareham's eye to her fine neck. 'Love is such a trouble.' She pointed to the other side of the table, shifting Wareham's attention to Conrad, who was sitting next to Hester, his arm gently brushing hers in a way he thought no one would notice.

'Poor Mr Harris here is desperate to marry my sister, but without a fortune, she isn't allowed to have him. Even if he was rich, our parents would make her refuse him, because he isn't from the right kind of family, and that is simply unfixable.'

Amy stared at the napkin on her lap. Lucy had no idea of the ground she was treading on, still it was mortifying, not only for her but for Wareham too, not to mention for Conrad and Hester.

Mr Craig looked at Conrad, as if noticing him for the first time. 'What is it you do, Mr Harris?'

'I'm an architect, sir. As with most professions, it takes time to build a reputation. Without a reputation, I have no means of keeping a wife.'

'He's extremely talented and hard-working,' added Hester, squeezing Conrad's hand under the table. 'It's only a matter of time before New York society recognises him.'

Mrs Craig nodded, sympathetic to their situation. 'Have you considered a long engagement?'

'My parents have refused,' replied Hester. 'Conrad is only here now because Lucy invited him.'

Lucy grinned as if she'd scored a victory. 'You see the difficultly love brings, Mr Wareham? I believe we're all better off without it.'

Amy could stand it no longer. She was about to feign a head-ache and leave the table when Wareham beat her to it.

'You must excuse me. There's some business I need to attend to.'

Mr Craig frowned. Unlike Wareham, life appeared to have hardened him enough for him not to be offended by Lucy's disparaging comments about self-made men. 'Can't it wait until the morning? We haven't had our brandy and cigars yet.'

'I'm afraid it needs my urgent attention. Please stay and finish your evening without me.'

Marion nodded to Amy. 'See our guest to the door. Make sure he's given the right hat on his way out.'

There was a pause, during which Amy froze. She couldn't be alone with Wareham, not after everything he'd just said. Wareham must have had the same thought.

'There's no need to trouble yourself, Miss Eaton. I'm capable of finding my own hat.'

The door had only just closed behind him when Lucy clapped her hands and declared a victory.

'What a delightful man Mr Wareham is. I look forward to spending more time in his company and I'm quite sure he feels the same about me.' Her eyes burned into Mrs Craig, urging her to respond, until she finally gave in and humoured her.

'He did seem quite taken with you.'

'Charming as he is,' said Marion. 'He's not one of us and he never will be.'

Lucy scowled. 'Times are changing. I don't see why Mr Wareham shouldn't be considered a suitable husband in any area of society. He's rich and good-looking and in want of a wife. What else could I ask for?'

'A good family,' snapped Marion.

Amy glanced at Mr and Mrs Craig, mortified on their behalf over Marion's comments. 'You make him sound like a racehorse.'

'We only allow thoroughbreds in this family, and everyone would do well to remember it.' Marion raised her butter knife, jabbing it in Lucy's direction. 'If I allow either you or Hester to set your hearts on men who are below you, your mother will never forgive me.'

Now it was Conrad's turn to abandon the table. He'd been looking increasingly uncomfortable with the conversation and could stand it no longer. He offered a respectful nod as he stood up to leave. 'Please excuse me. I also have some urgent business to attend to.'

Denied permission to see him out, Hester remained seated at the table, her head turned from the remaining guests as she tried to hide her tears. Amy's heart bled for her. She wanted to soothe her with the promise of a happy ending, but it was beyond her powers to grant it.

After the men had retired to the study for a glass of brandy and a cigar, Lucy brought the conversation back to the only reason she'd arranged the dinner.

'Tell me, Mrs Craig. How did you meet Mr Wareham?'

Amy cringed at the forthrightness of the question, but couldn't deny she was as keen to know the answer as Lucy. As much as she tried to convince herself she was a disinterested party, her curiosity got the better of her.

'Fifteen years ago, our only son, Julian, was killed in a railway accident. It was a freak occurrence. He was dismounting the carriage at the end of his journey when he happened to slip off the edge of the platform. Some oil had been spilled and it took his feet from under him. There was no guard on the platform and the driver had no way of knowing he was trapped. The train pulled out of the station, unaware that Julian was caught beneath its wheels.'

Amy reached for Mrs Craig's hand. 'I'm so sorry.'

'It made us realise that there was a need to improve safety on the railroads. Not only for the passengers but also for the people who work on them. The number of accidents and deaths is quite shocking in these new industries. As no one else seemed prepared to do anything about it, Mr Craig and I decided that we would.

'We spent the following years scouting for ideas for safety features. We listened to any engineer who had come up with an invention to help prevent accidents on the railway and pledged to fund the most effective one when it came along.

'Seven years ago, we were approached by Mr Wareham, a young man who'd recently graduated from Columbia. He had nothing to his name and nothing to recommend him beyond his clever invention and a determination to make it succeed.'

This was the Wareham Amy recognised; smart, ambitious, hard-working and confident.

'What was the invention?' asked Lucy.

'It was a coupler for connecting railroad carriages to one another. Many railroad workers had lost their hands or suffered terrible injuries attempting to couple the carriages manually. This cleverly designed piece of metal promised to significantly reduce the risk of such accidents occurring.'

Wareham had always been destined to achieve something

worthwhile. If Amy had had the courage to stand by him when he asked her to, she'd still be sitting at this table, enjoying the company of Mrs Craig, only she'd be here as his wife, not as a stranger.

'Mr Craig and I were instantly taken with Mr Wareham. He was clever and charming and had invented just the kind of safety device we'd been looking to invest in. He needed help with the composition of the steel the coupler was to be made of. It had to be strong, but not too brittle. This was where Mr Craig's expertise came in. They spent months working on it. Once it was ready, the invention was patented, and the three of us set up the business for the manufacturing of the part. It was soon in demand from railroad companies up and down the country.'

Marion frowned at Mrs Craig. 'You said *the three of us*. Were you involved in the business too?'

'To keep the costs to a minimum, I helped to run the business in the early days, and managed the new investors we needed to fund our expansion into mass production.' She threw a pointed look at Amy, as if she expected her to know exactly what she was talking about. 'Mr Wareham was the inventor, and we provided the money to get everything up and running in the first instance, along with offering the expertise on the composition of the steel, making us equal partners. The company is now a great success and Mr Wareham's invention has prevented countless injuries. Our original, small investors are also doing very well with their dividends. It's a happy situation all round.'

'It's a real success story,' added Amy, unable to disguise how much pride she felt in Wareham's achievement.

'And the story continues,' said Mrs Craig. 'We've made the decision to relocate the business to New York from California, as most of our suppliers are in the area. It'll make running the business more efficient.'

'Will Mr Wareham be setting up home here too?'

There it was again, the curiosity Amy was unable to temper.

Why should it matter to her if Wareham lived in New York? It wasn't as if she'd have to see him.

'We hope he'll join us. We've worked so closely with him over the years, that we see him as part of our family. Since losing our dear Julian, he's the nearest we have to a son.'

Having shown no interest in Wareham's invention or the company, Lucy now perked up. 'He sounds delightful, and yet he's never married. I wonder why that is?'

'He's very focused on his work, and has little time for anything else,' said Mrs Craig. 'He once confessed that he'd been disappointed in love some years ago. I suspect it put him off risking his heart to anyone ever again.'

'That's unfortunate,' said Lucy. 'We'll have to do what we can to restore his faith in love.'

Was it possible to have such faith restored after being so cruelly used? Amy couldn't have broken his heart irredeemably. His life had been too full of challenges and successes for him still to be dwelling on the past. He was extremely eligible. It would only be a matter of time before a beautiful young woman such as Lucy captivated him and then he'd be lost, or perhaps saved, whichever way you looked at it.

'Do you still play an active role in the business?' Amy needed to know she wasn't alone in pursuing her work, that other women also found financial reward and satisfaction in their labour.

'The company has grown too big for me to manage single-handedly, although I like to keep my finger on the pulse. I insist on a policy of employing women wherever we can. It's important we all have the opportunity for financial independence, don't you think so?'

'I do,' replied Amy.

The expression on Marion's face said no, she didn't think so. Amy understood that Marion's view was based on her social conditioning and on the fact that she'd been fortunate in marrying well. Unlike Amy and Mrs Craig, she'd been neither inspired nor obliged to work for a living. Having lived a cosseted life, she failed to recognise that most women weren't lucky enough to be able to rely on their husband's inherited wealth, that it was vital they were given the right to their own earning power. After all, where would Eleanor and her father be now if Amy wasn't able to earn the financial means to save them?

The rest of the evening passed in a blur as Amy played Wareham's words over in her mind. He hadn't been able to bring himself to look at her, and yet everything he'd said had been aimed at her. Every thought and feeling he'd expressed about love was a consequence of the way she'd treated him almost eight years ago. He was still angry with her. Every gesture he'd made to avoid catching her eye proved how much he despised her.

Still, it was impossible to believe he had any interest in Lucy as his future wife. He'd shown her good manners and charm, but it was no more than that. Lucy's wishful thinking, the facility she had for always getting her way, wouldn't work this time. Amy would have been able to tell if Wareham was in love with her. He would have betrayed it in his eyes. She knew what he looked like when he was in love, and tonight he'd lacked all traces of it.

But this was the wrong way of thinking. He claimed to have given up on love and was prepared to marry without it, and Lucy, for all her inexperience, was wise enough to understand this. Would Wareham allow himself to be seduced by Lucy's youth and beauty and would it make him happy where love had failed?

Lucy's forwardness had created more than a little awkwardness in the room. She'd been too indulged and assumed the right to be given her way in all things. And yet, Amy couldn't help admiring her tenacity and her confidence. Lucy was determined to get what she wanted and nothing would stand in her way. If Amy had displayed such strength of purpose all those years ago, how different her life would be today. Now, instead, it would be Lucy taking the prize while Amy stood silently by and watched her do it.

Chapter 12

Before leaving the dinner party, Mrs Craig had taken Amy to one side and invited her to drop in for tea the following afternoon.

'There's something I'd like to discuss with you. I think you might find it interesting.'

There was enough intrigue in the invitation to make Amy look forward to the next day. Even if it turned out to be nothing, the prospect of getting to know Mrs Craig a little better pleased her. Based on their brief acquaintance, she had the promise of becoming a true friend. The fact that she was so closely attached to Wareham had nothing to do with it at all.

Knowing she had a social engagement worth looking forward to, Amy had made good progress on *Missing in Love* that morning, and for once, felt less guilty than usual for putting aside her writing for a few hours.

Mrs Craig greeted her with the same warmth she'd displayed the previous evening, softening much of the trepidation Amy felt at returning to her family home now it was in the care of strangers.

How extraordinary it was, being welcomed into the place where she'd always done the welcoming, how odd to have to wait to be invited to sit on her mother's sofa in the drawing room. She could only find comfort in the fact that the situation was temporary, that in the fullness of time, thanks to her own efforts, her mother's beloved home would be returned to her.

Everything was as it had always been, from the over-furnished rooms to the display of her mother's favourite gewgaws. It had been foolish to fret over anything being different.

'Apart from the removal of a few mirrors, nothing's changed,' said Mrs Craig, observing Amy's eyes scouring every corner of the room. 'When you reach a certain age, seeing your own reflection seems less necessary. I see no reason to remind myself of my mortality a dozen times a day.'

Amy understood Mrs Craig's sentiment and was glad to see the mirrors gone. Still, everywhere she looked, there were echoes of her past life; stains on the carpets from leaking ink wells, scratches on the furniture from childhood games, faded patches on the curtains where the afternoon sun had bleached out the colour. Each mark had its own story that those who lived there now would never know. Together they added up to a series of recollections that no one else would ever be a part of.

For the first time, Amy was able to look at her family life, her history, from the distance of someone standing outside of it. Every detail reawakened a memory, and each freshly reawakened memory brought into sharp focus the realisation that something vital had been taken away, prompting the grief she felt over her loss of her mother to come rushing back with full force.

Amy had a rewarding professional life and was surrounded by her family, so why did her loneliness feel so overwhelming?

'Are you all right, my dear? You're looking very pale.'

Mrs Craig was standing over her, a cup of tea rattling in her outstretched hand. The cup and saucer, made of fine porcelain, had been Amy's mother's favourite. The tea service, bought in Paris on a whim, had been the very devil to transport home without breaking it.

'I'm fine. Thank you for the tea.' She forced herself to smile at her hostess. None of what Amy was feeling was Mrs Craig's fault.

'I hope you don't mind, but I invited Mrs Canby to join us. I believe she's a friend of yours.'

'Well, I . . .' Amy would hardly call Mrs Canby a friend and couldn't imagine what connected her to Mrs Craig.

True to form, Mrs Canby eventually sauntered in. 'Forgive me, I'm late again. Isn't it always so?' She glanced at the drawing room, her eyes skimming the old-fashioned pictures on the walls, the familiar curtains. 'How strange it is to be here again and yet nothing's changed.' She threw herself onto the sofa next to Amy. 'Has Mrs Craig revealed why we summoned you here?'

'I wouldn't go as far as to say she was summoned,' replied Mrs Craig, her tone sharper than Amy had yet known it.

'I assumed I was invited to drink tea.'

The more Amy thought of it, the more Mrs Craig and Mrs Canby seemed a strange pairing. The strained look on Mrs Craig's face suggested she might be thinking the same thing.

'It was something you said over dinner last night that inspired me to bring us all together,' said Mrs Craig. 'Mrs Canby and I met recently. We're both members of a local group campaigning for women's right to vote. As a free-thinking woman and a working woman, it's a cause that lies very close to my heart.'

'And mine, too,' added Mrs Canby, pouring herself a cup of tea. 'If women are to be treated equally and fairly, we need to have a say in who governs us.' She popped a sugar-coated bonbon in her mouth and crunched it between her teeth. 'My father is Senator Frost, so I know what I'm talking about.'

'It's the women in less privileged positions in life who'll benefit most from suffrage,' continued Mrs Craig. 'The challenge we have as a campaign group lies in spreading the word. As things stand, it's probably not obvious to many women how having a vote would enable them to fight for improved pay and working conditions, better education and medicine. We have to find a way of exposing them to the discussion.'

These were the same sentiments Amy had expressed many

times. 'I've been thinking of adding a storyline in my new novel to raise the issue.'

Mrs Canby roared. 'We only got you here to try to convince you of that very thing. We could have saved ourselves the trouble.'

'You should only use your novel as a vehicle for our campaign if you're sure,' added Mrs Craig. 'You wouldn't want to risk losing readers over it.'

'That's exactly my concern.' Amy rescued the plate of bonbons from Mrs Canby's lap and fixed her with a steady look. 'I didn't realise the issue was so close to your heart. I've never heard you talk of it before.'

'I've tried discussing it with Eleanor, but she's not the slightest bit interested. I assumed you might feel the same way.'

It was true that Eleanor paid little attention to anything apart from her fine clothes and playing bridge. Amy wondered what she did all day beyond her social calls and interminable shopping, whether she had anything at all to satisfy her internal life.

'Does your father support your views?' asked Mrs Craig, returning the plate of bonbons to Mrs Canby's lap. 'It could be very useful having a senator on our side in Congress.'

Now Amy understood why Mrs Craig had befriended Mrs Canby and why she was being so generous with the bonbons.

'Absolutely not. He's cut me off without a cent. It's what prompted me to join the campaign in the first place.'

'You're doing it to cause him embarrassment?' asked Mrs Craig.

'I wouldn't go as far as to call it that, but he shouldn't have cut me off.'

'So this is your revenge?'

'Does my motivation matter all that much? The result will amount to the same thing, whatever the thinking behind it. What matters is that women win the right to vote. Isn't that so?'

Amy disagreed. 'Our motivation matters a great deal if it's something that can be used against us. It's vital that women prove they're responsible enough to be given the right to have a say in how our country is governed. If we come across as emotional, vengeful creatures, it will do the cause more harm than good.'

'It's not only about revenge,' snapped Mrs Canby. 'If we have the right to vote, we'll have the power to challenge our fathers and brothers over the control they have over our money.'

'You mean your allowance,' corrected Mrs Craig.

'That money should be mine. I was born into the family and have a right to a share in its wealth, just as my brothers have.'

'Your brothers all work in the family banking business,' added Amy. 'They earn their living. It's only fair that you should be given the opportunity to do the same.'

'So that's the reason you've joined the fight for women's suffrage,' said Mrs Craig, finally finding satisfaction in Mrs Canby's answers. 'You want the right to work alongside your brothers.'

For the first time since Amy had known her, Mrs Canby seemed unsure of herself. She glanced helplessly at the clock on the mantelpiece. 'Is that the time already? I really should be going.'

'Were my questions too harsh?' asked Mrs Craig after she'd seen Mrs Canby to the door. 'I don't want to put her off working for the cause. We need all the help we can get.'

'You were simply trying to get to the root of the matter.'

There was an awkward pause before Mrs Craig spoke again. 'I didn't only invite you here today to convince you to write about the campaign for women's suffrage. I hope you understand that.'

'I've learned not to pay too much attention to anything Mrs Canby says.'

She wondered what Wareham would think of her friendship with Mrs Craig. Would he suspect her of trying to work her way back into his life or would he care so little that he wouldn't even notice her presence? It was fate after all that had brought them together. Amy couldn't have known that Wareham's business partners would become the tenants of her family home, or that she'd end up living across the street from them.

It would be best if she avoided him. It would save any unnecessary awkwardness. Just because she was friends with Mrs Craig, there was no reason for her and Wareham's paths to cross any more than they had to.

'So tell me, Miss Eaton. Why did Mrs Canby's family cut her off? Did she do something terrible?'

'Not by everyone's standards, but by the rules of old New York society, it was unforgiveable.'

Mrs Craig leaned forward in her chair. 'My dear, you're going to have to put me out of my misery and tell me what it was. I won't sleep tonight otherwise.'

'After her husband's death, Mrs Canby left her two little girls with their nanny and went to live openly as the mistress of another man.'

'I can see why people wouldn't take to that. Was it the shock of losing her husband that prompted it, do you think?'

'She never loved him. Her family had persuaded her to marry him because he was from the right sort of family. It was also a way of keeping her from the man she really loved, who wasn't quite so useful to her father's business or his political ambitions.'

'And this was the man she ran to after her husband died?'

Amy nodded. 'It's not hard to understand why.'

'Are they still together?'

'It only lasted a matter of months. The pressure from her family was too much for him to endure, but it did enough damage to Mrs Canby's reputation to last a lifetime.'

'The poor woman.'

'It was only by cutting her off that her family could maintain their credibility and their social standing, not to mention her father's political career. They also had their business to protect as much as their personal reputations. Such digressions in our small society are not forgotten and are never forgiven. It's all credit to Eleanor for standing by her. She won't risk being seen with her in public, but she's never objected to receiving her privately at home.'

Mrs Craig frowned. 'What a strange society you have here, it's so narrow and unforgiving.'

'I suppose it is. But it's the only world we know. To challenge it would be to give up everything, including those we love. It takes a brave heart to do it. You only have to consider what happened to Mrs Canby to see that.' Amy forced a smile, trying not to betray the damage its restrictions had done to her own life. 'If nothing else, it gives me plenty to write about in my novels.'

Chapter 13

The first instalment of *Missing in Love* was to be published in that day's edition of *Scribe* magazine. It was too late to worry about how the story would be received. The words were printed and had been sent out into the world. If the readers didn't like it, they'd soon write to her, courtesy of Mr Farrand, and let her know. Whether the responses were good or bad, Mr Farrand would have something to say about them and expect her to bear them in mind.

She got up at dawn, determined to get ahead with writing the next instalment before the rest of the house was awake, settling at the small table in the drawing room with her pen and paper, catching the best of the early morning light, hoping the sun would help to shake off her tiredness.

She'd barely slept, thanks to Charles Junior, who after a bad dream, had crawled into bed beside her, insisting that only his aunt Amy was able to make sure the monsters conjured in his mind didn't return to torment him. Despite Charles Junior only having two arms and two legs, sharing a bed with him was like sleeping beside a restless octopus.

As soon as breakfast was over, the family started drifting into the drawing room. Marion sat at her bureau to write her letters, determined to inform all her friends about how awful Mr and Mrs Craig and Mr Wareham were. Demolishing their characters was the only way she could salvage her own reputation after having them to dine, while Lucy sat next to her, writing her own letters, praising Mr Wareham to all her friends, most of whom were the daughters of the women Marion was writing to.

Later, while Marion was having her regular meeting with the cook to discuss the menus for the following week, Conrad, who just happened to be passing, dropped in for tea. Amy didn't believe he *just happened to be passing* for a minute, but welcomed him anyway. Remembering love's need, she couldn't blame Hester for inviting him.

Amy had learned to work with the murmur of conversation going on around her, and without Charles Junior, who was taking a nap to make up for the sleep he'd lost during the night, she was able to make progress. By the time Mrs Rawle arrived, excitedly waving a copy of *Scribe*, she'd completed three reasonable pages and was feeling pleased with herself.

'Take a look,' said Mrs Rawle, pressing the magazine into Amy's hands. 'Aren't you excited to see it? I ran my eyes over it on the cab ride over. It reads marvellously. You've done it again, my clever girl.'

Mrs Rawle was Amy's greatest supporter when it came to her writing, giving herself credit for Amy's success and reminding her more often than was necessary that if she hadn't persuaded her to break off her engagement to Wareham, she wouldn't have become a successful authoress.

Amy checked the layout, pleased to see the story had been spread over seven pages, and nicely illustrated with line drawings of the characters, and the old-fashioned New York brownstone which served as the setting for the story. Mr Farrand had been as good as his word. He'd promised to present her work to the best possible advantage and he'd done just that. In that moment, she forgot the difficulty she'd had writing it and felt only satisfaction at the achievement.

She smiled at Mrs Rawle, grateful for her appreciation. 'Now I've established my star-crossed lovers, I'm planning to introduce a strong female character who campaigns for women to have the right to vote. She—'

Mrs Rawle threw her hands in the air at Amy's announcement. 'Good heavens, no. You can't write about that. Readers come to your work to be entertained, not lectured.'

'It'll still be entertaining,' said Amy. 'I'll raise the issue of women's suffrage in a second storyline to encourage readers to start thinking about the subject, if they aren't already.'

'Why would you want women to have the vote?' asked Mrs Rawle, clearly appalled by the idea. 'They wouldn't know what to do with it even if they had it. They'd end up voting the way their husbands or fathers told them, so you might as well just leave it to them.'

'I don't think that would be the case. America is changing rapidly and not always for the better. You only have to visit the poorer quarters of New York to see the terrible living conditions many families are forced to suffer. Women need to be able to fight for the right to improve their lives, to have a better education and the right to decent paid work. They're perfectly capable of thinking for themselves, of knowing what's in their best interests.'

Amy faltered as she said it. She considered herself to have a strong mind and a clear intelligence, and yet she'd allowed herself to be talked out of following her heart and taking her preferred route in life. Still, her singular mistake wasn't a reason for women to be denied a say in who was elected to run their country. She was surprised by Mrs Rawle's reactionary response. She wouldn't have expected it of her, given her own independent status as a widow of means. It was a lesson in the fact that, below the surface, people weren't always who you expected them to be.

'You're a grown woman now, Amy, and you know your own mind. It's not up to me to tell you what to do. It seems there are some things we'll never agree on, but don't come crying to me if your readers are put off by the social and political drum-banging in your novel. Most women want a sentimental story, with the lovers living happily ever after, even if you don't. If the novel fails, don't say I didn't warn you.'

The comment that Amy didn't want a happy ending stung more than she could say. All these years, she must have been better at hiding her heartbreak than she'd realised. Mrs Rawle's comments did however plant a seed of doubt in Amy's mind. This book needed to be a success if she was to clear the family's debts. Now wasn't the time to take risks with the story. She couldn't afford to lose her loyal readers.

No one in the room, apart from Mrs Rawle, took the slightest notice of the magazine. The family preferred to ignore Amy's work, even when it was placed in front of them, conscious that it degraded them in the eyes of their peers. By refusing to acknowledge its existence, Marion felt able to hold onto her position in society. Amy tried not to allow the snub to hurt her. As far as she was concerned, the pretence created a dishonesty that only served to make fools of them.

While Mrs Rawle pored over the magazine, Amy returned to the table in the corner to correct the three pages she'd written that morning. She'd only been settled for a few minutes, crossing out and making changes to the first paragraph, when Mr Craig arrived. He wasn't alone. Wareham was with him.

Amy hadn't been expecting to see him and his sudden appearance left her lost for words. Unwilling to face him, she gripped her pen and stared at the page in front of her. It was impossible to concentrate with him so close by, but there was no reason for him to know it.

Mrs Rawle buried her face deeper in the magazine. Wareham was doing his best not to pay her any attention, but his presence was enough to make her uncomfortable. His pointed determination to look the other way proved he hadn't forgiven her for persuading Amy not to marry him.

It wasn't in Mrs Rawle's nature to stand down, but nor was it in her nature to tolerate company she believed to be inferior. She glanced at Wareham once or twice. When her dragon stare failed to send him into a retreat, she tugged at her ear lobes, where two identical emeralds nested. 'Is that the time? I have an appointment with my jeweller. How silly it was of me not to remember.'

Within moments of Wareham arriving, Mrs Rawle had left the room, dropping the magazine in her fluster and forgetting her gloves. With all the coming and going, Mr Craig seemed to be the only one in the room who realised Amy was trying to work.

'Forgive us for the interruption, but I wondered if I might find Mr Harris here.'

At the mention of his name, Conrad, who'd been sitting on a sofa with Hester, discreetly positioned behind a large parlour palm, jumped to his feet. 'I'm here, sir.'

'Ah, there you are.' Mr Craig waved at him to sit down again. 'Mr Wareham and I have been talking this morning, and he has persuaded me that as Mrs Craig and I are planning to build a house on Fifth Avenue, I should consider giving an up-and-coming young architect the opportunity to prove himself by inviting him to bid for the commission.'

Despite the instruction to sit, Conrad once again shot out of his seat. 'That's a very good idea, sir. A new talent will bring fresh ideas and ambition to the project. You'd be guaranteed a good job and a house that would be the envy of everyone on Fifth Avenue.'

'That would depend on the talent of the young architect, of course,' replied Mr Craig. 'No matter what Wareham says, I'll take some persuading to venture so much money on someone who is untried.'

Conrad nodded furiously. 'Any ambitious young architect would work closely with you, sir, to deliver everything you required, and would strive to make sure you were happy with the finished house. After all, such a prestigious project could make a man.'

A sob escaped from Hester's chest. She pulled a handkerchief from her pocket and held it to her face, attempting to disguise the sound as a cough. No one in the room seemed to notice apart from Amy and Wareham.

Mr Craig took a moment to consider Conrad's words. 'I can't promise you anything, young man, but come and see me tomorrow. Mrs Craig and I will describe the sort of house we'd like to build and you can see what you make of it. How does that sound?'

'Thank you, sir. Thank you.' Conrad dashed across the room and shook Mr Craig's hand. 'Name the time and I'll be there.'

It wasn't only Conrad who appeared overwhelmed. Hester's shoulders were now heaving with suppressed sobs, although true to her nature, she did her best to hide it. The sight of the hope budding inside her brought tears to Amy's eyes. Even if Conrad was engaged to build Mr and Mrs Craig's new home, Hester's parents would take a good deal of persuading to allow them to marry, but it was a start.

When Amy glanced up, Wareham was looking directly at her. She held his gaze for a moment before he turned away, distracted by Lucy, who was pulling at his sleeve, demanding to know his favourite dance.

Their silent communication had only lasted a moment, but his message had been clear. Wareham's desire to help Conrad was rooted in their own history. Not all love stories should have the unhappy ending theirs had suffered. Times and attitudes were changing. She could only hope they were changing quickly enough to allow Hester and Conrad a chance of happiness. She couldn't stand to think of the two of them suffering the way she and Wareham had done.

She dipped the nib of her pen in the inkwell, preparing to change one of the sentences she'd written earlier. Her hand was shaking. The intensity of Wareham's gaze had unsettled her, but she forced herself to continue. The work needed to be completed and it was her only way of coping with Wareham's presence, with the sight of Lucy demanding his full attention. It was foolish to be so distracted by the two of them whispering and laughing, but she couldn't help it.

The conversation had settled to a low murmur when Charles Junior came charging in. If he was suffering any ill effects from his bad dream, he didn't show it. Full of energy, he ran straight to Amy.

Amy held out her arms to embrace him, but it wasn't enough. He demanded to sit on her lap, throwing out his arms and legs in practised octopus style until she relented.

'Mind the table, Charles Junior.'

Wareham's warning came too late. Amy reached out to steady the inkwell but Charles Junior's flailing hand reached it first, knocking it over and spilling ink over the freshly written pages.

Before Amy could react, Charles Junior was lifted from her lap, freeing her hands so she could rescue the work. Still, it was too late. The pages were spoiled. She picked up the inkwell and blotted the paper, but it was no good. The words had disappeared beneath the pool of spilled ink. She took a deep breath, fighting back tears of frustration before she looked up. The conversation in the room had carried on, with no one taking any notice of the disaster. It was only a little spilled ink, after all, and not worth crying over. The table had avoided ruin, so it was of no consequence. Only Wareham was paying her any attention as he held Charles Junior and tried to calm him down. She hadn't realised at the time that he'd been the one to lift him off her lap.

He frowned as he caught her eye. 'Your work. Can it be salvaged?'

She shook her head and looked away, not wanting him to see how upset she was. All those hours of labour had been wasted and would have to be repeated.

Wareham placed Charles Junior back on his feet and held him

steady. 'Charles Junior looks as if he could do with some fresh air and exercise. Why don't we all take him for a walk in Central Park and leave Miss Eaton to continue her work?'

Lucy jumped to her feet. 'That's an excellent idea. You can tell me more about your magical invention, Mr Wareham. Did you say it was something to do with train wheels?'

'It's to enable the safer coupling of the carriages,' corrected Amy.

The words had slipped from her mouth before she could stop them. Wareham gave her a surprised look, turning away quickly as she inadvertently caught his eye.

Having finished her meeting with the cook, Marion arrived just in time to hear the suggestion of a walk. 'Of course, but we must have Amy with us. I can't be expected to manage Charles Junior without her.'

Wareham looked confounded. 'Can no one else take care of him?'

Marion looked horrified that Wareham had dared to speak. 'Amy is a guest in our home and is expected to oblige us in exchange for our hospitality. She can finish the work later. It can't be that difficult.'

Once again, Marion was going out of her way to put Amy in her place, reminding her she was the unmarried sister. With no husband or children of her own to take care of, she was expected to work as the unpaid help to those with more responsibilities whenever it was required.

There was no getting out of the walk without causing a scene in front of the guests. Amy appreciated that Wareham had tried to arrange for her to have some time alone to work, even if the attempt had failed. Or perhaps it wasn't that. Perhaps it was that he hadn't wanted her company, preferring to spend time alone with Lucy. There was no knowing one way or another, but given the resentment he still so clearly felt towards her, she could only assume it was the latter.

Chapter 14

The weather had failed to fulfil its early morning promise, and by the time they arrived in Central Park, the sky had clouded over, the still air creating an oppressive heat that was impossible to shake off. They appeared a mismatched group as they strolled along the Mall, the adolescent American elms, planted less than two decades ago, offering shade where it was no longer needed. Polite conversation was thrown about at random by Mr Craig, Wareham and Conrad as they attended the ladies, who kept their faces hidden from the imaginary sun beneath their veils and their fringed parasols.

Amy fell back from the group, giving herself an opportunity to observe them. Wareham was doing his best to burn off Charles Junior's energy, teaching him how to throw and catch a ball as they walked, and pointing out the bugs on the plants, much to the annoyance of Lucy, who wanted Wareham all to herself. When no one but Amy was looking, Conrad and Hester slipped away, leaving Marion to fend off Mr Craig's attempts at conversation.

Glad to steal a little time to herself, Amy wandered down a side path and settled on a bench. With no one to disturb her, she took out a pencil and a notebook and began thinking about the next part of the story for *Missing in Love*. She'd have to find the time later to repeat the work that had been spoiled that morning, but at least if she could use these few stolen minutes to think about her characters and their motivations, her day wouldn't have been wasted.

She'd hardly begun when she heard the sound of Lucy's voice on the other side of the hedge.

'Tell me, Mr Wareham, why haven't you shown any interest in renewing your acquaintance with Amy? You behave as if she doesn't exist.'

'Is that what she said?'

There was an uncharacteristic edge to Wareham's voice that Amy didn't recognise. He was usually so cool, so measured. She couldn't help listening to what came next. It wasn't eavesdropping when they chose to hold the conversation in a public place, and Lucy had never been known to have a quiet voice.

'She says as little about you as you do about her. She changes the subject every time I mention you.'

'Then I suppose she has nothing to say about me, just as I have nothing to say about her.'

'Nothing matters to her except writing novels. She even turned down an offer of marriage in favour of them.'

'Did she tell you that?'

'She didn't have to. Everyone knows Charles proposed to her. When she wouldn't have him, he married Marion instead.'

There was a long silence during which Wareham must have been absorbing this new information. Amy held her breath. The wait for his reaction was agony.

'Do I understand you correctly? Did you say Charles proposed to Miss Eaton?'

There was a hint of disbelief in his voice. Amy leaned forward and listened harder, not knowing what to make of his response.

'There was great fuss over it at the time, but it's all forgotten now. I don't think Marion loves Charles, so I don't suppose she cares that she was his second choice. He's rich, after all, and she does exactly as she pleases now she's married. She's fulfilled her duty by providing him with an heir. She almost died giving birth to him, so there won't be any more children. Since Charles Junior was born, she won't allow Charles into her bed.'

'Why did Miss Eaton refuse him?'

Wareham still didn't seem able to move on from the original point, no matter how much Lucy ran away with the subject.

'Mrs Rawle talked her out of it, insisting she'd never have time to write novels if she had a husband and children to look after. She's so possessive of Amy. She behaves as if she's her mother. Amy hangs on her every word and won't go against her.'

Wareham's feet scuffed the ground as if he were kicking away a troublesome stone. 'It shocks me how people can be so influenced by others when it comes to making life-changing decisions. It shows a weakness of character.'

Lucy squealed. 'You'll find I'm very stubborn. Admirably so.'

'I was talking about Miss Eaton.'

'Let's not waste our time talking about Amy. She's old and dull.'

'She's younger than I am, and yet you're willing to give me your attention.'

'That's because you're a man.'

The voices grew nearer as they approached. Not wanting to be caught listening to the conversation, Amy moved away from the bench and went in search of Marion and Mr Craig. Only a brisk walk would shake off her agitation at what she'd just overheard. Wareham was unable to let go of the issue of her weakness of character, and seemed determined to raise it at every opportunity with anyone who would listen. The situation was insufferable. If he wanted to raise it with anyone, he should raise it with her. After all, it concerned nobody else but the two of them.

She'd walked off the worst of her annoyance by the time she found the rest of the party, standing on the upper terrace that overlooked the fountain at the end of the Mall.

'Amy, there you are,' said Marion with undisguised relief. 'We'd thought we'd lost you.'

Marion was hot and bothered, having underestimated the humidity when she chose to wear her heavy brocade mantle. Hester was standing next to her looking downcast, but Conrad was nowhere to be seen. The lovers' earlier disappearance must have been discovered and they'd been duly punished for it.

Mr Craig, whose sense of gallantry had prevented him from leaving Marion's side for the duration of the walk, looked over Amy's shoulder and waved at Wareham and Lucy as they approached. Charles Junior was tagging along behind them, his eyes focused on the handful of snails he'd collected. Amy guessed his new fascination was Wareham's doing. Marion would be appalled when she discovered his new interest and was sure to denounce it as disgusting, but at least it was keeping him occupied.

'What is it you have there?' asked Amy, placing her hand on Charles Junior's head to draw his attention. She'd already forgiven him for spoiling her work that morning.

He was proudly showing her his collection of snails when they heard a commotion from the lower terrace. When they looked down, a group of women had gathered at the fountain and begun shouting 'Votes for women!' at the top of their voices.

Marion pulled back her veil to get a clearer view. 'How could those women make such a spectacle of themselves? What must their husbands and their fathers think of them?'

'That's the point,' replied Amy, her eyes tracking their movements as they circled the fountain. 'Their behaviour is designed to provoke. It's the only way they can see to instigate change.'

As she spoke, one of the leaders stepped into the fountain and waded towards the bronze statue at the centre, her cambric skirt clinging to her legs as the water dragged at the fabric.

'She's heading for the Angel of the Waters,' said Lucy, jumping up and down with excitement. 'What do you think she intends to do?'

They watched the woman clamber onto the statue, her

saturated skirt weighing down the lower part of her body as she began to climb the figure. Halfway up, she delved into the canvas bag that was slung over her shoulder and retrieved a banner, which she draped over the angel's wings. The words *Votes for Women* were roughly painted across it. The whole proceeding was accompanied by encouraging cheers from her fellow campaigners.

Amy scanned the faces of the demonstrators to see if she recognised anyone. There was no sign of Mrs Craig, but there in the centre of the gathering, shaking a tambourine above her head and shouting for all she was worth, was Mrs Canby.

'There's that disreputable friend of Eleanor's,' said Marion, who must have spotted her at the same time as Amy. She covered her face with her veil. 'Don't let her see you, whatever you do. The last thing we want is to be associated with her kind.'

Wareham considered the scene with cool detachment. 'What's she guilty of, besides demanding the right to vote? Something less than terrible, I expect.'

'She's guilty of loving someone when she had no right to do so,' replied Amy. 'Judge her as you will. Everyone else does.'

It was an insensitive thing to say and Amy regretted it as soon as she said it. Wareham's look of cool detachment melted away as he turned from her, the hunching of his right shoulder indicating her words had touched a nerve.

By now, a crowd had gathered at the fountain. Everyone in Central Park wanted to know what all the noise was about, and why their peaceful stroll had been disturbed. It would only be a matter of time before the police arrived, and the protesting women were arrested and carried off to jail. Tomorrow their names would be in all the newspapers, and the city would be divided over whether they should be shamed or applauded.

'Those women are very brave to make themselves a public spectacle,' said Hester. 'I can't help admiring them for standing up for what they believe in.'

'Women won't be granted the right to vote unless they fight

for it,' said Amy. 'It's going to be a long battle, and this is only the start of it.'

The protesting women were chanting louder than ever. All around them, the crowd were jeering. Objects were being thrown at them by men and women alike. Wareham visibly flinched as a stone glanced the head of the woman who'd waded into the fountain and climbed onto the statue to hang the banner. 'You have to applaud the bravery of these women for putting themselves in such danger for something they believe in.'

'They need to find cleverer ways to do it,' said Amy, still thinking about how she could use her novel to raise a discussion about the cause.

Wareham nodded. 'You're right. They won't be taken seriously otherwise. If they're going to prove themselves worthy of the vote, they'll have to be exemplary, just as I had to prove myself before I was accepted as an engineer in a society and a profession that looked down on me.'

Amy's heart missed a beat. No wonder Wareham had so much sympathy for these women, fighting for equality and recognition. It must have reminded him of the personal and professional struggles he'd been made to endure.

Mr Craig rubbed his hands together. 'Wait until Mrs Craig hears about this. She'll have something to say about it, I don't doubt.' He gave Marion a cursory bow. 'If you'll excuse me, I must go home and tell her about it straight away. She'll never forgive me otherwise. She'll be sorry to have missed it.'

Wareham picked up another snail from a nearby shrub and handed it to Charles Junior, distracting him from the violence of the crowd before turning to Mr Craig. 'Perhaps you could walk Miss Eaton home, as you're going that way.'

Amy was astonished by his suggestion. What gave him the right to decide it was time for her to go home?

'Do you want to get rid of me, Mr Wareham? Or do you think I'm too old and too unfit to spend whole hours at a time outdoors.'

'No, no . . .' Wareham stammered. 'I only thought that the house would be quiet now, and it would give you the opportunity to write without interruption. I can only imagine how frustrating it must have been for you to have had your work ruined this morning. As you can see, Charles Junior is now fully occupied with his collection of snails.'

It was more consideration than she was used to. She should have thought more carefully before snapping at him.

'You're right, of course. Thank you for thinking of it.'

He gave her a polite nod, but she could see the slight remained. Beyond the cool look that passed between them, there was nothing more to be said. She took Mr Craig's arm as he offered it, and after saying goodbye to the rest of the group, they began the walk back to the house.

Wareham was rid of her, which was what he'd wanted. Whether it was so he could spend more time with Lucy without her presence, or whether his suggestion was genuinely intended to give her time to write uninterrupted was a question she would spend many hours mulling over.

She still wondered at his surprise when he'd learned she'd turned down an offer of marriage from Charles. Could he really believe her heart had recovered sufficiently for her to marry another man? Surely he must understand that a love such as they had shared didn't disappear into fine mist. There could be no feelings left for her on his part, otherwise he wouldn't have reacted the way he did when he learned she'd rejected another suitor. For Amy, marriage to anyone but Wareham was unthinkable, yet he'd made his intention to find himself a wife only too clear, and there lay the difference in their hearts.

Chapter 15

Amy spent the following week trying to concentrate on the second instalment of *Missing in Love*. There were fleeting moments when, having banished all thoughts of Wareham from her mind, she was able to write freely. The opening pages, which had been ruined by the spilled ink, were finally rewritten, although they would never recapture what she'd achieved the first time of writing them and she mourned their loss. No reader would know the difference, but to Amy's mind, the replacement pages lacked the spontaneity and freshness of the originals.

Since his walk in Central Park, Charles Junior had developed a keen interest in collecting snails. Together, he and Amy had filled a dozen glass jars with leaves and begun to build a colony in the nursery. Rather than causing him to lose interest, the slow, determined nature of their movements kept him fascinated for hours, making him less demanding of Amy's attention.

It was late one afternoon when Lucy burst into the drawing room with the suggestion that they all go to the opera, as if the plan had come to her on the spur of the moment. With both Charles Junior and her work under control, Amy was delighted by the prospect of the distraction, believing she deserved an evening out.

Along with all the other riches, Charles's parents had given him and Marion a box at the Academy of Music as a wedding present. Highly coveted by old New York society, such a thing couldn't be bought for any price, and although the gilding had tarnished and the red plush seats had grown shabby, they were handed down through families like treasured heirlooms.

Later that evening, seated high above the stage, waiting for the musicians to take up their instruments, Amy felt more like her old self again. Just for a few hours, she could almost forget the responsibilities she'd taken on to clear the family debts and the pressure she felt at having to produce a highly anticipated novel in monthly instalments.

Once the chapters were published, there would be no changing them. If something went awry with the story, she'd have to work her way out of it, because there was no going back. Any false steps she took would be in the public eye and she'd have to make the best of them. The first novel of hers to be serialised had been completed in advance of its publication and she'd been able to revise the beginning and the middle after writing the end. Every author knew that the opening pages of the story couldn't be fully realised until the final chapter had been written and the ending satisfactorily resolved. Now, writing and publishing in real time felt like walking along a high wire and there was no net to catch her if she fell.

Marion pushed her opera glasses onto her nose, scanning the audience in the orchestra seats below, the diamonds in the ladies' headdresses and the gentlemen's collar studs, glinting like the sun on a rough sea.

'What are we here to see tonight?'

'*The Marriage of Figaro*.' Amy made a point of lowering her voice as a hint to Marion, who insisted on speaking at full volume during every performance.

Ostrich feather fans and swansdown tippets flew in all directions as the last few people hurried to their seats. Lucy leaned over the balcony to take in the spectacle, giggling at the flying feathers until Amy told her to sit back in her chair. She was baring more shoulder and bosom than was respectable, even by the standards of the opera, and was drawing too much attention to herself.

The curtain was about to rise when the door to the box opened and Wareham entered. He was wearing an evening suit with a starched shirt and white gloves, a gardenia pinned to his lapel. Amy turned away as he caught her staring at him. She'd never seen him looking so fine.

'Mr Wareham, there you are,' said Lucy. 'I thought you were going to be late.' She snatched the gardenia and wedged it inside the neckline of her dress, poking the stem between her breasts.

The look of horror on Marion's face told Amy she wasn't expecting Wareham. Nor was she expecting Mr and Mrs Craig or Conrad, who followed behind, thanking her in grateful whispers for the invitation as they took up the last remaining seats in the box.

The overture struck up. Someone gave a loud hush, quietening the last murmurs of conversation in the auditorium. Amy sat up straight and focused her eyes on the stage. Wareham was sitting directly behind her and she was finding it impossible to concentrate with the heat of his breath on her neck. Why hadn't he sat beside Lucy while he'd had the chance? Was he determined to plague her with his presence every time she was obliged to be in his company? He'd made his feelings for her quite clear and there was no need for him to go on tormenting her.

'We haven't seen you all week. Where have you been?' asked Lucy, directing the question to the side of Wareham's head. Like Marion, she would never accept that the opera was a place for watching and listening, and not for conversation.

Wareham put his finger to his lips, his eyes fixed on the stage. 'I'll tell you during the interval.'

He'd always loved music. He'd once confided to Amy that it was his ambition to visit all the great opera houses in Europe if he ever had the money to do so. What a pleasure it would have been to have shared this moment with him now, to enjoy the music together and be swept away by the romance of it, but it wasn't to be. The best Amy could expect from Wareham was cool indifference, as he allowed his good manners to temper the passion he felt for the music.

There was a general belief that men of science and engineering had no interest in culture, but this wasn't true of Wareham. It was one of the reasons Amy had been so surprised by his disparaging comments about her novels. His distaste hadn't been aimed at the novel in general, of course, but at her.

As soon as the curtain fell at the end of the first act, Lucy tapped Wareham on the shoulder with her fan. 'You promised to tell me why you've neglected me so criminally this past week.'

'I went to Cape May to see Mr Belmont, an old friend from my student days at Columbia. He wanted my opinion on the design of a project he's working on, and to ask if I'd be interested in investing in it.'

'It's not to do with train wheels again, is it?'

'No.'

The Wareham Amy had once known had loved nothing better than to talk at length about engineering. When an idea excited him, she would hear no end of it. His one word answer suggested he thought there was no point discussing his work with Lucy, and Lucy herself seemed keen to change the subject.

'Did you enjoy your stay in Cape May?'

'It was very pleasant. I'm returning in a few days with Mr and Mrs Craig. I've asked for their opinion on Mr Belmont's project. If they agree with my assessment, I'll help him to refine the design and the three of us will invest in it.'

'He's been very persuasive,' said Mrs Craig, nodding at Wareham's words. 'Mr Craig and I are excited to take a look at the project.' She glanced at her husband, but he was too deep in conversation with Conrad to notice.

103

'We should all go to Cape May,' insisted Lucy. 'I long to see it now Mr Wareham has spoken so highly of it, don't you agree, Marion?'

'I don't know, I . . .' Marion looked to Charles, who sat with his eyes closed, his head resting on the back of the chair as he quietly snored. There was no point in relying on him to come up with an excuse for not going.

Taking Marion's indecision as agreement, Lucy flicked open her fan and waved it in front of her face, her eyes shining as if a small victory had been won. 'Then that's settled. We shall all travel together.'

Hester whispered to Amy. 'Will you join us?'

The last thing Amy wanted was to spend more time in Wareham's company. If she was to focus on her work, she needed to be as far away from him as possible. Having him near was too much of a distraction. 'I don't think so, I . . .'

'Of course, she'll come,' insisted Marion. 'I can't manage without her.'

Once the audience were back in their seats, the curtain lifted and the performance continued, but no aria, however beautifully rendered, would put Lucy off her mission.

'So tell me, Mr Wareham. Are you going to settle in New York and build yourself a fine house like Mr and Mrs Craig?'

'I haven't decided yet.' Wareham's eyes remained fixed on the stage as he tried to concentrate on the music, but Lucy refused to take the hint.

'You're going to wait until you've taken a wife and let her decide for you. Is that what you're saying? I warn you, if you choose someone from this city, she'll be reluctant to leave her family and settle in California. I hear it's wild out west.'

Wareham nodded, his ears trained on the music. 'As I said, I haven't made up my mind.'

After the performance ended, Lucy insisted Wareham stayed with them while they waited for a hansom cab to take them home.

The Craigs took Hester and Conrad in their private carriage, leaving Marion, who would rather hail a cab on the street than travel with the Craigs, Charles, Lucy and Amy to wait for the next available cab. Amy told Wareham there was no need for him to stay, but he seemed reluctant to deny Lucy's request. Amy didn't investigate too closely why his continuing presence annoyed her, but she couldn't let it drop.

'We're quite capable of getting ourselves home safely, Mr Wareham. We're unlikely to be hindered by a terrible accident.'

'You can't be too sure. It's the nature of accidents that you never know when they're going to strike.'

'Nevertheless, even if some misfortune occurs, we're unlikely to need your help.'

'It's been known before. You must remember the time you twisted your ankle playing croquet and I had to pick you up and carry you all the way across the lawn.'

He'd said it without thinking, resurrecting a shared memory of happier days. At the time, there'd been no serious damage to her ankle and he knew it. He'd used it as an excuse to pick her up and carry her away. Complicit in the pretence, she'd made a great display of limping as he came to her rescue, laughing through the whole charade.

It must have been a slip of his tongue. He regretted it as soon as he said it. She could see it in his eyes, in the way he looked away, as if he was ashamed that the recollection had caught him out and made him smile against his better judgement. He hated that he had such memories, that they'd once shared such happiness now he had the prospect of a future with Lucy.

A hansom cab finally rolled up and they piled in, leaving Wareham alone on the pavement and saving them from any further awkwardness. There hadn't been time for Amy to ask him why the memory had suddenly sprung to his mind, even if she'd had the courage to raise it. Now he'd mentioned it, it was destined to stay with her too. Not only the physical sensation of being in his arms as he picked her up, but the sound of his laughter as he'd carried her across the lawn, the happiness she'd felt, doubled by the fact that she knew he'd felt it too. Even though neither of them felt it now, the memory of it lingered, not only in her mind, but undoubtedly in his too. For all the pain of the regret, there was comfort to be had in knowing he held onto it, even if it was only because he was a prisoner of it.

Chapter 16

Amy didn't truly believe that Marion would leave Charles Junior behind until they were actually standing on the station platform at the Grand Central depot, listening for the clang of the bell that would announce the arrival of the train and mark the beginning of their journey to Cape May. It seemed cruel to deny the little boy the experience of playing on the beach and a sailing trip on the ocean, but Marion was adamant. The excursion was a holiday for all of them, a time for a little rest, which meant an escape from the demands of Charles Junior, who'd been left in the capable hands of the housemaids, who according to Marion, had nothing better to do while the family was out of town.

'I'm doing you a favour, Amy, giving you a few days where you don't have to run around after him. You should be thanking me for it.'

The train pulled into the station, announcing its arrival with a squeal of brakes, and filling the air with clouds of smoke, the smuts causing Marion to cough uncontrollably.

'You'll never convince me that this sort of progress is of benefit to mankind.'

Charles was unable to join them on the trip, having suddenly remembered he was required to have lunch with his second cousin at his gentlemen's club the day they were due to leave. On hearing that Marion, Amy, Lucy and Hester would be travelling alone, Mrs Craig had invited them to join their party. Lucy had accepted on their behalf once she'd confirmed that the party included Wareham.

Wareham slipped the porter a large tip as he struggled on board with Lucy's luggage, while acknowledging Marion's disparaging comment about the railroads.

'It's still early days. There'll come a time when they'll be powered by something much cleaner than coal and run much quieter, although probably not in our lifetime.'

Lucy leaned over the edge of the platform and peered at the carriage wheels. 'Show me your marvellous invention, Mr Wareham. Which bit of this iron monster did you create?'

The train gave a sudden jolt. Hester squealed as Wareham dashed forward and grabbed Lucy's arm, pulling her away from the edge of the platform. 'Please be careful, Miss Morton. I wouldn't forgive myself if you came to any harm.'

Undaunted, Lucy pulled away from Wareham's grasp and leaned over the tracks. 'It's so interesting. I have to see the bit you invented, the bit that made you a rich man.'

Mrs Craig covered her face with her hand, memories of her son's death flashing before her eyes. 'Please, my dear. Listen to what Mr Wareham says.'

When Lucy ignored the warning, Wareham stepped forward and held onto her arm. 'The coupler is positioned beneath the carriage. You can't really see it from here.'

The whistle blew, drowning out Lucy's comment as Wareham finally managed to encourage her away from the edge of the platform and onto the train.

By the time they'd settled in their private compartment they were already pulling out of the station. Lucy stared out of the window as the burgeoning New York landscape rolled by. New buildings seemed to be appearing by the day, stretching the boundaries of the city until it threatened to become a sprawl.

'Is that all there is to your invention, Mr Wareham?' she asked. 'It doesn't look much. I can't believe you made your fortune from something so simple.'

Amy had already opened her notebook and was trying to work. She looked up, affronted by Lucy's comment. 'The cleverness is in the composition of the steel and the mechanism. You won't see it just by looking at it. It has to be seen in action.' She focused on Lucy, refusing to catch Wareham's eye as he looked at her, his eyebrows raised in surprise. 'It's not in use all the time, only when it's needed.'

Mr Craig chuckled. 'Someone's taken the trouble to look into the workings of it.'

Amy blushed, realising she'd been found out. 'I find it interesting, that's all.'

'The more complicated things are, the more likely they are to go wrong,' added Wareham. 'The cleverness lies in its simplicity. It was more difficult to design, but it makes it more reliable.'

'Mr Wareham is right,' said Mrs Craig, giving Amy a meaningful look. 'It was all credit to the early investors that they had the belief and the foresight to fund the development of the coupler as it went through a number of design changes. It didn't look very promising to begin with, but we knew we had something. It was just a matter of perfecting it.'

Marion gave a loud yawn. 'Oh, do put that notebook away, Amy. It's supposed to be a holiday. I'd have brought Charles Junior along if I'd known you were going to be working.'

Amy closed the notebook and stared out the window, still avoiding Wareham's eye. She didn't have to look in his direction to know he was watching her. She'd said too much about his invention and now regretted it. It wouldn't do to give away that she'd pored over the patent when it was first published, and followed the coupler's progress all the way from its conception through the various stages of testing to mass production, or that she'd read all the technical papers and the specialist journals that had reported on it over the years.

She'd say no more about it. It would be too awkward, too revealing to have to explain why she was so interested in it, or betray how proud she was of Wareham's achievement. He wouldn't welcome her estimation of it, just as she couldn't let it matter that he had such a low opinion of her novels.

They'd arranged in advance for a carriage to meet them off the train and take them to their hotel, which was situated on a stretch of beach overlooking the Atlantic. After the mugginess of New York, the air was cooler and fresher, the ocean breeze a balm after the oppressive atmosphere of the city, and even though Amy had been reluctant to make the trip she instantly felt better for the change of scene.

The season was tipping into autumn and the streets were quiet. Most of the summer visitors had left, and there was little hope of any form of society or entertainment. The few visitors who remained stayed mainly for their health, or because the living was cheaper than in New York. It made Amy think of her father and Eleanor and how quickly they'd resigned themselves to living in what they continued to refer to as their *second home* in Newport.

The hotel where they were staying was one of the remaining splendours of the old town, rearing up from the edge of the shore like a great lemon and white iced cake, and was one of the few traditional wooden buildings to have survived the fire that had destroyed much of the town a decade ago. Although the community had repaired itself, there was still a sense of loss over the fact that many of the historical landmarks had gone. It was after all, the character of the town as much as the beaches that attracted the summer visitors that so many of the local businesses relied on.

Before they went up to their rooms, Lucy insisted on taking a walk along the beach. She was still sulking at having been parted from Wareham so soon after they'd arrived. He wasn't staying in the hotel, but with his friend, Mr Belmont. It was a reminder that he was here to discuss work rather than to take a holiday.

Without the distraction of Charles Junior, Amy was also hoping to get some work done, but for now, she allowed herself a moment to breathe, to enjoy the view and the ocean air. Sometimes, she needed to remind herself that there were wonderful things in life to be had, if only you looked for them. She watched the waves crashing in, storing up the feeling of joy their energy gave her. In her experience, happiness wasn't a permanent state of being, but something to be grasped in small moments, and this was one of those moments.

Marion hid her face behind a veil and insisted Lucy and Hester did the same. The rough breeze was known to add years to a woman's complexion and she refused to risk the slightest damage.

After only a few minutes of exposure to the air, she decided it was time to go inside and change for dinner. 'It's vital we make the right impression. We can't be seen looking red-cheeked and wind-blown. You never know who might be staying in the hotel.'

So far, Marion's promise to find suitable husbands for Lucy and Hester while their parents were travelling in Europe was proving to be a disaster, with both girls having set their minds, and possibly their hearts, on men who were far below them in the social hierarchy.

'I want you both to wear your coming-out dresses this evening. Let people see you are debutantes of the highest order. It'll send the right message to any eligible young man who might still be in town.'

'I want to stay out a bit longer,' said Lucy, her eyes scanning the road that ran parallel to the beach. 'The veil will protect me, and a little colour will show me to advantage.'

'Then Amy can chaperone you,' replied Marion, shivering in the breeze. 'No one will care how rugged she looks, and as she refuses to wear a veil, it's her own fault.'

A few minutes after Marion had left them, Lucy spotted Wareham's familiar figure in the distance. Her strategy of walking up and down outside the hotel, in a way that could only be described as loitering, had finally paid off.

'Mr Wareham, there you are.' She waved her arms above her head and jumped up and down, making it impossible for him to miss her. 'We've only been here an hour and you've already become a stranger.'

'It's hardly been an hour, I assure you.' Wareham gave the impression of being delighted to see her, while reserving a cold look for Amy. He turned to the man standing beside him. 'This is my very good friend, Mr James Belmont.'

Belmont raised his hat and gave a shy smile. He was about the same age as Wareham, but seemed more careworn, the sorry angle of his head suggesting he carried a great emotional weight across his shoulders. He was shorter than Wareham and more slightly built, while his expression gave him the appearance of natural reticence rather than vigour. His eyes were grey as opposed to the blue Amy had anticipated, his fair hair made lighter by the summer sun. Wareham had talked about him often in the past and although she'd never met him, Amy felt as if she knew him.

He took Amy's hand, his face lighting up with recognition. 'Forgive me for asking, but are you *the* Miss Amy Eaton, the famous novelist?'

Amy felt the familiar mix of awkwardness and pleasure she always experienced when a stranger mentioned her work. 'Yes, I . . .'

'I've read all your books. It was Sarah who introduced them to me, I . . .' His face clouded over for a moment, his voice stalling at the mention of the woman's name. 'I've taken out a subscription to *Scribe* magazine, just so I can be one of the first to read your latest novel.'

It was unusual for a man to be taken with her work. Most claimed it to be too sentimental for their tastes. It took a close reader to see the subtleties that hinted at a darker emotional journey beneath the surface. 'I hope it doesn't disappoint you.'

'It couldn't possibly.' He turned to Wareham. 'Why didn't you tell me you knew my favourite authoress, or that she was so pretty? You were hoping to keep her all to yourself, I suppose.'

There was a beat of silence as Belmont's words fell in the void between Amy and Wareham. The fact that Belmont didn't know of her connection to Wareham suggested he hadn't mentioned her name when they were engaged, and certainly not since. She pushed down the feeling of disappointment, trying to dispel it. It had all been so very long ago. It wasn't worth letting it bother her now.

Wareham was giving her a strange look, as if he were suddenly seeing her through his friend's eyes. Emboldened by Belmont's praise, she returned his gaze. 'Is something wrong, Mr Wareham?'

'No, it's just that . . .' he paused, seeming to make it up as he went along. 'Sometimes, I forget what you've achieved. You never talk about it.'

'That's because I'm too busy getting on with it to have the time to talk about it.'

Refusing to be left out of the conversation, Lucy grabbed Wareham's arm and challenged him to a race across the beach. She pushed back her veil, her eyes shining with excitement. 'What do you say? Do you dare risk being beaten by me?'

Wareham looked down at his city shoes with apprehension. 'I'm hardly . . .'

'To the nearest rock and back. Go.'

Already Lucy had shot ahead, her soft-soled shoes slipping on the sand as she ran, the satin ribbons on her bonnet blowing in the wind.

Belmont clapped Wareham on the shoulder. 'You'd better run, my friend, if you don't want to be beaten by a girl. Trust me; you'll never hear the end of it.'

Still uncertain, Wareham handed Belmont his hat and went chasing after Lucy, picking up speed as his feet learned to find purchase on the sand. He didn't need to put in too much effort.

As soon as Lucy knew he was following her, she slowed down, allowing him to overtake her.

Belmont remained at Amy's side, watching Wareham's and Lucy's progress. 'I hope you're not going to challenge me to a race, Miss Eaton. I'm not sure I'd win as readily as Wareham, or even if it would be the gentlemanly thing to do.'

Already Amy was warming to Belmont. There was a thoughtfulness to his manner and a sensitivity she'd rarely experienced in any man, apart from Wareham.

'You're perfectly safe. The last thing I'll demand of you is a race across the sand. If you ask me, Mr Wareham has no say in whether he'll win or lose.'

'Miss Morton certainly seems to be a woman who knows her own mind.'

And who is used to getting her way, thought Amy, although she knew better than to say it.

Pink-cheeked and breathless, Lucy finally returned to the starting point and came to a stop. She leaned on Wareham's arm as he offered it, making much more of the exertion than she could possibly have felt.

'I should have known better than to challenge you to a race, Mr Wareham, when you're clearly so much stronger than I am.'

Belmont raised his eyebrows at Wareham, indicating he knew a ruse when he saw one, but Wareham failed to react, concentrating instead on Lucy as she passed him her fan and instructed him to wave it in front of her face.

The drama had gone on for too long. Amy couldn't stand another minute of it. It was too hard, watching Wareham focus his attention on Lucy when she was once the only woman who'd mattered to him, the only one he'd had eyes for. She scolded herself for indulging in such jealous thoughts. She was tired, and the shine had gone from the day. She clenched her fists, burying her feelings deep, and declared it was time to go inside, but Lucy wasn't ready to let go of Wareham just yet.

'Won't you join us for a glass of lemonade?'

'It's a very tempting invitation,' replied Belmont before Wareham had the presence of mind to speak, 'but Wareham and I have business to discuss.'

Taking Belmont's hint, Wareham was quick to say goodbye, and despite Amy's earlier desire to make the most of the sea air, she was glad to return to the hotel. Her face burned from the relentless breeze and her shoes were full of sand.

It would have been better not to have come rather than be forced to chaperone Lucy while she played games with Wareham. It was impossible to tell whether he was pleased with the attention she was giving him or simply being polite. At one time, she could read his every thought and knew exactly what he was feeling at any given moment. These days, he was so practised in the art of concealment, it was impossible to guess what was going on inside him.

Alone in her room, she unpacked her pens and paper and tried to concentrate on her writing. Work was her only solace. It was the thing she was meant for, and there was nothing else.

Chapter 17

It had been arranged that Lucy and Hester would take a walk along the seafront with Wareham and Belmont the following afternoon. Marion refused to be seen with the young men any more than she had to, and insisted Amy went in her place to act as a chaperone. It wasn't as if she had anything better to do, after all.

'I want you to work on Lucy,' she whispered. 'Do everything you can to put her off Wareham. I don't like the way she's throwing herself at him. He isn't a good match.'

Amy and Marion had had this conversation before. If Lucy had set her heart on Wareham, there was nothing Amy would be able to do to talk her out of it. She was too strong-willed to listen to persuasion.

In the end, it was Hester who chaperoned Lucy and Wareham, while Amy and Belmont fell back from the group so they could talk without constant interruption from Lucy.

'I hope I didn't offend you yesterday, Miss Eaton. I've never met an authoress before. I might have been a little forward.'

'Not at all.'

'When I told you Wareham had never mentioned he knew you, I might have been mistaken. There was a time, years ago, when he talked constantly of a mysterious Miss A.E. He was completely in love with her, and determined to marry her. Then one day, she was gone, and he never spoke of her again. I now wonder if Miss A.E, who broke his heart, could possibly have been you.'

So Wareham hadn't been shy of mentioning her to his friend after all. Amy shrugged off Belmont's comment, taking advantage of the fact that he hadn't been bold enough to phrase it as a question. She wasn't prepared to discuss what had happened in the past.

'Such beautiful weather we're having.'

Her response was enough to encourage him to change the subject. 'You must have strangers coming up to you all the time and telling you how wonderful your work is.'

She warmed to his awkwardness, his attempts to flatter her without gushing. 'It doesn't happen every day, I assure you.'

Ahead of them, Lucy was running circles around Wareham like an excited puppy. Even against the wind, she could hear their shared laughter. In Lucy's company, Wareham was like a boy again.

'I mentioned Sarah to you yesterday,' continued Belmont. 'She's the reason I'm so attached to your books. We used to read them together. We spent many happy evenings discussing them.'

Amy looked up at him and smiled. There was a darker tone to his voice suddenly, and she knew to tread carefully. 'I'm glad they brought you both pleasure.'

'I read them alone now, along with other books, of course. There's solace to be found in good stories, don't you think?'

'In writing them as well as in reading them, I find.'

'I knew you'd feel the same. There's something in your words that told me you understand about grief and loss. And yet, your books are never without hope. It's the reason I find your stories so comforting. They've shown me I'm not alone, that I'm not the only one to feel such things.'

'I'm glad my work has been some help to you, even if only in a small way.'

'During those first few months after Sarah died, I didn't know what to do with myself. Burying myself in a book was the only thing that gave me any comfort or distraction.'

'I'm so sorry you lost her.'

'It was very sudden. A boating accident. She loved to sail and was an expert sailor, having grown up on these waters, but the ocean is a capricious mistress. I remind myself every day that she died doing what she loved most, but it doesn't make it any easier. It was too cruel to lose her on the eve of our wedding. I'll never get over it.'

'Losing someone you love is the most terrible thing. You have to give yourself time to accept it. They say patience and resignation are needed, although I'm the last person to be able to talk of such qualities, when I'm lacking in them myself.'

She hadn't realised they'd caught up with the rest of the group until she felt Wareham's eyes on her. He must have heard what she'd said. Now, he was staring at her as if she were a stranger, as if he didn't know her at all.

The silence was broken by Lucy. 'I want to hire a boat and go sailing, but Mr Wareham says the water is too rough. Will you persuade him to let me have my way, Mr Belmont?'

Of all the things she could have asked for, this was the worst. Belmont's eyes narrowed on the shifting waves. 'Wareham's right. It's too rough, and we have to go now. We have a meeting with Mr and Mrs Craig. I have to convince them my invention is worth investing in. Wareham has promised to put in a good word for me.'

Lucy pushed back her veil, making sure everyone saw her disappointment. 'None of you know how to have fun.'

Sensing a change in the mood, Amy moved on to another subject. 'You haven't told me what the invention is for, Mr Belmont.' If Wareham was supporting it, she knew it must be something worthwhile.

He seemed surprised that she was interested. 'There was a terrible fire in the town some years ago. A number of important buildings were lost. The firefighters did their best, but their hosepipes kept bursting and they were unable to get the water to the flames quickly enough. If the equipment had been better designed, more properties would have been saved.'

'Please tell me you have a solution.'

'I've designed a flexible mesh to line the inside of hosepipes, something that will spread the pressure of the water when they expand and prevent them from bursting. I was inspired by watching the fishermen weave their nets, here along the shore. They use rope, of course, but I think a similar idea would work with a fine net of steel. It's a matter of getting the composition of the metal right. Wareham has offered to invest in it. I'm hoping Mr Craig will share some of his expert knowledge in steelmaking in exchange for shares in the company.'

'You'll need to convince Mrs Craig as well as her husband,' said Amy. 'If you think your invention will save lives as well as buildings, emphasise that too.'

'I will. Thank you for the advice, Miss Eaton.'

Wareham shot her a surprised look. 'You seem rather certain of Mrs Craig's way of thinking.'

Irritated by his tone, she returned his look. 'Mrs Craig and I are not that dissimilar.'

'So it seems.'

He lowered his eyes from her face and checked his pocket watch, clapping Belmont on the shoulder. 'It's time to go. We don't want to be late for Mr and Mrs Craig.'

Both men were deep in conversation as they walked away. It was probably Amy's imagination but it seemed they turned around to look at her at the same moment. She might have been mistaken, but she had the impression they were talking about her.

Chapter 18

The women had just returned from their morning walk along the beach when they discovered Conrad checking into the hotel. Hester rushed to greet him, trying to contain her excitement when she realised everyone's eyes were on her.

'What a lovely surprise. I didn't know you were coming.'

Conrad blushed, fighting to keep the same restraint, his arms remaining firmly at his sides. 'Mr Wareham suggested I come and look at the architecture in the town. Mr and Mrs Craig are taken with the style of the old houses that survived the fire, and he thought it might be useful to find out what they like about them if I'm to propose a design for their place in New York.'

Wareham wasn't giving up on his campaign to help Conrad win the contract to design the Craigs' house. It seemed he wasn't devoid of romantic feeling, after all.

As if Amy's thoughts had the power to summon him, Wareham walked into the lobby. He went straight up to Conrad and greeted him warmly. She shouldn't have been surprised that he was too busy to notice her. The days were long gone when she was the only person in the room who mattered to him. She was too distracted by Wareham to notice that Mr and Mrs Craig and Belmont had also arrived.

'Miss Eaton. It's lovely to see you.' Mrs Craig took her hand. 'Don't you look well? The sea air suits you.'

In spite of Marion's jibes, Amy still hadn't been persuaded to cover her face with a veil, or carry a parasol. After the dull city air, she relished the fresh feel of the ocean breeze on her skin. She wasn't worried about it reddening her cheeks when the recent years had done so much to drain the colour from them.

Mr Belmont was quick to agree with Mrs Craig. 'Not only is she a beauty, but she also writes wonderful books.'

His voice was a little too loud and must have carried across the lobby to where Wareham was deep in conversation with Conrad and Mr Craig. Amy looked up just as he turned and caught her eye, holding her gaze to the point of impertinence. The scorn came off him in waves. How dare he interrogate her face in such a way? She wanted to march across the lobby and demand to know what he was looking at, but she'd made enough of a fool of herself over him in the past, and wasn't prepared to do so again.

She was about to return to her room when Lucy announced her desire to hire a couple of open-topped barouches and take a ride through the town.

'It's the laziest way to see the sights, but everyone will see us and know we've arrived.'

Marion, still relentless in her mission to find suitable husbands for Lucy and Hester, agreed. Having decided there was no one of worth staying in the hotel, the girls had to be displayed further afield. She turned to Mr Craig, who she'd taken to treating as some kind of manservant, and asked him to arrange it.

He responded with a more gracious bow than she deserved. 'You must forgive me. Mrs Craig and I are occupied with the gentlemen here. We have business to discuss.'

Lucy gave Wareham a doe-eyed look. 'Can't we convince you to join the carriage ride?'

Would he be persuaded to put pleasure before work? How much power did Lucy have over him? Amy watched the expression on his face as he tried to find a solution that would keep her happy.

Finally, he turned to the Craigs and Conrad. 'A carriage ride through the town would give you all the opportunity to look at the architecture together. You must join us as well, Belmont. Mrs Craig has some questions about your hosepipe design.'

Lucy linked her arm through Wareham's. 'Then it's settled. We'll ride side by side, Mr Wareham. Amy, go and arrange the carriages.'

Wareham scowled, unceremoniously dropping Lucy's arm. 'Don't trouble yourself, Miss Eaton. I'll do it.'

The following awkward silence was filled by Mrs Craig, who invited Amy to ride in their carriage, but the last thing Amy wanted was to watch Lucy fawn over Wareham. Her patience wouldn't stand it and she didn't trust herself not to scold one or other of them.

'I have to work on *Missing in Love*. You must excuse me.'

'You'll join us for the archery party this afternoon?' asked Belmont, frowning at the thought of her absence.

It had been a long time since anyone had wanted Amy's company simply for herself rather than for the service she could offer them. 'I shall look forward to it.'

Once everyone had set out on the carriage ride, she returned to her room and sat by the window looking out across the ocean. By missing the carriage ride, she wasn't missing anything at all. To sit here alone was all she needed. She relished the restless nature of the waves and the energy it inspired in her. To be in a state of fluctuation was to be alive. To strive, to want something, gave meaning to life, at least for the time that such longing could be endured.

Despite everything, it was still a half life she was living, her lack of fulfilment a permanent ache in her heart. During moments like these, she had to remind herself that her loneliness was a consequence of the choices she'd made. Choices that determined her life would always be lived on the sidelines. She would only ever be an observer. True happiness was destined for others, but not for her.

She'd been fine until recently, devoting herself to her family and fooling herself into believing her life was everything it could be, but the reappearance of Wareham had brought back the memories of past hopes, his gentleness and good nature reminding her of what might have been every time she was in his presence.

She refused to let him see how his coolness bothered her, how the attention he paid to Lucy left her stomach in knots. She had only herself to blame for her situation, and she had no doubt that, if pressed on the subject, Wareham would be the first to remind her of it.

It was a couple of hours later when Hester knocked on her door. 'May I disturb you?'

'Please do.' Amy put aside her work. Not a word had been written all morning. She forced a smile. 'How was the carriage ride?'

'Conrad and Mr and Mrs Craig took in all the fine houses and talked about them endlessly.' She wrung her hands in a gesture reminiscent of Amy's habit. 'Mr Craig seems a fair man. Do you think he'll commission Conrad to build his house on Fifth Avenue?'

'For Conrad's sake, I hope so.'

'It's kind of Mr Wareham to champion his cause. Why do you think he's doing it?'

'I guess he recognises his talent and ambition, and wants to help.'

'You don't think he's just trying to make a good impression, so the family won't object to him marrying Lucy.'

This was the last thing Amy had considered. She'd assumed his actions had been inspired by the disappointment she and Wareham had suffered in the past. She hadn't thought they might be intended to smooth the way for his future. 'Is that what he told you?'

'No, but everyone's saying it. You only have to see how Lucy and Mr Wareham behave together. There must be an understanding between them. It can only be a matter of time before their engagement is announced.'

The news was everything Amy had dreaded. Lucy wouldn't make Wareham happy. He'd be trapped in a loveless marriage. But wasn't that what he wanted? He'd already made it clear that he was done with love.

'Your parents won't allow it. They won't think he's good enough for her.'

'That won't stop Lucy. She plans to marry him before they return from Europe.'

The idea was ridiculous, unbearable. 'Marion won't give her consent. She and Charles stand as your guardians in the absence of your parents.'

'They have no power over Lucy. No one will change her mind. She's determined to elope if it comes to it.'

Did Lucy love Wareham enough to sacrifice everything for him? And did she understand what that sacrifice really meant? If they eloped, she'd lose her family and her friends. Even if they settled in New York, it would no longer be the same welcoming place it had always been for her, not as Wareham's wife. Money wasn't everything, and when there was nothing else, it would never be enough, but it would be too late for Lucy to discover this once they were married.

Hester sighed. 'We can only hope that things turn out as they're supposed to, and that everyone has a happy ending.' She glanced at the clock. 'Are you coming downstairs? The archery party has already started. Mr Belmont has been asking for you.'

Amy forced herself to walk tall as she crossed the lawn at the back of the hotel to where everyone was already seated in a semi-circle facing the targets. The breeze had died down and the sky had clouded over, tempering the heat from the afternoon sun.

It was time for her to put her best self forward, to behave as if nothing in her world had materially shifted, and in one way, it hadn't. She'd lost Wareham eight years ago. The fact that he was about to marry Lucy should make no difference to her now.

Belmont ran to greet her and offered her his arm. 'I'm delighted you could join us, Miss Eaton. Mr Wareham is envious that I've already claimed you for my team. He told me you're an excellent shot.'

They'd been talking about her while she wasn't there. It tormented her, not knowing whether it was Wareham who had brought her into the conversation, or Belmont. Dismissing the thought, she helped herself to a bow and arrow. It had been years since she'd practised and she was nervous of not living up to Belmont's expectation.

'I'll try a test shot before we begin.'

All eyes were on her as she positioned herself in front of the target. She lifted the bow and the years fell away, her muscles instinctively moulding her body to the correct position. She sucked in a breath and held it, steadying herself as she took aim and let the arrow fly.

A gasp went around the group, followed by spontaneous applause. Amy released her breath and blinked at the arrow, sitting in the centre of the target.

Belmont cheered. 'Well done, Miss Eaton. Is there nothing you can't do?'

Suddenly Wareham was beside her, handing her another arrow. 'You never failed to miss your target. I see you haven't lost your touch.'

'It was a lucky shot, that's all.'

'Belmont doesn't see it that way.'

Her lips twitched at the thought that he might be jealous. 'It's just a game.'

'That's what you said the day you beat me at croquet.'

He'd done it again, bringing back the memory of the croquet match. Did he mean to remind her of it on purpose, forcing her to remember the way he'd picked her up and carried her across the lawn, a lawn very much like the one they now stood on? Had he forgotten how it was, or was he trying to punish her, not only by reminding her of what it felt like to have his arms around her, but the sensation of the kiss that followed afterwards? If he still felt it as keenly as she did, he wouldn't be so cruel as to keep reminding her of it. She took the arrow and fired it. Once again it hit the target, dead centre.

'Well done, Miss Eaton. There really is no end to your talents.'

She acknowledged Belmont's compliment with a smile. The past was gone and there was nothing to be gained from dwelling on it.

Lucy, who had changed into a white muslin dress and wide leghorn hat, insisted on going next. Throwing aside her veil, she lifted the bow and fired without paying attention to her aim. Everyone's eyes followed the arc of the arrow as it flew too high and landed on the grass some feet beyond the target.

Mrs Craig, who'd been watching from the sidelines, gave her a conciliatory clap. 'Never mind, Miss Morton. Better luck next time.'

Wareham offered her another arrow. 'Would you like to try again?'

'No.' Lucy tossed aside the bow and stamped her foot, her face red with petulance.

Undaunted, Wareham tried to hand her back the bow. 'Why don't you ask Miss Eaton to give you a lesson? You'll never meet a finer shot.'

Despite the sincerity of his tone, there was something in Wareham's expression that suggested his words had been double-edged. If he thought Amy was trying to impress Belmont or anyone else, he was mistaken.

'Archery is so unladylike,' said Lucy, pulling her veil fiercely over her face, 'and it's far too hot for such games. I'm going to lie down.'

After she'd gone, Mrs Craig whispered to Amy. 'Well done, my dear. It takes a lot to put Lucy in her place, but you managed it beautifully.'

'I shouldn't have shown off like that.'

'You weren't showing off. You were simply allowing your true self to shine through for once, and I was delighted to see it.' She poured them both a glass of lemonade. 'You appear to have ruffled a few feathers, and I don't mean those in your sister's hat.'

'What do you mean?'

'Mr Wareham seems rather put out by your friendship with Mr Belmont.'

If Wareham didn't like her spending time with Belmont, it could only be because he didn't trust her not to break his heart. Not that it was in any way possible. Belmont's grief for his fiancée was still raw, and he was in no condition to consider becoming attached to anyone else. An understanding friend was all he needed, and that was all she was offering to be.

'Mr Belmont and I both know how it feels to lose the person we love most in the world, the one we counted on spending the rest of our lives with. It changes the way you look at everything, the way you react to everyone around you. Such a loss can be isolating. Sometimes, it helps to talk to someone who understands.'

'My dear, sweet child. You bring such joy to everyone around you. No one sees how you've suffered.'

Amy blinked away her tears, embarrassed that Mrs Craig might see them. She hadn't felt such tenderness since her mother's death. Even Mrs Rawle, for all her attempts at taking her mother's place, had never really understood her.

With Lucy gone, there was no real appetite for an archery competition. Instead, everyone lined up to ask Amy's advice on how to improve their aim with the bow and arrow. Wareham was the only one not to approach her. Accomplished as he was in everything he touched, he had no need of her help. She watched from the corner of her eye as he withdrew from the group, choosing to sit on the grass with Conrad and Hester.

Perhaps Hester had been right. Perhaps Wareham was trying to ingratiate himself with the family so they wouldn't object to him marrying Lucy, and yet, try as she might, she couldn't see it. She knew better than anyone how Wareham behaved when he was in love and there was still no trace of it. No matter what he said, she refused to believe he would marry for anything less. If he was flattered by Lucy's attention, surely he had enough sense to realise that was all it was before it was too late. He must be able to see for himself that she wouldn't make him happy, either with or without love.

The archery had been a test of Lucy's character, and as far as Amy was concerned, she'd failed. The sport wasn't about winning or losing, or acknowledging that someone else was better than you at a particular skill. It was about rising to the challenge with good grace.

Lucy's attraction lay in her youthfulness, and for now, that would remain, no matter how badly she behaved. Amy had no right to resent her marrying Wareham after she'd once refused him, or blame her for the fact that she'd lived to regret it. Lucy had no objective in life other than to find a husband. With no inner resources to fulfil her, there was nothing else for her, which meant that ultimately not even marriage to Wareham would make her happy. And if Wareham chose to take that path, then he was old enough and wise enough to know what he was getting himself into.

Chapter 19

The final race meeting of the season was due to take place the day before they left Cape May. Having never been to a horse track, Lucy decided they must all go. Amy tried to get out of it. She couldn't face another day observing Wareham courting Lucy, but Marion insisted she accompany them.

'I need you to keep an eye on the girls and help me to make sure they're introduced to any eligible young men who might be there. It's their last chance to hook someone before we return to New York. You know what they say, where there's horse racing, there's breeding.'

And gambling, thought Amy, *and generally too much drinking.*

The race track was out of town and they hired a couple of carriages to take them. Amy travelled with Mr Belmont, Marion, Hester and Conrad, while Lucy travelled with Wareham and Mr and Mrs Craig.

The racing was already underway by the time they arrived, the men and women in the crowd standing shoulder to shoulder, roaring at the horses as they raced to the finish line. The sun was too strong to linger alongside the tracks, and with no interest in the racing, Marion insisted they squeeze themselves into the busiest hospitality tent, her eyes following every young man who happened to pass, assessing their eligibility based on their looks, bearing and clothes.

The Craigs took themselves off to the grandstand, while Lucy, who was determined not to miss anything, had no trouble persuading Wareham to accompany her to the finish line so she could watch the races being won. Hester offered to go along as chaperone, quickly followed by Conrad, who made his way politely through the crowd to catch up with them. Amy's heart panged, seeing how Hester and Conrad couldn't bear to be out of one another's sight for even a minute, remembering how she and Wareham had once been the same.

Belmont, who had remained at Amy's side all day, was going through the list of the horses for the next race.

'Here's one for you, Miss Eaton. It's called Darcy's Delight. It must be named after the character in *Pride and Prejudice*. You said Miss Austen is your favourite authoress. I shall put a small bet on the horse for you. The literary connection is too close to ignore.'

A man standing to their right must have heard Belmont's comments. 'Forgive the interruption, but did I overhear a racing tip?'

Belmont laughed. 'I'm afraid I can't answer for the form of the horse. I only referred to the coincidence of the name being linked to a famous authoress, when my friend here, Miss Eaton, is also a famous writer.'

The stranger raised his hat. 'Then I'm delighted to meet you. The Right Honourable Crawford Spencer Willmott, the Earl of Hokeham, at your service.'

He was English. Amy gathered that from his cut-glass accent as much as from his title. He was also tall, very good-looking and immaculately dressed. His kid gloves were soft as he took her hand and kissed it, his eyes never once leaving her face.

Suddenly hot, Amy cleared her throat. 'It's a pleasure to meet you.'

'The pleasure is all mine. Now if you'll excuse me, I'm off to put a wager on that horse. I'll be back in less than a minute.'

Marion fanned her face furiously as she watched him weave his way through the crowd. 'He's an earl, God bless us. He's one of the English nobility. What were the chances of meeting him here, like this? Who would have believed it?' She grabbed Belmont's arm. 'Go and fetch Lucy and Hester. We have to introduce them. Their mother will never forgive me if they miss this opportunity.'

It was every American mother's wish that their daughter marry into the English aristocracy, and as far as Marion was concerned there was no higher form of life. A connection like this would put them at the top of New York's social hierarchy. They wouldn't miss out on an invitation to a party or a ball ever again.

Belmont dashed off to do Marion's bidding, forgetting his promise to place a bet on Darcy's Delight. Once he'd gone, Amy tried to calm Marion down.

'Let's get to know the earl a little before we build up our hopes.'

'Don't be ridiculous, Amy. Imagine if he could be persuaded to marry Hester or Lucy. They'd be welcomed into the English royal court. They'd get to live in a castle.'

The horse race had been run and lost by the time everyone returned to the tent. Wareham frowned at the Right Honourable Crawford Spencer Willmott who was tearing up his betting paper. 'I trust you didn't lose too much.'

'A few hundred dollars.' He shrugged, as if it were nothing. 'It was worth it for the sport.'

'I'm so sorry, my lord.' Amy was mortified that she might have been the cause of such a loss. Darcy's Delight had come in second to last.

'No harm done. And to prove it, I insist you call me Spencer. All my friends do. *My lord* sounds like you're talking to my father.'

Marion manoeuvred herself into the small space between Amy and Spencer. 'Allow me to introduce Lucy and Hester Morton. They've just debuted in society and are as fresh as daisies.'

Spencer barely cast them a glance. 'Weren't they a little late?

Debutantes come out much younger in England' – he winked at Amy – 'but if you ask me, the first bloom of youth is overrated.'

Marion's lips quivered. 'We set our own rules here.'

In truth, Lucy and Hester had been out for much longer than Marion would admit to. The problem lay in the fact that they refused to accept the eligible men presented to them, choosing instead to follow their hearts. As far as Marion was concerned, it was turning into a battle of wills on a monumental scale.

Undeterred, Marion handed him a calling card. 'We return to New York tomorrow. You're welcome to visit us any time you're in town.'

He slipped the card into his pocket. 'I plan to be in New York very soon. I'll look forward to calling on you.' He took Amy's hand for a second time and kissed it, holding it longer than was strictly necessary. 'In the meantime, I shall read every one of your books and prepare to discuss them with you in detail the next time we meet.'

'You might want to try reading just the one first and see how you like it before you commit to reading all of them.'

'You do yourself a disservice. I'm determined to love every one. How could I not, now I've met the charming authoress?'

Amy tried not to laugh. Perhaps it was the habit of English manners, but to her mind, Spencer's behaviour bordered on the ridiculous and couldn't be taken seriously.

It was only after he'd gone that she realised Wareham was standing beside her, an unreadable look on his face, which she took to be criticism.

'Is there something I can do for you, Mr Wareham?'

Her question was enough to snap him out of whatever thoughts had caused him to frown. He paused for a second, as if he were searching for an answer which, despite his efforts, seemed beyond him. Defeated, he gave her a slight bow before he finally walked away without saying a word.

As they waited for their carriages to take them back to the

hotel, Marion could talk of nothing but Spencer. 'Did you see the way he shrugged off losing his bet, as if it hardly mattered? If he can afford to risk such a great sum of money he must be very wealthy indeed.' She retied the bow on Lucy's bonnet, which had come loose during the excitement of the day. 'You must pay him more attention when he comes to visit us, Lucy. And you must remember to call him Spencer, not *my lord*. He said we could call him Spencer. That's a sign of intimacy, is it not?'

Lucy remained silent, her eyes fixed on Wareham, who'd been remarkably quiet all day. Amy sensed his frustration. He'd come to Cape May to help Belmont gain Mr and Mrs Craig's backing for his invention, but the trip had turned into a holiday and there'd been too much distraction for important decisions to have been made.

'It's not Lucy he's interested in,' said Hester, ducking out of Marion's reach as she made a grab for the ribbons on her bonnet, which had no need of retying. 'He only had eyes for Amy.' She cast a telling glance at Belmont. 'His isn't the only eye she's caught recently.'

'Don't be ridiculous,' replied Marion. 'Amy's far too old to attract the attention of a man, especially a *lord*.'

Amy placed her hand on her forehead. The hospitality tent had been hot and crowded and she could feel a headache coming on. 'Please don't talk about me as if I'm not here.'

Lucy laughed. 'The gentlemen talk about you even more when you're not here.'

The carriages finally arrived, rescuing Amy from the conversation. She wasn't used to being the centre of attention and, as far as she was concerned, it was unwarranted. Wareham stepped forward and offered her his hand, helping her into the carriage.

'The sea air has served you well. You seem to have made at least two conquests.'

'It wasn't my intention, I assure you.'

Once she was seated, he checked the carriage door was securely closed and stepped away, folding his arms as he considered her. 'You couldn't help it, I suppose. You're so practised at breaking men's hearts that it's become second nature.'

He considered her a flirt, and was accusing her of playing with men's hearts for sport. His comments about how she hadn't lost her touch when it came to archery, how she never missed her target, had been a reference to this too. If he believed she went through life deliberately making men fall in love with her, only to then reject them, he was mistaken. It proved how badly he'd misjudged her character, how his bitterness and anger had marred his opinion of her in the years they'd been apart. He'd convinced himself she'd never loved him. No wonder he was so angry with her.

She opened her parasol, shielding her face from the other occupants in the carriage, so they wouldn't see the confusion and the rage that played out on her face. She hadn't wanted to come on this trip. The sooner they were back in New York, the better she'd feel. At least in the city, she wouldn't be obliged to see so much of Wareham.

Chapter 20

They were to return to New York that afternoon. After breakfast, Lucy sent a message to Wareham, asking him to arrange for them to go riding along the beach. The day at the races had made her suddenly mad for horses and she was determined to make the most of their last remaining hours in Cape May.

Marion refused to join them, insisting her corset wouldn't stand the strain, and she wouldn't be seen dead without it, even in Cape May. Mr and Mrs Craig had already returned to the city, accompanied by Conrad, who hoped to use the journey to discuss the ideas he'd been working on for their house on Fifth Avenue. He'd already made a series of drawings inspired by the style of the European Gothic revival houses, including the intricate gingerbread woodwork that was particular to the area and which seemed to appeal to Mrs Craig. Mr Craig, on the other hand, talked of nothing but limestone mansions in the French style with fancywork iron railings and gargoyles above the windows. The Craigs' marriage might have been a meeting of minds, but their taste in architecture couldn't have been more different.

After a tearful goodbye, Hester was ready to throw herself into any activity that would take her mind off Conrad's departure and was keen to be included in the excursion, even though, like Lucy, she had little experience of riding.

Belmont advised Wareham on the best livery stables where he could hire the horses and insisted on joining him. There was no word yet on whether Mr and Mrs Craig were prepared to invest in his invention or advise him on the composition of the steel for the mesh hosepipe liner, and as he confided to Amy, he wanted to get as much advice as possible from his old college friend before he returned to New York.

For once, Amy was pleased to be invited to join the group. The idea of riding across the beach, of feeling the freedom and the power of the horse beneath her was enough to bring back memories of the times she'd spent riding with her mother in Central Park, to remind her once more of the special bond they'd shared. No one had ever loved Amy as unconditionally as her mother. No one that was, apart from Wareham.

'Miss Eaton, I selected this bay mare for you to ride. She's quite placid.'

Belmont was standing beside her, offering her an aged horse. 'Thank you, I . . .'

Before she could take the reins, Wareham stepped forward and interrupted them.

'This bay is no good for Miss Eaton. It's far too tame.' He pointed to a black horse held in check by a nervous-looking Hester, and glanced at Amy. 'I chose this stallion especially for you.'

The stallion threw back his vast head and gave a snort, his hooves pawing the ground with suppressed energy. Amy moved slowly towards him and ran her hand along his flank to settle him, thrilled by the feel of his firm muscles beneath his silky coat. He was perfect. She could feel the excitement building inside her. Wareham hadn't forgotten how she liked to ride.

'Are you trying to kill me, Mr Wareham?'

Wareham gave her a startled look. 'I . . .'

Before he could continue, Lucy dashed forward and snatched the reins. 'I'll take the stallion if Amy is too scared to ride him.'

'I didn't say I wouldn't ride him, I was only . . .'

The stallion reared up on its hind legs, fighting Lucy's inexpert handling, and knocking her off-balance as she struggled to steady him. 'I want to ride him.' She turned to Wareham. 'Don't you think I should be allowed to ride him?'

Wareham rubbed his palms together, clearly flustered. 'Are you as strong a horsewoman as Miss Eaton?'

'Anything Amy can do, I can do.'

This wasn't strictly true, but Amy knew better than to point it out. 'You should take the bay, Lucy. It will suit you better.'

Lucy sniffed. 'Don't assume you know what's best for me.'

Wareham gave Amy a questioning look. Even if he trusted her on nothing else these days, he would trust her when it came to horses. 'You should listen to Miss Eaton's advice and take the bay.'

'Don't pay any attention to Amy,' snapped Lucy. 'She's such a bore. I know what I'm doing, Mr Wareham.'

'Are you sure?' he asked, keeping his voice level. 'The bay is a perfectly fine horse. Mr Belmont selected him.'

'Then he can ride her. I want the stallion.'

Wareham sighed, giving in to Lucy's demand, and helped her to mount the horse. Amy took the bay, much to Belmont's satisfaction. Hester and Wareham took the two chestnuts, leaving the white mare for Belmont.

Once they'd all mounted, Wareham pointed to the cliffs at the end of the long stretch of beach. 'I suggest we take a gentle walk up to that point and back, so we can get a feel for the horses.'

Everyone agreed, apart from Lucy, who insisted they head for the shoreline, so they could canter through the shallow waves. 'It would be such a romantic thing to do. Don't you agree, Mr Wareham?'

Before Wareham could answer, Lucy began tugging at the reins, forcing the stallion in all directions. Confused by the commands, the horse began to turn in circles.

'Don't pull so hard on the reins, Lucy,' warned Amy. 'He's

trained to respond to the gentlest appeal.'

Resenting Amy's advice, Lucy rocked backwards and forwards in her saddle, trying to persuade the confused horse to go in the direction she had in mind. 'There's no need to give me instructions, Amy. I have ridden before, you know.'

Belmont gave Hester a knowing look, as if to indicate he didn't believe it, before turning his attention to Lucy. 'Would you like me to lead you? I could take your horse's reins and we could walk side by side at a gentle pace.'

Lucy thumped her fist against her leg in outrage. 'No, I would not like you to lead me. I'm not a child.'

Distressed by Lucy's violent behaviour, the stallion reared up once again on its hind legs. Lucy let out a scream and clutched the horse's mane as the startled creature threatened to throw her.

'Hold on, Lucy, I'm coming.' Amy brought her horse slowly alongside Lucy's, so as not to cause the animal any further alarm, and reached over, grabbing the reins, while making gentle sounds to soothe him.

'Breathe deeply, Lucy, and try to relax. The horse is sensing your panic and it's making him restless.'

'Pay attention to what Amy's telling you,' added Hester, who had dismounted from her own horse, fearing Lucy's stallion might upset it.

'Don't be absurd,' snapped Lucy, her voice growing ever louder with irritation. 'To hear you speak, anyone would think the beast had feelings.'

The distraction of the conversation was enough to stop Lucy wriggling in her saddle, and by degrees, the horse began to settle. Relieved to see the creature growing calmer, Amy handed Lucy the reins and demonstrated how to hold them softly in her fingers, just as her mother had taught her.

'Let me lead you in a gentle walk up and down the beach to get you used to the horse.' Amy dismounted from the bay, all the while talking to Lucy to distract her from upsetting the horse again. The creature was skittish enough without any encouragement from Lucy. 'Sit up straight and look directly ahead.'

But Lucy was in no mood to take instruction. Mischief sparkled in her eyes as she grinned at Wareham, pacing quietly up and down on his horse, waiting to begin the gentle walk to the cliffs he'd originally proposed.

'Come on, Mr Wareham, I'll race you.'

Before Wareham could reply, Lucy dug her heels into the stallion's ribs and hallooed at the top of her voice. Quick as lightning, the stallion set off across the beach, his hooves beating against the sand. Unprepared for the sudden movement, Lucy's body began bouncing uncontrollably in the saddle. She let out a great scream, throwing her arms around the horse's neck as she struggled to hold on for dear life. No matter how much noise she made, begging the horse to stop, the creature continued to carry her away, his speed increasing with every stretch of ground they covered until he was at full gallop.

'Dear God, she's let go of the reins.' Wareham threw an astonished look at Amy and set off after Lucy as fast as his horse would carry him, all the while cursing under his breath.

Amy climbed back onto her horse and followed as quickly as she could, encouraging the aged bay to pick up speed.

'Hold on, Lucy, I'm coming.'

If she could get alongside the stallion, she might be able to grab the reins and gently encourage him to a halt.

'Hold on tight.'

'I can't hold on any longer. Help me. Somebody help me.' Lucy's cries rang out across the deserted beach. Amy's eyes scanned the shoreline, but there was no one close enough ahead to intercept the horse and take the reins.

Amy's bay slowly gathered speed as she urged him on, encouraging him to catch up with Lucy's stallion, but the poor animal was no match for the speeding horse, who was as quick as lightning. Wareham was just ahead, steadily gaining ground on Lucy.

139

Another minute at his current pace, and he would catch up with her. He called out, begging her to stay calm.

'I can't stay calm. I simply can't.'

There were tears in Lucy's voice as the stallion thundered along the beach, his hooves throwing up great showers of sand in his wake.

'Pick up the reins, Lucy. Once you've got them, pull on them gently.'

But Amy's instruction came too late. There was a terrifying scream as Lucy's strength gave out. Unable to hold on any longer, she slipped from the saddle by degrees, finally tumbling from the horse and landing heavily on the sand, her head crashing against a rock.

Wareham reached her first. He quickly dismounted and knelt beside her. It was only a matter of seconds before Amy joined him, a shock of fear running through her as she saw the trickle of blood escaping from the back of Lucy's head.

'Lucy, can you hear me?' Wareham whispered, gently touching her arm, but there was no response. He covered his face with his free hand. 'This is my fault. I should never have let her ride the stallion. I knew she wasn't a strong rider, but I let her persuade me otherwise.'

Amy checked Lucy's pulse. 'She's still alive.' She turned to Belmont, who had finally caught up with them. 'Fetch a doctor, quickly.'

Hester dismounted from her horse and stood over them, wringing her hands and sobbing. 'What can I do to help?'

Amy gripped Lucy's fingers, willing the life back into them as she spoke to Hester. 'Go to the hotel and tell Marion what's happened, then go to the livery stables and ask the grooms to collect the horses. Hurry.'

She slipped off her jacket and rolled it up, placing it gently under Lucy's head. All the while, Wareham remained at her side, the shock of the accident having rendered him helpless.

'How could I have been such a fool? I'll never forgive myself if she doesn't recover.'

A sudden breeze whipped up and wrapped itself around them. Amy shuddered. 'Don't think about that now. We have to concentrate on doing what we can to help her. Will you give her your coat?'

Following Amy's instruction, he peeled it off and placed it over Lucy's body. All at once, she was a child frozen in time, a sleeping beauty, her pale face the only part of her visible beneath Wareham's coat.

'What if I've killed her?'

His eyes were full of self-recrimination. He'd chosen Lucy's obstinacy of self-will over Amy's steadiness of principle and this was where it had got them. Amy felt her heart give at the sight of Wareham's obvious distress. She placed a reassuring hand on his shoulder, offering comfort where she wanted to offer love. It was wrong to think of her own happiness when Lucy's life was in danger, when Wareham was so wretched. She took a steadying breath, forcing herself to concentrate on Lucy, lying on the sand. Whether she recovered or not, the look of despair on Wareham's face told Amy there was no going back. Everything that had once been between them was lost forever.

Chapter 21

The doctor arrived within minutes, dashing along the beach behind Belmont, his bag clutched to his chest. After a brief examination, he confirmed Amy's suspicion that Lucy had suffered a concussion. Although she'd regained consciousness, she appeared disorientated and weak-limbed. As far as the doctor could tell, there were no broken bones, something he attributed to her youth and the give of the sand as she landed on the ground. It was bad luck that her head had hit a rock.

Hester soon appeared, breathless from her dash around the town, complaining that Marion was nowhere to be found, and accompanied by the grooms, who quickly rounded up the horses to return to the stables, their eyes averted from the patient lying on the ground.

Still in shock, Wareham stared into the distance, while Amy took careful note of everything the doctor said. 'Is it all right to take her back to New York? We were planning on travelling this afternoon.'

The doctor got to his feet, brushing the sand from his hands. 'She's in no state to undertake the journey. Given the unpredictable nature of a concussion, it's important that she has a prolonged period of rest.'

Lucy moved her head, her eyelids fluttering against the light as she tried to focus on the doctor's face. 'I don't want to be any trouble to anyone.'

The sound of her voice brought Wareham out of his reverie. 'We need to get Lucy inside while we decide what to do. She can't stay out here in the cold.'

Belmont clapped Wareham on the shoulder. 'Let's take her to my house. We can carry her between us.'

'There's no need. I can manage her myself.' Wareham brushed off Belmont's hand and gathered Lucy in his arms, cradling her as if any sudden movement might cause her to shatter. Compliant as a kitten, Lucy snaked her arms around his neck, resting her cheek against his chest as he carried her across the beach, fighting to keep them both steady on the shifting surface of the sand.

It was the croquet match all over again. On that day, it had been Amy that Wareham had carried off in his arms, her head tilted as she looked up into his gentle face. Then, there'd been laughter and the pleasure of a secret kiss when no one was looking. Today, there was only tears and pain. When Amy thought about it, she realised the memory was nothing like this moment at all.

They made quick progress through the town, and Lucy was soon settled on the sofa in Belmont's drawing room, with a blanket pulled up to her chin and a feather bolster to support her injured head. Once Hester had made sure her sister was comfortable, she went in search of Marion for a second time, while Amy worked out what to do next.

An hour passed before Marion finally arrived, with Hester at her side, murmuring under her breath to keep her calm. After taking one look at Lucy lying on the sofa, Marion covered her face with her hands and began swaying as if she were about to faint.

'This is too much for me to stand. Whatever shall I do?'

Belmont offered Marion a steadying arm and guided her to a nearby chair. 'Lucy is welcome to stay here until she's well enough to travel. I'll make sure she's comfortable and has all the medical attention she needs.'

'I'll pay the doctor's bills,' added Wareham, his voice full of anguish. Since the moment of the accident, he'd refused to leave Lucy's side. Now he sat on the floor beside the sofa where she lay, the very incarnation of a faithful dog. He gave Amy a desperate look. 'Will you stay with her? I won't trust her care to anyone else.'

The request landed like a spear in Amy's heart. 'Of course. I'll be glad to.'

'Don't be ridiculous, Amy. You're needed at home.' Marion shuffled in the seat, running her hands irritably along the folds in her skirt. 'I'll stay and look after her. Lucy's parents left me in charge of her care. I can't abandon her now.'

Wareham gave her a determined look. 'I think Miss Eaton would be the best person to look after her.'

'I don't care what you think, Mr Wareham. Lucy is my responsibility. It's up to me to decide who takes care of her.'

'Please don't argue.' Lucy started to cry, as if the sound of the voices was too much for her to stand.

Seeing Lucy's distress, Amy tried to appease the warring pair. 'I don't mind staying.'

'You can't possibly stay,' said Marion, her voice growing high-pitched. 'Charles Junior needs you.'

There was no arguing with Marion. Wareham wasn't a part of the family and couldn't be expected to have a say in who should care for Lucy. Not yet, anyway. His shoulders sagged as he conceded.

'In that case, I'll accompany Miss Eaton and Miss Morton back to New York tomorrow and make sure they get home safely.'

Marion sniffed, resplendent in her small victory. 'I'm sure I can trust you to do that, at least.'

There was no more to be said. Wareham expressed his need for some fresh air and left the house while Belmont arranged for his maid to make up the spare rooms and provide everyone with tea. Amy was touched by his kindness. Still mourning the death of his fiancée, it couldn't have been easy for him to cope with another tragedy, and she was grateful for his help. Even before Lucy's accident, she'd been conscious of how hard he'd worked to be cheerful, doing his best to make their brief holiday pleasant. Every now and again, when he thought no one was watching him, she'd witnessed his face cloud over as the memory of his loss returned to him with full force and refused to be pushed away.

He was a good man. She trusted there'd be more happiness for him in the future, that one day he'd find someone else to love. Knowing his heart was so full of kindness, she had every hope for him.

It was late in the afternoon and Wareham still hadn't returned to the house. Amy had expected him to come back by now to check on Lucy. He was so distraught when he left, that she worried for him. He was wrong to blame himself for the accident but it wouldn't stop him doing so. Lucy was strong-minded. It was the thing that had attracted him to her in the first place.

Made restless by the knowledge that he was out there some-where, nursing his troubled thoughts, Amy set out to find him. She wandered the streets of the town, but there was no sign of him. Guessing he'd headed to the ocean, she made her way to the beach and scoured the broad sweep of sand, desperate for a sight of him, needing to reassure herself he was all right.

She was about to give up when she spotted him, sitting with his back to her on one of the low-lying rocks and looking out across the ocean, so close to the water, he must have felt the spray of the waves as they crashed around him. He'd probably been there for some time, and now the tide was coming in.

She watched him from a distance, trying to read his thoughts in the curve of his spine, the hunch of his shoulders, but it was impossible to know what he was feeling. Lucy's accident had shaken him more than she'd expected. Was it because he truly loved her, or because he felt responsible for what had happened? After all, he was the one who'd chosen the stallion, the one who'd given in to her when she insisted on riding it.

Wareham had selected the stallion for Amy, and she should have accepted it without comment, rather than questioning his motives and turning his gesture into a joke. At one time, he'd have known she was teasing him, and seen the jest for what it was, known she was secretly delighted that he'd selected a horse for her. Whichever way she thought about it, there were mistakes on all sides.

She sat on the sand and waited to see if he noticed her. If he sensed her presence and turned around, it would mean he still loved her. It would only take one simple movement of his head, a glance over his shoulder, and then she'd know. It was a pointless game, but still she played it.

The sun was going down. She watched its slow descent on the horizon, disappearing as if it were a ball of fire melting into the ocean. Wareham's eyes must have been fixed on it too, because despite Amy's hopes and wishes, he didn't turn around.

The air grew cold without the sun to keep it warm. Amy scrambled to her feet, shivering as the gentle breeze whipped up to something more. He was never going to turn and look at her. Whatever love he'd once felt for her was long gone and would never reignite.

Chapter 22

Amy sat up all night, watching the progress of Lucy's every breath as she slept, desperate for a sign that she was improving, that there'd be no lasting effects from the accident. She woke just before breakfast, but was more subdued than usual, which was only to be expected after such a shock. Apart from a few bruises, she'd suffered no other injuries that anyone could see, which was largely thanks to a good dose of luck. It was too soon for the doctor to know if there'd be any permanent damage from the concussion. The best he could say at this moment was that she was out of danger.

They left for New York directly after breakfast. Amy, Wareham and Hester boarded the train in silence, each lost in their own thoughts. As soon as they'd settled in their compartment, Amy took out her notepaper and a pen. She'd promised Marion she'd write to Eleanor and her father, informing them of Lucy's accident, and was glad of the distraction the task offered. Hester stared out of the window, watching the landscape roll by, while Wareham read his newspaper.

The tension created by the unbroken silence was unbearable. It was all Amy could do not to scream, to beg Wareham to say something, anything that would make things more tolerable. Did he hate her so much, that he chose to ignore her? Was it because he blamed her for Lucy's accident? Had the fact that, after taking one look at the stallion, she'd asked if he wanted to kill her, cut that deeply? She'd meant it as a joke and had never expected it to be so fortuitous.

Hester suppressed a yawn. 'Shall we have tea?'

Neither Amy nor Wareham had the stomach for it. Exhaustion and worry had killed their appetites. Wareham offered to fetch some for Hester, but she insisted on going herself. He waited until she'd closed the door behind her before he spoke.

'She reminds me of you, in so many ways.'

Because of the constant wringing of her hands, she wondered, *or because of her devotion to a man her family believe to be an unsuitable match?*

'It's good of you to help Conrad. Hester loves him very much. I hope they're able to marry one day.'

He nodded, staring at the floor between them, his foot no more than an inch from hers. The slightest move and they'd be touching. 'I hope so too, although I have little faith in happy endings. New York society hasn't changed in all these years. It remains as prejudiced as it ever was.'

For a moment, she thought he was talking about their broken engagement, but he must have been referring to his intention to marry Lucy. After all, Marion hadn't hidden the fact that she thought him an unsuitable match.

'Lucy is strong-willed. You should have faith in her.'

'If she doesn't recover, I'll never forgive myself.' He leaned across the carriage towards her, his eyes still fixed on the floor. 'Will you do something for me?'

She nodded, nervous of what was coming next.

'Will you write to her parents and explain what happened? I know you'll break the news in a way that's least likely to cause alarm.'

'I'll be happy to.'

There was a beat of silence while he took a breath, as if he were preparing to make a speech. 'I just wanted to say—'

Before he could continue, Hester charged into the compartment, complaining there was no tea to be had and regretting she hadn't accepted an extra cup from Mr Belmont's maid before they left. The moment of intimacy was broken. Wareham leaned back in his seat and returned to his newspaper, indicating the conversation was over. His courage had failed him, or else he wasn't prepared to express what was on his mind in front of Hester.

Tormented by the thought of what might have been left unsaid, Amy pretended to write, even though she was in too much turmoil to compose even a simple sentence of her letter to Eleanor and her father. A quick glance told her Wareham wasn't reading the newspaper, but was using it to hide behind, just as she was hiding behind her pen and paper. She knew then that he'd withdrawn from her for good, that there was nothing left to be said between them. He was only interested in how she could be of service to him and Lucy.

At Grand Central, he handed them into a hansom cab and instructed the driver to take them home, trusting him with the last part of their journey, so he could return directly to Cape May. Barely a word passed between them while he made sure their luggage was placed at their feet and tested the driver's understanding of where he was to take them, as if Amy wasn't capable of organising such things for herself.

She wanted him to stop making so much fuss, and yet there was something comforting about his small attentions, a lovingness that made her long for more. His actions didn't imply he thought her incapable of making her own arrangements, but rather that he took pleasure in acting for her. It was fanciful thinking on her part. He was simply behaving as the gentleman she'd always known him to be, and yet still she couldn't help feeling touched by his kindness, whatever the meaning behind it.

He held onto the door as he closed it, ensuring it was secure. She caught his eye, and just for a moment, she thought he was going to say something, but the intention, laid bare in his expression, quickly faded and the moment passed. Perhaps she'd imagined it. Perhaps he had nothing to say to her at all, or perhaps he was considering asking her to do something else for Lucy before thinking better of it.

He would never forgive her for breaking his heart. He was lost to her forever, and as she watched him turn and walk away, beginning his journey back to Lucy, and the new life he was set to make with her, it felt as if he was taking the best part of herself with him.

Chapter 23

The house was unusually quiet without Marion's and Lucy's voices ringing through every room. Charles, who believed in taking all family dramas in his stride, remained largely in his study, emerging only for meals and to retire to bed now he was no longer required to attend Marion's constant social engagements.

Hester looked after Charles Junior, taking him for long walks in Central Park to help him enlarge his snail collection, freeing Amy to concentrate on writing the next instalment of *Missing in Love*. Amy suspected Hester was using the excuse of the walks to meet Conrad, but didn't question her over it. Charles Junior was always with them and she trusted Hester to behave appropriately when he was in her care. Amy wouldn't stand in the way of her seeing Conrad. She was too familiar with the agony of missing someone to wish it on anyone else.

They'd only been back from Cape May a few days when Amy received a note from Mrs Craig.

My Dear,
There's to be a rally in Central Park tomorrow afternoon at two o'clock. Come and join the march demanding votes for women and help us to spread the word!

Amy considered the invitation. The group of women who'd previously been caught protesting in Central Park had been arrested and fined, their names printed on the front pages of the newspapers, all apart from Mrs Canby, who either by accident or cunning, had managed to avoid public exposure. Amy suspected her father might have had some influence in keeping her name out of the papers, not for her sake, but for the sake of his political career. After all, it wouldn't do for the daughter of a senator to be seen challenging the political system.

The protester who'd hung the banner on the fountain was still being detained and was likely to face a prison sentence once the powers that be had come up with a charge that would be worthy of a severe punishment. The law was still young and unformed when it came to such things, and Amy suspected they were making it up as they went along, although the suppression of women's voices was as ancient as history.

The way the women had been treated was a salutary lesson. It was all well and good, protesting to bring attention to the cause, but at what personal cost? Amy had so much to lose, not only her reputation as a writer, but more importantly, her livelihood. She couldn't risk upsetting the readership of *Scribe* magazine or Mr Farrand when she was relying on the income from the serialisation to support the family and clear their debts.

There had to be a cleverer way of helping the campaign. If she remained a popular author, and her work continued to be a success, she could use her position to put out the message in a more measured way. Surely this would be more useful to the cause in the long term. A considered, respected voice was more likely to be listened to than someone shouting and waving a banner in a public park.

On the other hand, it would be cowardly to avoid direct action and leave it to others to campaign for her rights on her behalf. If the cause was worth fighting for, then someone had to do it. Women's lives wouldn't improve otherwise. If she joined Mrs

Craig on the rally, she didn't have to draw attention to herself. She could appear as just another face in the crowd, another voice demanding the right to vote. She spoke to Hester about it later that evening, testing her view on it.

'I don't know, Amy. Look how those poor women were publicly humiliated. I'd rather die than have my name printed in the newspapers while they accused me of being a criminal. There's no saying how brutally the women were treated after they were arrested. Think of the effect it must have had on their families.'

'So you won't join me on the march if I decide to go?'

Hester's eyes widened, displaying her panic, while she thought of an excuse to refuse the invitation. 'Tomorrow is the afternoon for my charity visit to the orphanage. I've promised to show the girls how to sew on a button.'

It could be argued that this activity was of a more practical use than waving a banner in Central Park. At least the young women would gain a tangible skill from Hester's efforts. And yet, something had to be done if things were to change.

Hester dropped her embroidery in her lap and stared at Amy. 'You're not actually considering going, are you?'

Mrs Craig called for Amy at eight minutes to two the following afternoon. Dressed for all aspects of the weather, she was wearing sturdy overshoes, a linen duster coat and a straw bonnet. She rubbed her hands together through thick leather gloves. 'Are you ready?'

An advance party of organisers had gone ahead and herded the sheep from the meadow they grazed in Central Park and returned them safely to the barn where they spent their nights, freeing up the large area of grassland for the rally.

Hundreds of women were already gathered when Amy and Mrs Craig arrived, banners and flags waving above their heads like tethered birds. Drums were being thumped and tin whistles blown. It was disorientating being among so many people and if there was any organisation, it was hard to see it.

'What happens now?' Amy raised her voice to be heard above the noise. 'Is there a plan of action?'

'We walk the length of the Mall, all the way up to the fountain. The general idea is to get in the way and make as much noise as possible.'

Mrs Canby must have spotted them while they were talking. She jostled her way through the crowd towards them, shouting above the noise to catch their attention. 'There you are, Miss Eaton. When Mrs Craig said you might come, I didn't believe it.'

She was dressed from head to foot in crimson silk. If anyone was determined to make herself seen, it was Mrs Canby.

'I see you're suitably dressed for the occasion,' joked Mrs Craig. 'After the lucky escape you had last time, I thought you might want to keep a lower profile.'

'What would be the point of that? We're here to make a nuisance of ourselves, aren't we? We can't do that if we're invisible.'

Amy didn't believe that was the reason they were there, but given the level of noise, it wasn't the time or the place to debate tactics.

There was a sudden surge in the crowd as someone hollered an instruction. Amy's feet shifted from under her as she was swept along, one small part of a huge animal, carried by its own momentum.

'Hold on, my dear,' cried Mrs Craig, grabbing Amy's hand. 'We don't want to become separated.'

As the moving crowd found its rhythm, Mrs Canby drew Amy's attention to the large can of whitewash she was carrying. 'I'm going to break ranks and cause some mayhem. Do you want to help?'

'What do you intend to do?'

'Those statues along the Mall are all men. It's time they had some white faces, don't you think?'

Amy considered the bronze figures of Shakespeare, Robert

Burns and Walter Scott in Poets Walk. They'd earned the right to be there and didn't deserve Mrs Canby's disrespect.

'Vandalism won't help the cause. It will only hinder it.'

Mrs Canby shrugged, shouting to be heard above the noise. 'You worry too much.'

'If you won't consider the damage to the statues, think of the damage to yourself. If you're caught, you'll be arrested and end up in jail.'

'The police won't dare to touch me. They know who my father is. How do you think my name was kept out of the newspapers the last time?'

She laughed as she forced her way through the crowd, heading in the direction of the statues. Whatever Mrs Canby might say, her campaigning wasn't about gaining votes for women, but about taking revenge on her family by causing her father as much embarrassment as possible.

Amy turned to Mrs Craig, but she'd already drifted away, their hands having come unclasped in the ever-shifting motion of the crowd. She strained to look over the heads of everyone around her, but there was no sign of her anywhere, only a sea of bonnets and banners that stretched as far as the eye could see.

It was impossible to fight against the will of the horde and the noise was growing ever more erratic. The steady rhythm of the drumbeats and the whistles that had kept everyone in step was slowly being drowned out by something much worse. Abandoning any hope she had of locating Mrs Craig, Amy allowed herself to be carried along until she was able to slip onto a side path, away from the route of the march. She could sense the growing danger in the atmosphere. Even from a safe distance she could feel the violence in it.

It wasn't only women now demanding their rights, but people who disagreed with their views making a disturbance. Insults and missiles were being thrown through the air, hauling threats with deadly intentions behind them. Already the policemen were arriving in great dark clusters, like meat flies homing in on a feast, clubs in hand and determined to restore order, no matter what it took.

Shaken by the atmosphere of hostility, Amy walked briskly through the quieter areas of the park, taking a roundabout route that would eventually lead her home. There was nothing to be gained from being a part of such chaos when the message of the campaign was destined to be lost beneath the violence. It would be futile to go back and try to find Mrs Craig, who was capable of taking care of herself, and Mrs Canby had put herself beyond saving. Set on a path of self-destruction, there was nothing that could be done to rescue her.

As Amy approached the house, Hester was climbing out of a hansom cab. Amy waved to catch her attention, acting as if she were returning from her usual stroll in the park, as if nothing out of the ordinary had occurred.

'How was your afternoon at the orphanage?'

'Fine. The girls are quick to learn. I only wish I had better skills to teach them. They'll need to be able to do more than simply sewing on buttons if they're to make their way in the world.'

The chanting and the banging of the drums carried on the breeze all the way from Central Park. Things had to change. Even Hester, wrapped up in her love for Conrad and her tiny cloistered world was ready to admit that, even if she was too preoccupied with her own concerns to do anything about it.

But what should be done? Protest marches and acts of vandalism weren't going to change the world. If Amy was to play her part in the liberation of women, she had to employ the weapons she had; her pen, her voice and her creative spirit. She'd be treading a fine line between upsetting her publisher and engaging her readers in the fight for the cause, but if it was the most effective way she could help the campaign for votes for women, then she had to consider whether there was a way to do it.

Chapter 24

During the following week, the newspapers were full of the story of the rally. Amy had only witnessed a small part of it, and was shocked to learn how quickly it had got out of hand after it had started so peacefully. If the women had been allowed to protest without interference, the newspapers would have reported on the message they were trying to express, rather than on the clashes, but human nature being what it is, it had never been destined to happen that way.

The names of the women who'd been arrested were listed on all the front pages, and although there was no mention of Mrs Canby, it was reported that a woman in a crimson dress had thrown whitewash over the statue of Walter Scott before one of her fellow protesters had apprehended her, thereby saving the statues of Robert Burns and Shakespeare from the same assault. The perpetrator wasn't named, nor was it made clear whether she'd been arrested.

Amy hadn't seen Mrs Craig since the day of the rally. There'd been a brief exchange of notes, confirming they'd each got home safely and avoided the skirmishes, but she'd heard nothing from her since. Although she was fond of Mrs Craig, she was too close to Wareham for Amy to risk becoming too friendly with her. Her sharp mind missed nothing and it wouldn't take much for her to guess her feelings for him. The humiliation, added to Mrs Craig's sympathy would be unbearable, especially if Amy's suspicions were correct, and there was already an understanding between Wareham and Lucy.

It was during this time that Marion sent a letter, bringing Amy up to date on Lucy's condition.

Dear Amy,

There's hardly been a minute to sit down and write. You can't imagine the strain Lucy's indisposition has put on me. I dare not leave her alone for a minute. We have a nurse to watch over her day and night, but even so, it's still too much.

They say Lucy is out of danger and my poor heart can only take the doctor's word for it. He is the expert, after all. Her bruises have now faded, and there appears to be no sign of any lasting physical injuries, although she must continue to have complete rest, beyond the small walks she is now advised to take.

Each morning, Mr Belmont accompanies her on her stroll along the beach. Lucy has become quite fond of Baxter, his little dog, and she insists on him going with them. As you can imagine, the responsibility of taking her out would be too much for me, with my sensitive constitution. I'm still not recovered from the shock of what happened, and doubt I'll ever be able to look at a horse or a beach in the same way again.

Mr Wareham is not the only one to blame for the accident and I trust you're feeling suitably remorseful now you've had time to dwell on it. It was nothing if not irresponsible of you to allow poor Lucy to ride that wild stallion when she's barely been on the back of a horse in the whole of her life.

It pains me to say it, but you would not recognise Lucy if you saw her. It's not her looks, which remain the same, but her character. Gone is the carefree child we knew and loved, and in her place is a placid, withdrawn creature. I fear this is partly Mr Belmont's fault for introducing her to quieter pastimes. It's not my place to criticise what a man does in his own home, but it's hard to remain silent when he insists on teaching her to play Jack straws and is even encouraging her to read!

Mr Wareham is no longer here with us, having finally retreated to his home in California, although he's no great loss. As you probably know, he returned to Cape May immediately after escorting you and Hester to New York, and was determined to stay close by, interfering in anything I tried to do. He's paying the doctor's bills for Lucy, just as he should, as well as for the twenty-four-hour nurse. It's the very least he can do, given the circumstances.

Marion

Amy studied the letter, trying to read between the lines, gleaning as much as she could from the things Marion hadn't said. Wareham was no longer in Cape May with Lucy, but had returned to California. There could only be one reason for it. He'd gone to make his home ready for his new bride. Knowing how much he disliked New York society, he wouldn't want to settle there once he was married. If Lucy was more pliable, as Marion suggested, Wareham would probably have little trouble persuading her to leave New York to begin a new life with him elsewhere.

He wouldn't have returned to Cape May and stayed for so long if Lucy meant nothing to him. It could only be a matter of time before the engagement was announced. They were probably only waiting until she was strong enough to travel. Whatever Marion thought about the match, it wouldn't be in her power to stop it. Hester had already mentioned that Lucy was prepared to elope if necessary. The next time she heard from Marion, Lucy and Wareham would probably already be married.

She sat down to write to Eleanor and her father, to pass on the news of Lucy's improvement, but found it impossible to concentrate. How was she supposed to put on a good show, to hide how deeply troubled she was by the turn of events?

Her thoughts were interrupted by the arrival of Mrs Rawle, who charged into the drawing room, gripping the latest edition of *Scribe* magazine.

'Don't mind me for disturbing you, but I had to come and congratulate you on the latest instalment of *Missing in Love*.'

Amy pushed Marion's letter into her pocket. She couldn't bring herself to mention its contents to Mrs Rawle, who would insist that Wareham's attachment to Lucy only went to prove she'd had a lucky escape from him all those years ago. 'I'm glad you enjoyed it.'

'The story is really getting under way now, but what I don't understand is why you're keeping the lovers apart. They hardly speak to one another.'

'It's only the beginning. They both have long emotional journeys ahead of them. It's not as if they live in a society where men and women can speak freely to one another. It would compromise the woman's reputation too much and it's not in the man's nature to speak out.'

'Your *so-called* romantic hero shows no interest in her in any way.'

'There's a reason for that. You'll have to wait until the end to find out what it is.'

Mrs Rawle frowned, unimpressed at being kept out of the secret. 'It's a bit flimsy, if you ask me.'

But I didn't ask you, thought Amy. 'I've purposely left space to bring in new ideas and situations to broaden the story once the main characters are established.'

'What exactly do you have in mind?'

'As I said, you'll have to wait and see.'

Even if Amy had worked out where the story was going, she

wouldn't share it with Mrs Rawle before it was published. Newly formed ideas were so brittle the slightest knock could shatter them.

'It would be a mistake to concentrate on anything other than the love story,' said Mrs Rawle, drumming her fingers on the cover of the magazine to emphasise her point. 'I'm telling you this for your own good. You understand that, don't you? I'm only doing what your mother would have done.'

Amy offered Mrs Rawle some tea, hinting as politely as she could that the subject of her work wasn't open for discussion. She respected her too much to imply any kind of criticism, or to seem cool in any way. It was enough to distract Mrs Rawle from expressing her opinion, at least for the time being.

'Is there any news on Lucy? Is it true she's attached to Mr Wareham?'

'If the rumours are true, yes.'

If Mrs Rawle thought Wareham and Lucy's situation a suitable subject for gossip, she either lacked sensitivity or had misunderstood the depth of Amy's attachment to him all those years ago. It had probably never crossed her mind that she might still be in love with him.

'How could he be interested in someone as flighty as Lucy after knowing you? There's no comparison.'

'He'll be looking for different qualities in a wife now than he did then.'

Amy tried to sound matter-of-fact, playing down the subject to avoid any further discussion. She needn't have worried. Mrs Rawle's mind had already moved on, as if Amy's broken heart was just another item on the long list of subjects she wanted to discuss. As far as Mrs Rawle was concerned, Amy and Wareham's attachment was firmly in the past.

'Did you see today's news? Someone set fire to an effigy of the president next to the fountain in Central Park.'

This was the first Amy had heard of it. 'Why would anyone

do that?'

'It was a protest by one of those mad women demanding the right to vote. As if such an extreme act would win them any favours in the eyes of Congress.'

'Do they know who did it?'

'No one was able to identify her. Apparently, she was wearing a veil and got away before the police arrived. Congress is outraged. The police have been charged with hunting her down and putting her on trial.'

'They'll have to find out who did it first.'

'She'll reveal herself sooner or later. Women like that can't resist making a show of themselves. It wouldn't surprise me if it was Mrs Craig.'

It was impossible to believe Mrs Craig would resort to such a reckless act when she had the reputation of the business to protect. Amy was appalled Mrs Rawle could even consider it.

'It could have been any number of women, or even a man for that matter. If they were wearing a veil, there's no saying who it was.'

'I wouldn't be so quick to defend Mrs Craig if I were you. She was seen at the rally in Central Park, demanding votes for women. They say she was right at the front, waving a banner.'

'Is that so terrible?'

'It's a disgrace.'

Knowing how rumours could be embellished with the spreading of them, Amy took Mrs Rawle's report on the event with a pinch of salt. Mrs Craig hadn't been at the front of the crowd when Amy was with her, nor did she have a banner. Her note had confirmed that, like Amy, she'd slipped away from the march and gone home soon after they'd become separated. She couldn't dispute Mrs Rawle's words without admitting she'd been right there, shoulder to shoulder with Mrs Craig. Still, she couldn't resist a little mischief.

'I wonder where she got the banner.'

Mrs Rawle looked aghast. 'Doesn't it bother you that disreputable people are living in your home?'

'They're keeping it very nicely. I have no complaints.'

'But, to be at the forefront of political demonstrations, to make a public spectacle of oneself like that. It's simply not done.'

'Women are poorly served in this society. The situation will only improve if we stand up and fight for our rights. Women like Mrs Craig are working on behalf of us all. The fact that she plays a significant role in running the business alongside her husband and Mr Wareham makes her a great example to women everywhere. It shows there's nothing we can't do if we put our minds to it. I must make a point of thanking her when I see her.'

'What nonsense you talk.'

'It's not nonsense. In fact, I'm still thinking of introducing a storyline about the campaign for votes for women in *Missing in Love*.'

Mrs Rawle stiffened as if someone had stuck a pin in her. 'You'll do no such thing. I don't know where you get your ideas from. Your mother would never approve.'

'I think she would.'

Amy had relied on Mrs Rawle to guide her on all the important decisions in her life, trusting her assurance that her advice was in accordance with what her mother would have wished for her. Now she was beginning to question it. Mrs Rawle was conditioned by her own views and prejudices, not her mother's, and perhaps they weren't always in Amy's best interests. Mrs Rawle had had many reasons to talk Amy out of marrying Wareham all those years ago, including not wanting to lose her, especially as she considered her to be the daughter she'd never had. Even by becoming a successful novelist, Amy was fulfilling Mrs Rawle's dreams.

Perhaps she was being too harsh. Each generation created their own rules and standards. It wasn't Mrs Rawle's fault that the values she lived by were rooted in the past, or that her comfortable life had given her no cause to look beyond the confines of her privileged society. Now, as Mrs Rawle stared at her across the room, her face pinched with disapproval, Amy wondered why she'd never worked this out before.

Chapter 25

Amy was walking in Central Park with Charles Junior, trying to work out what should happen next in *Missing in Love*, when she met Mrs Craig strolling along the Mall.

'My dear, it's been so long since I saw you. I hope you haven't been working too hard.' She took Amy's arm, encouraging her to walk with her. 'Mr Wareham has been asking after you in his letters and I had nothing to tell him.'

Wareham had been asking about her. How could it be, when he could hardly bring himself to look at her or have a conversation with her whenever she was in his company? He'd only spoken to her during the train ride from Cape May because he'd wanted her to write to Lucy's parents to inform them of the accident. He was only interested in her when she was useful to him.

She didn't share any of these thoughts with Mrs Craig. 'I've been working on the new instalments of *Missing in Love* and have rarely left the house.'

'Your hard work is paying off. It's better than anything you've written before. I can't praise it more highly than that.'

'You're very kind.'

'Not at all. I know talent when I see it and I believe in speaking plainly. Life would be a lot less complicated if everyone did the same.' She smiled at Charles Junior, happily trotting beside them as he hunted for snails. 'Will you both walk with me a little further? There's much to catch up on.'

'I want to hear everything.'

'Mr Wareham . . .'

There it was again, Wareham's name. Would her stomach ever cease to turn over every time it was mentioned? Would she ever be free of his effect on her?

'Mr Wareham has been helping his friend Mr Belmont with his revolutionary new hosepipe design and we're now confident enough to invest in the development of the expanding steel mesh lining.'

'That's excellent news.'

'Belmont is such a dear man. It takes strength of character to come back from heartbreak such as he suffered with the death of his fiancée. It's a credit to him, the way he's thrown himself into his work. I have every confidence that we can make a success of the new venture.'

She could have been talking about Wareham, throwing himself into his work and achieving so much after Amy broke off their engagement all those years ago. If Mrs Craig hadn't been such a straight-talking person Amy would have suspected her of hinting at it. She kept an eye on Charles Junior as he knelt down to search for snails in an overgrown cluster of hostas. She had to stop bringing every conversation around to thoughts of Wareham, or reading too much into every exchange with Mrs Craig.

'Have you decided who'll be designing and building your house on Fifth Avenue?'

'If you mean have we given the contract to Conrad Harris, then no, we haven't. Not yet. He still has a way to go to prove himself.'

'He's a determined young man.'

Mrs Craig gave her a guarded smile. 'As I said, I know talent when I see it. The other news is that Mr Wareham is developing a safety hat to be worn while riding horses.'

Amy stopped in her tracks. 'He's working on a riding hat?'

'The design is based on the bowler hat you see so many young men wearing these days. He got the idea after he noticed the railroad workers wearing them. As they'd already adopted them to keep the sun off their faces, it seemed an obvious step to make the crown into a protective shell for the head.

'The main challenge will be convincing ladies to wear it. Most are only interested in how fine they look on a horse and have no thought for safety. It was Lucy's fall that provoked it, of course. If she'd been wearing head protection, she might not have suffered her concussion. At the very least, if the impact had been cushioned, the injury might not have been so bad.'

Here was an example of remorse on the grandest scale. Wareham still hadn't forgiven himself for Lucy's accident and was doing everything he could to make up for it, from paying for her care, to developing safety measures to minimise the risk of it happening to anyone else. Everything he did was noble, selfless. Amy's heart dipped at the thought that Lucy remained at the forefront of his mind, that she'd become his muse.

'I have every confidence that both new projects will prove an asset to the company and to mankind,' continued Mrs Craig.

Lucy had become Wareham's muse. Amy couldn't get the idea out of her head. She had to change the subject before she betrayed herself.

'Are there any plans for another protest march?'

'Not for now. The mavericks have done the cause more harm than good.'

'Whoever burned the effigy of the president went too far,' said Amy. 'I don't know what they were thinking.'

'They're sorry for it now, I can tell you.' Mrs Craig lowered her voice, checking there was no one to overhear them before she continued. 'It won't surprise you to learn it was Mrs Canby who did it. She came to me for help the following evening. Her aunt has cut off her allowance, and her father, Senator Frost, can't promise to protect her any longer. He's used his influence to keep her name out of the papers until now, but there's no guarantee he'll be able to do so forever. If someone exposes her, there'll be a scandal, and he'll have no choice but to publicly condemn her for the sake of his own political career. If you ask me, he's gambling on this threat being enough to keep her in line.'

'Where is she now? Is she still with you?'

'I advised her to leave town until the fuss dies down. I gave her money, so she could afford a decent place to stay in the meantime, quite a lot of money, in fact.'

'Where was she planning to go?'

'She didn't say, and I didn't ask. I thought it best not to know.'

'Her family will want to prevent any hint of a scandal getting out, for all their sakes.'

There were buried misdemeanours in any number of families; inappropriate love affairs, or emotional breakdowns, children conceived outside of marriage that resulted in extended trips abroad to hide a pregnancy, the mothers only returning after the resulting baby had been weaned and placed in a suitable home. Such things happened every day. It was how these secrets were contained that made the difference, how far families were prepared to close ranks to avoid a scandal and protect their social standing.

'I should have discouraged her from treating the cause as part of her vendetta against her father,' said Mrs Craig. 'She might have been wronged by her family, but using the campaign as a public platform to get her revenge was only ever going to end in disaster for her and the cause.'

'What's to be done now?'

'We're trying to distance ourselves from all subversive actions, but it's not enough. We'll have to work more cleverly in future if we're to win the right to vote.'

'I want to feature the campaign in *Missing in Love*, but if the story doesn't work out, there'll be no going back on it.'

'You're worried it will upset some of your readers?'

'Does that make me weak?'

'Taking a controversial stance isn't a decision to be taken lightly, but as a respected authoress, you have a voice and the opportunity to be heard more than the rest of us.'

'That's what I've been thinking.'

'You should honour your own beliefs and do what you consider to be right. If what you decide to do turns out to be a mistake, then you own up to that too.'

The decision seemed easy when Mrs Craig put it so clearly. Amy had been under the influence of Mrs Rawle for too long; even though their views were different on so many things, she'd always held her in too much regard to go against her advice. Her mother would have wanted her to follow her heart. It was too late where Wareham was concerned, but while she had influence as an author, she would strive to use it for good.

Chapter 26

Marion returned to New York at the first sign of winter. She crashed into the house unexpectedly one afternoon while Charles Junior was having his nap. Amy looked up from her work, surprised to see her.

'Is Lucy with you?'

'The doctor says she's still not strong enough to travel.' She unpinned her hat and called for tea. 'I couldn't stand another day in Cape May, not with the social season under way in New York.'

'I should go to Lucy. She can't stay in Mr Belmont's house without a chaperone. It isn't right.'

'There's no need. It's all taken care of. Mrs Stern, the woman Mr Wareham employed to nurse her, is staying on as her companion.'

'Is Mr Wareham still paying for her care?'

'He insisted on it. He might as well put all that money he has to good use.'

Why would Wareham pay for Lucy to have a companion unless he'd assumed the role of her protector, or if there wasn't an understanding between them? Amy pushed the thoughts away. There was nothing to be gained from dwelling on what was lost.

'Mr Belmont said to congratulate you on the latest instalment of *Missing in Love*. He likes that you've brought in the new storyline about the fight for women's right to vote.' She took off her fur mantle, shaking the sleet from it. 'I can't see why, when he's a man.'

'Universal suffrage will benefit the whole of society, not just women.'

Marion rolled her eyes and dropped onto the sofa. 'Why isn't the tea here yet? Won't you go and see to it? After that, you must write to Eleanor and Father for me and update them on Lucy's condition.'

It was only a few days after Marion's homecoming that Spencer appeared. Amy guessed there was no coincidence in the timing of his visit. Since Amy had returned from Cape May, he'd left a calling card on four separate occasions, hoping to procure an invitation, but each time, she'd chosen not to respond. Now he was sitting in the drawing room with Marion, while poor Hester was paraded in front of him like a prime pedigree in a dog show.

After the third summons, Amy finally joined them. 'There you are,' said Marion, greeting her with a false smile. 'Spencer has been asking for you. I began to think you were too busy to join us.'

'I was helping Charles Junior to catch a spider from the corner of the ceiling.' Charles Junior's fascination with snails had now spread to spiders and Amy was happy to indulge him in any pastime that encouraged him to sit still and be quiet.

Spencer got to his feet as soon as she entered and began emptying the contents of his portmanteau onto the rug. 'I've been as good as my word, Miss Eaton. As you can see, I've bought every one of your novels. Not only that, but I've read them too.' He gestured to the heap on the floor. 'Here are five copies of each. Count them if you don't believe me.' His moustache twitched as he looked at her. 'I hope you'll do me the honour of signing them for my friends in England.'

It wasn't unusual for Amy to be asked to sign her books and she was always glad to do it, but there was something about the nature of his request that made her uncomfortable. There was

171

far too much show to it.

'Are you planning on carrying them all back to England with you?'

If they were gifts for his friends back home, perhaps he was leaving soon. The idea left her feeling relieved, although she couldn't have explained why.

'I'll have them sent over. I'm not planning on returning just yet. There's far too much to interest me here in New York.'

While everyone was distracted by Spencer, Hester tried to slip out of the room unnoticed, until Marion called her back, nodding to the piano in the corner. 'My dear, why don't you play something for us? I'm sure Spencer would love to hear it.'

The piano was never used and hadn't been tuned for as long as anyone could remember. The panic on Hester's face was palpable. 'I need to check on Charles Junior, in case he needs rescuing from another spider.'

'Not now, Hester. Amy checked on him only a minute ago. Stay and play for us.'

Spencer angled himself away from the piano as Hester started playing. Anyone observing him with a critical eye would have thought he was trying to block out the noise.

'Tell me, Miss Eaton. What are you planning to write next? I want to know everything about it.'

'I'm working on a serial for *Scribe* magazine. It's about—'

'I think you should write about English lords and ladies. It'll guarantee you enormous sales in England, and your American readers will love to read about the aristocracy. I can tell you everything you need to know, so you'll get every detail right.'

He hardly knew her, and yet he had the audacity to tell her what she should be writing. He even thought he had the right to tell her how to do it. Next, he'd insist on having his name on the cover as co-author.

'I prefer to write about what I know.'

'You have an English aristocrat sitting right in front of you.

What else do you need to know?'

'Are you suggesting I write you into one of my novels?'

He threw up his hands as if the idea had never crossed his mind. 'If you insist. I make the perfect hero, don't you agree?'

'Most heroes have dark secrets they wish to conceal, or a tragic flaw that leads to their downfall.' She leaned forward and lowered her voice. 'What is it you're hiding from us?'

Spencer gave a nervous laugh. 'I see you're having a joke with me.'

'You mustn't take any notice of Amy,' said Marion, giving her sister a sharp look. 'She loves nothing more than to tease the people she's most fond of. She has a lively mind. Sometimes, it runs away with her.'

'Please don't apologise for your sister. I like a woman with spirit.'

Hester gave up playing the piano and closed the lid with a crash. Marion gestured behind Spencer's back, ordering her to sit next to him. There was an awkward silence as Hester pushed Amy's books aside to make room for her feet before she sat down, her face flushed with fury. She might have been sitting next to an earl, but he was nothing compared to Conrad.

When Spencer failed to take any notice of Hester, Marion tried him with a different temptation. 'Won't you have a cream slice?'

She dropped a cake onto a small plate and pushed it under his nose, forcing him to lean back, his moustache twitching at the prospect of so much cream and sugar. Amy couldn't decide whether it was his abstemiousness or his vanity that caused him to refuse it. Whatever the reason, his response made her question whether it was possible to be entirely comfortable in the company of a man who turned up his nose at the prospect of a cream slice. She was mulling this vital question when she realised he was talking to her.

'Would you accompany me to the opera tomorrow night, Miss Eaton?'

Marion pinned him with her eyes. 'Do you have a box?'

Only the very best people had boxes. Anyone who sat in the orchestra stalls wasn't worth knowing. Amy waited to see if Marion would make an exception for an earl.

'No. Do I need one?'

'A man of your social standing would never sit in the orchestra stalls. Not in New York. We have a box. Why don't you come as our guest?'

'That's very kind, but you misunderstand me. I'm inviting Miss Eaton as my guest, so it wouldn't do if we all went together, don't you see?'

There was a loud sniff as Hester suppressed a giggle. Amy didn't dare to look at her. The situation was getting more awkward by the minute.

'It's good of you to invite me, Spencer.' Amy found it peculiar, calling him by a name better suited to a dog, when he had a perfectly good title, even if she wasn't impressed by it. 'But I'm leaving New York tomorrow. I've stayed too long already. It's time I joined my father and sister in Newport.'

'I see.'

He glowered at the untouched cream slice, piling the books into his portmanteau and snapping it shut. It didn't seem to have crossed his mind that Amy hadn't yet signed them.

'Perhaps another time,' he murmured. 'Our paths will cross again soon, no doubt.'

Marion jumped to her feet, following Spencer as he made his way to the door, the weight of the books in his portmanteau pulling at his arm. 'Hester would be happy to accompany you to the opera. She adores music. You could probably tell from how beautifully she played the piano.'

He smiled, forcing a gallantry that seemed to pain him as much as the sight of the cream slice had previously done. 'As I said, perhaps another time.'

As soon as he'd gone, Marion collapsed onto the sofa beside

Hester, as if the last few minutes had cost her a monumental effort. 'What a charming man.'

Amy wasn't so sure. 'Do you think so?'

'We must get to know him better. I'll invite him to dinner.' She patted Hester's knee. 'You must work a little harder with him, my dear. There's no need to be so shy. Men like a woman to show a little interest in them. Next time, ask him about his pastimes. Find out about his castle in England.'

'He might not have a castle.'

'Don't be silly, Hester. He's an earl. They all have castles.' She crossed the room to her writing desk. 'I must send a note to your mother right away and let her know you've made a connection with the English aristocracy.'

'It's not me he wants to know,' said Hester. 'It was Amy he invited to the opera.'

'Don't be ridiculous. No man would be interested in Amy. She's far too old. He was just being polite about her novels. Some people's heads are turned by such things, but it's not real. You're the reason he came here today, Hester, whether he realises it or not. We'll make a countess of you yet.'

Chapter 27

Amy was packing her trunk, ready to leave for Newport the next morning, when one of the maids knocked on her bedroom door.

'There's a Mr Farrand to see you, ma'am. He's waiting in the drawing room.'

It was after nine o'clock. What could he want with her so late in the evening? And what could be so important that he'd gone to the trouble of coming to see her rather than sending a note? He'd seemed happy enough when she delivered the latest instalment of *Missing in Love* a couple of days ago and had had nothing urgent to speak to her about then. That was before he'd read it, of course.

She checked her hair in the mirror and smoothed the worst of the creases from her house dress with the palms of her hands before going downstairs to greet him. He was standing in front of the window, squinting at the rainy night through the lace curtains when she entered.

'Mr Farrand. This is an unexpected surprise. What can I do for you?'

'Forgive me for interrupting your evening, Miss Eaton, but I need to speak to you as a matter of urgency, and I remembered you telling me you were leaving New York tomorrow.'

By saying *a matter of urgency*, she guessed he meant there was a problem. She beat down the feeling of dread rising in her stomach and forced a smile. 'Won't you sit down? Shall I send for some tea?'

He shook his head as she went to pull the bell cord to summon the maid. 'That won't be necessary. I won't interrupt your evening for any longer than I have to. This isn't a social call.'

Everything that passed between them was always strictly confined to business. Unlike the male writers commissioned by the magazine, Amy wasn't considered *clubbable*, and was never invited to any of the regular lunches or dinners at Delmonico's hosted by Mr Farrand. She hadn't worked out whether the slight was due to the fact that she was a woman in a male-dominated world, or whether it was because they considered her work inferior, or worse, that they knew it to be superior, and were worried that if they met her, they'd be forced to admit it.

After a spell of nervous throat-clearing, Mr Farrand finally declared the purpose of his visit. 'It's about the last two instalments of *Missing in Love*.'

'Was there something wrong with them?'

'As you know, I think your work is terrific. I'm just not sure about the change of emphasis in the story.'

'What is it you don't like?'

He held up his hands, suddenly defensive. 'I didn't say I didn't like it. The romantic element of the story is proving very popular. I'm just concerned that the political ideas you've introduced might be putting people off.'

'Have any of your readers complained about it so far?'

'There's been a few letters, yes.'

'I take it they don't like that I'm encouraging women to think about the importance of them having the right to vote.'

'That's about it.'

'I see.'

There was no point asking who'd written the letters. In Amy's experience, they were just as likely to have come from women as from men. No matter what quarter they came from, the resistance to change was real. Some women, it seemed, didn't want the responsibility of deciding who was elected to govern them, or of holding them to account for what they stood for.

'Speaking as your editor, Miss Eaton, I'm not against any of it. What you write is very compelling. I'm just worried about how any controversy might affect the reputation of the magazine. We can't risk alienating our loyal readership. We rely on their subscriptions to keep us afloat.'

Amy understood his position. She also needed to keep him on her side if she wasn't to lose her contract. If there was no contract, there would be no more monthly cheques to pay the rent on the house in Newport. 'How are the sales these days?'

'They're sky high. Better than ever. It's all the more reason not to upset anyone.'

'If the sales are continuing to grow then it suggests the readers approve of the material we're providing.'

He dropped onto the sofa and scratched his head. 'I had considered that. But there's still a voice of dissent. They may be in the minority, but they're very loud.'

'So those who shout the loudest get their way.'

'I didn't say it was fair, Miss Eaton.'

'If new readers have been attracted by the political content, we might lose them again if we remove it. Not everyone simply wants a love story. Some people want to be challenged by other ideas too. A novel can be more than one thing.'

'It's certainly getting us talked about. We're the first mainstream magazine to tackle the subject.'

'It's impossible to please everyone. You just have to please enough readers to make what we do worthwhile.'

'Profitable, you mean?'

'That as well.' She watched him as he stared at the backs of his hands, allowing him time to think. 'Thanks to my story, more people are talking about your magazine than ever before. What else is it you want me to do, Mr Farrand?'

There was a long pause while he thought about her question. 'It's a bit too . . .'

'Too what?'

'Radical.' He winced as he said it, as if the word was poison on his tongue. 'If we go too far with this, I worry we'll be jeopardising not only the size of our readership, but the future of the magazine itself. Thanks to the recent spate of vandalism inflicted by the suffragettes, Congress is scrutinising all campaigning much more closely. If they don't like what we're doing, they'll find a way to shut us down.'

This was Mrs Canby's doing. Throwing whitewash at statues and burning an effigy of the president might all be part of her vendetta against her family, but her behaviour was having far-reaching effects. Amy had no doubt that it was Senator Frost who was encouraging Congress to scrutinise the campaign. How else was he going to limit the damage to his reputation inflicted by his daughter?

'I understand your position, Mr Farrand, I really do. It seems we find ourselves caught up in a much bigger conflict than we anticipated.'

'I don't want to be in a position where I'm forced to sacrifice you and *Missing in Love* to ensure the magazine's survival.'

Amy nodded. She couldn't afford to lose the work, nor could she risk the damage it would do to her reputation. Above all else, it was vital that her publishers and her readers kept their faith in her. And yet, if she was to keep faith in herself and her work, she had to stay true to her principles.

'What do you propose we do, Mr Farrand?'

'I'll leave it up to you to decide. My advice would be to tone down the storyline involving the campaign for women's right to vote. Make the characters as sympathetic as you can, and perhaps devote less time to them on the page.'

179

'I'll have them rescue an injured dog. How does that sound?'

'Don't do anything too upsetting. Our readers don't like it when animals are seen to be suffering, even if it's only make-believe.'

Amy suppressed a smile. 'Of course. Then I'll think of something else.'

He took her answer as his cue to leave. 'Thank you for your understanding. I have every confidence that you'll find a way to keep controversy at bay without compromising your principles.'

Principles. It was her principles that had got Amy where she was now. She'd broken off her engagement to Wareham on principle, believing it was the right thing to do, so she didn't get in the way of his ambition. Now her determination to highlight the campaign for women's right to vote was another principle, and it was putting her livelihood at risk. Once again, she was faced with a dilemma. This time, she'd strive to find a middle ground. There had to be a way of raising the issues that needed to be brought to public attention without causing everything in her life to collapse around her.

Chapter 28

The train to Newport was almost deserted, which was only to be expected, given the time of year. Mrs Rawle insisted on travelling in her fur mantle, even at the risk of it picking up the smuts from the engine, and in the knowledge that the smell of soot would be the devil to remove from the fine fibres of the chinchilla.

The relationship between the two women had cooled since Amy had ignored her advice on not including a storyline about the campaign for votes for women in the recent instalments of *Missing in Love*. Now, with Mrs Rawle refusing to admit the idea was a success with the majority of her readers, they'd reached an unspoken agreement not to discuss Amy's work at all, which left them little to talk about, and the journey seemed very long indeed.

Newport was a different prospect in winter compared to the summer. The colourful birds had flown, the leaves had dropped from the trees and with so many houses closed for the winter the avenues were almost deserted. Even the fountains and the garden ornaments had been boarded up to protect them against the cold now the fair-weather residents had left.

The sight would have depressed many visitors, but Amy was glad to have escaped the busy streets of New York, where Wareham could appear at any moment. Here, there was no risk of seeing him, no energy wasted on hope or dread. She looked ahead to the long winter, to the cold days and the chilling ocean breeze. Here, there'd be just the right amount of society for distraction and enough solitude to finish the final instalments of *Missing in Love*. Newport out of season offered seclusion and peace of mind. It was all she could ask for, and she would expect nothing more.

After the hansom cab had dropped Mrs Rawle at her villa, Amy's mood lifted. It troubled her how far their once-close relationship had unravelled. It wasn't only *Missing in Love* that was to blame. Wareham's return to their social circle was another reason for the awkwardness between them. Mrs Rawle made no secret of the fact that she disapproved of his presence, and Amy worried how she would react if she knew she still had feelings for him.

Lately, the differences between the two women had grown more numerous than the things that bonded them, and it broke Amy's heart to know that the person who had once claimed to love her more than anyone else, had now become her harshest critic.

The colonial-style clapboard house chosen by Eleanor and their father was as smart as she'd imagined. Painted in a muted shade of grey to emphasise the neo-Gothic design, it had just the right lived-in feel about it, while the dried bones of last summer's clematis and briar roses, still clinging to the veranda, added to the mournfulness of its character. The lawn that sloped down to the beach was dotted with clover and the last of the daisies, the ferns erupting in an artful arrangement of evergreen clusters along the path. At that moment, the contained disorder of it all seemed perfectly in tune with Amy's heart.

Although Amy had written regularly to Eleanor and her father during the past months, there'd been almost no communication in return. They still resented her for exiling them in this semi-paradise, and the atmosphere when she walked through the door was as chilled as the ocean-blown air.

'You look well, I must say,' commented her father as she stood in the hallway removing her bonnet. 'You've gained a little weight.'

Mr Eaton was as lean and well-dressed as ever, the jasmine and orange-flower scent of his expensive pomade, shipped directly from Paris, giving him the aura of a pampered dog. Amy failed to recognise his fine woollen trousers or his silk waistcoat, the quality of which were more suited to an evening party than a quiet afternoon at home. He wasn't the only one who was well-dressed in the middle of the day. Eleanor was wearing a loose-fitting velvet tea gown and a pair of matching high-heeled slippers, none of which Amy had seen before. In spite of their promises to cut back on spending, there was a suspicious whiff of extravagance about both of them.

'Is that a new dress from Paris?'

Instead of answering the question, Eleanor's eyes ran over every inch of Amy's outfit, even though there was nothing she hadn't seen her wear a hundred times before. 'You've changed your hair.' The words sounded more like a rebuke than an observation.

'It's a little longer, that's all.'

'Your face is different, and your eyes are brighter. Have you been using belladonna?'

The visit to Cape May had brought a little colour to Amy's complexion, which Marion said made her look common. Since returning to New York, it had stubbornly refused to fade, mainly due to her reluctance to wear a veil when she took the air in Central Park. Not only did a veil restrict her vision, but it made it difficult to breathe when a brisk walk was the only thing that would calm her mind. Had she looked so terrible before, she wondered, that they now felt compelled to comment on the change in her?

Mr Eaton put on his coat, just as Amy was removing hers. 'You must excuse me. There are some fellows I've arranged to meet.' He picked up his tall hat, his silver-topped cane and his gloves, and was gone before Amy could ask if he was well.

Her absence had done nothing to make him feel more fondly towards her. He hadn't missed her, and appeared to think no better of her for all the things she'd done for him. However hard she tried, there was no getting through to his heart.

The house lacked the old-age splendour of their home in New York. The pale wood panelling and large windows gave the rooms an airy feel that lifted the spirits, even on a winter's day. The French-style furniture seemed lighter without the context of heavy velvet drapes and brocade covers, or the gilt-framed mirrors and Turkey rugs that had for years given their New York home an atmosphere of being over-filled.

Whoever had designed the interior had been inspired to bring the outside in, decorating the walls sky blue and white, adding just a hint of gilding for the sake of glamour. The plants, over-flowing from jardinières, and the many Wardian cases filled with exotics, gave a hothouse feel to the downstairs rooms, while the atmosphere remained temperate. After the stuffiness and the filth of New York, the farmyard smell of the streets, the place was a breath of fresh air.

They'd just settled in the drawing room when Amy heard a pair of heavy feet clattering down the stairs. 'Do we have a guest?'

'I was just about to tell you . . .'

Before Eleanor could finish, the door flew open and Mrs Canby charged in. 'Miss Eaton. Welcome. Forgive me for not being here to greet you when you arrived.'

Ever a martyr to her good manners, Amy forced herself to smile. 'I heard from Mrs Craig that you'd left New York, but had no idea you were here. Are you staying in Newport?'

Mrs Canby threw back her head and roared. 'You could say that. I'm staying right here in this very house.'

The woman caused trouble everywhere she went. What was Eleanor thinking, inviting her to stay? Amy glanced at her sister, her raised eyebrows silently demanding an explanation.

Eleanor took Mrs Canby's hand. It was an unassailable gesture of solidarity that could even have passed as friendship. 'Poor Mrs Canby has no money and nowhere else to go. She's had a dreadful

184

row with her family. None of them want to know her.'

'My beloved aunt has cast me out and cut me off without a cent. Not only that. My father made such terrible threats against me that I had no choice but to leave New York.'

Taken in by every word, Eleanor gave her a sympathetic look. 'She's such a dear friend. I couldn't turn her away when she came to me for help.'

Amy surreptitiously examined Mrs Canby's fingernails for signs of whitewash, checked the ends of her hair for singeing, but too much time had passed for there to be any evidence of her misdemeanours.

'Have you been staying long?'

'It's been a while now. I'm cosy as a bug in your guest room. Eleanor has made me very welcome.' She rolled her eyes. 'I don't think your father has even noticed I'm here.'

How much had Mrs Canby told Eleanor about what she'd been up to in New York? And what had happened to the considerable amount of money Mrs Craig had given her?

'Are your children here too?'

Mrs Canby gaped at the suggestion. 'Goodness, no. I left them in New York with my aunt.'

'Is there anything else you'd like to know?' asked Eleanor, her tone as sharp as splintered glass. 'Your questions are beginning to sound like an interrogation.'

'I'm catching up with what's been happening, that's all. I'm surprised you didn't write to let me know Mrs Canby was staying as our guest.'

'I didn't realise I was obliged to tell you everything.'

Mrs Canby's eyes darted from one sister's face to the other. 'You must excuse me. I have letters to write. If you want me, I'll be in my room.'

'I don't know what you expected me to do,' continued Eleanor after Mrs Canby had left them. 'She had nowhere else to go. I couldn't turn her away.' She sank onto a rosewood sofa and sighed. 'You don't begrudge me having a friend to stay, do you?'

'It was a surprise to see her, that's all.'

'You'll soon realise how dull it is here out of season. You'll be glad of company then, no matter who it is.' She picked up a rope cord that had been abandoned on the sofa, and began twisting it with clumsy fingers into a spiral knot. 'Look at me. I'm reduced to making macramé plant pot holders for charity to keep myself occupied.' Frustrated with her efforts, she cast it aside and changed the subject. 'I was stopped in the street by Mrs Tyler the other day. She owns the bookstore downtown. She asked if you'd drop by to sign copies of your books.'

'I'll talk to her about it.'

'It's all set for Saturday at four. She's put up a sign in the window. People will be expecting to see you. You might want to wear something more interesting than your usual grey dress.'

'Then it's all arranged.' Amy tried not to make it sound like a criticism. For once, she was glad her sister was being supportive of her work.

'You keep saying you need to sell more books. How else are you to pay the rent on this place?'

Eleanor was behaving like a deposed queen sent into exile. Newport was meant to be an expedient change, not a punishment.

'It sounds like you've made new friends.'

'I've become a member of the local ladies' charity institute. That's how I met Mrs Tyler. We get together in the afternoons to drink tea and eat a variety of fruit pies while we try to come up with ways to raise money for the women in the town who would like to become dressmakers or milliners, but have no means to train for it.' She held up the straggling piece of macramé. 'This will be one of the items on sale at the forthcoming fundraising bazaar.'

The pot holder was the first thing Amy had ever seen Eleanor create and she didn't want to cause her to abandon it by saying the wrong thing. 'Is Mrs Canby involved in the fundraising too?'

'She's reluctant to be seen around town. She's afraid her father will find out she's here and come after her. I don't know what went on between them, but it must have been bad. The day she arrived, I'd never seen her so scared.'

'She can't stay here forever. Does she have any plans?'

'None that I know of.'

Amy watched Eleanor struggle with a rope knot. The rogue strands seemed a long way from becoming a plant pot holder. 'You must let me know if there's anything I can do to help with the charity.'

'There's to be a fundraising auction. You could donate a signed copy of one of your novels. Your work is popular with the ladies here. It's sure to go down well.'

'Then I will. It's good to see you getting involved in the local life.'

'It's not much by the standards of New York, but there are regular musical evenings and dances. Father's joined a gentlemen's club. It seems to have enough whist, gossip and port to keep him occupied. That's where he was going when you arrived.'

Despite Eleanor's complaints, they were building their lives here and trying to make the best of it. There was no need for Amy to have fretted so much over whether they were socially isolated or lacking entertainment. And no doubt, for good or bad, Mrs Canby was making life interesting for them. Eleanor didn't seem any less happy than she'd been in New York. The cold shell of stoicism she'd developed over the past few years still remained impenetrable. She and Amy might as well have been strangers for all the intimacies they exchanged.

'You don't regret agreeing to come?'

'How can I be expected to regret a decision that wasn't mine to make? You and Father worked it all out between you. I never really had any say in it.' Her fingers toyed ineffectually with the limp strands of macramé. 'These past months have made me realise more than ever what my life amounts to without a husband. It's fine being the lady of Father's house, but he won't live forever. When he dies, my social standing dies with him. What will happen to me then?'

Eleanor might have been the eldest sister, but Amy felt more responsible for her than ever. 'If we clear the family debts, and you're sensible with your allowance, you'll be able to live independently and comfortably enough.'

'But I won't have the same social standing, and I won't be rich.'

'You'll be better off than most. Think of those poor girls, and their ambitions to become dressmakers or milliners. As long as you're careful, you won't have to work like that.'

'But you do, Amy. Doesn't it bother you that you're looked down upon?'

'I'm proud of the novels I've written, and not everyone looks down on the fact that I'm an author.'

The situation wasn't Eleanor's fault. There was no future for either of them in a society that discarded women because they were still unmarried at twenty-three, let alone at twenty-nine like Eleanor, a society that saw no value in women who failed to become wives and mothers, and made it almost impossible for them to earn a decent living for themselves.

Amy suspected Eleanor had given up hope of ever marrying, even if she was too proud to say it. Whether she had or hadn't, this was the first time she'd betrayed her fear of the future, and it was a fear that must have been felt by almost every woman in the country.

Alone in her room, Amy unpacked her portable writing desk and set out her paper, pens and ink. Decades of spinsterhood lay ahead for both her and Eleanor, years of looking after other people's children and taking care of the sick, duties that would have to be enough to satisfy their emotional lives. Love would never play a part in their future. Gratitude and a little respect from those they helped willingly and freely would be the best they could hope for.

She scanned the half-written page where she'd previously left off, and forced all other thoughts to the back of her mind. Her life would have been filled with love if she hadn't been persuaded not to marry Wareham, but there was nothing to be gained from dwelling on that now. She'd made a success of her life as an author and she must take all her satisfaction from that. Wareham was many miles away and about to marry Lucy. The most important thing now was to make sure no one guessed how much the fact that she'd lost him continued to matter.

Chapter 29

Mrs Tyler went to all sorts of trouble on the day of Amy's book-signing, decorating the store with hothouse flowers, and laying out tea and plates of marble cake. All six of Amy's published novels were displayed in the window, along with the latest edition of *Scribe* magazine. There was already a queue of people waiting to have their books signed when Amy arrived. Some had been purchased that day, others, going by the beaten-up look of the covers, had been read many times over.

'Thank you for coming, Miss Eaton. It's an honour to have you in my bookstore. I would also like to thank you for donating a signed first edition of one of your novels to our charity auction. There's sure to be a good deal of interest in it.'

Despite her slight figure, Mrs Tyler managed to look stylish without succumbing to fussiness. Her high-necked navy dress, edged at the collar and cuffs with a lace trim reflected her sensible manner, while the fine lines that had settled around her eyes suggested she was a woman of wisdom and humour. Amy took to her immediately. Women such as this, women of business and good sense, were America's future.

Amy's books greeted her from almost every surface as she glanced around the store. 'It was good of you to go to so much trouble for me.'

'Nonsense, my dear. You're one of our biggest sellers. News of your appearance has brought in more customers than I've ever known.' She led her to a table in the corner, where dozens of books had been piled up in neat stacks, ready for her to sign. 'Won't you sit and we'll get started.'

Eleanor and Mr Eaton had come along for the amusement, not really knowing what to expect, although there'd been a rumour of tea and marble cake. Surprised by the length of the queue, they loitered in the poetry section to watch the spectacle from a distance. It wouldn't do to be too closely associated with the authoress when she drew so much attention from strangers. The more popular she was, the more demeaning it appeared. Still, there was something fascinating about the scene that made them unable to take their eyes off it.

Twenty minutes into the signing, Amy was dedicating a book to 'Dearest Aunt Minnie' when she heard a familiar voice, its cut-glass tones rising above the general hubbub of the busy store.

'Miss Eaton. I saw the notice on the door and guessed I'd find you here. What a wonderful surprise.'

It was unmistakably Spencer. His tall figure loomed over her as she looked up, his arms laden with fresh copies of her novels. What was he doing in Newport so far out of the season? She handed Minnie's niece her book and forced herself to acknowledge him.

Taking her nod as an invitation, he dropped the pile of novels onto the table and gestured to the woman next in line to wait her turn. 'You must sign these for me. You forgot to do the last lot when I brought them to your sister's house in New York.'

Amy looked at him with dismay. 'Don't tell me you've bought more copies of my novels. What do you intend to do with them all?'

His largesse was verging on the vulgar and it made her uncomfortable. She'd done nothing to warrant so much attention from him.

'I gave the others away. I intend to keep these for myself. You wouldn't begrudge a fellow a few personalised copies of your books, would you, signed by your own fair hand?'

The people in the queue were growing impatient. Spencer hadn't bothered to wait in line and the mutterings about his ill manners were getting louder. Amy mouthed an apology to the woman at the front who'd been waiting to meet her for at least half an hour. It would be quicker to sign Spencer's books than to try to convince him to join the back of the queue. She hated to indulge him, but it was the fastest way to get rid of him. He hadn't asked for a dedication, so she simply added her initials to the title page of each one and handed them back, trusting him not to look at them until much later.

'I see you're busy,' he muttered, scowling at the length of the queue, which seemed to be growing longer by the minute, largely thanks to the fact that he'd held it up. 'I'll wait on the other side of the shop until you've finished.'

By the time Amy had signed the next customer's book, Spencer had introduced himself to her father and Eleanor, and the three of them were in animated conversation. His appearance felt too pre-meditated. When she'd turned down his invitation to the opera, using the excuse of coming to Newport, he hadn't mentioned he had a connection to the place or any plans to visit. Now, seeing him ingratiate himself with her family, she wondered what he was playing at.

It was ridiculous to suspect he'd followed her here from New York. He was a wealthy English aristocrat, a man of the world. He couldn't possibly be interested in her. He could have the pick of any young woman he fancied. And yet, his attention was so intense, it was almost suffocating.

Half an hour later, Amy looked up to greet the last customer, surprised to see another familiar face, although this one was much more welcome. 'Violet, how lovely to see you. I had no idea you were in Newport.' She instantly corrected herself. 'Sorry, I should call you Lady Stephens.'

Violet waved away the apology with her cotton glove. 'Violet will do.' She glanced around the store, taking in the multiple displays of Amy's books. 'Congratulations on your success. I've been following your career most carefully.'

They'd known each other since they were six years old, and for years had been as close as friends can be. They'd attended school together in New York and come out into society in the same season. During their debutante year, they'd been inseparable, attending dances and dinners together, until Violet, who was always the prettier one and more outgoing, married an English aristocrat who'd recently inherited his father's title. After Violet went to live in his ancestral home in Surrey, the two of them had lost touch. Amy had no idea that Violet was back in America, and this was the first time they'd seen each other in almost a decade.

Time had taken its toll, and although Amy would never say it, she was shocked by how Violet had changed in the intervening years. Her once-chestnut hair was now more brown than russet. Her eyes had lost their spark, and her complexion, which had once been the envy of every girl in their set, had grown dull.

Her dress appeared drab against the bright colours of the bookstore. The once-black bombazine fabric, now faded to grey, seemed dowdy, even compared to Amy's sensible pale blue linen outfit.

A few customers still lingered over the tea and marble cake, despite Mrs Tyler making gestures to indicate she wanted to close the store. Violet gave Amy her calling card. 'My lodgings are only a few streets from here. Come and visit me soon.'

Once Violet had gone, Amy glanced around the shop, surprised to see Spencer had left without saying goodbye. She guessed he wasn't used to being kept waiting, and wasn't prepared to do so any longer. Relieved she wouldn't have to suffer his company again that afternoon, she put him out of her mind.

As they left the bookshop, Eleanor linked her arm through

Amy's. 'You didn't tell us you were on such friendly terms with the Earl of Hokeham.'

Her sister was fishing for information. Amy should have guessed there was a reason behind the unaccustomed gesture of fondness. 'I'd hardly call Spencer a friend.'

'You know him well enough to call him Spencer,' said Mr Eaton. 'He says you met in Cape May, and that he visited you in New York.'

'Yes, that's true. I—'

Eleanor dug her fingers in Amy's arm. 'As you were too busy signing books, it was left to Father to invite him to call on us.'

This was the last thing Amy wanted. 'Didn't you think to check with me first?'

Eleanor almost screamed. 'He's an earl. What more is there to check?'

When it came to it, Amy couldn't say what it was about him that made her uncertain. The feeling was instinctive and not necessarily to be trusted. Perhaps it was his forwardness, the way he was always so eager to please her. It made her uncomfortable that he'd begun to turn up unexpectedly wherever she happened to be. Perhaps he wasn't guilty of any of these things. Perhaps it was only her suspicion that made it seem so. He was wealthy, good-looking, charming and an aristocrat, things that justified his self-importance in the eyes of everyone else.

'He's agreed to drop by this evening after dinner,' said Eleanor, more animated than Amy had seen her in years. 'We told him to come as soon as he could. It's not every day we meet an eligible aristocrat.'

So that was it. Spencer had wormed his way into her family and there was no way of getting rid of him. It wouldn't be a bad thing if she could interest him in Eleanor. Perhaps Amy could bring them together and help her to find a happy ending. After all, if anyone had the countenance to become a countess, it was Eleanor.

Chapter 30

Dinner that evening was a simple meal of clam broth with stewed celery. Ever conscious of their figures, Eleanor and Mr Eaton picked at their food like a pair of wounded sparrows. Mrs Canby, who was now used to their dining habits, had charged the maid with preparing her a side dish of boiled potatoes, which she diligently worked her way through without offering to share them with Amy.

As soon as they'd got up from the table, Eleanor changed into one of her newest Worth dresses of emerald watered silk, which she set off with a diamond pin that sat on her breast like an explosion of shooting stars. Spencer was due to call at nine o'clock, and she was ready on the stroke of the hour, her upright figure, made sterner by her corset, propped on the rosewood sofa, her feet elegantly poised in her high-heeled slippers and open lacework stockings.

Not to be outdone by Eleanor's finery, Mrs Canby presented herself in canary yellow silk, the style of which suggested it had also recently arrived from Worth. Amy couldn't help wondering if some of the money Mrs Craig had given her had gone towards its purchase.

After the effort she'd put into greeting her readers that

afternoon, Amy was too tired to change either for dinner or for Spencer, choosing instead to remain in the pale blue day dress she'd worn to the bookstore.

'Is that what you're planning on wearing?' Eleanor looked at her in disgust, her fingers blindly fiddling with the macramé pot holder which was still no nearer to being completed.

'It's perfectly acceptable for an evening at home.'

Suddenly the model of decorum, Mrs Canby pursed her lips as a sign of her disapproval, while choosing to say nothing.

The walnut box containing Mr Eaton's best Havana cigars had been placed on the table next to the port. Made restless by the late arrival of their guest, their father poured himself a drink.

'So what can you tell us about this earl of yours?'

Amy cringed at the implication. 'He's not *my* earl. I've only met him a few times. He's fond of horse racing and novels. That's all I know.'

Eleanor's face fell. 'Then I suppose we'll have to talk about horse racing.'

The clock had already struck the half hour when Spencer finally arrived. The lazy movements of his eyes suggested he'd already enjoyed a bottle of wine or two elsewhere. After he failed to offer an apology for his lateness, Amy assumed it must be the English custom and tried not to hold it against him, even though she was tired and wanted to go to bed.

Her father fussed around him, offering him a glass of port and a cigar, trying any number of subjects for conversation until they finally settled on horse racing, just as predicted.

Eleanor's eyes never left Spencer's face, although she said little, sitting very prettily with her ankles crossed, showing her hourglass figure to advantage and hoping he'd notice her as she fiddled with her macramé plant pot holder. All the while, Mrs Canby remained beside her, speaking only when asked a direct question. Her tight-lipped manner suggested she was unimpressed by him, and for once, whole minutes passed when it was possible to forget she was in the room.

Unsettled by Spencer's unexpected appearance, Amy wanted to know what he was doing there. It was one thing to turn up in New York, but quite another to appear in Newport out of season.

'Are you staying long in Rhode Island?'

He took a long draw on his cigar while he thought about it. 'It depends on the company. Will you be staying long, Miss Eaton?'

There could be no mistaking his directness. If she told him she was here indefinitely, she might never be rid of him.

'Nothing's settled yet.'

'Then you must let me know when it is.'

'We're very dull here. You wouldn't want to change your plans on my account.'

'It's not a matter of changing them, Miss Eaton, but a case of not settling them.'

The silence in the room landed like a heavy frost. Amy passed off his comment as a joke. 'You mustn't waste your time searching out my company. I'm far too busy with my work to go out much into society.'

There was an audible gasp from Eleanor. 'You mustn't take any notice of my sister. We'll always be honoured to welcome you here, and I hope we'll see you at the local musical evenings or one of the dances.'

He turned to Amy, behaving as if Eleanor hadn't spoken. 'What do you say to dancing?'

Was she over-sensitive, or was his behaviour too much, too pointed? His approach was beyond good manners, but nobody else in the room seemed to mind. 'My work keeps me busy. I never commit to social engagements.'

Mrs Canby let out a barking laugh. 'Nobody in their right mind would choose work over dancing.'

Spencer gave her a pointed look. 'You don't approve of Miss Eaton's work?'

'I come from a very rich family. I have no need to have a view on work of any kind.'

'Mrs Canby's family owns one of the oldest banks in America,' said Eleanor, moving the conversation away from the vulgar subject of wealth. 'Her father is one of our most important senators.'

'I know as little about your political system as I do about your society,' said Spencer, helping himself to another glass of port and turning his attention back to Amy. 'You must be too busy with your work to concern yourself with politics.'

Tired of his constant attention, Amy suppressed a yawn. 'It's been a very full day. If you'll excuse me, I'll say goodnight.'

Before Spencer could persuade her to stay, Amy slipped out of the room. Her heart was beating far too rapidly and she could feel her cheeks burning. Spencer couldn't possibly be trying to court her. It was too ridiculous to even consider it. She went upstairs and prepared for bed. With the flame in the gas lamp turned down low, she moved around quietly, listening to the noises of the house, searching for clues that would tell her Spencer had finally left. She'd been invisible for years. It was too unsettling to think any man might be interested in her now.

A few minutes later, Eleanor burst into her room, her eyes wild with fury. 'How could you be like that with him?'

Amy sat up in bed, blinking at the sudden intrusion. 'What are you talking about?'

'Spencer, the *Earl* of Hokeham. How could you be so rude to him when he's trying to be friendly?'

'His attention makes me uncomfortable.'

'Don't be ridiculous.'

'It's up to me to decide whether I want his attention or not.'

'You should be honoured that he's trying to court you, especially at your age.' She sat on the corner of Amy's bed, her shoulders slumped. Even the constriction of her corset couldn't hide her attitude of defeat. 'I'd give anything to have him look at me the way he looks at you.'

'I'm sorry. I've done nothing to encourage him.'

'What if he likes you?'

'Then he'll be disappointed.'

Eleanor wiped away a tear with the back of her hand. 'You don't have to make it personal. If he wants to marry you, you should consider it simply as a transaction. Think of the title you'd gain, the castle you'd live in, the fortune your children would inherit. There'd be no more little Miss Eaton, forced to write novels to ease her family's financial troubles. You'd be wealthy beyond all dreams.' She reached across the coverlet and took Amy's hand. 'If you won't think of yourself, think of me and Father. We'd be able to live in style again, to hold our heads up in New York society. One encouraging word to Spencer and you could save us all.'

'If you feel that way, you must try for him yourself.'

'Do you think I haven't? He's made it clear to Father that it's you he's interested in.'

'Then I'm sorry if I disappoint you.'

Eleanor sighed, pulling at her hair that had taken hours to pin and curl. 'What gives you the right to keep turning down eligible men? At least Charles had the good grace to marry Marion after you refused his offer of marriage. How many more potential husbands are you going to reject in favour of spinsterhood?'

There was nothing Amy could say. If she mentioned Wareham, it would only give Eleanor something else to criticise. There was no need for her to know anything about that whole sorry episode, especially as he was expected to marry Lucy as soon as she was strong enough to leave her bed.

'This isn't only about you, Amy. If a rich man of the right social standing says you're worth marrying, they might begin to think the same about me.'

Everything Eleanor said was true. What was it about Spencer that she couldn't trust? Perhaps there was nothing at all, but the fact that he wasn't Wareham. She was long resigned to not having him, yet she still couldn't bring herself to consider any other man, even if it meant the absence of love in her life. If she couldn't have Wareham, she wouldn't have anyone.

Chapter 31

Amy was surprised to find Violet living in a small lodging house near the edge of the town. It was the kind of place inhabited by the wives of sailors while they waited for their husbands to return from sea, where down-at-heel governesses resided while they tried to secure a position in a decent family. It certainly wasn't the kind of place she expected an heiress who had married into the aristocracy to be staying. Tucked away in a side street, the building was clean and respectable, but that was all that could be said of it.

Violet welcomed her into her small sitting room, made more pleasant by the swathes of English chintz, which had been used to disguise the threadbare furniture. Amy gave her a bunch of hothouse lilies which she'd bought from the florist on the way over. Instantly, she regretted the grand gesture, realising how vulgar they looked in the shabby surroundings.

'Such beautiful flowers. You shouldn't have gone to so much trouble.' Violet sniffed them as if such a gift were a rare thing. The strong scent brought tears to her eyes. It was only then that Amy realised she was in mourning. It explained the faded black bombazine dress, the dark shadows beneath her eyes and her sunken cheeks. She should have known better than to be so quick to judge her appearance when they last met.

'I'm sorry, Violet, I didn't know. I should have guessed you were in mourning when I saw you at the bookstore.'

'There's no need to be sorry. Edgar's death was a while ago now. In my case, mourning my husband has become a matter of appearances rather than anything else.'

'Was his death unexpected?'

'He was run down by a carriage on Piccadilly as he left his London club. They say he walked into the road without looking where he was going. He was drunk at the time.'

'So it was a tragic accident.'

'I'd be surprised if it was an accident. He owed money to all kinds of people, many of whom he should have known better than to cross.'

These weren't the words or the attitude of a grieving widow. Something must have changed during the years of her marriage. Violet had been so in love at eighteen when she and Edgar had announced their engagement. It had been the match of the season. Even today, it was still talked about by envious mothers whose only purpose in life was to see their daughters marry into the English aristocracy.

'You never wrote after you married and left for England. I always wondered how you got on. I imagined you living happily ever after in a castle, like a princess in a fairy tale.'

'I should have written to you, but I guessed you'd have romantic ideas about my new life and I didn't want to ruin them. The fairy-tale castle turned out to be a cold, damp country house, miles from anywhere. There were holes in the roof, no running water, no bath and a house full of servants who looked down on me.'

'You married for love. There must have been some consolation in that.'

'It was all a big lie. I married Edgar because my father said I must. As soon as the honeymoon in Europe was over, he returned to his mistress in London, leaving me alone in the country house.

I knew no one and no one wanted to know me. Everyone I spoke to made fun of my accent or pretended not to understand me.'

'But Edgar seemed so besotted with you here in New York.'

'It was my fortune he was besotted with. Most of the capital I took into the marriage was swallowed up by his debts the moment it was handed over. The rest, he gambled away or used to run his London house and keep his mistress. By the time he died, there was nothing left.' She waved her hand at the shabby sitting room. 'So this is where you find me now.'

'I'm so sorry.'

'Despite any romantic notions you may have, the English treat their dogs and horses better than they treat their wives.'

'I had no idea.'

'Why would you? I was too ashamed to tell anybody.'

'Didn't your father put anything in place to protect your financial independence before you married?'

'He thought such safeguards were unnecessary. He took Edgar to be a man of honour because that was how he wanted to see him. He wasn't the first wealthy American to have his head turned by an English aristocrat. Father jumped at the opportunity to secure a title for his only daughter, and failed to look too closely into Edgar's reasons for wanting to marry me.'

'Did he leave you anything at all?'

'I failed to provide an heir, so the estate went to his younger brother.'

'So you were left with nothing.'

'Only a pile of debts, which I left behind when I sailed for New York.' She touched her throat as if the memory of a necklace resided there. 'I sold my jewellery to pay for my passage and for my lodgings when I arrived.'

They were silent while Amy took in everything she'd been told. 'How are you managing to live now? Do you have help from your family?'

'Father and Mother both died while I was living in England. I never told them how bad things were, so at least they were saved the shame of knowing they'd been swindled. Since I came back, my brothers refuse to know me. They think I should have stayed in England and made the best of my life as the widow of a man from a noble family.'

'Noble.' The word stuck in Amy's throat as she said it.

'There was nothing for me in New York, so I moved to Newport. Everything is much cheaper here, and I like to be near the ocean. I get by, teaching etiquette to the daughters of ambitious mothers. They have an unshakeable belief that a little social polish will gain them wealthy husbands. I try to temper their ambitions, while at the same time, teaching them secretarial skills and the ability to think for themselves, things I've had to learn along the way, so they're equipped to earn their own living if it should come to it.'

'If I can help in any way, just say it.'

'Believe it or not, you already have. Your story in *Scribe* magazine, with the call for women to have the vote, has sparked an interest in better education for women. I've had enquiries from half a dozen young ladies, asking me to teach them stenography. It seems there's a new generation out there ready to move with the times and take up gainful employment.'

Amy thought of Mrs Rawle's disparaging comments, the letters she'd received from readers, warning her that women should know their place, how they were outnumbered by those thanking her for highlighting the issue of women's rights and for raising the debate. 'It's gained me a lot of criticism as well as praise.'

'Don't let the critics put you off. Not everyone will be pleased by your success, or agree with your views, but you're an inspiration to many of us.'

'The next generation of women need to aspire to more than just marriage. They deserve the right to be able to provide for themselves.'

'You never married?' asked Violet.

'No, but it doesn't mean I'm against it. Experience has taught me it's not every woman's destiny.'

After they parted, Amy wandered back through the town, considering everything Violet had told her. It was appalling to think she'd been seduced into leaving her country and her family and been treated so badly. Most of the American girls who married into the English aristocracy never returned. Over time they'd gained an almost mythical status. She now wondered why it was they chose to stay away, whether the fairy-tale ending they strove for ever really existed.

Her mind returned to Spencer. Compared to Edgar, he seemed a decent man after all. Considering his lifestyle, and the number of her books he'd bought, he couldn't be in need of money, and it was rare for a man to be so enthusiastic about her work. Travelling without companions, he cut a lonely figure, which might explain why he was always so eager to please.

Perhaps she'd misjudged him. Perhaps he was more deep thinking and sensitive than he appeared. She would never consider him for herself, but it was worth encouraging him to pay more attention to Eleanor. Amy was more convinced of it now than ever.

Chapter 32

Mrs Rawle arrived at the same time as Spencer, their carriages turning off the coastal road and stopping in front of the house almost simultaneously. Amy watched from the window as he handed her out of the hansom cab, muttering something under his breath that made her throw her head back and laugh in a way Amy hadn't seen her do in years. There was no denying his charm, his easy manner. He certainly had the knack of pleasing everyone.

'My dear, look who I met outside.' Mrs Rawle beamed as Amy greeted them at the door. 'It's the Earl of Hokeham come to call on you.'

Having heard the commotion, Eleanor rushed to the hallway to help Mrs Rawle off with her mantle. 'Spencer, how good of you to visit. Father's not here. He's gone wild bird shooting. It's just us ladies, I'm afraid.'

'That's all well and good, as it's the ladies I've come to see.'

The colour rose in Eleanor's cheeks, making her appear more beautiful than ever. Spencer couldn't have missed it. All was not lost. From now on, Amy would do everything she could to throw her sister and Spencer together. Despite Eleanor's cool exterior, he couldn't fail to notice her charm.

Amy gave her an encouraging look. 'Will you entertain our

guests in the drawing room while I make tea?'

At first, it had been an adjustment, relying on just one house-maid, but Amy had grown to appreciate the uncomplicated nature of the arrangement, and didn't mind doing more for herself and for her father. Eleanor, on the other hand, went into a sulk if she was asked to carry out the slightest household task or was expected to pin up her own hair.

By the time Amy returned to the drawing room, Eleanor was staring out of the window and looking stone-faced. Whatever attempt she'd made to get Spencer's attention had clearly failed and the atmosphere between them was as leaden as cold porridge.

Spencer jumped to his feet, offering to help as Amy struggled with the tea tray. 'Miss Eaton, I was just saying how wonderful it was to see you signing all those books for your readers in the store the other day. It must be reassuring to see your work selling so well.'

No wonder Eleanor was looking put out if all Spencer had talked about was Amy's novels. She humoured him with a smile. 'It's always nice to meet my readers. Of course, it was the first time you met Eleanor and my father.'

He nodded, his eyes still fixed on Amy. 'The reason for my visit today, is to ask if you'd join me for a carriage ride along Ocean Drive. You must be familiar with the views, but they're still a novelty to me. You can show me your favourite spot to watch the sun go down.'

'What a wonderful idea,' said Mrs Rawle, squeezing a slice of lemon into her tea. 'Amy, go and fetch your coat and gloves before the weather changes.'

The last thing Amy wanted was to be alone in a carriage with Spencer. 'It's a very kind offer, but the latest instalment of *Missing in Love* won't write itself. I have to get back to it right now. Why don't you take Eleanor? She knows the landscape far better than I do and can show you the most scenic spots.'

'I'd be delighted to come with you,' said Eleanor, scrambling to her feet. 'I only need a minute to change my shoes and fetch my coat.'

Spencer glanced at Eleanor, alarm registering in his eyes. 'I wouldn't want to interrupt your afternoon with Mrs Rawle.'

'It's no interruption at all,' insisted Eleanor, smiling and talking over his excuses. 'Mrs Canby is resting in her room. I'll ask her to come down and have tea with Mrs Rawle. I ought to have called her when you arrived.'

'Don't disturb Mrs Canby on my account.' Spencer knocked back his scalding tea and stood up to leave, pulling on his gloves on his way to the door. 'I'm sure Mrs Rawle would prefer to spend her afternoon with you. Mrs Canby's company is, after all, an acquired taste.'

He was gone before Eleanor could reduce herself to begging. She sank onto the sofa, consoling herself by dropping another lump of sugar into her tea. Amy wanted to cry for her.

Through the window, Mrs Rawle's eyes followed the progress of Spencer's carriage as it disappeared along the coastal road. 'That was badly done, Amy. Would it have hurt to give the man a little encouragement? Any fool can see how taken he is with you.'

No one else in the room seemed to have noticed the disparaging remark he'd made about Mrs Canby, or they were too blinded by his title to question it. She shrugged off Mrs Rawle's criticism. 'I have too much work to do to think about carriage rides and sunsets.'

After her recent conversation with Mr Farrand, Amy was trying to be cleverer about the way in which she presented the scenes of political activism in *Missing in Love* to ensure the message didn't either detract from the story of the estranged lovers, or become lost within it. Finding the right balance as she wrote and rewrote was taking up a good deal of time and had set her back with the next instalment.

'You wouldn't have to work so hard if you let Spencer take care of you,' said Mrs Rawle. 'Rumour has it, he's one of the richest men in England. He's an earl, for heaven's sake. You could ask for no higher social standing. This might be your last chance to get a husband. There's no better prospect.'

The only prospect Amy had ever wished for was Wareham, but that opportunity was long gone, thanks to Mrs Rawle's interference, although she didn't dare say it.

'I hardly know him.'

'Only you can remedy that. You're always complaining that your books aren't making enough money. Think how well they'd sell in England if you married into one of their finest families. Not that you'd need them to do well if you married into that kind of wealth. You'd never need to lift a finger again.' She waved a hand at Eleanor, who was dropping more lumps of sugar into her tea. 'You wouldn't only be doing it for yourself. Think how it would help the rest of your family.'

'I'm managing well enough without resorting to marrying for money. If Eleanor likes Spencer, she should try for him herself.'

Mrs Rawle scowled. 'You've already given your younger sister one of your cast-offs. Don't you think that's enough?'

'Marion is content with Charles.'

'Of course she is. That's why she treats you like one of her servants whenever you're in her home.'

'What do you mean?'

'Revenge, my dear, revenge.'

Amy turned to Eleanor and frowned. 'Is that really what Marion is about?'

Eleanor shrugged. 'It's just Marion being Marion.' She was too wrapped up in the humiliation of being refused a carriage ride by Spencer to pay much attention to the conversation.

Was Amy behaving selfishly? Mrs Rawle had been correct in what she'd said. Marrying Spencer would enable her to improve the lives of everyone in her family. Since her mother's death, Amy had seen it as her duty to look after them. If she couldn't get Spencer interested in Eleanor, should she consider sacrificing herself on the marriage altar? Given the society they lived in, marrying into money was the only way to ensure their lives were financially secure.

There was a good deal to consider. She stepped outside onto the veranda and sat on the bench, hoping a breath of air would help her to think more clearly. There was no saying Spencer was interested in marrying her. Just because he was paying her attention, it didn't mean he had serious intentions. He seemed more interested in her novels than in anything else. He was a rich young man, playing away from home. For all she knew, there could be someone waiting for him in England. Amy was probably nothing more than a bit of sport for him, a conquest to report back to his friends at home. She could imagine him regaling them with the tale of his affair with a famous authoress, laughing over how he made the creator of love stories fall for him, and then broke her heart. *I'll give her some meat for her next story.* She could hear him saying it now. After all, he'd already hinted that she should write him into one of her novels.

It was best to do nothing, think nothing of him. If Spencer was serious about her, he'd make it known, and if he wasn't, he'd soon get bored and move on to someone else. She wouldn't allow Mrs Rawle to influence her way of thinking the way she'd allowed her to in the past. She'd become more overbearing than ever lately, trying to influence her work as well as attempting to persuade her into the arms of a man she couldn't care for.

Perhaps she'd always been like this. Perhaps Amy was simply growing more independent in her thinking and moving away from Mrs Rawle's influence. Whatever the truth might be, it was time to put a little more distance between them. She didn't have the mettle to rebuff her, but Amy was old enough and wise enough to make up her own mind about marriage.

Chapter 33

Amy was still on the veranda, doing her best not to think about Spencer or Wareham, when Mrs Canby appeared from inside the house. Her step faltered when she realised Amy was sitting on the bench, her fingers picking absently at the brittle winter stems of the rambling rose that snaked its way across the sun-blistered trellis.

'Forgive me, Miss Eaton. I didn't know you were here. I'll go somewhere else.'

Amy called her back as she turned to leave. 'It's fine. Why don't you join me?' She shifted along the seat to make room for Mrs Canby's voluminous skirt and gestured to her to sit down.

'I don't want to be a nuisance.'

Her hair hung loose about her face in strands, as if she hadn't bothered to pin it up since her afternoon rest. Her skin was pale and her eyes swollen from either too much sleep or from sustained crying. It was rare to see her looking so out of sorts and for once, Amy felt a pang of sympathy for her. She was too social a creature to thrive in hiding.

'Are you all right?'

She settled on the bench next to Amy, huddling into the cash-mere shawl Eleanor had left on the back of the seat earlier in the day. 'I hope I didn't seem rude, not coming down to have tea with Mrs Rawle and the Earl of Hokeham.'

'Not at all. I should have called you.'

'I wasn't in the mood for company. And anyway, I'm sure I wasn't missed. Spencer fails to notice anyone else in the room when you're there. For an English lord, his manners leave a lot to be desired.'

She was quiet for a minute, as if she were making up her mind to do something, before she pulled a folded square of notepaper from her pocket. 'I received this letter from my father this morning. Someone must have told him where to find me.'

There was no accusation in Mrs Canby's tone, only resignation. As far as Amy knew, no one in the family had mentioned her situation to anyone. 'Does he say who it was?'

'It could have been any number of people, from a local police officer to a shopkeeper. My father's influence stretches far and wide and his pockets are deep. Few people are able to resist a bribe for the amount he's usually willing to offer. He has the whole of the New York police force doing his bidding.' She sighed, her eyes tracking the ocean as it made its retreat across the beach. 'I've tried to live as quietly as I can here, but I have to leave the house from time to time. I'd go mad otherwise.'

'Have you thought what you'll do next? You can't spend your life in hiding.'

'That's what my father says.' She shivered against the sudden upsurge in the breeze, forcing the letter back into her pocket before it blew away. 'He wants to resolve things between us.'

'That's good, isn't it?'

'He says if I do anything further to disgrace the family or to damage his career, he'll have me arrested and imprisoned. I call that a threat, not peace-making.'

'But that's—'

'Don't think he doesn't have the power to do it, because he does. As far as he's concerned, distancing himself from me is the only way to save his political skin. If he has to resort to publicly condemning me, then he'll do so.'

'I'm sorry.'

She pushed her hair from her face as the wind blew it, indifferent to her appearance. 'He's removed any right I have to the family fortune and left me with no choice but to give up my children, all because I wanted to be with the man I loved rather than the man they persuaded me to marry. Still he refuses to acknowledge how my convenient marriage benefitted the family business. They're all much richer thanks to my personal sacrifice.' She sniffed at the wind, tears brewing in her eyes. 'Your wedding day is meant to be the happiest day of your life. I stood at the altar, feeling like a piece of meat, sold to the highest bidder.'

'I assumed you'd chosen to leave your children in the care of your aunt when you came here.'

'It was made clear to me that giving them up was the only way to guarantee they kept their inheritance. I was told that if I took them, they'd be cut off without a cent. It wasn't for me to push that fate onto my two little girls. If they want to give up the money, they can make up their own minds to do it when they're older. Personally, I wouldn't wish being a woman without a cent to her name on anyone.'

'Is there no way back for you, even if it's only for the sake of being with your children?'

Mrs Canby laughed as the tears ran freely down her cheeks. 'Even if they could forgive me for running to the man I loved after my husband's death, burning the effigy of the president was a step too far. The family will never forgive me for it.' She wiped the tears away with the back of her hand. 'Can you imagine how humiliating it was for my father, having his daughter set fire to a symbol of everything he stands for? No wonder he's gone to great lengths to keep my identity out of the newspapers. He's protecting himself, not me. Now, if I do anything else to jeopardise his political career, he'll throw me to the wolves.'

'What made you do it?'

'Frustration, anger. A belief in the cause. In one way, I'm sorry for it, but I also love the fact that it's brought my father so much trouble.'

'Thanks to your actions, people now see suffragettes as vandals. They think women are too disrespectful of the law to be given the right to vote.'

'What do we have to do to win equal rights in this country, to have the means to stand up for ourselves without being threatened with prison or vilified in the newspapers and on the streets?' She threw up her hands to emphasise her point, her voice growing louder. 'Why should my father have the right to choose who I marry? Why should he be able to dictate whether I can be a mother to my children? The change has to start somewhere. As I see it, it starts with winning the right to vote and we have to fight for it using whatever means we can.' She paused for breath, dropping her voice to a whisper. 'You don't think my father got where he is by lawful means, do you?'

'I didn't realise you felt so strongly about the cause.'

'Honestly, I'd rather marry a rich man and be taken care of, but there's very little chance of that for me now.'

It was hard to know when Mrs Canby was being serious, whether her actions were for the common good, or whether she was simply trying to avenge the way she'd been treated by her family by ruining her father's political career. Her moods seemed to change like the wind, and it was impossible to know if she was an ally or a liability. Whatever it was, she was too inconsistent, too unreliable for Amy to have confidence in anything she said.

Chapter 34

Amy was taking an early morning walk along the beach when she spotted Mrs Craig's familiar figure coming towards her, her sturdy brown duster coat protecting her from the relentless breeze. She increased her pace, trudging across the damp sand to greet her.

'Mrs Craig. I didn't know you were in Newport.'

'We arrived late yesterday. I was planning to call on you this afternoon. I saw your sister before I left New York. She asked me to pass on a letter.'

Panic ran through Amy's veins at the thought that Lucy might have taken a turn for the worse. Marion wouldn't have written to her for any other reason.

'Is it bad news?'

Mrs Craig retrieved an envelope from her purse and handed it to her. 'You must read it for yourself.'

Amy,

I wouldn't usually consider asking favours of that dreadful woman, Mrs Craig, but she stopped me as I was passing her in the street and insisted on engaging me in conversation. Nevertheless, I kept our exchange short and I don't think anybody saw us.

She mentioned that she and that husband of hers were taking a trip to Newport, and so rather than going to the expense of posting you a letter, I thought she might as well deliver it and save me the cost of the postage.

Prepare yourself, for I have news to impart. Our own dear Lucy is to be married! I would go as far as to say, that by the time you read this, she might already be married. Can you believe it? Our own dear Lucy is to be the wife of an engineer!

Amy looked up from the letter and blinked at the big sky, staring at its brightness as the tears came. Wareham had done it. He'd married Lucy. Or if they weren't yet man and wife, they soon would be. He would never be hers. Whatever tiny hope she'd harboured had to be quashed. This wasn't one of her novels. There wasn't to be a happy ending, not for her and Wareham anyway. For all they'd been thrown into each other's company again, they were never destined to find their way back to one other.

'Are you all right, my dear? You look terribly pale.'

Amy had forgotten Mrs Craig was there. 'I'm fine.' She sniffed back her tears, blaming them on the sting of the ocean breeze and returned to the letter.

What a shock it is to us all. To think she'd marry James Belmont, just like that! I blame it on them being together so much during the long months of her convalescence. It goes to show he wasn't interested in you after all, so you can drop your hopes where he's concerned. By all accounts, he's been very attentive to her. It's his dog, I believe, that brought them together, and novels, of all things. Can you believe our dear Lucy has become interested in reading books!

Amy dropped the letter. Lucy wasn't marrying Wareham, but Mr Belmont. The news was too much for her to take in. The relief that Wareham was free after all was overwhelming. The tears came now in great heaving sobs.

Mrs Craig led her to a nearby rock and encouraged her to sit down before retrieving the letter as it tumbled across the sand.

'I hope it wasn't bad news.'

'Not at all. It's the very best news. Lucy is to marry Mr Belmont. In fact, they might already be married.'

Mrs Craig handed back the letter. 'That's very good news indeed.'

Amy still couldn't believe it. She turned over the page, scanning Marion's last few scrawled lines.

It doesn't reflect well on Mr Belmont, if you ask me. His fiancée has only been dead a matter of months, and now here he is, committing himself to Lucy. It just shows what fickle hearts men have.

We're appalled that she's marrying someone as lowly as an engineer, and one without a fortune, at that, but she won't be talked out of it. She says, if we don't give our permission, she'll marry him anyway, and an elopement will only bring more disgrace on the family. I don't know how I'll explain it to her parents, but Lucy is set on her course and there's nothing to be done. I've been assured by Mrs Craig that Belmont's new invention, which is something to do with hosepipes, is likely to make him a rich man. No doubt the Craigs will do well out of it too. Still, we can only hope she's right for poor Lucy's sake.

Marion

How the world was changing. Only eight years ago, Amy had been persuaded not to marry Wareham. Now Lucy was set to become Belmont's wife and no one was going to stop her.

The difference lay in the fact that Lucy was determined to follow her heart, and wouldn't be persuaded out of marrying the man she chose. It wasn't only about circumstance and a changing society, but her strength of character that made the difference.

No wonder Wareham despised Amy after she'd failed to stand up and fight for their love, for their future together. She'd thrown away their chance of happiness and she only had herself to blame.

How did Wareham feel about all of this? It had seemed to the world that he was set on marrying Lucy. Now he'd been usurped by his friend. He didn't deserve to have his heart broken a second time. She turned to Mrs Craig, trying not to sound too invested in her question.

'How did Mr Wareham respond to the news of the marriage?'

'He's delighted to know Mr Belmont has found love again after the tragedy of losing his fiancée so recently.'

'He wasn't disappointed at all?'

'From what I gather, he's enormously pleased for his friend.'

It was just as she thought. Wareham didn't love Lucy, and he never had. Nor had he been inclined to enter into a loveless marriage with her. She'd known, deep down, he wasn't capable of such a thing and she'd been right. Her feelings hadn't led her to misjudge the situation after all.

'He's still looking for a wife, though?' Once again, Amy tried not to seem too interested in the answer to her question.

'I believe he is.'

Mrs Craig was silent for a moment, her eyes looking out across the ocean as the waves rolled in. 'This is such a lovely place, especially in winter. I should invite Mr Wareham to join us. The weather will be a welcome change from the California sun.'

Amy said nothing, not wanting to give away how anxious she was to see him, or her happiness at knowing he wasn't attached to Lucy, that he never had been. If Mrs Craig invited Wareham, he was sure to come. She could hardly contain her excitement. Wareham was coming, and she'd be waiting for him. Soon, he'd be on his way, and she'd be counting the days until he arrived.

Chapter 35

The charity auction was set to take place in the ballroom of Newport's grandest hotel. The weather was stormy, even for the time of year, the wind shaking the trees of their last leaves and tossing the grey rolling waves of the ocean onto the beach like discarded dreams. Even the rain, coming down in sheets and sharp as pins, did nothing to put off the best of Newport society, who turned out in great numbers, in overshoes and sensible dresses, their brocade mantles protected from the rain by fringed umbrellas.

Amy sat at the edge of the room near the back, so as not to be seen while the auction took place. She didn't want to risk being accused of influencing the bidders, or be subjected to public humiliation if nobody bid for the signed first edition of the novel she'd donated. Eleanor had joined Mrs Tyler and the rest of the ladies from the charity committee on the front row, and with Mr Eaton spending the afternoon at his club rather than attending the auction, Amy was left to observe the room alone.

The auction was already on its third lot when a side door opened and someone slipped in, placing himself on the end of a row. It was Spencer, late as usual. Amy leaned back in her chair and tilted her head so she could watch him without being seen.

As always, he was alone, but what was he doing here?

His purpose became clear as soon as the bidding started on her book. The first to make a bid, he offered much more than the previous lots had sold for, and went on to raise the amount in increasingly higher increments each time someone bid against him. With each bid, a gasp went around the room. Few people in the town could match his wealth. Amy sank lower into her chair as the attention in the room focused on Spencer. It was good for the charity, but his ostentation verged on the vulgar and it made her uncomfortable.

Finally the gavel came down. Not surprisingly, Spencer had won the day. A signed first edition of one of Amy's novels was his, as if he hadn't already purchased enough copies of her books, but at least the proceeds from this one would go to a good cause.

Once the final lot had been auctioned, Amy slipped out of the hotel, hoping to get away unnoticed while all the attention was on Spencer. She hadn't realised Mrs Tyler had followed her until she was outside waiting to cross the road.

'My dear, you've done us proud. I don't know how to thank you. Your book has raised more money for our cause than all the other lots put together.'

'You have the Earl of Hokeham to thank for it. He's been very generous.' Amy tried to end the conversation, eager to get away before Spencer appeared. She wasn't in the mood for his Lord Bountiful act, but Mrs Tyler was too excited, too grateful to let her go so easily.

'I hear he's a particular friend of yours. He wouldn't have bid so generously otherwise.'

'He knows the money will go to a good cause.'

'He's very taken with you. Everyone in town is commenting on it.'

Amy glanced at the hotel entrance, expecting him to appear at any minute. Mrs Tyler must have guessed her thoughts and jumped to the wrong conclusion.

'He's inside, paying for the book, if you're wondering where he is.' She grinned. 'Goodness, what a lot of money he's pledged to us.'

Was it wrong of Amy to suspect it was only Spencer's vanity, his desire to impress her and everyone else in the town that had motivated him to bid so much for the book? She checked herself for her ungenerous thoughts. Whatever reason lay behind his actions, the charity would benefit from it, and that was all that mattered.

After a brief respite, the rain was beginning to fall again, dampening Mrs Tyler's enthusiasm to continue the conversation. She put up her umbrella and said goodbye. 'Come and see me at the bookstore whenever you're passing. I have a new stock of your books waiting to be signed.'

Amy looked up and down the street, watching the passers-by hurrying to get out of the rain. She'd forgotten her umbrella and there was little chance of hailing a hansom cab in this weather.

'Miss Eaton, Miss Eaton.'

Two elderly ladies she recognised from the auction room came dashing towards her, their sturdy leather boots making short work of the puddles. The taller one, dressed in a navy velvet coat and matching bonnet, placed a hand gently on her arm, her eyes sparking behind her tiny round spectacles.

'You mustn't mind the interruption. My name is Esther. My sister, Gladys, and I are great admirers of your work and we both wanted to congratulate you on *Missing in Love*. We've taken out a subscription to *Scribe* magazine, so we can be the first to read the new instalment every month. We have a boy deliver it to us.'

It was responses like this that made Amy's work worthwhile. 'Thank you. It means a great deal to know you're enjoying it.'

'We love the character of the young woman campaigning for women's votes. She's a call to arms to us all. I never thought before how the right to vote could lead to improvements in all areas of women's lives, particularly education and employment.'

Gladys, in a matching coat of light blue velvet, leaned in and whispered, 'That's all very good, but what we're most interested in is the love story. Will the estranged lovers finally find each other again after so many years apart?'

Esther batted away her sister's question. 'What we want to know is, are they still in love? Will they forgive themselves and each other for the mistakes they made in the past and will they live happily ever after?'

'And will the charming earl who bid so fiercely for your book in the auction have any influence on how the story ends?' added Gladys, her face suddenly serious.

Amy had asked herself these questions many times over. Still she hadn't found the answers. How was she supposed to settle on an ending for her characters, when each ending was only the beginning of a new chapter in their lives? How was she ever supposed to say *this is the end*, and let them go? She'd become too invested in their fates. They weren't simply characters on a page, but living, breathing people. They were as real to her as she was to herself, and their challenges and joys were as vital as those she experienced in her own life.

Gladys gave her sister a warning nudge. 'Don't tempt Miss Eaton to give away the ending. The enjoyment lies in not knowing what's going to happen next. I love to be kept guessing. It makes the story so much more fun.'

The rain was growing heavier. As Amy watched the ladies depart, she spotted a familiar figure standing nearby on the pavement, his face partly hidden by his umbrella. At first, she thought her eyes were deceiving her, that the rain had blurred her vision, until he tilted his umbrella just enough to reveal his face. He must have been watching her all this time, overhearing her conversation as it drifted towards him on the breeze. Wareham. Wareham was here, standing right beside her. Mrs Craig had invited him and he'd come.

As soon as he saw her looking, he pushed the small volume he'd been holding against his chest into his coat pocket. She'd have sworn it was one of her novels. She recognised the particular shade of maroon calfskin her publisher used for the binding.

Having caught her eye, he approached and handed her his umbrella. 'You're getting soaked. Take this.'

'Then you'll be wet.'

She tried to hand it back but he refused to accept it. Still, he remained beside her, the silence an agony between them as she struggled to find something to say.

'How do you find Newport?'

'It's too soon to form an opinion. I only arrived yesterday.'

He seemed reluctant to leave, and yet he had nothing to say. His eyes searched every line of her face, just as they'd done when they met in the street outside Mr Farrand's office. She cringed inside, knowing he was disappointed by what he saw.

She tried once again to return his umbrella. 'Please take it. You don't want the rain to soak through your coat and ruin the book I saw you stow in your pocket.'

She hadn't intended to mention the book, but the devil in her couldn't resist it. He'd become far too serious for his own good. She'd caught him in possession of one of her novels and she wanted him to know it.

His hand instinctively moved to his pocket as if such a gesture could banish the contents. 'It was Mrs Craig . . .'

'If she forced one of my novels onto you as a gift, then I'm sorry.'

'Not at all. It's . . .'

She held up her hand before he could say anything else. 'You don't have to tell me what you think of it.'

'I was only going to say how glad I am that your novels are a success. I know how much your writing has always mattered to you, the sacrifices you've made for it.'

This wasn't what she'd expected him to say. He'd been so dismissive of her work when they met over dinner that she thought he'd be disparaging. Perhaps she'd misjudged his previous comments and taken them too personally.

'We've both achieved so much these past years.'

She regretted mentioning the past as soon as she said it. He wouldn't want reminding of what had happened between them and she hadn't meant to bring it into the conversation. The silence returned to create a cavern between them.

This time it was Wareham who came to the rescue. 'I was very pleased to hear about Mr Belmont and Miss Morton's engagement. It's good news, don't you think?'

'I do. Do you?'

He nodded, his eyes drilling into hers. 'I'm very happy for both of them.'

Wareham had never had any intention of marrying Lucy and he wanted her to know it. Why else would he be making such a great point of telling her how pleased he was about her marriage to his friend?

'When Belmont said I'd never mentioned I knew you, he was mistaken.'

Amy nodded. 'He later recalled you mentioning a *mysterious Miss A.E.*' She couldn't resist the gentle tease, despite Wareham's obvious embarrassment.

'You must understand I referred to you that way out of delicacy. I had too much respect for you to talk about you freely to my male friends. At the same time, I was incapable of not mentioning you.'

The confession left Amy lost for words.

'Belmont is a good man,' continued Wareham. 'He's very kind to his dog. Some might criticise him for marrying so soon after the death of his previous fiancée, but I don't think his haste should be held against him.'

'I hope he's found happiness with Lucy.'

'All he wants is someone to love and to be loved. That's all any of us want.'

She stared at her feet. Already the rain was seeping through her overshoes. She looked up at him, unable to avoid his gaze.

The shoulders on his greatcoat were beginning to sag with the weight of the rain.

'You're soaked.'

Still neither of them made any effort to move.

She tilted the umbrella towards him, but they were too far apart for it to offer him shelter. It would have been unseemly to step any closer. 'Do you have any plans for your stay in Newport?'

'None at all.'

'Even out of season, there are things to do.' She spoke rapidly, filling the empty space between them before it could once more become a gulf. 'There are regular musical evenings and dancing.'

'Then perhaps . . .'

Before he could continue, Spencer strode out of the hotel and came straight up to them, placing his hand on Amy's arm.

'Here you are. I was afraid you'd left without me. You have no idea how much it has cost me, bidding for your little book in that auction.'

Amy stepped away from him, easing herself from his grip. 'It's for a good cause. A lot of people are grateful for your generosity, especially the women who'll benefit from the charity.'

'I didn't do it for them. I did it for you, my dear Miss Eaton.' He grinned, casting a satisfied look at Wareham. 'You're worth that amount of money, and a whole lot more, and I want the world to know it.' He scowled at the weather. 'You're getting soaked. No gentleman of honour would leave you standing in the rain. My carriage is waiting around the corner.' Once again, Spencer grabbed her arm. 'I'll take you home before you ruin your beautiful hat.'

His grip was firm. Any resistance on Amy's part would only have resulted in a struggle. 'I'm fine. Mr Wareham has lent me his umbrella.'

'That won't do.' He snatched the umbrella and thrust it at Wareham as if it carried something contagious. 'Let's get you home.'

Wareham took the umbrella without a word, his eyes never leaving Amy's face. She held his gaze as Spencer tried to lead her away, willing him to read her mind, delaying her departure just long enough to offer a few final words.

'There's an exhibition opening tomorrow night at Shaw's gallery. Mr Justin Jones is showing the portrait he painted of me in New York, among many other lovely things. Won't you come along? I'll ask Mr Shaw to send you an invitation.'

He made a gesture that could have been a yes or a no, before raising his rain-soaked hat to her and dashing into the hotel.

Amy watched him go, wondering what business he could have there, the rain running down her face in rivulets now she no longer had his umbrella to protect her. Suddenly cold, she shivered, while for the sake of good manners, she reluctantly allowed Spencer to lead her to his carriage, regretting every step that took her further away from Wareham.

Chapter 36

They'd only just set off in the carriage when a hooded figure in a dark cloak stepped out from a side street and dashed in front of them, waving desperately in an attempt to flag them down. Spencer leaned forward in his seat and rang the bell, signalling for the driver to stop. The wheels sprayed mud in all directions as the horses were brought to a sharp halt causing the whole carriage to jolt.

Amy looked through the window at the cloaked figure, the hood obscuring the woman's face as she stooped against the rain that was coming down in torrents, her ivory satin shoes already ruined by the downpour. There was something familiar, almost carefree about her gait as she dashed towards them. It wasn't until she'd climbed inside the carriage that she revealed herself to be Mrs Canby.

'Thank goodness you stopped.' She pulled the hood back from her face and smiled at Spencer. 'As soon as I spotted your coat of arms on the side of the carriage, I realised it was you. How grand it appeared from across the street compared to all the merchants' wagons and the hansom cabs clogging up the road.' She looked down at her feet with dismay, tugging at her skirt to reveal the determined curve of her ankles. 'These shoes have travelled all the way from Paris, only to be ruined on their first outing on the streets of Newport, and I have little hope for the fate of my stockings.'

She was breathless as she spoke, the rain from her cloak soaking the red plush upholstery and the leather trim of the seat. If the water damage bothered Spencer, he was too well bred to show it.

'This is cosy. I hope I'm not interrupting anything.'

Amy felt the stirrings of annoyance at what Mrs Canby was implying. 'Spencer kindly rescued me from the rain, just as he's rescued you.'

Impervious to the admonishment, she patted her hair to check the pins were still in place. 'What would we women do without these wonderful English baronets and their impeccable manners?'

'I'm an earl,' corrected Spencer, his moustache twitching with suppressed indignation. 'Not a baronet.'

'Forgive me. I know nothing of such titles. Those of us who hail from the American aristocracy refer to ourselves as plain old Mr, Mrs or Miss.'

Spencer brushed a raindrop from the back of his hand as it dripped from the edge of Mrs Canby's cloak. 'I didn't know America had an aristocracy.'

'It's not an aristocracy in the sense that you would know it. It's based on money, not breeding. Inheritance and inter-marriage still play a part, of course. It's how we keep things in the family.'

She retrieved a package from beneath the folds of her cloak and made a great show of checking it was still dry. 'Thank goodness. It would have been too bad if my new mantle had been ruined before it had even been worn.'

The purchase was beautifully wrapped, the expensive paper tied with a silk ribbon. Mrs Canby had extravagant shopping habits for a woman who claimed to have been cut off by her family and left without a cent.

'You've treated yourself to something new?' asked Amy, trying not to sound critical.

Mrs Canby tore at the corner of the fine paper to reveal a patch of dense mahogany-coloured fur. She grabbed Amy's hand and pulled off her glove, forcing her fingers to stroke the silky strands.

'It's mink. Feel it.'

It was like nothing Amy had ever felt, more luxurious than even one of Mrs Rawle's furs. She wondered if it was Mrs Craig's money she'd used to buy it, and if it was, whether she'd be pleased to see her spending it in this way.

'It must have cost a great deal.'

'There's no harm in a little treat now and then.'

Spencer was looking out of the window watching the rain as it landed in spikes on the road and paying no attention to all the talk of clothes and shopping. It was a short ride from downtown and already they were pulling up in front of the house. Mrs Canby clutched her parcel to her chest as she climbed out of the carriage.

'Will you come in for tea, Spencer? It's the least we can offer you after you were kind enough to see us safely home.'

'Yes, do come inside,' added Amy, reclaiming her rightful position as hostess. 'At least until the rain stops.'

His mind appeared to be elsewhere, and it was a moment before he responded, checking his pocket watch as if he were searching for an excuse within the workings of its gold case. 'Another time, perhaps. I have some business to attend to on the other side of town.'

Amy nodded, secretly relieved she wouldn't have to entertain him. She still hadn't forgiven him for interrupting her conversation with Wareham. 'Of course. We've already taken you out of your way. Thank you again for bidding so generously on my book.'

'It was nothing.' He closed the carriage door behind them and rang the bell, instructing the driver to turn the carriage around. By the time Amy and Mrs Canby had reached the front door, he was already gone.

Once they'd changed out of their wet clothes, Mrs Canby tried on her new mantle, inviting Amy to take a closer look at it. The mink draped around her shoulders so smoothly, it could almost have been a second skin.

'Isn't it the most glorious thing you've ever seen?'

'It's very eye-catching.'

Mrs Canby spun on her heels, her eyes narrowing on Amy. 'You think it's too much?'

'I'm sure it'll be perfect for the right occasion.'

'But it's too grand for Newport out of season?'

'I know very little about fashion. You should ask Eleanor. She'll be home soon.'

Mrs Canby's shoulders slumped beneath the weight of the mink. 'You were right when you said it was eye-catching. It's exactly what I intended it to be. Appearances are so important and have to be kept up. I can't let people suspect I'm down to my last few dollars. I have to appear wealthy if I'm to snare a rich husband. No one must guess I've been cut off from my family's money. Time's running out. If my father carries out his threat to publicly denounce me for setting fire to the effigy of the president, or for running straight into the arms of a lover even before my husband was cold in his grave, no decent man will have me.'

She dragged the mantle from her shoulders and held it at arm's length, as if it might turn and bite her at any minute. 'Desperate times call for desperate measures.'

Amy could see her predicament. She could also see her fool-hardiness. 'There's no need to rush into anything. You can stay here with us for as long as you need.'

'That's good of you, but one way or another I'll get myself out of here and back to the kind of life I deserve. I have no intention of living frugally, and refuse to be part of your conclave of spinsters for the rest of my days.'

She swept out of the room, leaving Amy stinging from her comments, and pondering whether Mrs Canby was a victim of her society, or of her own character.

Chapter 37

The art gallery was owned by Mr Logan Shaw, the third son of Cornelius Shaw who had made his fortune in meatpacking during the Civil War. At the age of seventeen, Logan spent a year in Italy, where he fell in love with a young sculptor named Roberto. During the course of a long, hot summer in Florence, Roberto introduced Logan to the treasures of the Uffizi Gallery and the wonders of Renaissance art, among many other things. They parted at the end of the summer, but Logan was never the same. Instead of joining the family meatpacking business and working alongside his father and his brothers, he left New York and used the generous allowance settled on him by his father to open a gallery in Newport.

Knowing there'd be little interest in art of the Italian Renaissance, he compromised, and in honour of his Italian lover, devoted his gallery to contemporary works. Every month, he offered an up-and-coming artist the opportunity to hold a small exhibition, and this month, it was the turn of Mr Justin Jones.

To raise more interest, the invitation to the opening mentioned that a portrait of the famous authoress Miss Amy Eaton would be the highlight of the show. Amy was happy to support Mr Jones by attending the exhibition opening, even if it meant putting aside the awkwardness she'd felt that day in his studio when she'd finally come face to face with her portrait and realised he'd failed to capture her character.

Having already seen something of the artist's work, and thought little of it, Mr Eaton declined his invitation, leaving Amy and Eleanor to attend without him. Having heard so much about Amy's portrait, and keen to show off her new fur mantle, Mrs Canby claimed Mr Eaton's invitation for herself. Now that Senator Frost knew of his daughter's whereabouts, there was no longer any need for her to avoid being seen in public and every reason for her to make a show of herself.

Spencer had offered to send his carriage for them, but Amy had politely refused. She couldn't stop him attending the exhibition, but she could avoid being seen arriving with him. Despite his growing popularity in the town, which was mainly due to the large amounts of money he spent everywhere he went, she didn't want to become too closely associated with him.

The gallery, which had once been a milliner's shop, was made up of a series of interconnecting rooms, and fronted by a row of large windows that looked out onto the main street, allowing passers-by the opportunity to view a few choice pieces of art without having to go inside. The prominent price tags meant Mr Shaw was less troubled with time-wasters, and saved the less wealthy customers the embarrassment of setting their hearts on a work of art before realising they were unable to afford it.

Amy put on a rose silk gown especially for the occasion and curled her hair, combing it out so it fell in soft waves around her face. Before she left the house, she checked her appearance in the mirror, satisfied that she'd made the best of herself, wondering if Mr Shaw had invited Wareham as she'd suggested, and if he had, whether he'd be tempted to attend.

Their chance meeting outside the hotel the previous day had caught her off guard. She hadn't expected to see him and had been flustered by his sudden presence. Tonight, she'd be better prepared to talk to him, to prove she was the same woman he fell in love with all those years ago. It was time to throw off her fear, to find the courage to reveal her feelings and try to win him back. She had nothing to lose but her dignity and her heart, and both had already been lost to him many years ago. She was tired of living with regret. It was time to mend the mistakes of the past, and if she failed, at least she would have tried.

The gallery was already full when they arrived. Mrs Canby left them at the door and headed straight for the canapés, sidestepping Mr Jones as he ran up to Amy and thrust a glass of lukewarm champagne into her hand.

'The guest of honour is here.' He offered her a florid bow. 'Thank you for coming, Miss Eaton. It's a pleasure to see you.'

He was too focused on Amy to notice Eleanor, who was left without a welcome or a drink, or else he remembered how she'd snubbed him in his studio and couldn't forgive her for it. Whatever the reasons for his lapse of manners, Amy prepared herself to suffer Eleanor's complaining about it later.

'Thank you for the invitation and congratulations on the exhibition.'

'I told you I'd be showing your portrait all around the country, and I've been as good as my word. It's already gained me half a dozen new commissions. If it carries on like this, I'll be able to move out of my shabby little attic studio in Hell's Kitchen and take premises in a better part of town.'

Amy raised her glass to him and smiled. 'I wish you every success.'

As far as Amy was concerned, anyone brave enough to embark on a creative profession deserved success. She knew what courage it took, how much it cost to bare one's soul for the amusement of strangers. She'd experienced the pain of rejection, knew how criticism, often made off the cuff, could cut to the bone. Anyone prepared to risk exposing the deepest part of themselves to such an insensitive world deserved to prosper.

While Mr Shaw was distracted by the arrival of yet more guests, Amy handed Eleanor her untouched glass of champagne and wandered off to look at the paintings on display. Eleanor followed, sipping the drink and making disparaging comments under her breath about everything they looked at.

Amy's portrait had been hung at the far end of the main room. She cringed when she realised a group of people were gathered in front of it, waving their champagne glasses in the air to emphasise their comments as they picked over the details. She wondered how they could have so many opinions on it when none of them knew her. Unlike many authors, she refused to have her picture printed on the title page of her novels. It had always been her nature to choose anonymity over self-promotion, to stand back in the shadows and let her work speak for itself, which is why she found the idea of the portrait excruciating.

She was about to move away when she spotted Wareham standing alone at the edge of the group. His arms were folded and his head was tilted to one side as he considered the portrait. She watched as he gazed at it in silence. He was the only one in the room not to voice an opinion on it.

Having lost Eleanor to a plate of lobster canapés, she wandered over to him, trying to appear matter-of-fact, as if she hadn't been searching for him. He appeared startled as she said his name as if he'd been too lost in his own thoughts to realise she was there.

'Amy, I mean, Miss Eaton. I was so busy considering your portrait, I didn't notice you were standing beside me.' He glanced at her and then back at the painting, repeating the action two or three times.

She tried to make light of his intensity. 'Are you going to tell me what you think of it?'

He looked at her again. This time, his eyes remained fixed on her face. 'It doesn't do you justice.'

'Some people would say it was flattering.'

'I'm not talking about how he's painted your hair or the colour of your eyes. Any half-decent copyist could do that. It's your spirit he's failed to capture. I look at it, and I see a picture of you, but I don't see you.'

Her cheeks grew hot from the steadiness of his gaze. 'Those were my thoughts too the first time I saw it.'

'No one who doesn't truly know and understand you could ever hope to capture you.'

'Then I make a bad subject for a portrait.'

'I'm being too critical of the artist. Nothing could ever compare to the real you.'

He handed her a glass of champagne as it was offered to him by a passing waiter before taking one for himself. 'I have a confession to make. When I saw you outside the hotel yesterday, you were right. The book you saw me slip into my pocket was one of yours.'

'I knew it.' She couldn't help smiling at her triumph, at his obvious embarrassment. 'I hope it didn't get too wet in the rain when you tried to hide it from me.'

'Not at all. And I'm enjoying it immensely. There's a lightness of touch to your work, a tenderness in the words, and a humour that's unmistakably you.'

This from a man who never read novels, who claimed they were the folly of the leisured classes.

He referred back to the painting. 'It's those elements of your character that Mr Jones has failed to capture in the portrait.'

'They say every writer reveals herself in her writing, however hard she strives to make it a fiction.'

'I see you in your work as clearly as I see you standing here.'

There it was again, his intent gaze bringing fire to her cheeks, setting alight every part of her. 'How terrible that must be for you. You have my permission to throw the book aside, whenever you find it too annoying.'

The change in his expression told her the joke had misfired. She'd meant to encourage him, not demolish him with her wit.

Just for a moment, he'd seemed to open himself up to her, as if he was about to let her back into his heart, but the moment had passed as quickly as it came.

He took a sip of champagne. 'I must thank you for responding so quickly the day Lucy fell from the horse in Cape May. I was so shocked by what had happened, I couldn't think clearly. You made sure she was comfortable and sent Belmont to fetch a doctor. It was thanks to your actions that she was able to recover the way she did.'

'I only did what anyone would do.'

'I was too busy blaming myself for the accident to help her. I shouldn't have let her ride the stallion. I should have known she wasn't a strong horsewoman.'

'Lucy can be very persuasive when she wants to be. You mustn't blame yourself. We all fall prey to influences that we later regret.'

'Allowing my better judgement to be influenced by others showed a weakness of character on my part. It was unforgiveable. Look at the harm it caused.'

'It was a mistake. We're all guilty of them from time to time. If we're to survive them, we have to learn from them so we can do better in future. It means forgiving ourselves as well as others.'

The way he looked away from her told her she'd touched a nerve. If she wasn't to lose him altogether, she had to move the conversation onto safer ground.

'How are Mr and Mrs Craig? I'd hoped to see them here tonight.'

'They had a prior engagement. Although Mrs Craig looks forward to seeing your portrait before someone buys it and takes it away.'

'Please don't let her buy it. I'd never forgive myself.'

He cleared his throat, suppressing a laugh as he changed the subject. 'You might be interested to know that Mr and Mrs Craig have approved Conrad's plans for the house he proposes to build for them on Fifth Avenue and have engaged him as the architect on the project.'

This was Wareham's doing, even though he wouldn't admit it. Hester had written and told her how closely he'd been advising Conrad to help him win the contract. 'That's wonderful news. Hester will be delighted.'

'It's an opportunity for him to make his name.'

'Thank you. I know how much you've done for him.'

He looked surprised that she'd paid so much attention to his efforts to help. 'I'm thinking of asking him to design a house for me too; that's if he's able to take on a second commission.'

It was the first time he'd mentioned anything about his personal life. She jumped on the subject, urging him to reveal more, desperate to know if she had any chance of featuring in his future. 'The houses in California must be very different to the ones in New York.'

'Yes, they—'

'Miss Eaton, there you are. I've been looking for you every-where.'

Spencer's voice bellowed through the gallery as he bounded up to her like an over-excited puppy. 'Why are you hiding in this gloomy corner? You're here to be seen and admired. Take my arm and I'll lead you around the rooms. Let me show you off.'

Affronted by his overbearing presence, Amy did her best to step away from him. 'Tonight is about Mr Jones's paintings. I just happen to be the subject of one of them.'

'It's the best one there is.' He glanced at the portrait. 'He's captured you perfectly. It's you, through and through. Can I buy it, or has it already been snapped up?'

The idea that Spencer might buy her portrait was too alarming, 'You mustn't even think of it. It's very expensive.'

'I don't care about that. It'll look spectacular at the top of the main staircase in my family's ancestral home in England. I can see it now, the lady of the house, looking down on everyone as they make their way to bed.'

Amy blanched at his words. 'You're getting carried away.'

'Forgive me, Miss Eaton. I wouldn't want to bid against you if you want to buy it yourself.'

'It's far too much for my limited pocket.'

She glanced at Wareham, silently pleading with him to rescue her, but once again, he misread her meaning. Avoiding her eye, he turned away, muttering under his breath.

'You must excuse me. I've stayed too long.'

Instead of rescuing Amy from Spencer's unwanted attention, Wareham knocked back the last of his champagne and made his way towards the door, his head bowed as he weaved through the crowd.

Amy's heart clenched as she watched him disappear from the room. She was too conditioned by her upbringing to snub Spencer or to run after Wareham and beg him not to abandon her, when all she wanted to do was continue their conversation, to find out if there was a chance of salvaging anything from the wreckage of their past love.

Spencer smoothed his moustache with his fingertips, his lips twisted to demonstrate his distaste. 'If that's a display of American manners, I don't think much of them.'

'You presume too much.'

He brushed off her comment with a shrug, his eyes scanning the room. 'There's Mrs Canby. Isn't that the artist she's talking to? She'll be commissioning him to paint her portrait now she's seen yours. She won't want to be outdone by you.'

Amy cared nothing for Mrs Canby's pretence. 'You must excuse me.' She couldn't stand Spencer's company a minute longer. Abandoning him in front of her portrait, she went in search of Wareham. Somehow, she had to find the courage to speak her mind to him. She couldn't let him leave in anger and with a misunderstanding between them. Did he harbour so much resentment against her that he couldn't see what she was feeling?

The gallery was packed with guests enjoying the free champagne, the noise of the revellers growing louder with each glass that was sipped. Amy strained to see over the fancy feathered hats of the women as she searched for Wareham among the crowd. Despite her urgency, he was determined not to be found.

As she checked the last of the rooms, Mrs Canby came up to her. 'There you are.' She hiccoughed as the bubbles from the champagne fizzed at the back of her throat, her words slurred from one glass too many. 'You're the talk of the gallery, thanks to that painting of yours.'

'I don't think so,' replied Amy, sidestepping her in a bid to escape. She wasn't in the mood to humour a drunken Mrs Canby, and if she didn't catch up with Wareham soon, he'd be lost for good. She forced a polite smile as she turned away, narrowing her eyes and scanning the room. The noise of the gallery was unbearable, the heat stifling as the guests clustered around the paintings to shout their opinions above everyone else's.

Wareham was just leaving the gallery when Amy finally found him. She called his name, but he refused to turn around, increasing his stride as he stepped out into the street.

Throwing off all pretence of good manners, Amy went after him. 'Mr Wareham. Mr Wareham.'

When he failed to answer, she picked up her pace, determined to catch up with him, and not caring how ridiculous she looked chasing a man down the street.

'Mr Wareham.' She was level with him before she finally forced him to acknowledge her. 'Are you leaving already?'

His face was set like stone. 'I've seen everything I need to see.'

The change in his manner almost broke her, but she refused to let him see it. 'We were having such a lovely evening. It's a shame for it to end so abruptly.'

'I thought so too, but now I realise there's nothing worth staying for.'

Amy sighed, betraying her exasperation, hoping he'd realise how much his answers frustrated her. Could he not see what

Spencer was playing at?

'You haven't seen the rest of the paintings. Why don't you come back inside and we can look at them together?' She held out her arm, encouraging him to take it, but he remained unmoving.

'As I said, I've seen everything I need to see.'

It was his stubbornness that prevented him from giving in, but Amy refused to give up on him. She grabbed his wrist, holding her ground and causing him to stumble as he tried to pull away. Did he not know how much she wanted to be seen on his arm? Would it really humiliate him to stand next to her in public?

'You were about to tell me about your plans to build a house. Will you settle in New York near Mr and Mrs Craig?'

'I was thinking of it, but not anymore.'

She was losing him. She could see it in his eyes, hear it in his words, but she wasn't ready to give up, not yet, not without a fight, not this time. 'Why's that? Aren't you tempted by the delights of the city?'

'There's nothing to delight me in New York, or anywhere else for that matter.' He disentangled himself from her grasp and stepped away, as if her closeness offended him.

There was nothing more to lose. All she could do was lay herself bare to him. If only she had the courage. 'Mr Wareham, I—'

'Something I've learned too late in life, Miss Eaton, is that you should always listen to your instincts, because they will never betray you the way others might. I implore you to learn from my mistakes.'

What was he trying to say? Was he still blaming her for breaking off their engagement all those years ago? Could he not let it go? Was he saying he wasn't prepared to give her a second chance, or could he not see she was trying to put things right between them? How more blatant could she be without getting on her knees and begging him to love her?

She took a deep breath, trying to regain her composure. 'Will you not come and look at the paintings with me?'

Already he was walking away, his head bowed as he murmured his parting words. 'I've wasted enough time here. Goodnight.'

There was no choice but to let him go. Across the street, a couple of young men had stopped to observe the scene. She'd already made a spectacle of herself. She wouldn't embarrass herself further in front of strangers, and in spite of everything, she had too much pride to beg, even in whispers.

It pained her that the man who was once so reluctant to leave her side now couldn't get away quickly enough. She considered the sudden change in his manner after they'd talked so pleasantly in front of the painting. He didn't have an irrational bone in his body, so there was only one other explanation.

It wasn't resentment or anger Wareham was displaying, but jealousy. Her good sense told her it was ridiculous, yet there was no doubt about it. She'd suspected it before, but now it was indisputable. She could see it in his eyes, however much he tried to hide it. It bled from every part of him. She wanted to laugh and cry all at the same time. How could she make him understand that he had nothing to fear from Spencer? That the Englishman's attentions were as unwelcome to her as the plague?

She stood alone in the street, oblivious to the critical stares of strangers, while she ran their recent conversation through her mind. If Wareham was jealous, then he must still have feelings for her, however deeply they were buried beneath his anger and his pain.

Wareham still loved her. She was almost certain of it. The acknowledgement burst upon her heart like the sunrise on a winter's day. And yet, if he refused to talk to her, how could she persuade him that, in spite of all the years that had passed, in spite of all the misunderstandings and the recriminations that confounded them, she still loved him too?

Chapter 38

Amy was in her room, putting the finishing touches to the latest instalment of *Missing in Love*. It was due on Mr Farrand's desk in New York by the end of the week, and if it wasn't to be late, she had to send it that morning.

She was waiting for the ink to dry on the final clean copy when her father knocked on her bedroom door. He'd been absent from breakfast, and she was surprised to see him up and about. She'd heard the hansom cab arrive outside the house just before dawn, returning him from the gentlemen's club in town where he preferred to spend most of his evenings. It was too dull for him at home these days with just Amy, Eleanor and Mrs Canby to talk to, and she couldn't blame him for craving male company.

He gave her a weak smile. 'Don't let me disturb you. I just wanted to ask if you'd seen Spencer lately.'

'I saw him briefly at the exhibition opening a couple of nights ago. Why do you ask?'

'I beat him at a game of cards last week. He'd bet more than he had to hand at the time, but promised to send it over the next morning. I waited, but nothing arrived. A few days later, I sent a message to his lodgings to remind him of the debt. All I got in return was a note, pledging to pay me, but with no indication as to when that would be. I expected something better from an English lord.'

He pulled the note from his pocket and stared at it. His face crumpled with disappointment. 'He seems to be a particular friend of yours. Perhaps you'd have a word when you see him. Explain how things are done. No one respects a man who fails to honour his debts.'

Despite the hypocrisy of his comment, Amy hated to see her father disappointed. 'It must have slipped his mind. I'll remind him of it when I next see him.'

The thought of having to speak to Spencer sat uneasily with her. She was reluctant to do anything he might see as encouragement, and talking about money would make the situation even more awkward. Still, it was unreasonable of him to leave the debt to her father unpaid, and if it came to it, she wasn't afraid of initiating uncomfortable conversations.

Her father had only just left when Eleanor burst into her room, gripping the latest edition of *The Newport Daily Times*.

'The rumours have been all over town, but now it's in the newspaper, so it must be true. How could you have kept something like this from me?'

'Whatever it is, can we discuss it later? I have to send this work to Mr Farrand. The payment for it will be late if I miss the deadline.'

'You can't dismiss the news as easily as that, and no, it won't wait.' Eleanor turned to the society page, thrusting it in front of Amy's face. 'Read it.'

Famous Authoress to Marry Charming English Aristocrat?

Amy blinked at the headline, unable to believe what she was seeing. At least they'd had the decency to put a question mark at the end of the statement, which only went to prove the story was pure speculation.

Tears of rage, jealousy and disappointment were burning on Eleanor's cheeks. 'Why didn't you tell me?'

'Because it's not true. Someone must have heard the rumours and now they're guessing. There's no more to it than that. It's the kind of speculation that sells newspapers and they know it.'

'There's no smoke without fire. Spencer followed you here directly from New York. Before that, he followed you from Cape May. He's made no secret of his interest in you. There's talk about the two of you everywhere I go.'

'It's none of my doing. It's not him that I'm—' Amy stopped before she betrayed herself. 'I'll drop by the newspaper office and make them print a retraction. They have no right to use my name in such a way.'

It must have been Spencer who'd started the rumours. He loved nothing more than to be the centre of attention. If he thought she'd be flattered seeing her name linked to his in the newspaper, then he'd misjudged her.

Her heart dipped as she thought of Wareham. There was no doubt he'd see the article. Even if he didn't buy the newspaper himself, someone would show it to him. She couldn't stop thinking about how he'd stormed out of the art gallery after Spencer had talked of hanging her portrait in his family home as if there was an understanding between them. This article would only confirm his suspicions and reduce his opinion of her even further.

Her hands shook as she pushed the loose pages of *Missing in Love* into the envelope without checking to make sure the ink was dry. What gave Spencer the right to behave in such a way? If he had any respect for her reputation he wouldn't have made her the subject of such speculation. Was this why he hadn't honoured his debt to her father? Did he think that if they were soon to be family, it would no longer stand? Whatever his reasoning, these were not the acts of a decent man.

Mrs Rawle arrived at the house just as Amy was leaving. She threw out her arms with joy, believing a victory had been won.

'My dear, let me be the first to congratulate you. I knew it was only a matter of time before news of your engagement to Spencer was announced.'

The misinformation had already spread and it was too late to stop it. Amy tempered her reply, trying not to betray her indignation. 'It's not what it seems. There's been a misunderstanding.'

'There's no need to be coy. Everyone will be enormously pleased for you.'

There was no time to stop and talk. Amy had to ensure the story was corrected in the next edition of the newspaper. Wareham needed to know there was nothing between her and Spencer.

'I can't explain now. I'm in the most terrible hurry.'

Amy couldn't reveal the full truth, knowing the scorn she'd suffer if Mrs Rawle discovered how she felt about Wareham.

Instead of waiting for a cab, she walked into town, trusting the exercise to burn off the energy generated by her rage. The offices of *The Newport Daily Times* were just off the main street, and a world removed from the oak-panelled grandeur of the New York offices of *Scribe* magazine. This was the lower end of the publishing market, where two-bit stories and half-truths were peddled in a desperate bid to gain advertising revenue, and it didn't matter how many situations were misrepresented, how many lives ruined in their bid to improve the bottom line.

As Amy approached the front desk, the steady thump emanating from beneath the floor indicated that the printing press was in the basement. Every process of producing the paper was carried out in this single shabby building, keeping the damage they inflicted on innocent individuals in-house. The thoughts tossed around Amy's mind like dead fish on the ocean waves. The brisk walk into town had done nothing to cool her anger. She needed to be calmer if she wasn't to make a difficult situation worse. Further bad press wouldn't win Wareham back.

'Good morning, I'd like to see the editor, please.'

The young man on the desk looked at her from under the peak of his flat cap and wrenched the pencil from his mouth.

'Who shall I say wants him?'

'Miss Amy Eaton.'

He blew out his cheeks as if to indicate her request was too much trouble, before turning his back on her and yelling.

'Chief. There's a Miss Elton to see you.'

'Eaton,' hissed Amy, to no effect.

The young man had already returned his pencil to his mouth and was staring at the large sheet of newsprint in front of him. Before she could try to correct him again, a man appeared from somewhere at the back, forcing his stocky arms into his jacket as he greeted her.

'Miss Elton. I'm Mr Robbins, the editor of *The Newport Daily Times*.'

'It's Eaton. Miss Amy Eaton.'

'Ah, the famous authoress. What an honour this is. What can I do for you?'

'Can we speak privately in your office?'

He nodded, winking at the young man as he led her into an adjoining room filled with rows of grubby desks. Here, reporters pored over tomorrow's headlines and wrote up their tittle-tattle, each trying to catch her eye as she hurried to keep up with Mr Robbins before he disappeared into his office in the far corner.

Windowless and airless, and with an overpowering smell of must, Mr Robbins's office wasn't quite the cupboard Amy had expected, but it wasn't far off it, with piles of paper and ledgers cluttering the shelves and spilling over onto the floor and every other available surface. Seemingly unconscious of the state of chaos in which he wallowed, Mr Robbins cleared a chair and gestured to her to sit down before returning his vast bulk to his own seat on the other side of the desk.

'It's not every day we have such a distinguished person in our office.' He picked up his spectacles and pushed them onto his nose, peering through thick lenses at the envelope containing the latest instalment of *Missing in Love*, which Amy held close to her chest. 'Tell me what I can do for you. Have you fallen on hard times? Do you want me to print one of your little stories, is that what it is?'

She couldn't decide whether he was naturally overconfident or simply determined to humiliate her. 'It's regarding the story you printed about me in your newspaper this morning.'

'Ah, yes. It was a particularly good headline, don't you think?'

'I'm here to ask you to print a retraction.'

He leaned back in his chair, folding his hands behind his head. 'What is it you'd like me to retract?'

'The hints you made regarding a supposed attachment between me and the Earl of Hokeham.'

'You saw the question mark at the end of the headline? We're simply asking the question, floating the idea to titillate our readers' minds. We didn't say you were attached to this fancy English lord, just as we didn't say you weren't.' He gave her a satisfied grin. 'Have you come to set the story straight? Would you like me to make an official announcement on your behalf? I can promise you tomorrow's front page if you're willing to give me that.'

The man was insufferable. She had to be careful not to give him anything that could lead to further speculation. She could see the headline now. *Does the lady protest too much?*

'Would you be good enough to tell me who suggested the idea of the story to you?'

He folded his arms across his vast stomach and considered her. 'I can't give you any names, you must understand that. An editor has to protect his sources.'

'Can you tell me anything at all?'

'On one condition; that you give me the exclusive rights to print any forthcoming announcements regarding you and the English lord.'

'If the Earl of Hokeham and I decide to marry, you'll be the first to know about it.' This was an easy promise to make, because it was never going to happen.

Mr Robbins leaned forward and lowered his voice, even though there was no one else to overhear them beyond the spiders hiding in the crevices and the mice scratching in the walls.

'All I can say is, I was approached by a certain senator, who had a story to tell me about the activities of a particular widow, who he knew for a fact was responsible for the burning of the effigy of the president in Central Park.'

Amy forced herself to appear composed. 'I see no connection between what you're telling me and the story you printed about me and the Earl of Hokeham.'

'That's because I haven't told you everything yet.' He cleared his throat before continuing. 'What the senator told me was a very compelling story, but it seemed only right to get the other side of it before I went to print.'

'You like to get your facts right?'

'Every time. Anyway, the widow in question was understandably very upset at the prospect of being accused of committing such a terrible crime in the newspaper. As I'm sure you know, if such a story was published in my little rag, every other editor in the country would pick up on it, and in no time at all, it would be on the front page of every newspaper in America.'

'You made this clear to the widow in question?'

'I didn't have to. She knew it already. And so, after a certain amount of discussion, we came to an agreement.'

'And that agreement involved me?'

'And the English lord, naturally.'

'So she gave you the story of the supposed attachment between me and the Earl of Hokeham, and in return you promised not to print anything damaging against her.'

'That's about it, yes.'

'And you didn't think to check the facts with me first?'

'As I said before, I stated no facts. I only raised the question. I leave the rest to the imagination of my readers.'

Amy had to admire his cunning. The deployment of a simple

question mark at the end of the headline had absolved him of all responsibility.

Mr Robbins continued. 'The certain widow has bought herself a little time, but not much. The senator is most keen for his story to be broken. I won't be able to hold him at bay forever. And even if I choose not to print it, there are plenty of other newspapers out there who would.'

'So why did this senator come to you, rather than expose his victim in one of the New York or Washington newspapers?'

'You'll have to ask him that. Now, unless you've got a story for me, I'll say good day to you.'

He got up from behind his desk and showed her to the door, making the point that he wasn't prepared to discuss the matter any further. Clearly her last question had been a question too far and was too close to the nub of the matter.

Back on the street, Amy tried to work out the reasoning behind Senator Frost's plan. He must have offered the story to the editor of the local newspaper where Mrs Canby was hiding, on the condition that she was given the opportunity to prevent it from being published.

This deadly game of brinkmanship gave the senator the means to threaten his daughter with the public exposure of her crime, but without actually carrying out the deed. After all, it wasn't in the interests of either of them for the story to come out. The senator was gambling on the immediate threat of exposure being enough to rein in his daughter's behaviour, and if that failed, he would only then resort to publicly denouncing her to save his political skin. Even after all this time, and at a distance of so many miles, he was still determined to control her.

In turn, Mrs Canby had no misgivings about throwing Amy's reputation to the wolves to protect her own name, and had given Mr Robbins a story about her and Spencer as a means of buying Mr Robbins off, to save her own scandalous story appearing in the press. It seemed that father and daughter weren't so different

249

after all.

Amy shivered in the midmorning winter sun. The whole thing was more involved than any plot she could have conceived for one of her novels.

'Miss Eaton. What a coincidence that I should see you this morning.'

Mrs Tyler from the bookstore was dashing along the street towards her. Amy gritted her teeth, hoping she wouldn't raise the subject of the newspaper article. Everyone would have read it by now, or at least have heard about it. It was a small town and gossip spread like wildfire. She could only hope she'd offered Mr Robbins enough to prevent him spreading any further spurious stories about her and Spencer.

'Is that the next instalment of *Missing in Love* you're holding?' Mrs Tyler stared hungrily at the large envelope tucked under Amy's arm.

'I'm on my way to post it to *Scribe* magazine.'

'The new character you've introduced. I'm not sure whether he can be trusted or not. He's very charming but . . .'

Amy knew exactly what she meant. 'I haven't quite worked him out yet, either.'

Mrs Tyler laughed. 'I can't believe I'm taking it so seriously. I won't keep you from your important errand.' She gripped the leather satchel that hung from her shoulder as if the contents were precious. 'I'm on my way to deliver the novel you donated to the charity auction to the winning bidder.'

Surely Spencer had collected the book directly after the auction. When he met her outside the hotel afterwards, he'd indicated he'd already paid for it. She hadn't seen him carrying it, but the small volume would easily have fitted into the pocket of his greatcoat and would have protected it from the rain.

'I assumed the Earl of Hokeham already had it.'

'The earl made the highest public bid, but when it came to paying, he was unable to honour it. He contacted his bank, but

I gather they refused to extend his credit.'

The failure of Spencer to honour his debts was beginning to sound like a familiar story. 'I'm sorry to hear that. What happens to the book now? Is it going to the next highest bidder in the room?'

The closest bid was considerably lower than the one Spencer had pledged, but if he couldn't honour it, then at least it had still sold for a fair sum. Spencer's bid had, after all, been extravagant and out of proportion to the value of the thing itself.

'Someone offered to match the winning bid, so the charity hasn't lost out.'

Amy was astounded. 'That was very generous of them. I don't recall anyone else in the room bidding that kind of money.'

'The person in question wasn't in the room. They approached one of the charity board members privately after the auction and pledged to match any bid on the book if the winning bidder failed to pay.'

'May I ask who it was?'

She hoped it wasn't Mrs Canby, as this too was likely to have been an unsubstantiated bid. It could have been Mrs Craig. It was in her nature to make such a generous gesture and she made no secret of admiring Amy's work.

'I was asked to keep their identity a secret.'

Now Amy was more intrigued than ever. 'I'd very much like to know who was prepared to pay such a vast sum for my book.'

'Of course you would. It's only natural. I know you won't say a word to anyone.'

Amy leaned in closer and lowered her voice. 'Who was it?'

'It was Mr Wareham.'

'Mr Wareham?'

Wareham was the last person Amy had expected to come to her rescue. But of course, it wasn't she he'd rescued. It was the charity.

Mrs Tyler blanched, as if the shock on Amy's face had made her regret betraying Wareham's secret. 'I understand he's an acquaintance of yours.'

So that was where Wareham was going that day in the rain when he dashed into the hotel after the auction. He must have had a suspicion that Spencer would make a ridiculously high bid on her book, just for the show of it, and then fail to honour it. He'd already worked out his character and knew he couldn't be trusted.

No one else had had the foresight or the means to step in and save the situation the way he'd done. Even if he didn't want anyone to know about it, his generosity had to be acknowledged. He'd saved her the embarrassment of the book not being sold, and ensured the charity received a hefty donation, and for that she was grateful.

'Will you allow me to write a personal message inside the cover? It's the least I can do after Mr Wareham has been so generous.'

Mrs Tyler handed over the book. 'I'm sure he won't mind that I've told you. You are the author, after all.'

Amy took out her pen and inscribed a message to Wareham on the flyleaf, with a sentiment that only he would understand. There was no saying he'd ever see it, or even care what she'd written, but it would always be there, just in case he ever felt like opening the pages and taking a look at it, just in case he ever went in search of a reason to give her a second chance.

Chapter 39

It had been a day of revelations. Amy was still reeling from the news that Spencer had been unable to honour his winning bid on her book, and that Wareham had stepped in and rescued the situation. Not to mention what she'd learned about Mrs Canby's deal with Mr Robbins to keep her name out of the papers at the expense of Amy's reputation.

Mrs Canby's behaviour had always made her uneasy, and from the first moment she met Spencer, she'd suspected his charm was too unflinching to be sincere. There'd always been something controlling about his niceness that made her wary. If only she'd trusted her instincts, and not been persuaded by those closest to her to entertain him, she might have saved everyone a lot of trouble.

The more she considered it, the more she began to see the similarities in the behaviour between Spencer and Violet's late husband, Edgar. Having lived among the English aristocracy for almost a decade, Violet was the best person to confirm her suspicions regarding Spencer's character and his motivations behind his attempts to court her. It was time to pay her a visit.

Violet was drinking tea with Mrs Fairchild, the mother of one of her pupils, when Amy arrived. Too out of sorts to accept a drink, she sat at the table, staring at the plate of scones as if they were the cause of her confusion.

Mrs Fairchild put aside the report Violet had compiled on her daughter's progress, and turned her attention to Amy. 'I hear the opening of the exhibition at Shaw's gallery was a great success.'

'I imagine so,' said Amy, 'judging by the number of people who attended.'

The exhibition was the last thing on her mind. She was more concerned that Spencer was going around the town promising money he didn't have to people who couldn't afford to do without it.

'I believe the Earl of Hokeham was there.'

Mrs Fairchild must have seen the article in *The Newport Daily Times* and was trying to bring the conversation around to the subject. Amy would have to find ways of shutting down the rumours everywhere she went until they finally blew over.

'I saw him briefly.'

Violet raised her eyebrows. 'Should we be offering you our congratulations?'

'For what?'

'For your forthcoming engagement to the Earl of Hokeham.'

'There is no engagement.'

The words came out sharper than Amy had intended. It was the consequences of the speculation that angered her more than anything, the effect the rumours would have on Wareham when they reached his ears.

'Not yet, perhaps,' prompted Violet, leaning forward and encouraging Amy to be less discreet.

'Not now or ever, I assure you.'

'But everyone's talking about it.' Violet glanced at Mrs Fairchild, as if to reassure herself of the truth. 'We both saw the article in the newspaper.'

'They had no right to hint at an attachment when Spencer and I are nothing to one another.'

Mrs Fairchild rolled her eyes, unconvinced by Amy's assertion. 'I appreciate you wanting to deny the rumours about the two of you. Discretion is everything, of course, but perhaps you can tell me where I can find him?'

'Why would you expect me to know that?'

'Because whatever you might say, Miss Eaton, he's known to be a particular friend of yours and he owes my husband a great deal of money.'

'He has gambling debts all over town,' explained Violet, a sorry note creeping into her voice. 'He's left his lodgings without warning and without paying his bill. Nobody knows where he's gone.'

The news didn't come as a surprise to Amy, knowing what she already did of Spencer, and only served to confirm her worst fears. 'I'm sorry, but I don't know where he is. If I knew, I'd tell you.'

Spencer wasn't mentioned again until after Mrs Fairchild had left. Violet insisted on pouring her a cup of overbrewed tea from the pot and offered her commiserations.

'I'm sorry about Spencer. I hope he didn't give you any expectations and leave you disappointed.'

'Not at all. If he's gone, then I'm glad of it.'

'Do you mean it?'

'Of course I do.' Amy saw a look of relief pass across Violet's face. 'Is there something you're not telling me?'

'I wanted to know if you were attached to him before I spoke.'

'And if I were attached to him?'

'Then I'd be telling you this as a warning.'

Amy took a sip of the cold tea, tasting its bitterness on her tongue. 'You'd better tell me what it is you've been keeping from me.'

'I knew Spencer in England. He was my husband's closest friend. They'd known each other since their school days, and as young men, they were inseparable. Thanks to the feckless lifestyle of Spencer's father, and the poor management of the estate, the family was almost ruined by the time Spencer came of age. Determined to keep up the standard of living he believed was owed to him, he persuaded Edgar to lend him large sums of money over the course of a number of years, which he never repaid. He also encouraged Edgar to gamble, which is why he ended up in so much debt.'

'That was the debt he used your capital to settle?'

'Most of my capital went that way, yes. He and Spencer, along with Edgar's mistress, quickly burned through what remained of it.'

Amy was silent while she took it all in. 'Spencer never mentioned he knew you.'

'I watched him enter the bookstore the day you were there signing books. He left as soon as he saw me. I don't think he stayed long enough to work out that we were friends, otherwise I suspect he'd have tried to turn you against me, to make sure I didn't tell you what he's really like.'

Amy thought back to the day in the bookstore. Spencer had promised to wait for her while she signed the books for the people in the queue. She'd been relieved when he left without saying goodbye, assuming he'd grown tired of waiting, and had thought no more of it. Now she realised he must have left to avoid an awkward meeting with Violet.

'Thank you for telling me.'

She was relieved to know he'd gone, that he wouldn't be bothering her again. It was Eleanor who would be the most disappointed. She'd tried so hard to get his attention. If only Amy had realised at the time how wrong she'd been to encourage it. Rather than seeing his disappearance as a disappointment, they should consider it a lucky escape.

'Don't assume it's over,' warned Violet. 'He's a charmer and a trickster. If he's set his sights on you, it's obviously for a reason. He might have left Newport to avoid paying his debts, but it doesn't mean he's given up on you.'

It was just as she suspected. Spencer wasn't interested in her at all, or her literary fame. It was only her money he wanted. He'd probably come to America to find himself a rich wife to cover his gambling debts and fund his extravagant lifestyle, just as so many English aristocrats had done before him. If he'd discovered she wasn't as wealthy as he'd assumed, and neither was her family, it would explain his sudden disappearance. She was unlikely to ever see him again. It wasn't an unwelcome thought.

Amy only had to consider what had happened to Violet to know how disastrous such a match could be. Still, American parents threw their innocent daughters at any man who stepped off the boat with a title and tales of their family estate in the English countryside. Social climbers loved nothing better than to be associated with the aristocracy, even at the cost of ruining their daughters' lives and squandering their fortunes.

She took a deep breath, trying to hide her fury that so many people had been taken in by him. 'There's no need to worry on my behalf, Violet. I have the full measure of Spencer and he won't be getting anything from me.'

Chapter 40

Instead of going straight home, Amy took a walk along the beach to gather her thoughts. Everyone had been taken in by Spencer apart from Wareham. He'd worked out his character and made sure the charity didn't suffer for his dishonesty by fulfilling his pledge to them, even though it wasn't his responsibility. If Amy had suspected Spencer couldn't be trusted, then Wareham had known it for certain.

This must have been what he was trying to say at the exhibition opening when he advised her to trust her instincts. He wasn't referring to her breaking off their engagement all those years ago as she'd assumed. He was warning her against Spencer's character. It wasn't jealousy that inspired his words, but his wish not to see her exploited.

As Amy drew near the house, she spotted Eleanor sitting on the veranda looking out across the ocean, her cheeks reddened by the relentless breeze. Lately, she'd given up wearing a veil to protect her complexion and Amy wondered if it was a sign she'd given up hope of finding a husband.

There'd been a change in her since leaving New York, and in many ways, it was for the better. Encouraged by her association with the women on the local charity board, she was beginning to see beyond the narrow confines of the old New York society and its rules. Whether Eleanor found a husband or not, Amy hoped she'd eventually find her place in the world, just as Amy had done with the success of her novels. Work could never satisfy every longing, but it was something, and sometimes, it had to be enough.

Eleanor raised her hand and waved. 'There you are. Come and join me. You're already windswept, so it hardly matters.' She removed her sewing basket from the bench, making room for Amy to sit down. 'Did you get an apology from the editor of the *Daily Times*?'

'No, but I don't think he'll print a story like that again. Is Mrs Canby here?'

Eleanor straightened the woollen blanket as it threatened to slip from her knees.

'She's gone to stay with a friend in Providence. She left this morning.'

The timing of her departure was no coincidence. She knew Amy would find out she was responsible for the article in the newspaper and would want to confront her over it.

'Did she say when she was coming back?'

'No. Is something wrong?'

'Nothing at all.'

There was no point relating the story to Eleanor when she was always so quick to defend her friend. It was bad enough that she had to break the news about Spencer without starting any other difficult conversations. She settled on the bench, pulling her mantle tighter around her shoulders to cut out the breeze. 'It's a fine view from here.'

A strand of hair blew across Eleanor's eyes and was gone again before she could brush it away. 'It's better living here than in New York in some ways.'

'But not in every way?' Amy squeezed her sister's hand. 'We'll go back someday, I promise.'

'It'll be too late for me by then. It probably already is.'

'Just as it is for me.'

Their eyes met, and an understanding passed between them that had never been there before. Amy sensed a hint of the closeness she'd longed for every day since their mother's death, and for a moment, she thought something precious had been captured.

A seabird cried overhead and the moment passed. Eleanor looked up at the sky and frowned. 'All those beautiful dresses from Worth are wasted here. There's not a single man worth catching. It's new money or no money everywhere you look. I wouldn't be surprised if old New York society didn't find a different place to spend their summer next year. Then we won't even have the season to look forward to.'

Perhaps it was losing their mother at such a tender age that made them unable to love each other the way other sisters seemed able to. Would they have learned to be kinder to one another if she'd been there to guide them, or was it only Amy's wishful thinking? Perhaps it was just that they were different people. Despite Eleanor's physical closeness, a surge of loneliness washed over Amy, and it was as grey and thunderous as the ocean waves that beat against the shore.

It was Eleanor who finally broke the silence. 'I had the strangest conversation with Spencer at the exhibition the other night.'

'What did he want?' He would have wanted something. It seemed he was all about *want*.

'I can't say, although he asked some odd questions.'

'What kind of questions?'

'He wanted to know why you hadn't bought your portrait from Mr Jones.'

'What did you tell him?'

'The truth. That you didn't like the painting. Somehow, he got me to confess that you or Father couldn't afford to buy it even if you'd wanted it.'

'What else did he want to know?'

'Whether you made a lot of money from your novels. He didn't ask directly, because that would have been impolite, but it's what he was getting at.'

'How did you answer?'

'I said you worked very hard, that sometimes you could work on a story for a year, only for it not to be sold, and that would be a whole year of work for which you weren't paid.'

'How did he take it?'

'He was surprised. His reaction suggested he thought you were rich.'

'Then it can only have been an assumption on his part.'

'He also wanted to know why we'd let the house in New York and moved here, even though it was out of season. I told him what we tell everyone, that we wanted a change from New York.'

It wouldn't have taken much for Spencer to work out the real reason behind the move. There'd been whisperings all over town, and they weren't the only family in financial difficulty to resort to such measures.

It was just as she'd guessed. Once he realised she wasn't wealthy enough to fund his extravagant lifestyle, he'd disappeared.

'Are you all right, Amy? Did I say the wrong thing to Spencer?'

'You said exactly what needed to be said.'

'I hope I haven't spoiled your chances with him. I know I was jealous of the attention he gave you at first, but as long as he marries one of us, we'll all be all right, won't we?'

'Rumour has it, he's left town. I don't expect we'll be seeing him again.'

'I hope you're not too sorry.'

Amy leaned over and kissed her sister on the forehead. 'He wasn't the answer to our fortunes in the way you'd hoped, but don't worry. We'll be just fine without him.'

Chapter 41

Marion and Charles arrived in Newport without warning. Amy and Eleanor were having a light lunch of boiled ham and pickles when they burst in. Amy stood up to greet them, wringing her hands as she always seemed to when she was in Marion's presence.

'This is unexpected. You should have told us you were coming.'

'I thought I'd save the cost of sending a letter and surprise you.'

'You've certainly done that.' Amy looked around, but there was no sign of the boy. 'Where's Charles Junior? Don't tell me he's already gone to play on the beach.'

'We left him in New York.' Marion's shoulders sagged, exaggerating her sadness. 'We've had to employ a nanny since you abandoned us. It didn't seem worth dragging her all this way when she's perfectly settled at home with Charles Junior. You wouldn't believe the expense involved when you travel with the hired help.'

Marion was still complaining about the cost of the nanny when a second carriage pulled up outside. Amy looked out of the window just as Lucy, Hester and Conrad were disembarking.

'You didn't tell me the rest of you were coming.'

Hester was wearing one of last season's dresses, and had a simple brocade mantle draped around her shoulders. She burst into the house ahead of the others and threw her arms around

Amy.

'I'm so glad to see you.' She waved her hand under Amy's nose. The chip of ruby in her ring glinted in the cool midday light. 'Look what Conrad gave me. I told him he shouldn't spend his money on a ring, but he insisted on buying it anyway.'

Hester and Conrad were finally engaged, and would live the life Amy and Wareham had missed out on. If Wareham hadn't helped Conrad win his first big commission as an architect, it wouldn't have been possible. It explained the economy of Hester's dress, the simplicity in the way she'd pinned her hair. She no longer saw herself as a debutante, the trophy of a rich family, but as the future wife of a professional working man. Given time, and the influence of women like Mrs Craig, she might even grow to see herself as a person in her own right. Amy wiped away a tear, hoping Hester would think she'd shed it out of happiness for her and Conrad, rather than out of regret for the life she and Wareham had missed.

It was only then that Amy realised Lucy was in the room. She'd crept in when no one was looking and settled herself on the rosewood sofa. Her pink velvet dress hung from her shoulders in folds, her corset hardly doing any work to create her tiny waist. The hourglass figure she'd previously taken such pride in was reduced to skin and bone.

Amy sat beside her and took her hand, searching her face for the Lucy she used to know. It was the first time she'd seen her since her accident in Cape May and she was shocked by the change in her. What a difference a few months could make, and it was all down to one ill-considered action. If only she could have been persuaded out of her recklessness, her life would be set on a different course.

'How are you?'

'I'm much better, thank you.'

Her voice was little more than a whisper. Her complexion no longer a blend of milk white and blush, but ashen. The spark that had lit her eyes had been doused, leaving behind an emptiness that made Amy uncertain. The Lucy she'd once known had gone and a stranger had stolen in and taken her place.

Marion was circling the table, picking at the cold cuts of boiled ham. Amy realised she'd been remiss and rang the bell for the maid. 'You must all be hungry after your journey. Let me get you something to eat.' She did a quick calculation in her head, trying to work out what was left in the kitchen that they could present at short notice as a decent meal. She hadn't been expecting guests and such was their economy, there was only enough food in the house to feed the three of them.

'Don't trouble yourself,' said Marion, crunching a pickled cucumber between her back teeth. 'We've taken rooms in town. They're expecting us for a late lunch. I just wanted to drop by as soon as we arrived, to let you know we're here, and to invite you all to Hester and Conrad's engagement party.'

Hester produced an invitation from her purse and handed it to Amy. 'Marion thought we should hold it here, rather than in New York.' Her forced brightness betrayed she was trying to make the best of it.

'Why would you choose to hold the party in Newport?' asked Eleanor, grabbing the last pickled cucumber before Marion claimed it.

'Because most of the family is here,' said Marion. 'And we thought the trip would make a nice change.' She turned to Conrad, who was looking out of the window at the vast expanse of beach. 'You don't mind having the celebration here, do you?' It wasn't so much a question as a statement.

Conrad turned from the window and shrugged, fixing his eyes on his fiancée. 'I'll go anywhere as long as I can be with Hester.'

As far as Marion was concerned, everything was settled. She gave Hester a shove. 'You should give Amy the other invitation too. She can pass it on when she sees him, as she undoubtedly will, from what we've been hearing.'

For a moment, Amy assumed she was referring to Wareham. Hope fluttered at the thought of having an excuse to contact him, but it wasn't that at all. If anyone would invite him to the party, it would be Conrad. Apart from Lucy, no one here knew of Amy's connection to him, and these days, there was no connection. The fluttering in her heart turned to something else altogether as Hester passed her the second invitation and she read the name on it. *Spencer.*

Amy held it at arm's length, gesturing for her to take it back. 'I won't be seeing him again. I heard he's left town.'

'What do you mean, he's left town?' Marion's face was like stone. 'I'm relying on him to add a touch of respectability to the celebration. If people hear an English earl attended the engagement party, they might not look down so much on the match.'

Amy glanced at Conrad, who turned his attention once more to the view, his shoulders stiffening at Marion's words.

'Rumour has it, Spencer owes money all over town and nobody seems to know where he is.'

Marion bristled. 'There must be a misunderstanding. That can't possibly be the case. You should know better than to pay attention to the gossip on the streets.'

'It's not gossip,' snapped Eleanor. 'I know for a fact that he owes Father the money he lost to him in a card game.'

A gasp escaped from Marion. For a split second, her jaw refused to close. 'As I said, it's sure to be a misunderstanding.'

The conversation came to a halt as the maid entered the room and handed a letter to Amy. While she read it, Marion ordered the lunch plates to be cleared away and for fresh tea to be brought to them.

Hester watched Amy's reaction to the note with concern. 'It's not bad news, is it?'

'Not at all.' Amy shook her head, unable to believe it. 'It's from Mr Jones. My portrait has been sold. Someone saw it in the exhibition and bought it. He thought I might like to know.'

'Who in the world would want to buy your portrait?' asked Marion, the pitch of her voice rising with her indignation. 'They must have thought it was of someone else. They'll return it once they realise their mistake. After all, no one who reads your books would recognise your face, and you've passed the age when anyone would want to look at you.' She peered over Amy's shoulder, squinting at the letter. 'Who was fool enough to buy it?'

'He doesn't say. The buyer has asked to remain anonymous.'

If it was Spencer making another empty gesture, as he'd done at the charity auction, then poor Mr Jones wouldn't be paid. Wareham wouldn't be there to mop up after him this time or come to the rescue of his unpaid debt. She had to trust that Mr Jones or Mr Shaw, the gallery owner, wouldn't be foolish enough to hand over the painting to the buyer until the money had changed hands.

While Amy was worrying about Mr Jones being swindled by Spencer, Lucy leaned over and whispered to her. 'Will you come outside and sit with me on the veranda for a while?'

Bundled in blankets, they settled on the bench, listening to the sound of the waves as they blew in across the sand. Amy worried that the sight of the beach would remind Lucy of the accident, but she appeared more relaxed on the veranda than she had in the house, where the noise of the family seemed to have put a strain on her.

'Why are Hester and Conrad holding their engagement party here in Newport?' asked Amy. 'I can't believe it's for the reasons Marion suggests.'

Lucy rested her head on Amy's shoulder as if she was already exhausted by the subject. 'Marion refuses to hold the party in New York because she disapproves of Conrad. By holding it here, out of season, she's hoping no one will find out who Hester is marrying. There's also no obligation to invite anyone who'll look down on the match.'

'If she feels so strongly, why did she give her permission for the marriage to go ahead?'

'She had no choice. It was either a family wedding or an elopement, and Marion wouldn't want to have to explain that to our parents when they return from France. She promised to find us wealthy husbands from old New York society. As far as she's concerned, she's failed us and our parents. She sees only shame in the fact that we're both marrying men who have to work for their living.'

'At least she hasn't stopped you both following your hearts.'

'That's because we've refused to be talked out of it. We might appear compliant on the surface, but we know our own minds.'

If only Amy could have had the same strength of purpose as these young women when she was their age how different her life would be now. Seeing them stand up for what they believed in gave her hope for the future. Theirs was the generation that would secure the right to vote, the generation that would make a difference to the lives of every woman who came after them.

'Have you and Belmont started planning your wedding yet?'

'There's little to plan. It'll be a quiet affair, in Cape May. I hope you'll come.'

'Of course.' Amy blinked back her tears. 'Will you have a party to celebrate your engagement?'

'Belmont thinks we should, but I can't cope with being in a crowded room these days. I've lost the habit of society. I blame it on all those long quiet days of convalescence.'

'You suffered quite a knock when you came off that horse. It'll take time until you feel like yourself again.'

Lucy reached for the spot where her head had collided with the rock. The way she tensed suggested it was still tender. 'I don't think it's that. I'm perfectly fine. The accident has left no trace. I've grown up, that's all.'

The spirit of Lucy's youth had flown. Perhaps something more stable, more capable of finding happiness had taken its place. And yet, if she wasn't clear-headed enough to have worked out that the accident had caused the change in her character, was she in her right mind to have made the decision to marry?

'You're happy with Mr Belmont? You're sure he's the right choice? It's not too late to call off the engagement.' It wasn't Amy's intention to talk Lucy out of the marriage. No one should assume the right to do that. She simply needed to be sure Lucy was making the right choice.

'Belmont is offering me a quiet home by the sea and space to breathe. A place where I can be myself. He has a wonderful little dog too. Have you seen his dog?'

'It'll be a very different life to the one you're used to in New York.'

'When I look back at the person I was before the accident, it's like looking at a stranger. Everyone insists the head injury has changed me, but I think it's the life I've found with Belmont that has made the difference. Whatever caused it, I don't suppose it really matters.'

'Not as long as you're happy.'

There was a long pause before Lucy spoke, as if she was trying to find the right way to express what she was thinking, where the old Lucy would have stormed in.

'I want to thank you for everything you did for me after the accident. Belmont told me how quickly you reacted, making sure I was comfortable, and sending him to fetch a doctor when no one else knew what to do.'

'Anyone would have done the same.'

'But it wasn't anyone. It was you. You sat by my bed and held my hand, and made sure I was comfortable. You took control in a calm, steady way.'

'You were asleep for most of the time.'

'Not always. I observed more than you know. As my world slowly started to come back into focus, I realised you were the kind of woman I want to be. Living as Belmont's wife, away from my family, and away from New York, I think I have a chance of becoming that woman.'

'There's little in me to admire. I'm as guilty of making mistakes as anyone.'

'Our lives are better in so many ways because of you, Amy, and yet we take you for granted.'

'If you knew the things that went through my head, you wouldn't think so generously of me.'

The wind had brought the colour back to Lucy's cheeks and already she seemed brighter. 'Looking back, I'm ashamed of the way I treated Mr Wareham. I demanded his attention because he was a rich man, and I took advantage of his good nature, even though I didn't like him in the least. Not in the way of marrying him, anyway.'

Amy pushed down her anger. There was no point expressing the hurt Lucy had caused her, and the way she'd treated Wareham was unforgiveable.

'I tried so hard to make Wareham fall in love with me,' said Lucy, 'and yet whatever I did, it had no effect.'

'You can't make someone love you, however hard you try. That's not how the heart works.'

'I think his heart belongs to someone else, or else it's broken beyond repair. It's as if he's built a hard shell around it that nothing will crack.'

The wind was making Amy's eyes stream. She turned from Lucy and wiped away her tears. 'Perhaps you're right.'

'Belmont said Wareham was mightily pleased when he told him of our engagement. He blamed himself for my accident when it was actually my fault.'

Amy didn't contradict her, even though it was what Lucy wanted to hear. 'There's no point dwelling on the past. It will only make you unhappy.'

How many times had Amy told herself these words? Every night she'd whispered them over and over again, trying to settle her mind when sleep wouldn't come. What was done was done, and no amount of wishing could change it. The future, however, was still hers to grasp. If Wareham still loved her the way she suspected, then his heart was there for the taking. All she had to do was find a way to convince him she loved him too.

Chapter 42

Hester and Conrad's engagement party was held in a private room at the seafront hotel where the family was staying. As Marion had said, it was to be a small affair, without music or dancing, unless Amy could be persuaded to play the piano.

It was Lucy who usually supplied the music for family occasions, but despite Amy's entreaties, she refused to attend. By the time the evening of the party arrived, she'd already returned to Cape May to prepare for her own wedding.

It was important for Hester's sake to make an effort for the party, and Amy put aside her usual grey silk in favour of the oyster dress with the lilac wrap she'd worn for her portrait sittings. Knowing Wareham had been invited to the party, she wondered if he'd recognise the outfit and whether it would prompt him to speak to her, whether he'd be surprised to learn someone had purchased the painting after he'd expressed how much he disliked it.

Eleanor knocked on her door to let her know the carriage was waiting to take them to the party. She admired Amy's dress, and the satin shoes that would be ruined if it happened to rain. Eleanor was wearing one of her Worth dresses that had so far failed to see the light of day. The bold shade of the silk leeched the colour from her cheeks, the overly starched lace at the neck and cuffs giving it a brittle edge that did nothing to flatter her.

'Do you think it will ever be us, Amy, celebrating our engagement?'

Amy saw the despondency in Eleanor's expression, the defeat. She was nearly thirty and already she believed her life was over. What kind of a society would treat women so cruelly? The upcoming weddings of Lucy and Hester, both nearly ten years younger than Amy and Eleanor, brought their plight into sharp focus. Amy had her career as an author, but what would become of Eleanor? Since discovering Spencer's true character, she'd withdrawn into herself, stepping back from the charity work that Amy had hoped would give her a purpose in life. His deception had cut deep and sent her into a retreat, as if he'd been her last hope of salvation, the last hope either of them had of achieving a different life. Now, with all hope gone, she had nothing beyond the family home, nothing beyond being her father's daughter.

'Let's not think about that now,' said Amy. 'Tonight, we must celebrate Hester and Conrad's happiness.'

The gathering was a small affair, just as Marion had intended. Conrad's family lived too far away to make the trip, and on his side, there was only Mr and Mrs Craig, and Wareham.

Amy, Eleanor and their father were the last to arrive, thanks to Mr Eaton's insistence on having his coat pressed a second time to ensure it sat smoothly across his shoulders and showed off his figure to greatest effect. Amy had hoped that removing him from old New York society might have quashed his vanity, but if anything it had made it worse. With less competition, he considered himself the best-looking man in Newport.

Mrs Craig greeted Amy as soon as she arrived, eager to discuss the latest instalment of *Missing in Love*.

'The story of the thwarted lovers is perfection, but the work is so much more than that. The way you're showing your characters fighting for votes for women has the potential to change your readers' lives. If you ask me, this is your most important novel to date.' She nodded to Wareham, who was standing near the piano sipping a glass of champagne. 'I was only saying to Mr Wareham the other day what great work you're doing.'

Wareham looked away, pretending not to have heard, but Mrs Craig was determined to draw him into the conversation, beckoning him to join them with a forthrightness that verged on a summons.

Amy stared at her glass as, reluctantly, he wandered over. She didn't have to look at him to know he was making every effort not to catch her eye. He was still furious with her. She could tell by the way he held his shoulders, by the shallowness of his breath. If Mrs Craig sensed the awkwardness between them, she chose to ignore it as she continued with the conversation.

'Mr Wareham insists it isn't my place to mention it, but perhaps you could address the issue of the poor working conditions in the factories and on the railroads. Not in this novel, of course, but in your next one or in the one after that. I appreciate that if you put too many social issues in one story, you risk losing your readers and that can't be allowed to happen. Your primary aim is to entertain and that must never be neglected.'

Amy nodded, hardly taking in Mrs Craig's comments. Did Wareham really believe she'd attached herself to Spencer? Is that why he was so furious with her? He knew the man for what he really was. Surely he couldn't have been taken in by his talk of hanging her portrait in his stately home in England?

If Wareham knew anything of her character, he must know she wouldn't be so easily influenced by Spencer's overbearing charm. But of course, that wasn't the case. He considered her to be weak-minded. Why else would she have let Mrs Rawle talk her out of marrying him all those years ago? There was no reason for him to believe she was any different now, and for all her efforts, she'd failed to show him how much she regretted it.

If it wasn't anger he was holding onto, then perhaps it was

jealousy. She'd suspected him of it the night he stormed out of the exhibition, but knew better than to let herself believe it. Nevertheless, it kept alive a glowing cinder of hope that was just enough to keep her heart warm. After all, he was still here, when his work required him to be elsewhere.

'I'm surprised to see you still in Newport, Mr Wareham. Last time we spoke, you seemed very keen to leave.'

The slant of his lips told her he was chewing the inside of his cheek. It was something he always did when he was uncomfortable. She wanted to tell him to stop, that his mouth would be sore if he carried on.

'You're quite right, Miss Eaton. I did say that.'

She grinned, unable to resist teasing him. 'And yet, you're still here.'

He knew what she was playing at and it piqued him. 'So are you.'

'Unlike you, Mr Wareham, I have no alternative.'

Mrs Craig had been watching their exchange with amusement. She leaned her head towards Amy. 'We're having a little gathering tomorrow night. Nothing fancy, just a quiet dinner for a few friends. Mr Wareham will be there. Won't you come?'

She extended the invitation to Marion, who was standing off to one side, listening to their conversation. 'Bring the whole family. You're all welcome.'

Marion was silent while she thought about it. If they'd been in New York, she'd have refused instantly, but in Newport, with the best of society not there to witness it, it was harder to turn down the prospect of a good dinner, especially as she wouldn't be required to pay for it.

'I don't know, I . . .'

'Don't forget, we have tickets to a musical evening tomorrow night,' said Charles, coming to her rescue. 'Best seats in the house. Not a box, of course, but you can't expect anything better outside of New York.'

'Of course we have,' said Marion. Unable to make a decision, she turned to Amy. 'What should we do? Would you prefer to attend the musical evening or have dinner with Mr and Mrs Craig?'

'It would be a shame to refuse an invitation to dine with Mr and Mrs Craig,' said Amy, trying not to seem too eager. 'We can go to a musical evening another time.'

An evening in Wareham's company was much to be wished for. Amy gave him a pointed look, hoping he'd read more into her response than she was able to openly express. She enjoyed the company of the Craigs, but the opportunity to spend time with Wareham was her real reason for wanting to be there and she needed him to know it.

'That's all well and good,' said Marion, 'but the tickets are bought and paid for.'

'Perhaps we could change them for another evening,' said Amy, trying to find a solution to Marion's dilemma.

'But is it worth the trouble?' asked Marion. 'The musical evening is already agreed on.' She tapped Mrs Craig on the shoulder with her fan. 'You could always change your dinner to another night. Then we could attend without having to cancel our original plans.'

'I would gladly, but we have other guests joining us. I wouldn't want to put them off.'

Marion sighed. The idea of a good dinner was very tempting. 'Honestly, I don't know what to do.'

'We should accept Mrs Craig's invitation to dinner,' said Amy, repeating her assertion. 'We can attend a musical evening another time. Don't you agree, Mr Wareham?'

He couldn't ignore her direct question. It would appear rude when so many sets of eyes were on him, waiting for his answer. He cleared his throat and stared at his glass. 'There are enough people here capable of influencing your decision, Miss Eaton. Whatever I say will make no difference.'

'Then that's settled,' said Charles. 'We'll go to the musical evening. Thank you for your invitation, Mrs Craig. Perhaps we can do it another time.'

Marion looked at her husband, visibly relieved that, for once, Charles had said something useful, even if it did mean they were missing out on a good dinner.

Mrs Rawle, who had observed the whole exchange, took Amy aside, lowering her voice so as not to be overheard. 'You should be a little more discerning about the company you keep. You wouldn't want Mr Wareham to get his hopes up again where you're concerned. He might be rich, but that still doesn't make him a suitable match.'

Now it was Amy's turn to bite the inside of her cheek. She no longer cared for Mrs Rawle's opinion, even if she was too polite to say so.

More than anything, she wanted to have dinner at the Craigs, to sit for one evening at the same table as Wareham, even if he despised her. It might be the last opportunity she'd ever have to be in his company, her last chance to rescue the situation between them; that was, if there was any chance of rescuing it at all. Even if there was no hope of a reconciliation between them, was spending a few final hours with him too much to wish for? Clearly it was. Sensing his eyes on her, she turned to look at him.

'I was right,' he whispered. 'Once again you allow a disinterested person to influence your decision.'

The words stung more than she could say. If only he could see what was in front of him. If only she could tell him what she really felt. The shame couldn't be any worse than what she was suffering now. But what good would it do? His anger was as raw and blinding as ever. And if it was jealousy, then it was proving to be just as destructive as his rage. The pain she'd caused him had cut his soul to pieces. He would never love her again. He didn't even like her.

She was rescued from her thoughts by Hester, begging her to play the piano, so they could roll back the carpet and dance.

'I would have asked Lucy to play, but she's not here.'

Lucy's absence was the only blight on Hester's happiness. Every time she looked at Conrad, the love shone from her eyes. 'All right, but I haven't played in a while. Don't listen too closely.'

It wasn't the music that mattered, but the dancing. The opportunity to focus on the one you loved, to move to the rhythm with a single purpose, to feel connected in body and soul.

Amy had only played the first few bars when she felt Wareham's presence beside her, his eyes following the notes on the sheet music as he leaned forward, ever so slightly, at her shoulder.

The tension between them subsided, as gradually, their breaths began to match the tempo of the tune, as if they too were dancing. She tried not to let his closeness bother her, concentrating harder, defying her fingers to grow clumsy at his nearness. She knew how much he loved music, remembered how many evenings they'd spent together in this manner. She'd never been an expert player, but in those days, she'd always been good enough, good enough for him, at least.

'May I?'

He turned over the sheet music at exactly the right moment. She carried on playing, wordlessly, reliving the joy of those past evenings eight years ago, wallowing in his passion for music, recalling how his enjoyment had made her want to play better. Now, she fought to keep the rhythm steady, trying not to rush the piece, wanting to make it last forever.

She took a deep breath as she reached the end, flexing her fingers to take away the ache. She'd never been so tense when playing a popular song. She turned to him and looked up, surprised to see his eyes still fixed on the piano keys.

Desperate to keep him near, she said the first thing that came into her head. 'Thank you for buying my book at the auction. The money will do an immense amount of good for the charity.' She didn't mention that she knew Spencer had failed to honour his winning bid, that she knew he'd stepped in to save the day.

'It was for a good cause. I was glad to help.'

He hadn't run away when she spoke, so she pushed him a little further. 'Have you opened it?'

She didn't care whether he'd read it. She only wanted to know if he'd seen the dedication, whether he'd understood the message she'd risked all by including.

'No, I . . .' He began chewing the inside of his cheek again.

'Of course, you're a busy man. I wouldn't expect you to read it, and I'm not looking for praise.' Her mouth had run away with her and she'd said more than she'd intended. He would think her vain, expecting compliments for her work.

'You must forgive me, Miss Eaton, for not having read the book. It's just that I . . .' He picked up the pile of sheet music and started sifting through it. 'Will you play something else? Hester and Conrad are looking restless and are keen to dance.' He placed a sheet of music in front of her. 'I think you'll find this is familiar.'

It was a tune she'd played for him endlessly at one time, the one that had been his favourite. She nodded, fighting back the swell of tears. 'I remember it well.'

'No one plays it like you, Amy.'

Amy. No longer *Miss Eaton.* The familiarity, the fondness had slipped out without him realising and she held the memory of it close to her heart as she played. She knew the piece well enough not to need the music, but she paused anyway at the right moment, prompting him to turn over the page, the light tapping of his forefinger as he rested his hand on the piano drawing him in, making him a part of the performance, and once again, with nothing spoken between them, it was as if they were one.

When the piece came to an end, he went to fetch her a drink. Amy tried to compose herself as she watched him make his way across the room with a steadiness of purpose that was all for her benefit. Was it real? Was Wareham really paying her attention? It was easier when they didn't speak, when they just let themselves be. Everyone else in the room was chatting and drinking. No one was taking any notice of them, apart from Mrs Craig, who smiled and raised her glass the moment Amy happened to catch her eye.

Eleanor had set herself aside from the gathering and was looking out of the window, idly observing the comings and goings of the street. Suddenly she let out a squeal, as if a spider had run across her foot. But it was much more terrible than that.

'Look, it's Spencer. There he is. He's just climbed out of a hansom cab. If I'm not mistaken, Mrs Canby is with him.'

'It can't be Mrs Canby,' said Amy. 'You told me yourself, she's in Providence.'

'Are you sure it's him?' Mr Eaton rushed to the window to see for himself. 'It's not his usual carriage.'

Amy didn't wait for an answer. She brushed aside the drink as Wareham tried to hand it to her and ran out of the room. Spencer was a swindler, but he wouldn't get away with it. She was determined to catch up with him and make him pay the debt he owed her father. And if Mrs Canby was with him, she wanted to know what she was playing at.

Her eyes scanned left and right as she left the hotel, squinting at the blinding pools of light spilling from the gas lamps that lined the deserted road. There was no sign of Spencer or Mrs Canby anywhere, no sign of the carriage that had brought them here. Undaunted, she widened her search, marching determinedly through the town, scouring every street and checking every blind corner.

When she failed to find them, she moved farther afield, increasing her pace as she scouted the coastal road, shivering all the way in the damp night air. She didn't doubt Eleanor's sighting, but Spencer was as slippery as an eel, and wherever he was, he was determined not to be found.

The rain that had threatened all day finally began to spit. Retracing her steps along the shoreline, she sensed a storm brewing. She could feel it in the air, feel the weight of the thunder clouds gathering overhead as with each step the rain grew heavier, until finally, she had no choice but to admit defeat. There was no point in continuing her search in foul weather when Spencer would already have gone to ground.

By the time she returned to the hotel, she was soaked, her dress and shoes splattered with the dirt from the road. As she entered the lobby, she spotted Wareham on his way out, his face as stormy as the ocean breeze whipping up outside. She rushed forward to intercept him, the rain dripping from the ends of her hair.

'Are you leaving already?'

He glanced at her shoes, at the trail of wet footprints she'd left on the tiled floor. 'There's nothing to stay for. I was a fool to ever think there was.'

She couldn't let him leave now, not after they'd been getting along so well. 'There's a storm brewing. At least wait until it blows over.'

He continued towards the door, his eyes still focused on the floor. How could she delay him without resorting to begging? What words could she summon to make him stay? Frustrated by his pride, and her failure to find Spencer and hold him to account, she shouted after him.

'Why do you always leave?'

The question was enough to make him stop and turn around. 'You can't expect me to stay and watch you run after another man.'

'It's not what you think.'

'I saw the determination in your eyes, the speed with which you ran after him.'

'But—'

'I saw the article in the newspaper. Mrs Tyler took great pride in showing it to me when she delivered the book I'd won at the auction. She glowed over the fact that now you were to become a titled lady, my prize would increase in value.'

'The information in the article was false.'

'I was at the exhibition when Spencer talked of hanging your portrait in his ancestral home in England. Now, one hint that he's outside the hotel and you run after him.'

He pulled on his gloves, stepping around her as she tried to block his way to the door. 'He's an earl. He'll make you a countess. I could offer you many things, Miss Eaton, but I can't compete with that.'

'If only you'll let me explain.'

But already he was gone, leaving her standing in the doorway. She considered going after him, but there was no getting through to him in this mood, and after he'd seen her running after Spencer, he would only condemn her for it.

People in the lobby were staring, murmuring about her unseemly behaviour. She shook the rain from her skirt, trying to restore her dignity. She didn't realise Marion was watching her until she heard her voice.

'Come back to the party at once. You're making a spectacle of yourself.'

'I'll be there in a minute.' After her exchange with Wareham she was too wounded to face anyone.

'You'll come with me now.' She grabbed Amy's arm and began dragging her back to their private room, away from prying eyes. 'How could you behave so shamefully in front of everyone?'

'I went to confront Spencer over the money he owes Father.'

'Eleanor now thinks she might have been mistaken, that it wasn't Spencer she saw after all, but some other fine man. The situation is not good. We need to find something to occupy her mind and break her of this obsession she has with him.'

Amy took in little of Marion's words. All she could think of was Wareham. After what he'd just seen of her, he'd be more determined to leave Newport than ever, and she'd never see him again. She thought back to the night at the exhibition. As he left the gallery, he'd proclaimed there was nothing for him to stay for. He must have come tonight to see if they had another chance, and her determination to hold Spencer to account had ruined it. After the way he'd perceived her behaviour, he'd be more certain than ever that they had no future together.

Chapter 43

Eleanor and Mr Eaton were out of sorts the morning after the party, thanks not so much to the champagne, but the inferior brandy that followed it, while Amy was still reeling from yet another fraught exchange with Wareham.

It was almost lunchtime when Eleanor wandered into her room looking pale and still in her nightdress, her hair unpinned.

'I've just received a letter from Mrs Canby. It's the most curious thing.'

My dearest Eleanor,
By the time this letter reaches you, the Earl of Hokeham and I will already be married and on our way to England! I told you I'd snare myself a rich husband before long and I've gone and done it!

What a whirlwind it's been, but given my particular circumstances, you can understand why I agreed to marry Spencer the very second he proposed. I had no idea he had such intense feelings for me until very recently. We only started to get to know one another after we were thrown together at the opening of the exhibition at Shaw's gallery. If you remember, Amy became unaccountably upset over something, but refused

to say what it was, and you both left without me, abandoning
me to make my own way home. Thankfully, Spencer came to
my rescue and offered to escort me back safely. Who would
have guessed that a simple carriage ride could lead to my life
changing in such a miraculous way?

You'll excuse my little white lie about visiting a friend in
Providence. That was Spencer's idea, dreamed up to save your
sister the humiliation of knowing we were planning to leave
town together. Please offer her my apologies, but Spencer has
assured me he never had any serious intentions towards her,
and I don't believe she cared for him anyway.

Thank you for having me to stay these past months, but I
won't be returning to your quaint little house in Newport ever
again. Help yourself to any fripperies I might have left behind,
or donate them to one of your charitable causes.

Yours
Mrs Olivia Canby (soon to be Countess!)

Amy read the letter, fitting together the loose pieces of Mrs
Canby's story. She seemed to have no idea that Spencer was penni-
less and in debt, that he'd probably only married her because she'd
led him to believe she was wealthy and an heiress to the family
banking fortune. It was hard to know whether to laugh or cry at
the foolishness of both parties. Each had married the other for
their money when neither of them had a cent.

'How long will it be before Mrs Canby works out Spencer is a
gold digger?' asked Eleanor, after Amy had read the letter.

'She'll realise it as soon as Spencer discovers she's no dollar
princess.'

Amy doubted they'd make it as far as England. Spencer would
abandon her as soon as he realised she had nothing to her name,
whether they were married or not. She was glad she hadn't fallen
for his charm. It was Wareham she had to thank for it. While
her heart still belonged to him, no one else had a chance of

capturing it.

Eleanor shifted about the room, restless now with nothing to occupy her and not even Mrs Canby for company.

'Are you writing today? Would you like to go out?'

Amy was too preoccupied, trying to figure out the ending of *Missing in Love* to notice Eleanor's question.

Whichever way she looked at it, she couldn't find a way to reconcile the estranged lovers. For all her efforts, they were still so far apart, still with so many misunderstandings between them. She couldn't allow coincidence to bring them together. Her readers deserved better from her at this stage of the plot and they would never forgive her if the ending wasn't meaningful.

Experience had taught her that the final chapter of any book made up the reader's mind as to whether they would buy her next one. It was the lasting impression that stayed with them, and Amy owed it to them to make it satisfying. There was too much at stake for things to end badly.

If only the rules of society were different. If only she could allow her heroine to stride up to the man she loved and tell him exactly how she felt, tell him his assumptions about her were wrong. If only she could grab him by the shoulders and shake him until the realisation struck, and he finally accepted that, for all the years they'd been apart, she'd never stopped loving him, that if anything, she loved him more than ever.

It was impossible, of course, constrained as they were by a society that disallowed an unmarried woman to be alone with a man, where the rules stated she couldn't cross the room to speak to him, couldn't seek him out. How was the truth to be made known if she had to risk being ostracised for speaking it?

She'd made her hero too stubborn, too blinded by his anger and his jealousy to be able to open his heart, to give her heroine an opportunity to prove her love. He wasn't the kind of man who would listen to reason when he was caught up in such a passion, or to see what she'd plainly set in front of him.

If only she could go back and rewrite the whole story from the beginning, then she could change things. She could plant something in an early chapter that would be the key to their reconciliation. She could make her hero less heartbroken, her heroine more assertive. But it was too late for any of that. Most of the novel had already been published and there was no going back on it. She had no choice but to work with what she'd created and find a way to make the best of it.

'Are you listening to me, Amy? What would you like to do?'

Amy finally looked up from her work. 'I'm sorry, Eleanor. What did you say?'

'I'm bored. I'm permanently bored. What use am I to anyone or anything?'

'Would you like to go back to New York for a while? Perhaps you could stay with Marion.'

'I'm tired of the rounds of dances and nights at the opera, tired of the same old people, the same old stories, and I'm tired of standing on the sidelines, watching the younger women being asked to dance. No one will miss me if I'm not there. Soon, I won't even be required to chaperone Hester.'

These days, Hester spent most of her time with Conrad, expecting Eleanor to act as her chaperone when Marion wasn't able to oblige. It hadn't crossed Hester's mind what a cruel thing it was to ask of a disappointed spinster. Amy sighed, frustrated by Eleanor's lack of motivation. 'What is it you want?'

'I want to be myself. I want to look in the mirror each morning and know I'm worth something.'

'How about your charity work? You seemed inspired by it until Spencer came along.'

'What difference will macramé pot holders make to anyone's life? Is that what I'm to be remembered for?'

Amy longed to tell Eleanor that her destiny was in her own hands, but given the society they lived in, it would have been a lie. 'Are you prepared to work, Eleanor? To dedicate yourself to a project the way you would dedicate yourself to a husband? Are you willing to worry more about others than you care about your Worth dresses?'

'I'm not like you, Amy. I can't write novels. I see how hard it is, the commitment it takes.'

'I'm not talking about writing novels. I'm thinking of something else.'

It was seeing the work Violet did that had given Amy the idea, that and the auction organised by the local ladies charity board to raise money for the women who wanted to learn skills that would equip them for the workplace. If they could form an institution to teach secretarial skills such as Violet was offering, and merge it with the training the charity board gave in trades such as millinery and dressmaking, it would broaden the opportunities for women to gain decent paid work.

'I'm suggesting we set up a night school for women to learn any number of skills to match their talents and enable them to get respectable, safe jobs. We'd need someone to organise and run it. It's a huge task. Would you consider doing it?'

No one had ever asked anything of Eleanor beyond planning the family meals for the week with the cook and ordering dresses from Worth twice a year. This would be the first time she'd stepped outside of her safe domestic environment and into the wider world.

Eleanor stared at the floor, uncertain of herself. 'I wouldn't know how to do it.'

'You've run Father's house and managed the staff since you were barely more than a child. Nobody taught you how to do that after Mother died. You worked it out as you went along. You can do the same with the night school.'

'I made such a mess of managing the household accounts. Why would anyone trust me?'

'Because you're smart enough to learn from your mistakes. If I can convince people to help us fund it, I can convince them to give you a chance to organise it. Their trust in you will follow, but it will have to be earned.'

Eleanor pulled her silk robe tighter around her body. 'What if I fail? What if nobody comes to the night school and I waste all the money that will have been raised? What if I make a stupid mistake and let everybody down?'

'What if you succeed? Think what the achievement will mean to you, the difference it will make to other women's lives.'

It might not have been the happy ever after Eleanor had hoped for, but it would give her a purpose and her efforts would benefit others.

'I couldn't do it alone. Would you help me?'

'I have to start writing another novel as soon as I've finished *Missing in Love*. Violet is already doing something similar to what I'm proposing. She might be willing to assist you, if you're prepared to give it a try.'

Eleanor was silent for a long time while she thought about it. 'We'd need rooms to teach in, books, pens and paper, materials and the tools for dressmaking and millinery, equipment for stenography. We'd have to pay the tutors and Violet, of course. We couldn't expect them to work for nothing. If the women who came to us to study had children, we'd want to be able to offer a nursery facility to look after them during their lessons. It would cost a great deal. How would we raise the money?'

Amy handed her half a dozen sheets of paper and a pen. 'Start making a list of everything we'll need and what it will cost, and leave the rest to me.'

For the first time in as long as she could remember, Eleanor offered Amy a smile. 'I'll try not to let you down.'

Amy reached out and gave her a hug, fighting back the tears as Eleanor's brittle exterior yielded to her touch. One day, they would only have each other to rely on, and if they couldn't be kind to one another, what kind of life would be left for them?

Chapter 44

Amy found Mrs Craig in the private drawing room at the hotel where she was staying. She was planning on asking her opinion on the idea of establishing a night school for the local women, and if she approved, she'd then ask if she'd be interested in helping to raise funds for it. Her proposal was all worked out. Equipping women with the skills needed for the modern workplace would benefit employers such as the Craigs, as well as the women themselves. Most importantly, women deserved the right to independence, so they were no longer completely reliant on men.

The Craigs were sitting around a table, poring over the plans for the new house with Conrad and Wareham when she arrived.

'Forgive me for interrupting, I . . .'

Amy hadn't expected to see Wareham. He'd made it clear more than once that there was nothing to keep him in Newport and she'd assumed that, by now, he'd already be on his way back to California or New York. At the sight of him, the speech she'd worked out to convince Mrs Craig to support the night school flew out of her head.

He glanced up from the plans as she entered, but looked away again without catching her eye.

Mrs Craig stood up to greet her. If she noticed any awkwardness, she was too polite to show it. 'How lovely to see you, Miss Eaton. Come and look at the plans for the new house and tell me what you think. Mr Craig won't be convinced that the dining room should have French doors leading out into the garden. Tell him I'm right.'

As Amy approached the plans, Wareham got to his feet and withdrew from the table. 'You may take my seat. I have a letter to write.'

Amy fixed her eyes on the vacated chair. 'There's no need to move on my account. There's plenty of room at the table for all of us.'

Ignoring her words, he retreated to the writing desk in the corner and reached for a pen. There was a subtle art to burying a snub in a gesture of good manners, but he'd managed to achieve it, and nobody appeared to notice apart from Amy.

Mrs Craig frowned at him from across the room. 'Can the letter not wait until later?'

'Mr Belmont needs answers to the questions he has regarding the steel mesh design for lining the hosepipes. If we're to move ahead with the project, I should address them sooner rather than later.'

Amy took his seat and looked at the plans with interest. If Wareham was determined to inflict a wound, she would show herself resistant to it. 'French doors leading out onto the garden are a lovely idea. Imagine the scent of roses and jasmine drifting into the dining room during the summer evenings.'

Conrad nodded, furiously scribbling notes on the drawing. Mr Craig rolled his eyes in a good-humoured show of defeat. 'I should have known you'd give my wife romantic ideas, Miss Eaton.'

'We're all romantics at heart, my dear,' said Mrs Craig, slapping him on the shoulder, 'even if some of us try not to show it.' She threw a look at Wareham, who failed to acknowledge what must have been a joke between them. Whatever conversation was taking place around the table, he seemed determined to remain focused on composing his letter.

'Talking of romantics,' continued Mrs Craig, 'I hope you didn't suffer too much at the hands of that conniving English earl.'

'Not at all,' replied Amy. 'We can only hope Mrs Canby has enough strength of character to withstand any trials he throws her way now they're married.'

'They're married?' Mrs Canby glanced at Wareham, who was too engrossed in his letter to notice. 'Who would ever have thought it?'

'My sister received a letter from Mrs Canby this morning, informing her of the wedding.'

Mrs Craig chuckled. 'Well, we wish them the very best of happiness. If you ask me, the man's a rogue, but Mrs Canby will be more than a match for him. It's you I'm most concerned about, Miss Eaton.'

'I always suspected he was too good to be true. His manners were too perfect to be real. I could never trust a man who consistently displays such an even temper. It suggests either a lack of feeling, or that he's hiding something. In his case, he turned out to be guilty of both.'

Mrs Craig glanced at Wareham. 'You're quite right. You can't know where you are with a man if he refuses to admit his true feelings.' She cleared her throat, turning her attention back to Amy. 'Rumour has it that Spencer owes money all over town.'

'I can't speak for others, but he owes my father a good deal. It's the reason I ran into the street the other night at Conrad and Hester's engagement party. Eleanor thought she'd spotted him climbing out of a hansom cab and I was determined to confront him.'

Mr Craig was still frowning at the plans. 'I doubt you'll see that money again.'

'I'm worried he might also have my portrait. Whoever bought it at the exhibition insisted on remaining anonymous. I can't stand the thought of Spencer possessing it, and Mr Jones can't afford not to be paid for his work. I hope he wasn't taken in by him, as many people were, including most of my family.'

'Not everyone was fooled by him,' replied Mrs Craig. 'Our dear Wareham here suspected him right from the start. It was thanks to his generosity that Spencer's bid on your book was honoured.'

Wareham turned the pen irritably in his fingers. 'That information was supposed to be kept between the two of us.'

'It's the worst-kept secret in town,' said Amy. 'The ladies on the charity board are very grateful to you and have insisted on telling everyone.'

Mrs Craig grinned, as if the devil had got into her. 'Mr Wareham is too shy to admit it to you himself, but he's read the novel from cover to cover, not once, but twice, and claims it was worth every cent he paid for it and more besides.'

Amy thought of the message she'd written inside the book. She watched him from across the room as he concentrated on finishing his letter, a seam of hope running through her veins. She was desperate to know if the sentiments she'd expressed in the dedication meant anything to him, but however much she tried to catch his eye, he refused to look up.

Mrs Craig was still grinning. 'He's also read every instalment of *Missing in Love* and is curious to know how it ends.'

Why would Wareham waste so much time reading her work when he was such a busy man? Or was he simply humouring Mrs Craig, who always showed so much enthusiasm for Amy's work, who even now, despite looking at the house plans, was more interested in talking about *Missing in Love*.

'We all want to know whether the estranged lovers will be reunited after so many years apart, when it's clear they are still in love, despite their misunderstandings and the obstacles that have been put in their way.' Mrs Craig waved her hands as she continued, warming to her theme. 'It bothers me that the fierce, independent spirit of the heroine might be too much for the

291

hero. He's so full of pride and feels very hard done by.' She gave Amy a pointed look. 'How will you bring them together when his stubbornness is preventing him from talking to her?'

'Honestly, I don't know. The ending troubles me day and night and I have very little time left to work it out.'

Conrad, who'd been concentrating on adding the French doors to the plans, suddenly looked up. 'Sometimes, people receive help from an unexpected quarter. For instance, if Mr and Mrs Craig hadn't engaged me to build their house, Hester and I would have no hope of ever marrying. Now look at us. The wedding will take place in the summer, and we have our whole future ahead of us. Before I received Mr and Mrs Craig's patronage, the best we could hope for was a long engagement, and even that was in doubt.'

Mr Craig patted him on the back. 'It's Wareham you've got to thank for it. He's the one who convinced us to employ you.'

Wareham looked up when Mr Craig said his name. Amy caught his eye, registering the hollowness lurking behind his expression. It was Conrad's mention of a long engagement that had triggered it. He must have been remembering the moment she'd turned down his suggestion of the very same thing, having been talked into breaking off their engagement altogether.

At the time, Mrs Rawle had persuaded her she was doing it for Wareham's sake, leaving him free to pursue his career. If he'd really loved her, he'd have come back for her once he'd made his fortune, but he never did. In all the years that had since passed, he'd failed to write her a single letter.

'Long engagements aren't the fashion these days,' added Mrs Craig. 'You only have to consider Miss Morton and Mr Belmont's determination to marry so quickly to see that. You have to wonder about the constancy of that young man's heart. His previous fiancée has only been dead a matter of months, and yet he's already found another and is all set to marry.'

'A woman wouldn't have recovered so quickly from her attachment,' said Amy, jumping on the subject a little too eagerly. 'We're more constant by nature than any man. We continue to love where all hope is gone.'

Mr Craig frowned. 'What proof do you have of that?'

'I have experience enough to know it. The rules of our society dictate that we women have to keep our feelings to ourselves. If we betray our hearts, or appear too forward in our behaviour, we risk public shame and the loss of our closest friends and family, who would cast us out at the slightest sign of impropriety to save their own social standing.'

'You're mistaken,' replied Mr Craig. 'It's men who feel it the most. You only have to read the work of the poets, or listen to the words of any popular song to know it.'

Wareham, who was still writing his letter, dropped his pen, quickly picking it up again before the ink bled onto the paper. He then sealed it in an envelope and immediately began writing another.

Amy continued, hardly noticing whether he was listening or not. 'One of the reasons I became a writer was to give women a voice. Men have always had the power of the pen, the freedom to put their side of the story down on paper for everyone to read, while women, apart from a few favoured authoresses, are required to stay silent.

'Even now, the work written by women is rarely read by men. Or if it is, it's simply dismissed as sentimental or condemned for dealing with domestic matters, when the home and the family are at the centre of almost everyone's lives, or they fail to see the underlying seriousness in the themes embedded within the stories. Until our voices are heard more widely, our stories read more closely, the world will assume women have nothing of importance to say, no feelings to express, when the truth is that we feel most deeply.'

Conrad looked up from the plans, affronted by Amy's comment. 'You say a man doesn't feel as deeply as a woman?'

'I'm saying that men are able to speak for themselves without judgement. They also have the ability to go out into the world and find distractions to help mend their broken hearts, while women are obliged to stay at home with nothing to fill their time but family duty and regret.'

'You're the exception to this though, Miss Eaton,' added Mr Craig.

'I am, but I'm looked down on for the novels I write and am accused of degrading my family by the people closest to me. Still, I won't let it prevent me speaking for the women who are unable to speak for themselves, so they can be more sympathetically understood.'

The conversation must have become too dull for Wareham, who got up from the desk. 'Please excuse me. I must see this letter is delivered immediately.' He strode out of the room and was gone before anyone had the opportunity to say goodbye.

Bewildered by the sudden change in his behaviour, Mrs Craig glanced at the desk where he'd been sitting. She frowned at the paper and the envelopes he'd left in disarray. 'What could be urgent enough to make him run off like that?'

Seconds later, the door flew open and Wareham dashed back into the room, more flustered than Amy had ever seen him.

'Forgive me. I left my gloves behind.'

He snatched his gloves from where he'd been sitting and made for the door, handing a letter to Amy on his way out, which he'd retrieved from beneath the scattered papers he'd abandoned on the desk. She caught his eye for a brief moment before he was gone, without a single word passing between them.

Mr Craig looked up from the plans at the sound of the door closing. 'Wareham is behaving most strangely. I don't know what's got into him lately.'

Amy tried to appear calm as she held the letter. Why would Wareham go to the trouble of writing to her while they were sitting in the same room? If he had something to say, why couldn't he just say it? Was he still too angry to have a conversation with her, even after all this time? She waited until Mrs Craig had returned to the discussion about the French doors before she opened it and read it.

I struggle to keep my hand steady as I write. I can remain silent no longer. You are too unjust, too harsh when you talk of a man's inconstant heart. Oh, how little you know of it. You have undone me with talk of a woman's constancy. Know a man can love long and deeply, even when all hope is gone.

The message you wrote in the book, and every word you have written in Missing in Love has renewed my hope. Do you think I don't recognise myself on every page? Let me be the one to help you find the happy ending you seek for your characters. Please do not mistake my despair for anger. I am yours and always have been. It is the chance of being in your company that brought me to Newport, the pleasure of hearing your voice that makes me stay. My love for you grows deeper, my admiration for you greater with each passing moment. I offer you my heart, fuller and stronger than when you broke it all those years ago. Tell me I'm not too late.

If I have mistaken your defence of a woman's constancy for a veiled expression of your enduring love, then forgive me. One word, one look from you will tell me whether I should stay in Newport or leave. I cannot watch you read this letter, but will remain close by in agony, in hope.

Wareham

Love, hope, despair. Wareham's words danced before her eyes. He loved her. Beyond everything, he loved her. Her hand shook as she clutched the letter, reading it over and over again. It was too much to take in, too much to expect after so many years of longing. Everything she wished for was here, laid out before her in a few simple words. Wareham was offering her his heart.

'Miss Eaton, are you all right? You're looking very pale.' Mrs

Craig was standing over her, one hand gentle on her shoulder. 'Shall I fetch you some water?'

Amy shook her head, trying to regain control of her senses. 'No, thank you, I'm fine. I need some fresh air, that's all.'

She had to find Wareham. He was out there somewhere, waiting for her, waiting for a sign from her. One look was all he was asking for when she had so much more to give him. She took a breath to steady herself, her legs almost giving way under her as she struggled out of the chair.

Mrs Craig watched her with concern. 'You're not well, Miss Eaton. Allow me a moment to fetch my coat. I won't let you go out alone while you're this unsteady.'

'Please don't trouble yourself, I'm fine.'

The last thing she needed was Mrs Craig's company. How could she speak openly, truthfully to Wareham while someone else was standing by?

'If you won't let me accompany you, then I'll send for a carriage.'

To be hidden in a carriage would be even worse. If she passed him on the road, he'd think she was running away from him.

'Thank you for your kindness, Mrs Craig, but I intend to walk. A little fresh air is all I need to clear my head.'

'Then I insist on coming with you. I'll never forgive myself if you had a bad turn on the street.'

'Honestly, I—'

'Give me five minutes to change my shoes and put on my hat and coat.'

'But . . .'

Five minutes more and Wareham could be anywhere. It could take hours to find him. They'd wasted too much time already. There wasn't another minute to lose.

Mr Craig looked up from the plans and grinned as his wife dashed out of the room. 'There's no talking Mrs Craig out of anything once she's set her mind to it, so you might as well resign yourself to accepting her help.'

Five minutes turned into ten. Amy read over the letter again, restlessly pacing the room while she waited for Mrs Craig. How long did it take to put on a pair of shoes, a coat and a hat? So much time had passed already. What must Wareham be thinking? And where would she find him? He could have wandered anywhere in the town by now.

'Here we are.'

Mrs Craig finally burst into the room. Not only had she changed her shoes, but her whole outfit. 'I thought it might be a little chilly for the house dress I was wearing, so I changed the muslin for a heavier cotton with long sleeves. Then of course, I had to find the right shoes and a coat to match.' She pinned her hat blindly in place as she talked. 'Are you ready to go?'

Amy nodded. Already she was waiting at the door, not thinking of her manners as she left Mr Craig and Conrad poring over the plans for the new house without so much as a backward glance. Nothing existed beyond her need to find Wareham. There'd already been too much agony, too many wasted years. It was time to start living again.

Chapter 45

'Where would you like to go, my dear? Shall I walk you straight home?'

Mrs Craig's question hung in the air, wrapped in her gentle concern. All Amy could think about was finding Wareham, but she had no idea where to start. He could be wandering the streets in the town or strolling along the beach. If he was on the beach, he could be anywhere. The sand stretched for miles in each direction.

She thought of the day in Cape May when she'd watched him looking out across the ocean, how still he'd seemed, how at one with the stormy landscape. If only she'd had the courage to approach him then, if only he'd turned around and looked at her, how different things could have been. And yet all was not lost.

'Let's walk along the beach for a while.'

She tried to sound like her usual self. It was unfair to cause Mrs Craig unnecessary worry. She wasn't ill. She'd never felt better, more hopeful in her life.

While she scoured the deserted beach for Wareham, Amy told Mrs Craig about her plan to establish a night school for women, and how she intended Eleanor to run it.

'It's an excellent idea. You must allow me to help you raise the funds. I know other industrialists who might be willing to get involved, and if they aren't, I'll make sure their wives convince them of the wisdom of it. We can advise on the sorts of skills we need in our workplaces, perhaps help to facilitate some of the training. I'll also consider employing any of the women you instruct.'

This was more than Amy could ever have wished for. 'Thank you. You're in a position to win the support of people I could never hope to reach.'

If the night school scheme was successful in Newport, there was no saying they couldn't roll it out in other parts of the country. Eleanor was going to be very busy.

As they talked, Amy's eyes continued to scour the beach for Wareham. Perhaps she'd made the wrong choice in searching for him here. Perhaps he'd walked into the town or returned to his hotel. For all she knew he'd had a change of heart and gone straight back to New York or was on his way to California, never to be seen again.

The wind had turned cold and relentless. Grains of sand blew into her eyes, forcing the tears to come.

Mrs Craig looked at her with concern. 'This weather's doing you no good. You're not yourself. I'll call a carriage to take you home.'

'Let's walk a little further.' Amy refused to give up her search so soon. She stopped to blow her nose, reaching in her pocket for a handkerchief. All the while, Mrs Craig kept talking, expressing her excitement for the night school.

'You and Eleanor must come to lunch soon, so you can tell me your plans and we can work out the best way to enable them.' She paused to catch her breath, her eyes squinting against the wind. 'Look, there's Wareham. I wonder what he's doing on the beach all alone. He must have taken a very odd route to post his letter.'

He was sitting on the edge of a rock, sheltered from the breeze, his elbows resting on his knees as he watched the waves roll in across the sand.

He looked up as Mrs Craig called his name, waving her arm above her head to catch his attention. As soon as he saw them, he stood up, the wind blowing the edge of his coat, not daring to approach until Amy began walking rapidly towards him, fighting her instinct to break into a run.

'I thought I might find you on the beach. I know how much you love the ocean.' She pulled the crumpled letter from her pocket and pressed it against her heart. 'Thank you for your letter.'

Mrs Craig shuddered against the wind. 'Miss Eaton wasn't feeling herself. She thought a breath of air might do her good.'

Wareham's eyes remained fixed on Amy's face. 'Are you feeling better, Miss Eaton?'

'So much better.'

A wave crashed along the shore, its bubbling foam catching the hem of Mrs Craig's skirt before retreating across the sand as quickly as it came. She looked at her feet and sighed. 'These city shoes won't survive another minute of this and neither will I.' She shook the water from her skirt and glanced at Wareham. 'As Miss Eaton is feeling better, you won't mind if I leave her in your care.'

Wareham dragged his eyes from Amy's gaze. 'Of course. Would you like me to walk you back to your hotel, Mrs Craig?'

'There's no need.' She gave them a knowing look. 'I think the two of you can put aside social conventions and do without a chaperone from now on.'

Once they were alone, Wareham offered Amy his arm. She gladly took it, her heart soaring higher than the seabirds coasting on the breeze.

'You read my letter?'

'More than once.'

'I hope I didn't say anything to offend you.'

'Not at all. I'm only sorry you didn't write to me sooner.'

She held onto his arm, a lost traveller returning home after so many years in the wilderness. There was so much to say, so much lost time to make up for, yet the silence spread out before them like the endless stretch of sand. Not strained, as it had been before, but companionable.

When the wind dropped, Wareham finally began to speak. 'I wanted to write to you immediately after we'd parted all those years ago, but found it impossible to find the words to express how I felt. As time went on, rather than dwelling on what I'd lost, I devoted myself completely to my work, determined to make the world a better, safer place.'

'You should be proud of what you've achieved.'

'My success has meant little without you at my side to share it.'

'If only you'd written to me.'

'I worked day and night, putting the symptoms of my broken heart down to my exhaustion. Eventually, I was able to convince myself I'd forgotten you. I was a fool to think it was ever possible.'

'It was a mistake to let Mrs Rawle persuade me to break off our engagement. I've regretted it ever since.'

'During these past years, everywhere I've looked, I've seen your novels. I saw them reviewed in the newspapers, and heard people talking about them wherever I went. Mrs Craig spoke of you constantly, even before she knew you. I came to realise you were no longer my Amy. You were a successful authoress and you belonged to everyone.'

'I wish you'd been there to share my success.'

'That day in New York, when I saw you across the street, I wasn't prepared for the shock of seeing you. As I stood before you, every bit of pretence I'd conjured to convince myself I no longer loved you fell away. There were so many things I wanted to say to you, but once again, I couldn't find the words.'

'You seemed so angry every time we met, so full of contempt.'

'I was furious with myself for having let you go so easily, and furious with you for allowing Mrs Rawle to ruin our chance of happiness. I was determined not to let you see how much you still affected me.'

'You succeeded.'

'Spending time in your company, witnessing your kindness, your intelligence and your wit, finally forced me to accept that the love I felt for you was stronger than ever.'

'If only you'd talked to me and told me how you felt.'

'You had so many admirers I didn't think you'd give me a second chance.' He paused, watching the sky as a gull flew low over their heads, settling on the high point of a nearby rock. 'You were still surrounded by the people who had persuaded you not to marry me all those years ago. I saw nothing to make me think they wouldn't have the same power over you again.'

'It won't happen again, I assure you.'

'That day at Cape May, when you saw me on the beach, looking out across the ocean at the sunset. Why didn't you approach me?'

Amy considered her answer, reliving the moment in her mind. 'I told myself that if you still loved me, you'd turn around and look at me, but you never did.' She paused while a seabird let out its plaintive cry. 'If you knew I was there, why didn't you acknowledge me?'

'I wanted you to come to me so badly, and when you didn't, I thought you didn't care. My heart shattered into a thousand pieces when you walked away. I was too much of a coward to go after you. I didn't want to humiliate myself by betraying my feelings, not knowing if you felt the same. I was in awe of your beauty and your kindness. You should know I've never felt worthy of you.'

'I was convinced you were planning to marry Lucy, even though I didn't believe you loved her.'

'I was a fool not to realise that my good manners towards her, which I only offered out of respect for you, would be misinterpreted as something more. After she fell from the horse, I knew I was honour-bound to marry her, if that was what she wished. I blamed myself for the accident, for allowing her to persuade me to let her ride the stallion. I believed I owed it to her to look after her, even at the sacrifice of my own happiness. It was only when I learned of her engagement to Belmont that I felt finally free of any responsibility towards her. From that moment, I was determined that nothing else would come between us.'

'And then Spencer appeared.'

'I should have trusted you to see him for what he was, but I was terrified of losing you a second time, even before I'd won you back.'

'I saw him as a suitor for Eleanor, not for myself. That was before I fully understood the kind of man he was.'

This was not the time for guilt or recrimination. If they were to be happy, they had to forgive themselves and each other for their past mistakes. She pulled Wareham closer, breathing in the familiar scent of him, feeling the warmth of his body.

'Thank you for honouring Spencer's bid at the charity auction.'

He threw his head back and laughed. Once again, he was the young man she'd fallen in love with, full of charm and good humour. 'How did I think I could ever keep it a secret?' He looked at her, suddenly serious. 'The message you wrote in the book gave me hope, and yet it was so elegantly written, so accomplished, I couldn't bring myself to trust it.'

'You thought it was simply a florid message from an author's pen?'

Wareham nodded. 'It was your speech about the constancy of a woman's heart that finally did it. I knew if I didn't find the courage to speak to you now, then I never would.'

There was a pause before he continued. 'There's something else I have to confess.'

She dreaded what it could be, but had to trust him, just as she should have trusted him all those years ago. 'What is it?'

'Your portrait. I was the anonymous buyer.'

'But you dislike the painting. You said it was nothing like me.'

'I know, but I couldn't stand the thought of Spencer possessing it. At that time, I was convinced you were going to marry him. If I owned the painting, it was one part of you he couldn't take away from me.'

'Spencer could never possess my heart. It has always belonged to you.'

He pulled her closer. 'You don't ever have to look at the portrait again if you don't want to. We can hide it in the back of a cupboard and never let it see the light of day.'

He talked of their future, of having a home together. They would never be separated again. The fact that they would marry was implicit in all of this. Neither of them doubted it for a second.

Chapter 46

Everyone was surprised when Amy took it upon herself to invite the family, and Mr and Mrs Craig to dinner. Since moving to Newport, entertaining had been considered too extravagant. Not only because of the cost of the food, but the Eatons no longer had the household staff to serve at the table. Even away from the prying eyes and gossiping jaws of old New York society, standards were expected to be maintained, even if it was just a family gathering, and if they couldn't maintain them, then it was best not to entertain at all. In the past, as the female head of the household, it had been Eleanor's role to arrange the social engagements, but this time, she knew nothing about it until Amy gave her the invitation.

As they settled in the drawing room, Amy overheard Mr Eaton suggest that Amy's sudden desire for a dinner party was due to boredom now she'd delivered the final instalment of *Missing in Love*. Marion and Charles agreed, while Eleanor, along with Mr and Mrs Craig, assumed it was to give them an opportunity to discuss the proposed night school in more detail.

Having set themselves apart from the rest of the group, Conrad and Hester appeared too caught up in each other to consider Mr Eaton's suggestion that there might be a particular reason behind

305

the invitation, while Mrs Rawle, who'd seen so little of Amy lately, expressed her delight at having been invited.

'Even though I've given it a good deal of thought,' she added. 'I've no idea what I've done to cause her to put so much distance between us.'

Wareham was the only one who knew the real reason for the gathering and if anyone thought he seemed particularly cheerful when he arrived, or was surprised that he was there, nobody commented on it.

Amy and Wareham waited until everyone had been served a glass of champagne before they announced their engagement. There was a beat of silence while everyone took in the news. No one, it seemed, had any idea that they were in love, and always had been. Mr Eaton had a vague recollection of Wareham as a young upstart, trying to claim Amy's heart before he was sent away with his tail between his legs, but that was all a very long time ago and nothing had been said about it since. Mrs Rawle was the only other person who knew of their previous attachment. Now, she gripped the stem of her champagne glass, slowly shaking her head as she took in the news.

'At last,' shouted Mrs Craig, letting out a great shriek of joy. 'I thought the two of you would never come to your senses. I hope this means that *Missing in Love* has also found its happy ending.'

Amy should have guessed that Mrs Craig had worked it all out. With hindsight, she could see how she'd been quietly trying to bring them together. 'How did you know?'

'I realised it the first moment I saw the two of you in the same room,' replied Mrs Craig. 'You don't see that level of tension between strangers. There had to be more to it than the two of you were admitting. Call me an old romantic, but that night over dinner, it was like a flame had been lit in our dear Wareham's heart.'

'It wasn't a particularly happy flame,' said Wareham, frowning at the memory of it.

Mrs Craig lowered her voice. 'You can't deny there was passion in it, even if it was disguised as rage.'

Marion knocked back the contents of her glass and pinned her glare on Wareham. 'You're marrying *him*? But you hardly know him.'

'I know him very well, and have done so for a long time,' replied Amy.

'But why choose *him*, when you could have had an English earl?' asked Marion, the pitch of her voice growing steadily higher.

'You seem to be forgetting that Spencer was a conman and a trickster.'

'Think how terrible it will look when people realise you rejected a member of the aristocracy to marry a man who made his fortune on the railroads, a man who has no family to speak of. No one will invite us to dinner or to a ball ever again.'

Amy resisted the urge to shout back. 'My future with Wareham is too precious to concern myself with the opinions of people who have never really cared for me.'

A gasp escaped from Marion's mouth. She placed her fist against her chest as if she'd been struck. 'If you won't think about your own reputation, you should consider Charles Junior. How is he to find a suitable wife after you've brought the family to such degradation?'

'Steady on, Marion,' said Charles, topping up her glass. 'Charles Junior is still in knickerbockers. I don't think we need to worry about marrying him off just yet.'

Marion ignored his unhelpful comment. 'As if it isn't bad enough that you've stooped to become an authoress, exposing yourself shamelessly to the public eye, now you do this to us.' She clenched her fist harder against her chest. 'I don't know if I can bring myself to consider you my sister anymore.'

Wareham gave Amy a heartbroken look. Amy squeezed his hand. With Wareham beside her, Marion could no longer hurt her. 'I can't force you to be pleased for us, Marion, but nothing you can say will persuade me to give up the man I love.' She glanced at Mrs Rawle, standing red-faced in the corner. 'I was fool enough to make that mistake once before. I won't do it again.'

Hester gave an uncharacteristic whoop as she ran across the room, planting a kiss on Wareham's cheek before throwing her arms around Amy. 'I'm so happy for you both. If it hadn't been for the two of you, Conrad and I wouldn't be able to marry. You deserve the same happiness you've given us.'

Confounded, Marion gulped her champagne and stared at Mr Eaton, urging him to say something, until he finally took the hint.

'Think carefully, Amy. You need to consider our social standing before you rush into this foolishness. This isn't only about Charles Junior's future. No one worth knowing in New York will associate with us if you marry into new money.'

Amy could feel her fury building. 'Wareham made his fortune through his cleverness and his hard work. Everything he's done has been driven by his integrity.' She turned to Wareham, chewing anxiously on the inside of his cheek. 'Above all else, he loves me as much as I love him.'

Mr Eaton curled his lip. 'New money is new money, Amy. You should never forget that.'

There was one secret Amy had been determined to maintain, but the anger driven by her father's words forced her to reconsider. Mrs Craig had been discreet enough never to mention it, but it was time everyone in the room knew the truth.

'Before you insult the source of Mr Wareham's wealth, you might want to ask yourself where the money has come from to subsidise your lifestyle here in Newport.'

'You've paid for everything, Amy, with the money from your writing,' said Eleanor. 'I don't know what we would have done if you hadn't come to our rescue.'

'I'm sorry to disillusion you, but the income from my writing alone hasn't been enough to support your lifestyle. Paying off your outstanding debts took almost every cent I had. It's Mr

Wareham you have to thank for most of what has been spent setting us up in Newport.'

Silence fell around the room. Even Wareham looked surprised. Amy gave Mrs Craig a knowing smile.

'I used the money I made from my first novel to invest in the fledgling company set up by Mr Wareham, and Mr and Mrs Craig. It was only a modest investment by the standards of many, but thanks to the success of Mr Wareham's invention and the clever management of the business by Mrs Craig, it has paid back many times over, and continues to do so.'

Tears were brimming in Wareham's eyes. 'You invested in my company?'

'I always believed in you. I had no way of showing you my love after I broke off our engagement, but this was the one thing I could do to prove it.' She glanced at Mrs Craig, gleeful in the corner. 'Mrs Craig has always looked after the financial side of the business. I don't suppose it took much for her to work out that Miss A. Eaton, one of the earliest investors, was me.'

'Of course I knew it,' roared Mrs Craig, 'just as I knew the two of you were in love the first time I saw you in the same room. It's taken you both long enough to come to your senses and admit it.'

Wareham shook his head, still struggling to take everything in. 'You were always there for me. If only I'd known it.'

While her father and Marion muttered frantically to one another, Amy went to speak to Mrs Rawle, who had retreated to the rosewood sofa and was knocking back her third glass of champagne.

'Please don't tell me my mother would disapprove of me marrying Mr Wareham. I think she would have wanted me to be happy.'

Mrs Rawle failed to meet Amy's eye as she toyed with her empty glass. 'I had no idea how much you loved him. I thought it was just a girlish infatuation, that one day, you'd thank me for saving you from marrying an impoverished nobody.'

'I should have been more strong-minded when you challenged my decision to marry him.'

'I let you down. I thought I was offering the advice your mother would have given, but I was mistaken. I misjudged you both. It seems I didn't know you at all.' She sniffed back a tear. 'I wanted so much to take your mother's place after she died. It was presumptuous of me to ever consider I was capable of such a thing.'

Amy patted her hand. Her mother wouldn't have wanted her to treat Mrs Rawle roughly. 'You did what you thought was best.'

'I've learned that the best intentions aren't always enough, especially when they're blinded by prejudice. Can you ever forgive me?'

'Your advice was well-meant.' Amy wished her mother was there to show her how to put things right. 'I hope you'll come to the wedding.'

Before they went in to dinner, Mr Eaton took Amy aside. 'Look here, Amy. Wareham's handsome enough and all that, and wealthy enough, but you don't have to marry him. If it's the money then . . . well . . . your mother wouldn't have wanted you to sacrifice yourself for our sakes.'

'I think marrying Wareham is exactly what Mother would have wanted for me. I hope one day, you'll grow to understand why.'

Eleanor came over to join them, clinging to her father's arm, just as she clung to the status of being the mistress of his house. 'Congratulations, Amy. At least one of us has a happy ending.'

Amy was touched by Eleanor's words, knowing how much it had cost her pride to say them. 'It's not the end, Eleanor. You must never think that.'

'I don't, not any more. I have other things to worry about now I have the challenge of getting the night school up and running.'

'There's one more piece of news I have to share,' said Amy. 'The popularity of *Missing in Love* has resulted in renewed interest in my previous novels and the income from the surge in sales means you'll be able to move back home to New York much sooner than I'd hoped.'

Eleanor gave her father a hug. 'We're going home. I can't believe it.'

'I must say, I'll be glad to sleep in my own bed again,' said Mr Eaton. He turned to Amy, his eyes full of suspicion. 'It's not Wareham's new money is it, that's responsible for this extra revenue you've suddenly acquired?'

Amy was saddened that he'd even think it. 'It's the money I've earned by my pen.'

Desperate for a breath of air, Amy wandered out onto the veranda. She needed to compose herself before she could face everyone again over dinner. Today was meant to be a celebration, but as always, certain members of her family had tried to ruin it for her.

'Are you all right, Amy?' Wareham had followed her outside. He sat beside her on the bench and placed his arm around her shoulder. 'Don't let Marion or your father spoil our happiness.'

'I'm sorry they find it so difficult to accept you. Perhaps in time . . .'

He put his finger to his lips, bidding her to listen. At first, she thought he was bringing her attention to the sound of the waves crashing against the shore, until she realised he was leaning his head in the direction of the house, smiling at Mrs Craig's words as they drifted through the open window and carried on the breeze.

'Our Wareham is so dear to us. Everyone admires him. You'll all feel the same when you get to know him. You'll never meet a man with gentler manners, or a kinder heart. Even dogs love him . . .'

Amy and Wareham were married in the quaint English-style church in Newport. Despite receiving invitations, none of Amy's family attended the wedding, apart from Eleanor, and Hester, who was delighted to be Amy's maid of honour, and excited to stand alongside Conrad at the altar as he served as Wareham's best man. The absence of Marion and her father did nothing to spoil the day. Amy and Wareham didn't seek the approval of old New York society and they required no one's blessing but each other's to make them happy.

It was the friends who turned out to see them take their vows who mattered most. Mrs Rawle sat in the front row, mouthing the words to the hymns and dabbing her eyes with a handkerchief. Whether the tears were a symptom of joy or regret was anyone's guess, as from that day on, her feelings about the marriage would remain unspoken. In contrast, the Craigs, sitting alongside her, couldn't have been prouder or happier if Wareham had been their son.

Amy and Wareham spent their honeymoon in Europe, visiting the opera houses that Wareham had longed to see since he was a boy. He'd put off the trip until now, waiting until he had the right companion to share it with.

While they were travelling, Amy gathered ideas for her next novel, inspired by the sights of London and Paris, Madrid and Rome. While they were away, Conrad oversaw the building of their new home, just off Fifth Avenue, similar in style and not a million miles away from the family brownstone, where Eleanor and Mr Eaton were now comfortably resettled.

For all they loved their New York home, it was Newport that had captured their hearts and it was there that Amy found the peace to write, in a modest villa overlooking the ocean on the edge of Rhode Island's easternmost cliffs. Soothed by the sun as it glowed through the mist, and the endless ebb and flow of the waves, it was a place where Amy and Wareham could be themselves, living without judgement or reproach, thankful that they'd been brave enough to grasp a second chance of happiness, and loving each other enough to forgive the mistakes of the past.

A Letter from Theresa Howes

I fell in love with Jane Austen when I was twelve years old after my mum gave me a hardback copy of *Pride and Prejudice* with a bright red cover and gold lettering on the spine. Designed for younger readers, the large text and colour plate illustrations meant the volume was a considerable size, and it weighed heavily on my legs as it lay open on my lap for hours at a time, the world of Mrs Bennett and her daughters revealing itself to my eager mind.

Soon, I was devouring *Emma*, and *Sense and Sensibility*, *Northanger Abbey* and *Persuasion*. At school, we studied *Mansfield Park*, discussing whether Fanny Price was truly the heroine of the novel, a debate which still rattles on today. At the same time, I set out to read other nineteenth-century classics, working my way through the Brontës and cherry-picking the novels of Dickens and Thomas Hardy, George Eliot and Louisa May Alcott, and although I loved them all, and so many more authors to varying degrees, my heart belonged, and still belongs to Jane Austen.

It's the humour in the books that keeps me going back to them, the way Austen portrays even her most annoying characters with warmth and love, the way she tenderly pokes fun at the narrow, genteel society in which she lived, while at the same time being only too aware of the social and political issues of the wider world.

When it came to my own retelling of *Persuasion*, my objective was to honour the things I love most about Austen's work, to bring out the same humour in my characters, showing the selfishness and the vanity of many of them, and doing it with fondness in a way that I hope Austen would recognise and approve of. The other objective was to pay tribute to the love story between Anne Elliot and Captain Wentworth. There's no greater heartbreak than a love forsaken, no greater feel-good moment than that love finally being restored. Although I've updated my heroine so she has more agency than Anne, giving her a successful career in a male-dominated world, I was determined to return her heart to the one man who most deserved it.

When it came to choosing a setting for this story, I was struck by how close the values and codes of behaviour of America's Gilded Age were to those of Jane Austen's world, with the distinctions between social class and wealth being the great determiners of everybody's fate.

Women in New York's privileged knickerbocker society had the same constraints upon them as the women of the middle and upper classes in Jane Austen's era, their main duties being to find a respectable husband and to provide an heir. Beyond this, they were limited to working for charitable causes and overseeing the running of the household. Ultimately, the position of women hadn't changed across the continents or from the beginning of the nineteenth century to the end.

The rapid industrialisation of America after the Civil War also proved an ideal setting to explore the evolving political situation of the day as the women who were hungry for change undertook the fight for the right to vote. It was also the perfect backdrop for the story of a successful female novelist and a self-made engineer who learn to resist the rules of the strict society that had once prevented them from marrying, so they eventually find their way back to each other.

Researching the Gilded Age, it was impossible not to take into consideration Edith Wharton, who having been born into its privileged society, portrayed the world so intimately in her novels. I also took inspiration from her life when depicting how Amy's success as an author is viewed by her family.

A *Matter of Persuasion* was written with love and a little playfulness, and always with respect for Austen and everything she stands for. If you haven't read the original, this novel is here for you to enjoy on its own terms. It needs no other explanation. I hope you find as much joy in reading it as I found in writing it. To paraphrase someone else's well-worn saying, with every word I wrote, I found myself standing on the shoulders of greatness.

The French Affair

A country at war. A dangerous secret.

After a failed honey-trap mission for British Intelligence leads to the breakdown of her marriage, French journalist Iris escapes to Dijon, seeking refuge in the cottage of her beloved aunt, Eva. But Eva is gone, the streets are full of distrust, and Iris is soon followed by the very last man she wants to see – the British civil servant and traitor she was tasked with catching, now keen to rekindle their affair.

Eva's home used to be a comforting place, where the locals sought out Eva's homemade tinctures and cures and gifted jars of fresh honey from the garden. Now it is a place of danger, where threats loom in every corner. And as Iris spends more time there, she discovers a secret that will change the way she sees her aunt forever – and the course of her own life too . . .

The Secrets We Keep

1944, the Cote d'Azur.

Artist Marguerite Segal is recruited by British Intelligence into befriending Etienne Valade, a local priest. Her mission is to persuade him to pass on information from the high-ranking German officers who attend his church: evidence of their war crimes.

Connected by a passion for art, Marguerite and Etienne soon fall in love, but their association increasingly puts her at danger of violent reprisals. With his church frequented by Nazis, Etienne is a suspected collaborator, and distrust is high.

And Marguerite is keeping her own secret too. Like the Jews whose identity cards she forges to hide them from the Third Reich, she is hiding behind a false name, her true identity and past known only to her closest friend.

Marguerite must get hold of the documents that will condemn the German officers but, in a world where everything is at stake, can she truly trust anyone – even the man she loves?

Acknowledgements

This book wouldn't have been possible without the work of so many people behind the scenes. To start at the beginning. Sincerest thanks to my fabulous agent Juliet Mushens for your continued guidance and encouragement. I wouldn't be writing this if it wasn't for you. Thanks also to Rachel Neely for your advice on pitching the idea for this novel to HQ Digital and for your brilliant follow-up support.

Also massive thanks to the rest of the amazing team at Mushens Entertainment. Emma Dawson, for your thoughtful notes on the first draft. Liza deBlock, Alba Arnau Prado and Catriona Fida for the great work you do in selling foreign rights, and to Kiya Evans and Den Patrick. Thanks to all of you for being so great at what you do, and for being so lovely to work with.

A huge thank you to Abi Fenton at HQ Digital for being so excited when I originally suggested the idea of this novel, and to Audrey Linton, for your incisive work on the early rounds of edits, and for helping to shape the story into what it has become today. Also, a big thank you to Sophia Allistone for your perceptive and sensitive line edit and for always being on hand to discuss shout lines and cover designs and everything in between. It's been a real pleasure and great fun to work with each of you.

I'd also like to thank Eldes Tran for the copy edit. You save my blushes once again with your attention to detail, and to Anne O'Brien for your proofreading skills. In production, thank you to Francesca Tuzzeo, and in publishing operations, thanks to Sarah Renwick and Tom Han. In Finance, thank you to Kelly Spells and Akifah Mendheria. Thank you to Louise de St Aubin and Emily Gerbner in marketing, Hannah Lismore, Georgina Green, Sara Eusebi and Lauren Trabucci in sales, and Georgina Hester in publicity, and to Charlotte Phillips for designing such a spectacular cover. Thanks to all of you for working so cleverly to make my novel stand out, and for striving to bring it to the attention of the reading public. I'm forever grateful for your creativity and your enthusiasm.

Thank you to Annabelle Thorpe for the long lunches during the course of writing this book, and for the fabulous parties, and to Aliya Ali-Afzal for the coffees and the chats. Thank you to Jessica Bull, who knows more about Jane Austen than I could ever hope to. Your support is wonderful and your work is an inspiration. Thanks to loyal friends, Rif Aslam and Ray Wood for the seaside breaks and the laughs, and to Soosan Atkins and Bronagh Taggart for inspiring trips to the V&A, and tea and cake.

Thank you to all the book bloggers, reviewers, booksellers and librarians who work so hard to bring the work of authors everywhere to wider attention. Your dedication makes a difference to us all. Thanks to all the readers who have chosen to pick up one of my novels, and to all those who make Book Twitter/X a familiar and friendly place to be. I love how the power of a good story can bring strangers together.

Thank you to Mum and Dad for being constant and unshakeable in your belief in me, and to Claude, our larger than life cat, even if stray strands of your fur did jam the S key on my laptop during the course of writing this novel.

Finally, thank you to my long-suffering husband, Bill, for explaining about nineteenth-century patents, railway couplers, the composition of steel, and the evolution of fire-hose design, as well as answering countless other engineering-related questions. If this novel doesn't prove an engineer can be a romantic hero, then I don't know what will.

Dear Reader,

We hope you enjoyed reading this book. If you did, we'd be so appreciative if you left a review. It really helps us and the author to bring more books like this to you.

Here at HQ Digital we are dedicated to publishing fiction that will keep you turning the pages into the early hours. Don't want to miss a thing? To find out more about our books, promotions, discover exclusive content and enter competitions you can keep in touch in the following ways:

JOIN OUR COMMUNITY:
Sign up to our new email newsletter: http://smarturl.it/SignUpHQ
Read our new blog www.hqstories.co.uk

𝕏 https://twitter.com/HQStories
❚ www.facebook.com/HQStories

BUDDING WRITER?
We're also looking for authors to join the HQ Digital family!
Find out more here:

https://www.hqstories.co.uk/want-to-write-for-us/

Thanks for reading, from the HQ Digital team